WAR OF
SECRETS

SPACE MARINE CONQUESTS

WAR OF
SECRETS

PHIL KELLY

BLACK LIBRARY

Many thanks for the sage advice of my inner circle of Company Masters: Phil Atherton, James Fox, Andy Meechan, Gavin Thorpe and his mechanical hamster Dennis.

A BLACK LIBRARY PUBLICATION

First published in Great Britain in 2018 by
Black Library,
Games Workshop Ltd.,
Willow Road,
Nottingham, NG7 2WS, UK.

10 9 8 7 6 5 4 3 2 1

Produced by Games Workshop in Nottingham.
Cover illustration by Neil Roberts.

See Black Library on the internet at

blacklibrary.com

Find out more about Games Workshop
and the world of Warhammer 40,000 at

games-workshop.com

Printed and bound by CPI Group (UK) Ltd, Croydon, CR0 4YY

It is the 41st millennium. For more than a hundred centuries the Emperor has sat immobile on the Golden Throne of Earth. He is the Master of Mankind by the will of the gods, and master of a million worlds by the might of his inexhaustible armies. He is a rotting carcass writhing invisibly with power from the Dark Age of Technology. He is the Carrion Lord of the Imperium for whom a thousand souls are sacrificed every day, so that he may never truly die.

Yet even in his deathless state, the Emperor continues his eternal vigilance. Mighty battlefleets cross the daemon-infested miasma of the warp, the only route between distant stars, their way lit by the Astronomican, the psychic manifestation of the Emperor's will. Vast armies give battle in His name on uncounted worlds. Greatest amongst his soldiers are the Adeptus Astartes, the Space Marines, bioengineered super-warriors. Their comrades in arms are legion: the Astra Militarum and countless planetary defence forces, the ever-vigilant Inquisition and the tech-priests of the Adeptus Mechanicus to name only a few. But for all their multitudes, they are barely enough to hold off the ever-present threat from aliens, heretics, mutants — and worse.

To be a man in such times is to be one amongst untold billions. It is to live in the cruellest and most bloody regime imaginable. These are the tales of those times. Forget the power of technology and science, for so much has been forgotten, never to be re-learned. Forget the promise of progress and understanding, for in the grim dark future there is only war. There is no peace amongst the stars, only an eternity of carnage and slaughter, and the laughter of thirsting gods.

DRAMATIS PERSONAE

PRIMARIS SPACE MARINES

OFFICERS

Lieutenant — Xedro Farren

INTERCESSORS

Brother — Lason Enrod

Brother — Danic Vesleigh

Brother — Jacardo Thrunn

Brother — Ropan Gsar

Sergeant — Galus Parvell

Sergeant — Dendon Orenst

HELLBLASTERS

Sergeant — Pietr Moricani

Brother — Nenst Lenkatz

Brother — Eoun Darrodan

THE UNFORGIVEN

DARK ANGELS COMMAND

Interrogator-Chaplain — Zaeroph

Company Master — Gabrael

Librarian — Dothrael

Apothecary — Vaarad

Techmarine — Autinocus

ANGELS OF ABSOLUTION

Master Castellan   Moddren

HERETICUS

Brother   Gohorael

IMPERIAL CITIZENRY

SALTIRE VEX

Rigswoman Prime	Jensa Deel
Rigswoman Prime	Kaita del Aggio
Rigsman	Derrod Markens

ALLHALLOW

Castellan Guard	Landers Harasen
Wallsman	Fenas Blentar
Wallsman	Vallac Vandersen

T'AU EMPIRE

Surestrike	High Commander of the Fourth Sphere Expansion
Tutor Twiceblade	Sub-commander
Kais	The Living Weapon
Aun'Shao	Ethereal Magister

PROLOGUE
THE TAKERS

Ferro-Giant Omicroid
Saltire Vex, Pelagic Industrial World
Chalnath Expanse

Sleet hammered on the prayer shack's rusted tin roof. The downpour pelted so hard that stray drops pattered through, setting the ring of candles inside sizzling like hot fat in a skillet.

'Oh mighty T'au'va, hear us.'

The riggers within raised their voices to compensate for the lashing storm. Robed in ochre sackcloth, they were kneeling around a statue crafted from cheap bars of soap.

The idol was sculpted well enough, showing the likeness of a faceless figure with far too many arms. One of its hands proffered a stylised cornucopia made from a crumpled tin rations pack; another held a stiletto made from a broken toothpick.

'T'au'va, hear our prayer,' called out the priestess in front of the statue. A tall woman with a sump-swimmer's build, her voice was clear and strong over the distant rumble of thunder. She turned an empty salve flask over and over in her hands.

The storm boomed in the distance, closer now.

'Hear us, and grant us salvation,' replied the bedraggled crowd of people around her.

The priestess noted with a pang of empathy that some of them were shivering, their twisted limbs wrapped tight to ward against the sodden air. She felt tightness in her chest, a vague notion that something bad was coming.

Something far worse than mere cold.

'Bring us the deliverance of the communal soul,' she said. 'We offer ourselves to you.'

'We join our strength with yours,' came the response.

'We do this not for gifts from the stars,' continued the priestess. 'Nor to escape the mind-plague. We do this so that we might serve you in the Greater Good, and be remade in its light.'

'For the good of all,' echoed the throng.

The riggers drew close, clasping their hands together until they stood in a tight circle, the statue and its candlelight beneath them. The priestess smiled through her consternation, making eye contact with each of her fellows.

With a shriek of tearing metal, a full half of the roof was ripped away, high winds blasting in a barrage of sleet that extinguished the candles and sent several of the riggers scattering to the walls like cockroaches seeking cover.

The priestess looked up in shock. In places, the night sky rippled like water, the outline of something huge and strangely transparent made visible only by the heavy rain rebounding from its contoured edges.

'Run!' she shouted, diving headlong behind Gravide, the largest of their number. She saw Ultrecht kick open the bolted door with a grunt, Aala scooping up the statue behind him and cradling it to herself before running through the sleet to flee out of the shack's bolted door. Gravide made after them.

Jensa Deel hesitated. Some instinct told the priestess not to follow close. Instead she turned back, making for a discoloured panel at the shack's rear.

A split second later, she felt something hot and wet cover her entire flank, then a backwash of heat accompanying a swelling tide of pain. As the animalistic need to run fought against the urge to turn and look, the priestess put her shoulder to the discoloured section of the wall – the same section she had divested of its rivets several months ago. For a moment, the panel held fast, but adrenaline and panic lent Deel a surge of strength.

Suddenly, the metal gave way. She tumbled out, grazing her shin on the frame at the base.

'Jensa,' came a cry from behind her. 'Wait!'

The priestess glanced back for a moment. Alaweir was behind her, slicked with blood amongst a scattering of torn corpses. Her eyes were wide in a crimson mask. Then a blinding explosion of light silhouetted Alaweir for a moment, and she vanished in a cloud of red mist.

Deel gaped. They were all gone. The only sign that her friends had ever been present was the blood painting the walls and iron floor. It was already being washed away by the sleet.

The priestess ran as fast as she could down the gantry, her steel-toed boots clanging on the walkway grilles. Driving rain lanced needle-like into her forehead. The chill of it numbed her face as she darted from stanchion to stanchion, hands reaching to cling onto the cold, hard and familiar uprights of the colossal promethium rig.

PHIL KELLY

She felt a terrible pressure building in her head, a grow-ing headache so intense it felt as if her skull might burst with the stress. That thing she had seen above the shack had been camouflaged so well it was invisible but for its outline. There was only one explanation.

The Takers had returned.

There was a shrill scream from above, cut ominously short. Deel doubled over and stumble-ran under the sill of an observation post. She took a look up through a half-grille to the next storey. Something moved, high above; she caught a glimpse of a slow, predatory advance.

Deel's breath heaved in her chest, heart pounding from exertion and panic. Forcing herself to calm down, she ran across an open expanse of gantry towards a ladder tube and jumped legs-first for the entry port, sliding over the lip and twisting straight down. She blocked her fall with her elbows extended. Shrugging off the impact, Deel grasped the rungs and started descending three at a time.

The pain came a moment later, thumping through her fevered brain, but she pushed it away. Black spots swam in front of her eyes, threatening to merge together and steal her sight entirely.

The thing that had killed Alaweir was close. She could feel its gaze on the back of her neck.

Deel jumped the last twelve feet, landing with an impact so hard it made her knees feel as though they had been struck with lump hammers. Recovering her balance, she grabbed the rigger wrench from a pressure release alcove. She brought it around like a sword, batting clumsily at her invisible assailant.

The blow did not connect, for there was no one there.

Her eyes darted into every corner and pool of shadow, but still found nothing.

Slowly, the pain in her head began to recede a little.

Shuffling sidelong, crab-like, down a tight maintenance passage, Deel reached another set of rung hollows and began to descend. These contingency routes were hardly ever used, but had been built into the leg of the colossal rig in case the main apertures were ever ablaze.

The smell of crude promethium filled her nostrils, its odour thick and powerful enough to sting the inside of her nose despite the mist of seawater that filled the air of the lower levels. With the noise of the storm above, there was no way she would be able to hear the approach of the Takers. An invisible enemy could snatch her away at any moment.

The thought made her squeeze her eyes shut, reaching out with her mind to feel for anything that came with deadly intent.

There was an explosion from high above. Deel opened her eyes once more on reflex, raising the wrench as if to strike. The rig shook as if hit by some colossal impact, toppling her sideways.

She reached out for a nearby grille on instinct. Its rust-sharpened edges cut at her fingers, but she kept her footing. Drops of her blood whipped away into the storm, some spattering the mesh of the gantry, others carried down into the iron depths of the rig's base.

Out to the west she could see the ocean, colder and crueller than she had ever seen it before. It had been thrashed into a frenzy of white-capped waves that hammered into the rig's thick stanchions.

Sleet whipped in from the edge of the rig, carried almost

horizontal by the storm. As she emerged to find the next ladder tube down, an icy blast of air and water hit her like a jet from a burst pipe. She stood firm and fought forwards.

For a moment, she thought she saw lights out there in the darkness, arranged in tight groups. They were moving too fast to be rig ships, too fast even for the Valkyrie carriers of the Astra Militarum.

More Takers, then, come to seal her fate. This time, it would be someone else that struck the names from the rigger's register the morning after the tempest, someone else that counted the cost and set in motion the prescribed period of grieving.

Something flickered in the edge of Deel's vision. On instinct, she threw herself to one side. She cried out as a burst of light and heat flung her along the gantry in a tangle of limbs. The rusted grille she had kept close had taken the brunt of the explosion, but the energies had washed through it. The back of her fatigues hung in rags, exposing long burns, ribbons of duracloth and ruined skin flapping in the wind.

Deel gave a long, keening cry. 'Please,' she said, her jaw shuddering in cold and pain. 'Just let me live.'

There was a crack of lightning and, almost simultaneously, a double boom of thunder. The storm was immediately overhead now.

In that strobing flash, Deel saw a light in the corner of her eye. She hefted her wrench and ran for the narrow corridor between two giant fusil capacitors, her lungs aching. The backs of her thighs were singing with pain, the icy rain stabbing its cold talons into her open wounds.

The priestess rebounded from the walls as she half-ran

down the narrow passage, cursing herself for a fool as she realised it led to the northern edge of the rig. Not good enough. The work platform on the other side was dangerously exposed.

Deel winced as she heard another scream, this time close by.

Wriggling through a triangular gap inside one of the rig's main supports, she used the criss-crossing diagonal bars like the rungs of a ladder, planting her feet at each junction so as not to lose her footing on the rain-slicked metal. She clung tight as she descended, avoiding scraping her wounded back and legs on the salt-encrusted uprights of the support.

Another dozen steps down and she would be able to crawl back out on the level below. Another two levels below that, and she had a shred of hope for survival. Perhaps, if she could make it to the pontoon, an evacuation craft might already be loading up.

Klaxons blared high above as the rig's auto-responses finally awoke to the fact it was under attack. The alarms came much too late, as usual. The Takers worked too fast and too stealthily for such conventional measures to thwart them.

In the distance Deel saw blurs of movement, a shadow briefly visible behind a ring-iron fence. Something massive had stalked past her position as she passed Level Tert-Epsilon.

There was a blaze of light, and a very human bellow of defiance. Another flash. The voice grew louder – she recognised Rotheran's phlegmy roar – before it was abruptly silenced.

The acrid stink of promethium grew almost unbearable

as Deel descended towards the vat farms, forcing herself to focus on her progress. 'Hand over hand,' she panted. 'Just take it easy. Can defeat the Takers. Just need a chance.'

She realised she was muttering into the storm, and forced herself into silence by biting her lip. She needed to conserve her breath. Another ten steps, and she would come out near the gate. Beyond that were the promethium vats. There, she would make it to the pontoons and the freedom they represented – or a death that would be swift and spectacular.

Perhaps the vats' sheer volatility would stop the Takers from risking a direct attack. Perhaps she could make it after all. Deel burst from her hiding place in the stanchion and sprinted the distance into the vat farm through the front gate.

The caulk-swathed servitor caryatids on either side of the promethium gate growled in confusion. It offended them to see her pass without the correct vocal offerings and blandishments. They set their hazard klaxons bleating an intruder alarm as she passed, so strident and aggressive that even a born killer might be scared away.

So much for stealth. At least she might draw a few of the Takers away from her colleagues before they put her down for good.

'Come any closer and I'll spark these up!' she shouted, waving her wrench at the promethium vats.

The only answer was the boom of waves pounding against the stubby, broad legs of the rig's main supports.

Deel sprinted to the rear of the vat farm, its monolithic cylinders looming on either side of the gantry run. She pushed into another triangular pillar through a slim aperture, blocking the pain from her mind as she slid one leg, then the other through the widest opening she could find. She got her hips through – no mean feat in itself – and dropped down to the lower level with a clang.

Biting back a sob of pain and self-pity, she desperately fought the urge to touch the ruin of skin on the back of her legs. She was safe, for the moment. She had to be.

Deel saw another flicker of movement, less than a hundred feet to the north on the other side of the gate. The tang of bile rose up unbidden in the back of her throat as she wiggled back and away, praying to T'au'va that she remained unseen. She emerged from the other side of the triangular pillar and ran on animal instinct, her hindbrain taking over to drive her away as fast as she could run. Putting the promethium vats at her back, she staggered out onto the reclaimant pontoon, hoping desperately to see an evacuation craft loading nearby.

Nothing.

Just an endless vista of crashing grey waves, the nearest slapping hard at the cylindrical fuel-siphons marching out to the sea.

Something massive loomed from behind the closest of the siphon pillars, its outline visible only because of the frozen rain pummelling into its flank. A Taker.

Deel screamed as a tide of pain swelled up from her spine to eclipse her mind. She went blind, staggering into a foetal crouch as her brain burned like a lidless eye bathed in simmerfuel. Then there was a sudden release, and a feeling like cool water dousing her aggravated nerves.

When she opened her eyes once more, the stanchions to her right had been carved apart, their edges glowing cherry-red as if slashed by some high-powered cutting laser. A crane rig, two of its legs shorn straight through, creaked ominously before looming, toppling and crashing down, its bifurcated top half spinning end over end into the violent waters below. A giant double wave rose from the impact, sending sea spray high before falling back with a crash.

Revealed behind the crane rig was a giant some twenty feet in height, its ochre mass seemingly frozen in place. It was inhuman and surprisingly bulky, its bulbous head set within a wide and powerful frame. Standing atop one of the promethium siphons, it had its arms poised as if it was about to leap. Strange lights flickered upon its extremities, and cords of electricity writhed around the dual scars of molten metal that cut diagonally across its torso.

Deel felt numb as the reality of the vision before her sank in.

The Takers were not ghosts, nor were they storm giants come from the sky to claim a feast of human flesh.

They were something far more formidable. Xenos.

The massive machine rippled as if underwater, its smooth-lined sophistication otherworldly next to the rugged Imperial constructions around it. Even as she watched, it shimmered, its outlines blurring to blend with the steel grey of the water behind.

'We are your allies!' shouted Deel into the storm, her words snatched away by the wind. She linked her hands, fingers twining in the sign of the Greater Good. 'We are gue'vesa!'

The giant machine took a gunner's crouch, swinging around the strange tripartite gun that formed its arm.

Horror swamped Deel's mind. She ran from the machine, leaped from the edge of the pontoon and dived headlong into the raging sea.

CHAPTER ONE
THE TIP OF THE BLADE

Ferro-Giant Omicroid
Saltire Vex, Pelagic Industrial World
Chalnath Expanse

'Battle stations.'

Xedro Farren opened his eyes, his hands automatically checking the critical points of his bolt rifle. His augmented senses pierced the amber gloom of the *Night Harrower*'s hold.

The lieutenant's battle-brothers sat in two lines around him, most of them as silent and still as crypt-statues. Some of them were looking around, taking stock just as he was, but the rest were evidently content to wait. The grinding growl of the Repulsor's grav plate engines filled the tank's interior, the racket so loud it almost drowned out the crashing boom of waves and the occasional roll of thunder from the storm outside.

'*Engagement range in eight minutes,*' came the clipped, disapproving tones of their superior, Zaeroph. The Chaplain was voxing through to the *Harrower*'s skull-like relay from the command echelon's Thunderhawk, *Sacred Mace*. *'Commend your souls to the Emperor and the Lion. Strike from a place bereft of doubt.'*

'Lieutenant,' hissed Sergeant Moricani. 'How do we commend our souls? Does it involve kneeling? Because I'm not sure I wish to be nose to nose with any of you armoured ogryns.'

Farren raised an eyebrow, cocking his head to one side. 'We want to impress our Dark Angels brothers, Pietr. Not make them think that Terra and Mars raise only boors.'

'Impress them?' scoffed Vesleigh. 'Primaris Space Marines are the closest gene-sons to the primarch. We have the true blood of the Lion in our veins.'

'Have some respect,' said Farren. 'These Dark Angels have given everything in the defence of the Imperium for thousands of years.'

'And what have you done in that time, Vesleigh?' said Enrod. 'Lain dormant in a stasis casket? Explain to me, how does that make you such a hero?'

'Wait and see,' mumbled Vesleigh, his heavy brows knitted together. 'I have nothing to prove.'

'Oh, on the contrary,' said Moricani, looking thoughtfully at his plasma incinerator. 'We have everything to prove. To them, we are new. We will be weighed and measured. It is likely that even this conversation is being monitored. You will already be marked as one to watch.'

At this, the Hellblaster sergeant leaned towards the servo-skull tethered via its spinal cables to the Repulsor's rear. 'As will I.' Features underlit, Moricani made the sign of the Aquila with his face an exaggerated mask of sincerity.

'Discipline, Pietr. Now is not the time,' Farren ordered.

'Where are we to strike again?' asked Thrunn, the youngest of either combat squad despite being the largest. He looked at Farren, eyes wide in a face ringed with dense sideburns and a strap of a beard. No doubt the affectation was intended to make him look mature, but it always reminded Farren of a startled hive owl.

Farren checked the data-slate to his left. 'The promethium rigs of Saltire Vex, specifically the structure known as Ferro-Giant Omicroid,' he said. 'There is evidence of xenos infestation there, and we are to expunge all sign of their presence.'

'Excellent,' said Enrod, his face creased and tight as if concentrating hard. 'My kind of mission.'

Moricani snorted in disbelief, casting a glance at Farren in the hope of finding a similar reaction. Farren shot him a warning glance instead.

'And exactly how many xenos have you killed, Enrod?' asked Vesleigh.

Enrod shook his head. 'More than you, no doubt.'

'Really?'

Farren was about to intercede when the Repulsor's interior lights increased to full. Its alarum chimes rang out. He stood up, bracing himself against the rolling, shivering progress of the anti-grav tank as it ground across the ocean's surface.

The storm was becoming violent now. He could feel it in the way the Repulsor's floor tilted and dipped every few seconds. Farren peered at the display slate, but with the wind and rain lashing outside, he could make out very little.

'I'm going for a visual,' said the lieutenant, donning

his Mark X helm and putting the mag-clamps under his boots to half yield.

'Good hunting, lieutenant,' said Thrunn, his expression grave. 'The Omnissiah watches over you.'

Farren hoped he was right. They were critically low on pertinent information here, and he didn't like it at all.

'This is not how we waged war on Mars, nor Terra,' muttered Enrod, echoing Farren's thoughts. 'Even when things went wrong, we had more insight than this.'

'Yet nonetheless, we will triumph,' said Farren. 'Or die in the attempt.'

'Perhaps both,' said Moricani, turning to Enrod with a smile. 'I have often thought the lieutenant would make for a truly impressive corpse.'

Farren shook his head and tapped the egress rune under the Repulsor's top hatch. He gave the bar beneath it a sharp quarter-turn with both hands. The automated systems took over to slide it open. Sleet slashed down into the tank's interior as Farren jumped up to catch his arm over the lip of the open hatch. He hauled himself up, legs dangling, to look outside.

The vista that greeted him was one of cold and impressive grandeur. Ahead was a massive promethium rig, its six main pillars holding aloft a multi-layered structure that reached high into the sky.

Ferro-Giant Omicroid.

Colossal chimneys vented bursts of flame, each volcanic plume sending a vast wreath of steam into the night. Siphon cylinders stretched out, linked to the main rig by masses of pipes and cable. In the far distance, Farren could just make out other such structures on the horizon, each capped with several tiny tongues of fire.

The Repulsor bullied its way through the surf towards the megastructure in an elongated trough of brine. Its anti-grav suspensor engines pushed down so hard on the salt-rich water that the tank was surrounded by crashing black waves of its own making.

As the *Harrower* drew closer, Farren could see a force field shimmering over the promethium rig ahead, a huge aegis dome of blue dots that fizzed where the waves crashed through it.

A Stygies pattern macro-field, thought Farren. Though an advancing craft could pass through it with little more than a frisson of electrical energy irritating its machine-spirit, against bullets and las-beams it was as stalwart as four feet of hypersteel, for it was calibrated to let nothing with higher velocity than a raindrop penetrate its hemispherical field.

The energy dome's readouts on Farren's autosenses were spiking so hard he doubted even a shot from the *Harrower*'s twin las-talon could penetrate it. To run such a massive shield generator for any length of time required an immense amount of power, enough Terra-watts to run a hive city. But if the Primaris Marines' data-slate briefing was true, power was not something the ferro-giants had in short supply.

Pushing his helm's scryer autosenses to maximum, Farren saw explosions of light amidst the tangled iron platforms of the megastructure. He saw a body falling with limbs flailing into the sea, then another.

There was no time to waste. The xenos attack was in full flow.

Farren opened a vox-channel to Gsar, the Repulsor's pilot. 'Maximum speed, if she will take it. Avoid the biggest waves, and ride out the others.'

'*Acknowledged, lieutenant,*' came the reply. '*We'll be there soon enough. I know what I'm doing.*'

'You have not failed me yet.'

Two other Repulsors flanked the *Harrower*. Together they bore the entirety of Strike Force Blacksword's contingent of Primaris Marines. Their insignia was emblazoned on the dark green hulls of each grav-tank, each numeral and icon displayed in pride of place along with the winged blade symbol of the First Legion.

On the right was the *Heaven's Troth*, Repulsor of Squad Orenst. The twin onslaught cannon in its cupola was drawing a bead on the rig looming ahead. It gunned forward as if to overtake – a blatant breach of spearhead protocol, and one typical of Dendon Orenst's belligerent nature. Farren made a mental note to address it, his jaw clenching in irritation.

On Farren's left was the transport of Squad Parvell, known as the *Dire Tidings*. The lieutenant's eyes narrowed as he made out the sergeant's bald pate glinting orange in the promethium fires. He too was taking a visual from the cupola. After the Noctan Glitchwar – a violent disaster that was supposed to be a regulation dune-hunt for a tribe of malfunctioning servitors – Galus Parvell had forsaken his helm whenever he could, despite Farren's explicit instructions he wear it in all battlefield conditions. Today was another infraction – since Farren's adherence to protocol had once cost them half their squad, there had been quite a few.

This far from Mars' cloying grip, Farren told himself, a little rebellion was understandable. He knew better than to dampen the fire of a Space Marine ready for the kill.

Introspections aside, the lieutenant could not help but

feel a swell of pride at the sight of the Primaris spearhead. He cursed himself for having any doubt about the battle to come, or the shadows of the past. There was nothing the Dark Angels could not accomplish. No foe they could not overcome through the pinpoint application of the Omnissiah's firepower.

The Primaris Marines themselves were the pinnacle of Mars' geneto-military machine, and each of their Repulsor transports was a miracle of Father Cawl's mastery of the technological. The stoic angles of the *Harrower*'s construction echoed Arkhan Land's iconic Raider design. Some amongst the Primaris Marines said that Archmagos Cawl had improved even upon that legendary engine of war, hard as it was to believe.

A spray of spume slapped Farren's helm as Gsar pushed through a tall crest of seawater. The lieutenant rode it out, knowing that even a tidal wave would be hard put to neutralise the transport. When on land, the tank was able to traverse the most rugged terrain at speed, leaving a trail of crushed rock behind it as its engines fought against the local gravity and won. Crossing a storm-wracked ocean was well within the Repulsor's capabilities. That versatility alone made it invaluable for the fast-striking forces of the Adeptus Astartes, and especially for the Dark Angels.

'*How's it looking, lieutenant?*' came Gsar's voice over the vox.

'Hostile,' replied Farren. 'But promising.'

The Primaris spearhead was not alone. In the middle distance were the Land Speeders of the Ravenwing, the onyx-hulled skimmers carving through the air like groups of raptors on the wing. Behind them came a cloud of murky darkness, and inside that was the haunting, gloom-bringing relic of technology that Farren's helm display recognised as the *Halo of Hidden Saints*. Similar in construction to the other skimmers but far more arcane in function, the Dark-shroud speeder carried a stone-carved statue atop it, barely visible at this distance. A relic of long-lost Caliban, that monument to the past was so thick with age and mystery its aura was like a cloud of ink spreading in water.

'All present and correct then, Farren?' shouted Moricani from the *Harrower*'s interior. 'You are letting in the cold air.'

'Then endure it, *Sergeant* Moricani,' said Farren, smiling despite himself. 'This is a view worth remembering.'

High above the Darkshroud soared two squadrons of compact but powerful jetfighters – Nephilim, Farren recalled, each pair escorting a priceless Dark Talon with its signature chin-mounted rift cannon glowing strangely in the gloom. Close behind the aerial hunters came two massive Thunderhawk gunships, their forest green livery appearing almost black in the night. Inside their cavernous holds were squads from the Dark Angels of the Third Company, each battle-brother a tried and tested warrior with years of experience in the crucible of war.

Farren felt a brief flicker of apprehension at the sight. The Primaris Marines of his command – though well trained before their incarceration in their cryo-caskets – had fought ten to fifteen large-scale battles in total. The vast majority of those had been in test conditions on Mars, and only a few of them had been lucky enough to fight on Terra. To fight in a true battle for the Imperium's cause, and to do so beside a strike force of veteran Dark Angels – the First of the Emperor's Legions – would be an honour indeed.

Farren had no intention of wasting the opportunity.

* * *

As the strike force closed in on the promethium rig, it split into three elements, with the squadrons of Land Speeders arcing around to the left flank even as their aerial wing took the right. The Primaris Marines continued to make a beeline for their target, aiming for the nearest of the gigantic cylinders that formed the legs of the promethium rig.

'*Squads Farren, Orenst and Parvell, Third Company,*' intoned Chaplain Zaeroph over the magna-vox. '*Stay the course on full ahead. You have the honour of the frontal assault. Root out the xenos. Send their corpses as ash into the sea.*'

'Aye, Chaplain,' replied Farren. 'We will win glory for the Chapter, for Terra, and for Mars.'

'*Speak not of Mars,*' said Zaeroph, his voice a low growl. '*I need no reminder of your divided loyalties. Just do your damned duty.*'

Farren felt Moricani's eyes on the back of his neck. This time, he turned and met his friend's gaze, giving the smallest of shrugs before turning back.

'At least you remembered to call the Dark Angels a Chapter, rather than a Legion, this time,' said Moricani. 'After millennia of lying around in stasis, I have a feeling the terms we learned as aspirants on Mars are not necessarily correct.'

'Easily baited, that Zaeroph,' said Vesleigh. 'They do not like it when we call the Emperor the Omnissiah, these ones. And especially not him.'

'Don't bait him too much,' said Farren grimly as he climbed back into the Repulsor's transport bay. 'You might receive a power maul to the back of the head.'

'*Crozius Arcanum,*' said Moricani, gesturing extravagantly. 'I believe it translates from High Gothic as "holy stick".'

'It means "arcane cross" in Low Gothic as you well know, Sergeant Moricani,' said Gsar over the interior vox.

'Enough,' said Farren. 'Moricani, brief your team. Ready firing solutions. Gsar, track and take down anything larger than an unaugmented human on approach.'

'Acknowledged,' said the Repulsor's pilot. 'Patching through battlefield schematics now.'

The Repulsor's sensor array, remote-linked to Farren's Mark X armour, filled his inbuilt relays with the STC data of the ferro-giant rig up ahead. Sturdy yet relatively cheap to build, the colossal rig was one of thousands of such megastructures across the planet. Its auto-defences were at high alert. The servitor-crewed heavy stubbers mounted upon the corners of its platforms scanned for targets as the waves crashed against its thick, rivet-studded supports.

Farren heard the muffled crump of distant explosions, and saw bursts of illumination from inside the rig. He zoomed in on the defence nests. Odd, he thought. It was clearly under attack, but none of its gun emplacements were firing.

'The xenos are well inside it already,' said Farren. 'They have bypassed its outer defences. We will have to make ingress.'

'Oh well,' said Moricani. 'A close-range firefight it is then. How unfortunate.'

'For them,' said Enrod.

The Repulsor shook hard, toppling Farren back into his seat with a clang. Every interior display fuzzed with static.

'We've been hit,' said Thrunn.

'Thank you for pointing that out, Thrunn,' said Farren. 'Gsar, how bad is it?'

There was no reply. The interior comms crackled with

static. Farren was glad to see Gsar's name-rune still green on his helm display, but the internal link had been cut.

Another impact, rocking the Repulsor to the side.

'Omnissiah's wounds,' swore Farren. 'That's an energy weapon. We're going to have to risk another direct visual.'

'Get out there,' said Moricani. 'Maybe a stray tidal wave will cool your hunger to show off.'

'A jibe about taking unnecessary risks from a Hellblaster?' Moricani guffawed. 'A solid hit at last, lieutenant.'

Farren was already moving, opening the hatch atop the Repulsor once more and poking his head out. Rain lashed his helm, his autosenses picking through the gloom to the rig beyond.

The ferro-giant loomed high now, all but blotting out the horizon. Gsar was opening fire with the pintle-mounted gatling cannon, its rotary barrels blurring as it stitched bullets into the second storey of the promethium rig.

Where they struck home, something shimmered – something that looked bulkier than a Space Marine, but bulbous, with one arm little more than an elongated weapon system.

'Contact,' barked Farren. Gsar panned the stream of bullets across, catching another xenos warsuit and sending it rebounding from a girder behind it to topple into the sea.

'These ones match a known anatomy,' said Farren, ducking back into the Repulsor as his autosenses fed a blurt of xenological data to his helm. 'They are a xenos breed known as t'au.'

'A physically feeble race made formidable by their blasphemous warsuit technology,' said Moricani. 'Native to the Eastern Fringe, I believe. The Ultramarines, Scar Lords, White Scars and Hammers of Dorn faced them in the Damocles Crusade.'

'That's them,' said Farren. 'The minor warsuits that Gsar just cut down were well armed, but I think the energy hits we took were from something much larger. Prepare yourselves for heavy firepower.'

'Let's see who carries the heaviest,' said Moricani, hefting his long-barrelled incinerator. 'Phobossian is the great leveller, even against giants.'

'He is indeed, though he has a temper,' nodded Farren. 'I promise you can take down one of the big ones, Moricani, when we find them.'

'Gladly.'

'There is a pontoon beyond those siphon cylinders, with an ingress point to the lower levels,' said Farren, motioning for his squad to get to their feet. 'Prepare to disembark in three.'

The Repulsor pushed its trough of water underneath the rig, flanked by its fellows. It pulled in close to the dock. Side hatches clunked open as Gsar adjusted its grav-push to make level with the iron pontoon.

One by one Squad Farren disembarked onto the swaying, brine-slicked metal platform. The mag-clamps on their boots kept them steady. Farren climbed out of the Repulsor's gunnery hatch, leaping up to grab hold of the pipes overhead with his bolt rifle clamped to his hip. He pulled himself up in one easy movement as the rest of his squad climbed up the stanchion ladder to the first storey in good order. He was first to gain the walkway, hauling himself onto the level above before unclamping his rifle and scanning his immediate environment along its barrel.

'Clear,' he said. 'Moricani, get your men up here. Parvell, Orenst, cover the rear.'

'Already en route, glorious leader,' came Moricani's reply. 'Nice entry technique.'

'Lieutenant,' said Orenst. 'This mission of extermination. Are there civilians aboard the rig?'

'There are,' said Farren. 'It goes without saying we should spare who we can. Still, collateral damage may occur. That is the price of war.'

'Rather a clean death than a lifetime spent in slavery to filthy xenos,' said Enrod.

'Fine words,' replied Farren.

The main body of the promethium rig had been built to endure the elements. Farren knew enough about material tolerances to know the main gantries would bear their weight easily enough. He was not so sure about the auxiliary structures and ersatz repairs on its outskirts, however. They would have to tread carefully if the battle took them out there. Even a Primaris Marine would struggle if pitched into the crashing waters below.

'To the west!' shouted Vesleigh, 'Target–'

Thick trails of light whipped across Farren's field of vision. He dived backwards on instinct, grabbing an iron pillar with his free hand and swinging around it to put the iron strut between him and the enemy marksman. He heard energy discharge sizzle on the other side of the stanchion.

In one smooth motion, the lieutenant crouched and calibrated his rifle for single round, maximum range. He leaned out, took the shot, then leaned back in to narrow his profile.

There was a distant boom, and a weird shriek that could only have been the scream of an alien.

'Centre mass shot,' said Vesleigh. 'First blood to the lieutenant.'

'Why didn't we see it?' said Thrunn.

'Camouflage field,' said Farren. 'The t'au specialise in them, cowards that they are. Stick to the outskirts for now, and watch for areas where the air is distorted, or the raindrops don't make it to the ground.'

'Acknowledged,' came the reply.

There was a dull clang from above, and the whirr of an alien weapon system powering up. Moricani was already there beneath it, letting fly a blinding burst of plasma. The searing orb burst through the iron grillwork above him, burning into something half-hidden in a blaze of energy. Two more plasma blasts came from those of Moricani's squad who had already made the climb, blasting apart a large section of the gantry overhead.

A bulky form fell down towards them amongst a scattering of mangled, red-hot metal. Moricani and his squadmates had to dodge sidelong to avoid the xenos warsuit crashing into them. It hit the gantry hard with a dull clang.

Farren cast around for more movement, finding nothing, before taking a closer look at his would-be assassin. There was something vaguely insectile about the xenos thing's hooded carapace. Crackling light played across the warsuit as its chameleon field attempted to reassert itself, the system still active despite the gaping hole that had been burned through its undersection.

Visible under the warsuit's smooth exoskeleton was a gangly blue-grey body, its innards cauterised around a black wound. The vile thing twitched, and the stench of burning alien flesh rose up to filter into Farren's nostrils.

'That is truly foul,' said Enrod. 'It must be slain in the Emperor's name.' He lowered the muzzle of his autorifle and put a bolt through the hole Moricani had opened. The projectile detonated a split second later, splattering both squads with alien blood and sending shards of alloy pinging from their power armour.

'So you bathe us in it?' said Moricani, wiping a gobbet of alien flesh from his helm's eye. 'Any more of this filth gets on my gun, and its machine-spirit would be well within its rights to malfunction. I would not be surprised if it took my arm off out of spite.'

'Enough,' said Farren. 'Let us complete a perimeter run. This one's kin will not be slow to respond, but the largest will struggle to get far inside.'

'They got through the force field easily enough,' said Enrod.

'Stealthers,' said Farren, shrugging by way of answer. 'And not the kind that wear foliage as their camouflage. This should be good hunting.' He set off at a loose run, autorifle held close at his shoulder.

As Farren darted from one bulkhead to another, there was movement over the ocean. He dived headlong for cover, some instinct telling him to leap forward instead of ducking low. The gantry behind him exploded into flame and scorched metal silhouettes, twisting girders blackening in a sudden conflagration of light. A whole section of flooring tumbled away into the cool waters beneath.

'Heavy xenos warsuits have a bead,' voxed Farren, checking his sight was still aligned. 'All squads hold position behind the bulkheads.'

Bright blurs of plasma sizzled past from deep inside the rig, each round small, but potent enough to kill. The lieutenant grimaced. If he moved into the open, he would be caught in a crossfire between the t'au stealthers and what-ever xenotech monstrosity had just taken out the gantry he had been crossing moments ago.

'Oaths and blood,' said Farren under his breath, draw-ing up the schematics of the STC rig on the interior of his helm. 'This won't be easy without support.' In truth, he would rather die than ask his brothers in the Dark Angels for help. The Primaris Marines had a reputation to win.

Another volley of plasma crackled past. The heavy iron grilles through which the firepower was coming were thick enough to bar his path to the alien stealthers, but the t'au within were clearly marksmen. They were skilled enough to thread their shots through the diamond-shaped gaps wherever the Primaris Marines appeared. Squads Farren and Moricani were caught between entrenched xenos infantry and whatever chameleonic warsuit was out there over the waves, all but invisible near the siphon cylinders.

There was still a way to close with the stealthers, and get further inside to a position of relative safety. There had to be.

Farren leaned out and loosed off a quick triple burst along the trajectory of the last few plasma bolts, thread-ing the shots through the diamond gaps with ease. The explosions of his bolts were gratifyingly loud.

A twenty-foot gap still yawned between Farren and his battle-brothers, but his suppressing fire had likely bought them a moment to regroup. He stowed his rifle, crouched and leaped directly upwards, making the jump to grab hold of the thick pipes beneath the next gantry. Pulling himself up, he mag-clamped the tips of his boots to the underside of the painted ironwork.

'Cover me!' he shouted to his squad. 'Bolter muzzles

into the gaps. Opportune fire only. Squad Moricani, cross and flank!'

'Aye, lieutenant,' came Moricani's reply. 'Already on course.'

The sergeant's second, Lenkatz, was the first to leap across the missing section of the gantry. He cleared the gap with a hand's span to spare. The other Hellblasters were quick to follow, with Thrunn striding forwards close to the diamond grille and loosing shots whenever he saw movement within the rig. A volley of plasma seared in, but the big warrior ducked back at the last moment.

By the time Moricani's whole squad had cleared the gap, Farren had climbed along the underside of the ceiling gantry, using a solid grip and the tips of his mag-plate boots to make his way to the steaming hole left where the Hellblasters had cored the iron structure above. Thankfully, the stealthers below had not reacted to him; they were too busy exchanging opportunistic fire with his Space Marine brothers.

Up on this level, another corridor, perpendicular to the gantry below, led further into the rig. This time there was no diamond-gapped wall to bar his path. Farren reached up into the hole. Pulling himself over the lip, he yanked himself through, using the momentum of his swing to get one knee over the still-glowing edges.

The gantry screeched in protest, the distorted metal giving under his weight. Farren's eyes went wide as he froze in place.

Inch by careful inch, he gradually climbed up and through, his fingers gripping through the metal grille to pull himself to safety. His armour's damage readout set a low-grade alert rune flaring, but he dismissed it, mouthing a silent apology to its machine-spirit.

As he got to his feet and ran along the second storey gantry further into the rig, Farren saw the muzzle flash of a t'au plasma weapon on the level below. The telltale explosions of bolt rounds boomed as Thrunn and Enrod returned fire. Farren could see two shimmering forms directly below him ducking into cover, their motion and heat signatures all but invisible to his Mark X armour's sub-auspex reader.

Grimacing at the breach of protocol, he took off his helm, mag-clamping it to his waist. Now he could see them as strange silhouettes, patchy ripples of non-colour below him. Xenotech witchery, and reason enough to kill them without a second thought.

The xenos warsuits fired another volley, the flashes of light clinching their position. Farren drew his broad-bladed power sword from its scabbard with a strange reluctance; it was the first time he had done so in battlefield conditions. He depressed its activation rune and cut away the metal of the gantry to leave a semicircle the size of his helm. The blessed blade sliced through the thick iron bars as if they were no more than hempen rope.

There was a thin shriek as he pulled the metal up and away with his other hand. Below, one of the t'au looked up sharply. The creature raised its gun, drawing a bead.

Farren's grenade was already primed and dropping. The deadly cylinder spun as it dropped towards the two t'au stealthers, then detonated a second before it hit the ground. The warsuits were flung sideways, chameleon fields haywire. One of them became fully visible as a heavy-set warsuit torn open from shoulder to hip.

Farren took aim through the hole and put a bolt right in the wound. A split second later, the warsuit's detonation sent pieces of armour flying amidst an explosion of gore.

The lieutenant moved the barrel of his gun swiftly to the other stealther, placing a shot right in the back of the neck. It hit at just the right angle to punch through the armour's weak spot, blowing clear the warsuit's head in a blossom of fire.

'Blessed be the Maker,' said Farren softly as he chambered another clip.

Below him, his squads were already running to the site, panning their own bolt rifles left and right. Enrod's voice rang out.

'Farren, target behind!'

The lieutenant ducked on instinct, turning in a pivoting crouch. Four finger-sized bolts of plasma sizzled a hand's breadth overhead, burning through the triangular stanchion behind him in a cloud of acrid-smelling steam.

Farren brought his rifle in tight and shot the only part of the corridor wide enough to house a t'au warsuit. He silently prayed to the Omnissiah his ballistics theory was sound.

His supposition was proved right when a bolt cracked against something nigh invisible, the ensuing detonation revealing another ochre warsuit as it toppled onto its back.

Farren ran. Another two warsuits emerged from the corridor behind the first, camo fields flickering as rain pelted down from a loading shaft above them. They sent volleys of plasma sizzling in, forcing Farren's squadmates into cover.

Glancing up, Farren saw a dangling, spider-legged winch lift linked by chains and pulleys to the stanchions three storeys up. The apparatus was typically Mechanicus in design, its main body in the shape of a stylised cranium. Farren calibrated for a moment before shooting at the heavy chains that held it aloft, one bolt following another.

Impacting upon one of the chains, the master-crafted weapon's ammunition exploded with force enough to tear its links apart. The entire apparatus swung down at a crazy angle, its sword-sharp appendages screeching across the gantry in a shower of sparks.

The t'au warsuits below raised their weapons. Presumably taking it for some giant Imperial servo-skull, they poured shots into it.

A heartbeat later they were consumed in fire as Moricani's Hellblasters sent a diagonal volley of their own through the gantry. The plasma volley took the first stealther right in the midsection, blasting through him in a shower of glowing gobbets.

The second was consumed from head to toe in white fire when Lenkatz's ball of superheated gas clipped the cover it skulked behind. Xenos remains toppled to the gantry in a clatter of alloy and high-tech plasteks.

Farren ran forward to crouch between the two stealthers. He looked for signs of life, even replacing his helm to scan their bio-rhythms, but his micro-scryers found nothing.

The stench filtering through the lieutenant's helm was awful, the scent of burning electrics mingling with that of cooked xenos meat. The gaping hole in the abdomen of the nearest warsuit had revealed a mass of cauterised innards; it had burned right through the alien in places. The molten armour around it had exposed much of the pilot within. It was a greyish wretch of a thing, its remains fragile and small to Farren's eyes.

With its dying act, the alien had clawed at the air in vain hope of seizing a second's more existence. Its hand was four-fingered, clumsy and stubby in proportion, compared to that of a human. No wonder the t'au felt the need to go to war in such heavy armour if their physiques were so pitifully underdeveloped.

'My thanks, Squad Moricani,' said Farren. 'You completed the trap without my needing to say a word.'

'A pleasure, brother,' said Moricani, eyes panning for the next target.

'Chaplain Zaeroph,' said Farren, engaging his helm's magna-vox. 'All Primaris squads have embarked and engaged the enemy successfully. No losses.'

There was no reply.

'Chaplain Zaeroph, this is Lieutenant Farren. We're going further in.'

Only static came in response.

'Squads Parvell and Orenst, you're clear,' said the lieutenant. 'Get inside, as deep as you can. That high yield warsuit is still out there, I believe.'

'Acknowledged,' said Parvell, his name-rune flashing in affirmation.

'And if I get a visual on that bald skull of yours without a helm, Parvell, you'll feel the flat of my blade.'

'You can try, lieutenant,' said Parvell, the wry grin in his voice audible even over the crackling distortion of the vox.

Raised voices filtered down from the gantry above. They spoke in Low Gothic – human in tone, though Farren could not quite make out their words. The speech had the intonation of a fierce argument, getting louder by the moment. Farren spiked his audio feed to maximum and looked straight at the source.

'You'll only make it worse!' shouted a hoarse voice. 'They *are* the Takers, fool! They are attacking us as we speak!'

'Then they are doing so for a sound reason!' came the bellowed reply. 'For the Greater Good!'

'There are civilians up there,' said Farren. 'Watch your aim.'

A moment later, the telltale crack of autoguns rang out. Farren looked up, spying dark silhouettes through the grate of the storey above. There was another shot, closely followed by a flash of light. A scream pierced the din of the storm.

'T'au weaponry,' said Farren. 'There are more xenos on the next storey, opening fire upon the riggers.'

'Then let us get up there now!' cried Enrod. 'Show these alien scum how it feels to be outclassed by superior firepower.'

Farren called up the rig's schematic within his helm once more, examining the standard template construct's architectural data. 'Yes. There is a stairway network to the right. Orenst, Parvell, consolidate this level. Watch the exterior for that heavy warsuit. Its stealth tech will almost certainly be better than that of its smaller comrades. Look for a shimmer in the rain.'

'Aye, lieutenant.'

'Acknowledged.'

Motioning for his squad to move out, Farren ran for the stairway at the end of the passage. He took the ridged stairs three at a time, canting his shoulders diagonally so he could fit his broad pauldrons through the top of the stairs before bursting out from the top with his rifle raised. He swept the barrel left and right to check the shadowed areas, and his gaze settled on a pair of riggers crouched low on the passageway, their wide eyes white in the gloom.

'Don't come no further!' shouted the smaller of the two, his long hair slicked over a pallid face. He was holding a long-barrelled rifle of unknown design, its wide rectangular shape unmistakably alien. 'Your fight ain't with us!'

The second rigger snarled. His expression was angry, savage almost, but fear clouded his eyes. He raised his own weapon, a blunt xenos carbine with a second rectangular barrel beneath the first. 'They're here to kill us, Gransen!'

Farren strode towards them, rifle held in a controlled firing grip as he reset the bolt in its barrel to be non-reactive on impact.

Time seemed to slow as the rigger's trigger finger began to clench.

Farren took the shot. His target squeezed off a streaking blur of plasma, but Farren had already read its trajectory from the barrel's angle, and darted left. The plasma streaked past him just as Farren's bolt struck home. With a wet thump, the human's shoulder came apart. Blood squirted high as the figure tumbled, insensate with shock, to the ground.

The rigger's compatriot screamed. Farren lowered his rifle and strode purposefully towards him.

'Leave this one alive, brothers, he–'

The human was hit under the chin by a pinpoint shot from behind Farren. The impact alone was so hard it almost took his head off. Then the bolt exploded, sending fragments of skull and brain pattering from the stanchions behind and to the right.

'Apologies, lieutenant,' said Enrod, half-emerging from the top of the stairs. 'I already had the shot.'

'You will pay for that, Enrod,' said Farren coldly. 'I explicitly said to leave him. You disobeyed my orders, brother. Censure is the–'

The sound of gunfire in the middle distance snatched

away his words, shortly followed by the gruff thump of an explosion.

'You think this is the optimal time for a lecture?' said Enrod.

Farren turned away, feeling bitterness in his throat. 'Vesleigh, cover us.'

Vesleigh took position at the end of the gantry as Thrunn pushed past, roughly elbowing Enrod aside as he approached Farren's position. 'Civilians are using xenos tech, lieutenant.'

'It looks that way. One of them took a shot with one of these plasma weapons, but the other held his fire. He clearly wanted to parley.'

'Perhaps they disabled a couple of the xenos riflemen themselves, and grabbed their weapons,' said Enrod.

'They looted their corpses,' said Thrunn.

'Almost certainly,' said Enrod. 'Thieves as well as blasphemers against the Omnissiah's works.' He kicked the cadaver of the smaller human, and a fresh spurt of blood drizzled from its wounds to leak down through the gantry to the level below.

'I'm not so sure about that,' said Farren. 'The t'au are infamously adept at bribing the common populace to their side.'

He leaned over the nearest cadaver, pushing the carbine from its grip with his foot, and took a brief pict of the weapons tech. There was something odd about it, something even stranger than the weird lines and unbalanced design that he could not place. 'Right now it matters not. We press on.'

The *clang-clang-clang* of hurrying footfalls came from a corridor running parallel to their position. Farren raised his rifle, then checked his sword in its scabbard out of completeness. More riggers; quite a few of them, by the sound of their steps, all wearing steel-reinforced work boots.

Farren motioned for his men to hug the wall. As one they moved to the side. The low hum of their Mark X armour was nothing to the crashing tumult of the storm. By keeping still in the lee of a ribbed munitorum crate, they made a passable attempt at stealth.

Farren watched as a group of five humans ran past at the end of the corridor, too intent on moving quickly to scan their surroundings. They were a motley collection, but every man and woman was sparse and muscular, clad in overalls and gauntleted jackets of heavy suede.

The last of them, a man with wild eyes and a scraggly black beard, looked down the corridor straight at Farren as he ran past.

He halted, staring in disbelief as his chest heaved hard.

'No lethal force,' said Farren across the vox. He held a hand up, a warding gesture. 'We are hunting the xenos invaders!' he called out. 'We have no quarrel with–'

'For the Greater Good!'

A sweat-slicked bear of a man, nearly as tall as Farren was in full battleplate, barrelled around the corner with a rigwrench in each hand. He screamed as he flung himself straight for Farren, but he was made slow by his own bulk, and too desperate to think beyond his all-out attack.

Farren stepped forward and swept away both of the rigger's wrenches with a circle of his bolt rifle. The heavy tools clanged into the gantry just as Farren's pauldron caught the big man under the chin, slamming his head back and knocking him out cold.

'Ultrecht!' shouted a woman clutching her belongings with one arm as she drew a makeshift throwing knife from her belt. 'You will pay for that, Taker!' At her side the straggle-bearded male sprang forward, a dagger in each hand and a strange light in his eyes.

Thrunn stepped forward to take the daggerman's blades on his forearm with a spray of sparks. In one smooth motion, he backhanded the human so hard he was flung into a stanchion, collapsing unconscious a moment later. Moricani flung a grenade at the female just as she drew her knife back for a throw. It hit her in the forehead with such force she went down with a crash.

Farren's heart leaped into his mouth for a moment as the grenade rolled away with a telltale tinkle of metal. He turned his shoulder with his head tucked in.

'Pin's still in it,' said Moricani with a shrug. 'But it's still a hard lump of metal.' Farren could hear the smile in his voice. 'Who says Primaris Marines can't improvise.'

Bursting out from a rusted grille behind them came a pair of knife-wielding humans, a bald male and a scruffy blonde female. Vesleigh swung his bolt rifle sidelong to swipe the female back into a stanchion, leaning into the blow. She collided with force enough to slam her into unconsciousness.

Enrod swung a punch, hitting the male in the face. The blow caved in his features and cracked his head open against the stanchion. Purple-grey matter oozed from the ragged red splits along his scalp.

'Omnissiah! I said *no* lethal force, Enrod!'

'I honestly did not realise they would be so weak,' said Enrod. 'Laughable, really, that they should attack those sent to save them.'

'Disobey me once more and you will never laugh again,' said Farren, fighting down the urge to throttle his battle-brother then and there. 'It is well for you that I have more pressing matters.'

The blonde female at Vesleigh's feet suddenly rose as if hoisted by some unseen force, arms and legs dangling as she hung in midair. She gave a horrible snort of blood from her nose, eyes blazing blue and matted hair sticking out. Her mouth opened, the jaw stretching far, far too wide. A column of azure energy shot from her maw and slammed into Farren's side, knocking him sprawling into the bald man's corpse.

For a second, Farren was lost. The pain cascading across his body was fierce, even agonising, but it faded quickly as his system's natural anaesthetic kicked in. His power armour flooded his bloodstream with stimms, and he vaulted upright, one hand clasped to his wounded side. The other brought his bolt rifle to bear for a kill-shot.

The creature that hung in the corridor, still levitating, had only a blood-jetting stump for a neck. Behind her, Thrunn placed her decapitated head against a stanchion, then wiped his combat knife clean upon the still-floating corpse.

'Psyker,' he said.

'Well spotted, Thrunn,' said Moricani. 'Xedro, that was too close. Never underestimate the power of the mind, as Father Cawl used to say.'

'I'm not sure this was what he meant,' said Farren grimly, shouldering his rifle. 'Thrunn, my thanks for the assist.'

'Lethal force authorised now, is it?' said Enrod.

Burning with frustration, Farren turned away and walked down the corridor through the bodies of the fallen riggers.

The female with the throwing knife, knocked cold by Moricani's grenade, had let spill her bundle of belongings to reveal a strange statue with too many limbs. Farren nudged the effigy out of the cloth wrapping with his toe, then took a quick pict from his helm lens for later assimilation.

The statue was a faceless, strange thing, somehow alien in its anatomy. It reeked of blasphemy against the Omnissiah. On a sudden impulse, he crushed it under his foot, kicking the remains through a hole in the gantry wall to tumble down into the amber-lit darkness.

Farren made his way onward through the rig, his battle-brothers scanning every corner and darkened crevice as they pressed further inside. In the depths of the mega-structure they could still hear muffled explosions as the rest of the Dark Angels engaged.

'We'll link up with the First if we can,' said Farren. 'Once the fighting is over, Zaeroph will see to those heretics. They aren't going anywhere.'

The Primaris Marines passed stacks of rust-flecked promethium drums and crane assemblies, hustled past blood-spattered walls and trod spent bullet casings flat against walkways as they passed. At one point, the gantry fell away to the right, exposing a long drop down to a docking platform below.

Farren furrowed his brow and engaged his helm's picter once more for later study. In places the metal had been sheared through. The edges were still glowing, as if the rig had been carved by some vast, superheated blade.

'Another energy weapon?' said Moricani as he and his squad brought up the rear.

'I honestly do not know,' said Farren. 'It could be

xenotech, but by the angle and sweep of it... It looks almost as if it was fired at random.'

There was a sharp crack of weapons discharge from the north.

'The other strike forces seem happy to engage without us,' said Vesleigh. 'You think they used us as a distraction?'

'Our battle-brothers are concentrating on their duty, as should we,' said Farren. 'Watch the flanks, let's link up with–'

'There!'

A burning white ball of energy crackled through the sheets of rain. Farren dived hard to the left. The blast's pressure wave caught him nonetheless, sending him tumbling over the rail towards the precipitous drop. He flung out a hand and caught a stanchion, his shoulder joint burning with sudden pain as it took the entirety of his weight.

Another deadly sphere burned through the air, forcing him to raise his legs a split second before the ball of energy shot underneath. He felt its heat along his thighs and back.

Servos whined inside his power armour as he swung out over nothing, then hoisted himself up to get both elbows over the gantry. Enrod extended a hand, but the lieutenant ignored it, pushing his bolt rifle away for a moment and hauling himself back onto the walkway. He grabbed his rifle once more before springing up to his full height.

'Where is that thing?' he shouted. 'I want it dead.'

There was a shimmer in the rain, perhaps a hundred yards distant.

'By the pontoons!' shouted Enrod.

Farren shouldered his rifle and took a shot. A heartbeat

later his squad followed suit, a dozen killing rounds searing through the rain.

The volley of bolts was met by tiny glowing motes, a storm of fireflies that flickered into life to collide with the self-propelled rounds. They detonated the projectiles well before they could strike their target. A chain of explosions flashed in the rain, and orange light caught the edges of the warsuit's massive bulk.

The battle engine was far bigger than a Primaris Marine. Bigger even than a Redemptor Dreadnought, come to that, and yet it was rendered all but invisible by its camo field.

Farren cast around, looking for something to tip the balance. He spotted a stack of promethium drums, a common enough sight on such a rig. Their potential made his pulse race. He tapped his lenses to infra-red, and felt his hopes dampen. They were reading empty.

Another burst of plasma seared in. This time, Farren and his brothers were ready for it, and got clear just before the sphere obliterated the stanchions behind.

Sergeant Orenst and his squadmates had finally made the gantry, levelling their bolt rifles and sending a tight volley into the rain. Once more, a swarm of intercepting firefly-things appeared from nowhere to meet them. The bolts lit up the night once more, their wrath as futile as the rain itself.

'Thrunn,' said Farren, motioning at the promethium drums some way back along the gantry. 'Grab one of those barrels and hurl it out there.' He ran some preliminary ballistics in his head.

'I can get it some of the way, lieutenant, but–'

'Do it!'

Thrunn's name rune flashed in acknowledgement on

Farren's helm display as the young warrior pounded over to the stack of barrels, manhandling one from the top before dropping it with a clang and taking another.

'They're empty,' he said.

'They'll still have the dregs, and traces of gas.'

'It won't reach the–'

'It doesn't need to! Just get one out there!'

Another ball of plasma hurtled towards them. This time Moricani and his team were ready, sending a volley of their own superheated energies from their plasma incinerators to blaze straight into the incoming shot. Farren heard Moricani laugh harshly as the air turned to spectacular inferno. His autosenses kicked in, dimming his lenses to keep him from being blinded entirely.

'Now!'

Spinning around on the spot like a Medusan hammer thrower, Thrunn whirled the heavy iron drum before releasing it with a roar. Farren knelt and took a bead as it curved through the air towards the site of the stealther's plasma discharge.

'Maximum yield, brothers,' said Moricani. 'And make ready.' Farren heard the telltale whine of the plasma guns reaching their highest output; a lethal risk in any situation, even for those as scrupulous in their maintenance rituals as the Hellblasters.

'On my mark...' said Farren. He mouthed a silent prayer to the Omnissiah, running his index finger along his gun's barrel to calm its machine-spirit.

His bolt rifle bucked as he took the shot. It struck the promethium barrel dead centre, the armour-piercing bolt punching straight through.

With a deafening crack, the promethium vapour ignited

and the barrel came apart in a puff of flame. Splintered wedges of metal burned in all directions. Once more the firefly countermeasures of the xenos stealther shot out, this time flitting to intercept the knives of shrapnel coming towards it. Illuminated by the flame of the detonation, the colossal warsuit had been made visible, a giant of smooth lines and glinting sensors.

'Fire!' said Farren.

The xenos-thing moved to evade, but with its countermeasures already launched it had no way to escape. The bolts fired by Farren and his brothers struck hard, each piercing shot punching through alien alloy to detonate with a loud boom. Smoking craters appeared in the machine's hull.

A moment later, Squad Moricani's blinding spheres of plasma energy struck the warsuit, burning away its front and melting its primary weapon limb to a drizzling, shapeless mass.

The machine, mortally stricken and with flame jetting from within its cockpit, toppled back from its perch into the heaving waves below.

Farren cast about himself, looking for signs of any xenos threat. The storm howled, but of the battle unfolding around the rig, he saw nothing.

'And so it goes,' said Moricani. 'Score one for the Hellblasters.'

The lieutenant tapped his lenses through every spectrum available, scanning for t'au presence. Though he could not see him nearby, Parvell would no doubt have taken off his helm by now, trusting his own senses to scan for more stealthers. Yet even he remained silent.

'Eastern quadrant neutralised, Chaplain,' said Farren over the macro-vox. 'Your orders?'

There was still no reply.

Baring his teeth in irritation, Farren made his way out onto a jutting girder. He pushed out until he felt the strain of the metal underneath him near its optimum tolerance. Part of the rig's core armature, it was built to last. But after the blazing energies of their fight with the warsuit, he did not push his luck too far.

Something caught his eye to the far left, vanishing from sight.

Farren frowned, risking another step out on the stanchion. It shuddered under his feet, a warning from the primitive spirit of the rig itself.

He increased his mag-clamps to maximum as the wind howled around him, each new gust tugging and pushing at him as he took the best vantage point he could. Steeling himself, he raised his bolt rifle to his shoulder and readied to jump back if the stanchion gave way. It would not help the Primaris strike force's already shaky command structure to see their lieutenant plunge down into the icy water.

Peering down the scryer-scope to the far left of their position, Farren made out a group of bone-armoured figures. Each was massive in bulk, and several were adorned with the tall feathered wing-pennants of the First's elite. The squad had taken up a full-circle firing stance as it was lowered into the sea by a winch-platform on the western pontoon.

The Deathwing, fabled First Company of the Dark Angels, were seeking to engage beneath the waves.

Farren frowned, theories clustering in his head, as he watched them descend to the base of the pontoon and down into the surging waves. They were still standing in weapons-ready position as the crashing waters closed over them. Before long, all he could make out was their armour-lumens, dimly glowing in the sea. Then even those were gone.

The sound of explosions came from the west. Lashing flames curled around the stanchions from a clash happening just out of sight.

Then the macro-vox crackled, laced with a fizzle of static but still intelligible.

'*Primaris elements,*' came the voice of Chaplain Zaeroph. '*You have done well. The xenos are in full retreat. Return to your transports and extract forthwith.*'

'Acknowledged,' said Farren.

Another explosion sounded from the west, this time a muffled thump that sent up a plume of water.

Farren opened the macro-vox line again. 'Forgive me, Chaplain Zaeroph, but it appears elements of our wider force are still engaged. Should we reinforce the Deathwing?'

'*Return to your transports and extract immediately!*' The Chaplain's tone had a note of rage that took Farren aback.

'Understood. Heading for rendezvous point now.'

The lieutenant heard indistinct voices over the vox, muffled ghosts that he could not discern. Then Zaeroph's voice came through once more.

'*Farren, you are to attend us in the octagonal chamber at the rig's pinnacle.*'

'Aye, Chaplain.'

'*Alone.*'

'Acknowledged.'

Farren motioned for his men to move out, but did not go with them. Moricani raised an eyebrow, but he waved his brother's concern away. 'Later, Pietr. I have a report to make.'

Within seconds, the Primaris Marines were retracing their steps. The lieutenant cast a glance over his shoulder as he left the gantry, staring back at the crashing waves where he had seen his Deathwing battle-brothers submerge.

Only the black depths, profound with unanswered questions, greeted his gaze.

CHAPTER TWO
COLD THOUGHTS

Ferro-Giant Network
Saltire Vex, Pelagic Industrial World
Chalnath Expanse

Jensa Deel was sodden and numb with exhaustion. She was free of the water at last, having climbed out of the stormy ocean up one of the rig's main stanchions with the last of her strength. She was not free of the rising tide of panic that threatened to consume her mind.

Her teeth chattered violently enough for her jaws to clack like those of a skeletal marionette. She clung to the stanchion of the promethium rig as tightly as she could, the sharp-spined shells of zebra limpets cutting into her fingers and wrists. But she was alive. Through sheer animal adrenaline – and through the inner strength of a lifetime spent braving the waters during her down cycles – she had made the journey from Omicroid without drowning.

Less than a few hours earlier, she had plunged from the crosshairs of a xenos gun into the stormy waters. The gambit had worked, for the Takers that attacked her had left her for dead.

Perhaps they weren't so far off the mark. She had been a prime target for the remora-mouthed saprays that writhed in the surf, having to kick them off her legs as best she could even as she swam. She had lost a lot of blood, and likely had the cold-ague at the very least. Given the number and depth of the wounds, scrapes and gashes she had sustained in the last few hours, she might not last the night. But for now, at least, she clung on.

Jensa forced herself to look upwards and assess the outside of the rig. The oval hollows in the outside of the stanchion led up higher than she could see, their height seemingly infinite as they stretched away into the rain.

The priestess imagined a warm bed with a dozen blankets, and stretched a shuddering hand up to the first metal hollow in the stanchion's side. Then she reached her other hand up to the second. It took her three tries to force the toe of her boot into another of the hollows below, but she made it, and pushed upwards to grab a solid grip.

'You… can… do it… Jensa,' stuttered the rigswoman, her throat thick with the acrid, salty taste of seawater. 'Done… it… a hundred… times… before.'

Muscle memory took over, her limbs so cold and tired that the pain in her joints and the back of her thighs was almost abstract. Some animalistic need for survival took over, and her movements became almost automatic. One hollow blended into the next. A deep black sleep threatened to snatch her away and drop her into the waters at any moment.

Half-blind with tiredness, Deel allowed herself a moment of rest. She locked her limbs into the hollows, pushing her thigh all the way through to sit half-astride. She wedged her shoulder into the hollow above, just as she had been trained to do on the first day of her indoctrination.

She hung there like a rag doll, head drooping. The only thing keeping her awake was the cold rain lashing her face. She knew she was still losing blood from the wounds on her legs. The freezing sea had caused her veins to contract to the point it would likely be a mere trickle, but if she opened them up too much, she would probably bleed out.

'T'au'va, spare me,' she whispered into the storm. 'T'au'va, give me strength.'

For a second, she fell into the sleep of the dead.

A geyser of water erupted from the sea near the northern siphon point, waking her up with a jolt. A black shape burst from its midst in a manner that reminded Jensa of a spine-whale breaching. With its wings swept in the manner of a soaring raptor, it roared up into the skies on twin trails of flame. She could make out two blunt cannons jutting from the cockpit. Trails of blue sparks crackled across one of its wings around a crater of battle damage that fizzed with energy.

Jensa watched it with a numb detachment. There was no such craft on her rig, nor the ones either side of it. Nothing happened on Ferro-Giant Omicroid without her permission, and little on the other rigs without her getting word of it. But right now, such concerns seemed a thousand years away.

There was a sky-splitting boom, and suddenly there were more black shapes jetting overhead. The din of their engines rose above the crash and thunder of the tempest. Three squadrons of three fighters, stylised pinions emblazoned across their wings, carved through the skies after the unknown craft like carrion crows pursuing a great black eagle. As they matched their prey's flight path, the flee-ing craft shimmered and disappeared from sight entirely.

Deel frowned. The vessel that had burst from the water had been nowhere near the cloudbanks. If anything, it had been heading for a gap in the thunderheads, its flight path leading it straight for the star she knew as the Scorpid's Eye. So how did it just disappear?

She felt the roar of the jetfighters reverberate in her chest as they engaged their afterburners. They drove hard along the same vector, then peeled off, three by three, before splitting up in a rising spiral that reminded her of a cyclone gathering force.

A search pattern, unmistakeably. She was not the only one to have lost the first craft's trail.

The jetfighters hurtled up into the storm clouds, and were gone.

Jensa Deel finally hauled herself onto the lowest dwelling-level of the rig. Still dripping, she sprawled on her face onto the cold metal, eyes closed and too tired to cry. She could hear the dull clang of footsteps, and they were get-ting louder. Only through the most tremendous act of willpower did she manage to push herself onto all fours.

She opened her eyes to see two massive, armoured boots. Their royal blue hue was so dark they seemed almost black, and they glinted with amber spots in the orange light of the sub-level.

They were far too large to be those of a human.

Deel blinked, gathered herself, and stood shakily. Adren-aline pounded in her neck, her chest, her spine as she took in the barrel chest and hulking, bear-like mass of an Imperial Space Marine.

She felt like a shivering child next to the immense armour-clad figure that stood before her, as impassive as a statue. The low hum of its power armour thrummed under the sound of distant waves. Deel could feel its gaze upon her, its disapproval mixed with idle interest.

She was suddenly aware that in some other circumstances, some animal part of her would have cowered, shrinking away from the terrifying apparition. But right now, she was too tired to do anything more than exist, and get to shelter by whatever means necessary. The adrenaline rushing through her system, by this point feeling stagnant and spiky rather than invigorating, made her feel more willing to fight than flee. It would mean less movement, for one thing.

Even though spots of exhaustion danced in front of her eyes, she forced herself to look up and meet its gaze.

A hooded figure stared back, as deathly and stern as if the Reaper had come for her himself. Only the lower half of the Space Marine's face was exposed, a jutting jaw made rough with dark stubble, but as her eyesight adjusted she could see a little way under its cowl. Strange cables framed the giant's angular features. His eyes, narrow and slitted against the wind, seemed to glow coldly in the shadows. She felt as though they bored into the centre of her brain.

'Deel,' he said, the word as sepulchral and deep as the black sea.

'Y-y-yes,' she chattered.

'You will come with me. Back to Omicroid.'

Xedro Farren stood in the octagonal viewing room at the top of the promethium rig. Opposite him were two of the most senior members of the Dark Angels Chapter, imposing even to one who had witnessed Archmagos Cawl in the flesh. Light flickered from the cage-lumens above, casting them all in a wan blue tint. Around him were cogitator banks and wide panoramic windows that showed the storm-wracked ocean beyond. Ferro-Giant Omicroid's fellow rigs dotted the horizon, churning excess power from the ocean to send tongues of flame into the night.

Farren's gaze was firmly fixed upon his fellow Dark Angels. Solid figures in ornate power armour, their presence and gravitas seemed to take up far more room than any mortal could ever hope to fill.

Chaplain Zaeroph's face was hidden behind a stylised skull helmet, grim and forbidding. Around his neck was a sacred Rosarius, the force-field amulet held on a string of pearled beads – for some reason three of them were black, but Farren had never mustered the nerve to ask why. Even with his features covered, the Chaplain managed to exude a disapproval so intense it felt like it stripped a layer of paint from Farren's armour with every glance.

Company Master Gabrael did not wear his helm, instead reinforcing his status with a long and elaborately embroidered cloak. He stared at Farren with an even and passionless expression, the stolid intensity of a castellan watching foes approach his fortress before giving the order to fire. The deep brown of his skin was that of a soul well used to fighting under a harsh sun. Three golden service studs in the shape of skulls jutted from his forehead in stark contrast, glinting in the flickering light beneath a receding hairline of cropped black hair.

Farren knew he was more physically imposing than the veteran Dark Angels officers he was reporting to, and he was clad in Mark X armour, the finest type of battle-plate yet known to the Adeptus Astartes. The implants in his body were superior to those of the traditional Space Marines, giving him greater endurance and swifter reaction speed. He had coils of hyper-durable metal around every sinew, a Belisarian furnace in his chest and the blood of the Lion pulsing in his veins. More than that, he carried the rank of lieutenant, an honour he had earned twice over. He had nothing to fear from his battle-brothers.

And still, in the face of the luminaries of his Chapter, Farren felt like a boy called to answer to his elders and betters.

There was a heaviness to them, the weight of centuries spent in battle. They bore it in their posture, their gaze, even the aura around them. To Farren, they seemed sculpted from stone, with he and his kin mere driftwood by comparison. Their presence was intimidating, even to one used to dealing with the half-human magi of the Adeptus Mechanicus.

'May I tell you of our fight?' said Farren, his voice coming out not nearly as strident and confident as he had hoped. 'It will be of interest.'

'You may not,' snapped Zaeroph.

'We await the return of Epistolary Dothrael,' said Gabrael, his eyes looking sidelong out the viewscreen window as if Farren was barely worthy of notice. 'His gunship just made it back to the skyshield.'

Farren kept his peace. In his mind's eye he saw Moricani laughing at him. How glad he was that his battle-brother had not been asked along to the debriefing.

'He is here,' said Zaeroph, turning to the doorway.

A gale of cold wind burst through the seal-hatch as the

epistolary flung it open, his massively built form holding the worst of the elements at bay. His eyes glowed blue, tiny traceries of lightning at each corner.

Shoved roughly before him was a human female, long-limbed and muscular of build, but small in comparison to her saviour. She staggered in, dropping to one knee with a grunt of pain. The human was already half-dead, by the look in her eye and the chattering of her teeth. Farren surreptitiously tapped his helm to infra-red; her life-signs were pitifully low. Even her core was barely registering amber levels of heat.

'This is the survivor?' said Zaeroph.

'Yes, Interrogator-Chaplain,' said Dothrael, the wind tugging at his cowl as he shut the bulkhead door behind him. 'Rigswoman Jensa Deel. Somehow she made it to the next rig.' Farren frowned at the Librarian's term of address. *Interrogator*?

'She is the only human still active from this megastructure, according to the Ravenwing,' said Master Gabrael, his cloak of office billowing around him in the last of the wind. 'Just as well.'

Zaeroph snorted through his helm-vox, a sound like that of an impatient stallion. 'Stand up, mortal. Let me assess you.'

The bedraggled human stood as tall as she could, her fists bunched and arms shaking.

'G-g-get…'

'Get what, woman?' said the Chaplain, moving in close to stare down at her with red-lit eyes.

'G-g-get to the s-sea's b-bed with y-you.'

To Farren, she looked on the point of despair, or madness. Her shivering was uncontrollable, almost hard to watch.

'Or get her a blanket,' he said, despite himself.

'What did you say?' said Gabrael, his tone incredulous. 'We are not nursemaids. Your kind is clearly too naive to realise it, Farren, but compassion is a weakness.'

'If she dies on us, it will be next to impossible to unpick what happened here,' said Farren, his tone level.

'We will have the answers we need before she expires,' said Zaeroph. Next to him, the company master turned and looked out of the window, already disinterested.

Farren moved over to Gabrael and grabbed his heavy cloak, yanking it so hard it tore away from the clasps on his shoulders with a loud rip. The company master spun, his face a mask of indignant fury. His power sword was already half way from its skull-work scabbard, glowing blue with a crackle of disruptive energies.

Zaeroph's hand shot out and grabbed the company master by the wrist, holding his sword arm in place. The Chaplain fixed Gabrael with an even stare, daring him to lash out.

Farren turned away without a word, wrapping the heavy cloak around the shivering woman until she was covered head to toe with only her face visible. She looked up at him, gratitude mingled with shock in her eyes as she pulled the velvety fabric in close.

'That cloak once swathed a relic of the Chapter's past,' said Gabrael, his voice cold and monotone. 'You will answer for that.'

'The matter can wait,' said Zaeroph. 'Farren is correct. The woman is more use to us alive, and intelligible, than as a corpse.'

Farren cast about the room, eyes alighting on a bullet flask wedged in between two of the cogitator banks. He walked over, ignoring Gabrael's dagger stare as he pulled the flask out and unscrewed the cap. He held it under his respirator for a moment; it had the bitter tang of recaf, mixed with the ester-rich scent of moonshine. Bad quality, and poisonous in the long term, but clearly the riggers found it warming enough.

'Here,' he said, handing it to the woman. 'Drink this.'

She took it with shaking hands, sipping at first, then gulping it down. She coughed hard, spat a thin gruel of seawater and moonshine onto the steel floor, and pulled the cloak tight once more.

'My... th-thanks,' she stammered. 'B-but really I n-need s-something hot.'

'Why must we suffer this nonsense?' blurted Gabrael. 'Time is of the essence!'

'However fast we pursue, we will not outdistance the Ravenwing,' said Zaeroph. 'Let them do what they were born to.'

'We shall find plenty of answers here,' said Epistolary Dothrael. 'Even if we have to resort to unusual methods to find them.'

'I am glad to hear it,' said Farren. 'I have many questions.'

The room went silent, its atmosphere suddenly growing so cold that Farren half expected to see his breath frosting in front of his face.

'Let him ask,' said the Librarian. 'We may gain some insight into the Primaris mindset, or perhaps even that of his ultimate sponsor, the Lord Macragge. Besides, after we get back to the *Blade*, what difference will it make?'

'There is that,' said Gabrael. 'Perhaps it is the teachings of Guilliman that leads him to disrespect the Sons of the Lion, stealing the belongings of his superiors and giving them to human serfs. Is that how the primarch told you to behave when you met him, Primaris?'

'It is the faultless logic of Mars, combined with the human decency of Terra,' said Farren. 'We still have some of that left.'

As Gabrael gave a short, barking laugh at the implied rebuke, questions blurred together in Farren's mind. What had the company master meant, about meeting the primarch? And what events were due to take place on the *Blade*? He had heard nothing.

'Enough,' said Zaeroph. 'Report. Whilst this one gathers herself.'

'My teams engaged the xenos at the southern pontoon,' said Farren. 'We took the first storey with ease before encountering resistance from a stealth team.'

'Fascinating,' said Gabrael dully.

'Let him speak,' said Zaeroph. 'Did you learn of their modus?'

'They struck as and when the opportunity presented itself, placing themselves in commanding ballistic positions. They relied on their adaptive camouflage to shield them from return fire. In this lies their weakness.'

'Go on.'

'They use the mindset of the ambush predator, Chaplain. Yet we are not prey. They little realise that if they do not kill us when they have the advantage, they invite a far deadlier retribution.'

'How many xenos fell to your teams?' asked Gabrael.

'Five warsuits in total.'

The company master snorted, turning away once more to look out at the ocean beyond.

'The last of them we engaged was some thirty feet tall, and cloaked with such sophisticated tech it was all but invisible. It had an ionic plasma weapon of some kind, judging by its proton yield, and countermeasures that intercepted our bolt rounds with ease.'

'So how did you kill it?' asked Dothrael. 'You Primaris Marines forsake heavy weapon troopers, do you not?'

'We have squads intended for engaging heavy targets. I improvised, occupied its countermeasures, and coordinated a dual strike with Sergeant Moricani that sent it below the waves.'

'Hmm,' said Zaeroph. 'At least you kept one heavy warsuit occupied, then.'

'We killed it,' said Farren. 'Whereas the Ravenwing, tasked with perimeter control, were nowhere to be seen.'

'The Ravenwing's business is their own,' said Gabrael. 'And you do not know that you killed it, if you merely saw it submerge.'

'On the subject of submerging,' said Farren, 'I saw members of the Deathwing descend into the water on a winch rig. When I offered my teams' assistance, you refused on their behalf. May I ask, in my capacity as the commanding officer of the Primaris contingent, what they were hoping to accomplish?'

'No,' said Zaeroph.

'We are discussing the xenos presence, and their capabilities,' said Epistolary Dothrael. 'Did you encounter any anomalies you could not explain?'

'Not from the xenos,' said Farren, giving Zaeroph a long stare. The Chaplain remained impassive. 'Although the site where we fought the macro-stealther looked as if it had been cut apart by an industrial lascutter, wielded more or less at random,' continued Farren. 'Whole sections of the rig were slashed away, and still glowing.'

Farren saw the human female glance up at this, but she looked away as soon as she felt his gaze.

'Anything else?' said Gabrael.

The lieutenant called up the pict-captures he had assembled over the course of the battle, coming to rest on the image of the fallen riggers that had fired upon them with xenos weaponry.

'On two occasions we encountered resistance from indigenous humans, once deep within the rig, and once on its outskirts. The first group were put down efficiently.'

A vision of Enrod's bolt detonating within an unarmoured human's neck filled Farren's mind. He was not sure he would ever forget the sight. When they had been shooting servitors on Mars that had been different, somehow. Those things were half-dead already, their true sentience long gone.

'And the second?' said Gabrael.

'The second group we intended to subdue for questioning,' he continued, 'but they fought hard, and we were forced to put them down too.'

'Such is the cost of war.'

Farren was about to mention the strange sculpture he had found in the bundle of the knife-thrower's belongings, but something in Gabrael's contemptuous tone made him keep that to himself. He had no desire to feel the lash of the company master's tongue again.

'One of them, on the brink of death, manifested some psychic ability,' said Farren. 'Seemingly spontaneous, and uncontrolled. Telekinesis, I believe. And some manner of biomancy that sent a beam of white energy from the mouth.'

'You slew this creature?' said Dothrael, leaning forward with his expression intense.

'Immediately,' said Farren. 'Summary decapitation.'

'Did any of your men come into physical contact with the ectoplasmic discharge?'

'No,' said Farren, putting aside the ghosts of pain that still ached in his flank from the psyker's beam. The answer was technically correct; after all, he was the commander of the unit, rather than a part of it.

Dothrael nodded solemnly. 'She was probably an unsanctioned witch that had come here for refuge,' he said. 'It is well she is dead, and the matter is closed.'

Odd, thought Farren. He had not told the Librarian the gender of the psyker.

'There was one other thing that made little sense to me,' said Farren, eye-spooling back through his pict-captures. He picked out the pict of a t'au corpse, four-fingered hand clutching at the air. He summoned the pict of a discarded t'au rifle lying near a dead rigger, and compared them against each other.

'Well?' said Dothrael.

'One of the riggers we encountered used a rifle of xenos make. I assumed he had recovered it from an alien corpse, and in his panic he was on the brink of using it against us. But its grip was for a five-fingered hand.'

'The roots of heresy penetrate further than ever, since the Rift,' said Zaeroph. 'But theft is a minor crime, compared to rebellion.'

'That's just it. The t'au are quadrodactylous. Four-fingered. I checked one of their cadavers up close.'

'Is this babble relevant?' said Gabrael. 'Or are you further wasting our time?'

'Have some respect,' sighed Farren. 'I am a Dark Angel too, and an officer at that. You may outrank me, Company

Master Gabrael, but one of the Adeptus Astartes should not talk to a fellow officer in that manner.'

'*Fellow officer?*' said Gabrael, incredulous. 'The only thing you and I have in common, *brother*, is the colour of our battleplate. To my mind, you Mars-loving bastards do not deserve even that.'

'The lieutenant's report is relevant,' said Epistolary Dothrael. 'And his perspicacity does him credit.' He turned to the shivering human woman, staring down at her. 'Jensa Deel. Did the populace of your rig ever treat with xenos ambassadors, and accept weapons customised for human use? Do not lie to me, for I shall know of it.'

'We did,' she said, her voice quavering.

'And was this something that was common to the planet of Saltire Vex?'

Deel said nothing, staring up at the Librarian with a mixture of defiance and terror.

'Answer him,' said Zaeroph. 'Or he will rip the knowledge from your mind, and leave you a drooling cretin for the rest of your short life.'

Stricken, she looked over at Farren.

'Comply,' he said.

'W-we sent our message boats decades ago,' she said coldly, her jaw jutting out. 'Even manned shuttles when we had the chance, and sent them to Qaru Non. We got nothing! The astropaths wouldn't even see us.'

'And?'

'The Imperium ignored our calls for medicine, for supplies, vitae-paste, fresh blood, everything! We had epidemics of bone-twist, of rickets, and outbreaks of ulcers inside and out. Even the supply ships stopped coming to take away the promethium we mined from the seabed.

What's the point of mining it if it's just going to get stock-piled and never used?'

Deel seemed to be warmed by her anger. Some of the colour was returning to her cheeks, and her stutter was gone.

'If it is your duty to mine it, then I do not see the issue,' said Farren.

'We can't turn the machines off. Our warehouse levels are packed to capacity. We're so overloaded we have to burn the stuff off each night, or we'd be drowning in it!'

'And that is cause to betray the Emperor?' said Chaplain Zaeroph. 'To flee into the arms of xenos scum?' He took a step forward, his fists clenched at his sides, and leaned forward as if he were about to bite her. 'You are already lost, human.'

'We had no choice!' said Deel, her voice high. 'Without them, without T'au'va, we would all be dead. This world's population would be nothing more than floating corpses.'

'Better that than xenos sympathisers,' said Gabrael coldly. 'You will die a traitor, and your kin will be put to death. But not until we have wrung every last iota of information we need from your worthless mind.'

'I mean no disrespect, but you don't understand what we went through,' said Deel. 'The Imperium is blind to Saltire Vex. It has forgotten we exist. And why? We have our tithes ready, and the Imperium needs fuel more than ever to wage its wars. So why are we being left to starve?'

'The galaxy is a big place,' said Farren. 'Sometimes mistakes are made.'

'Some comfort that is! With the Emperor's light taken from us, we can't possibly hope to survive. Malnutrition is one thing, but there's not much to do out here at night but stargaze. And there's something new in the sky, isn't there? That great purple scar?'

'It is forbidden to look upon it,' said Dothrael. 'Even you must know that.'

'I'm not surprised. Those who stared at it too long, they lost their minds. We had outbreaks of violent psychosis every month, then every week. We know what's in store for us here. Without the t'au's help, we would have wound up eating each other when the food ran out, and even then the survivors would freeze to death.'

'How so?' asked Farren. 'With that much excess prome-thium, surely fire is not a problem?'

'This planet's orbit takes us far from the sun,' said Deel. 'Barrel-fire's not nearly enough to keep that kind of cold at bay. The Great Cycle, we call it. In the past the Adepts have always evacuated us, taking us off world. They resettle the rigs once the cold time is over. But there's no reply to our data-psalms, no talk of evacuation now. Not this time.'

'The Emperor has more pressing concerns,' said Zaeroph drily. 'What does he care if a world of xenos-worshipping heretics dies out?'

'You aren't listening! Without a way off world, another five months go past and we'll all have frozen to death, or else gone mad and killed one another,' said Deel. 'When the t'au came offering help, what was I supposed to do?'

'Fight them to the last drop of blood, and then die in the Emperor's grace,' said Gabrael with a half-shrug. 'Only in death does duty end.'

'An industrial outpost world can't hold out against an alien empire,' said Deel. 'That's why the Emperor made peo-ple like you, to fight on our behalf.' She made a grimace. 'A lot of good you did us. The defenders of humanity indeed.'

'We saved you from the xenos that were corrupting you,' said Farren. 'Though you yourselves attacked us as we did so. One of your number turned xenos weaponry against us, and another used some manner of psychic assault.'

The lieutenant unconsciously moved his arm to cover his side, the scorched black ceramite clustered around a deep crater that exposed layers of shining alloy and reinforced fibre bundles around a pitted crater of flesh.

It looked much like a plasma wound, thank the Omnissiah. No one had questioned it thus far, but something about it felt wrong. He could feel the sting of the wound at the crater's centre, almost red hot with the process of accelerated healing as his advanced biology went to work.

'Those who attacked you likely thought you to be Takers,' said Deel sullenly.

'Takers?' said Zaeroph. 'Explain this term.'

'Over the last few months, thirty-four riggers have gone missing. Usually whenever the cloud cover comes in low, or when the storms roll in.'

'Collateral damage from the tempests,' said Zaeroph. 'Such an open structure is bound to take losses.'

'No. We know how to batten down the hatches. We train for that. This is something else entirely. We are being abducted.'

'Speak on,' said Zaeroph.

'No one knew how, or why, or by what. These Takers are invisible. They come down from the clouds, seize you, and they take you away. But then I saw one of the things with my own eyes.'

'They were the same breed of xenos you claimed had come to save you,' said Farren.

Deel looked at the floor.

'Yes.'

'See how your new masters reward you for your compliance,' growled Gabrael.

'You reap that which you have sown,' said Zaeroph, nodding. 'Treat with dark forces, and you will find yourself in the depths of the abyss.'

'So I see,' said Deel, her eyes flashing.

Zaeroph, Gabrael and Dothrael stared at her, saying nothing. She pulled the cloak tight around her once more, seeming to shrink.

'Was there any pattern to those taken by the xenos?' asked Farren.

'Yes,' said Deel quietly. 'The abductees were always those who had experienced splitting headaches beforehand.'

Zaeroph leaned forward. 'Elaborate.'

'There are those amongst us who had developed migraines, recently,' she said with a shiver. 'Migraines and memory loss. They were always the ones that were taken. I kept track, and marked the registers myself.'

'She's hiding something,' said Dothrael to Zaeroph.

'Woman, you had better speak the full truth,' said Gabrael. 'Your time is running out.'

Farren saw Deel's eyes dart over to him. He nodded, just once.

'She had these symptoms herself,' said Zaeroph, his tone sly.

'Yes,' she confessed. 'I had them too. When the Takers came for me... that was when I dived into the water, and swam to Thetoid.'

'An unaugmented human managed to escape a xenos warsuit?'

'Something happened. I... my head felt like it split open, and when I opened my eyes...'

'Yes?'

'The warsuit thing had been hit by some kind of weapon.'

'You mean you had manifested a psychic ability,' said Dothrael.

'All I know is the girders around me had been cut through, and the thing was suddenly visible, with two deep gashes across its chest.'

Dothrael and Zaeroph shared a glance.

'The site I spoke of,' said Farren.

'It was huge,' continued Deel. 'Far larger than any loader armature or sentinel array I had ever seen. It looked… advanced. There were these disc things flying around it, a little like servo-skulls, I suppose, but much bigger. But it wasn't moving.'

'And that is when you ran,' said Farren.

'Yes. I dived into the water, and swam. That's all.' She stared at nothing, and spoke as if to herself. 'I need to get to a fire. I must go.'

'Manifesting untrained psychic powers is amongst the most severe transgressions in the Imperium,' said Dothrael. 'So, no, you cannot simply *go*.'

'You will stay under our auspice,' said Zaeroph, nodding. 'Somewhere secure, and discreet. You are the self-confessed leader of a group of known t'au sympathisers. Having already been the target of one abduction attempt, you will likely be a priority target for whatever force tried to remove you.'

'In short, you make for good bait,' said Dothrael.

'I have to ask,' said Farren. 'Why did the members of your rig suddenly begin to manifest empyric phenomena? The data slate on these t'au says they are psychically inert.'

'That is enough in the way of questions for today,' said

Zaeroph, turning his back on the assembly to gaze out of the window to the rigs on the horizon. 'We will learn more soon enough.'

'But with all due respect, Chaplain, that information could–'

'Farren, leave us. Return to your squads. Dothrael, you will keep watch over this rigger, somewhere secure, and take any truths she has yet to give us. I expect a full report within the hour. We must rendezvous with the Ravenwing at the muster point once they have seen to their quarry.'

'Of course, Chaplain Zaeroph,' said Dothrael.

'Interrogator-Chaplain, wasn't it?' said Farren. 'That was what you called him earlier, isn't it, Epistolary Dothrael?'

Gabrael spoke through his teeth. 'It matters little, in the end.'

'Leave us, Farren,' said Zaeroph, his tone as cold as buried steel. 'Do not make me repeat myself again, or it will go the worse for you.'

'As you wish. But I would recommend keeping Mamzel Deel inside, as close to warm and dry as you can. If possible, you should get Apothecary Vaarad to see to her.'

Zaeroph and Gabrael stared long at Farren. The feeling of their dislike was so intense it was almost palpable.

'We must honour the tenets of the Lord Macragge,' said Dothrael dully. 'Of course.'

'Make ready your contingent, Farren,' said Zaeroph. 'We will leave this warzone within the hour.'

'We have business elsewhere,' said Company Master Gabrael. 'You will be briefed at the appropriate juncture. Now is the time to leave.'

Farren turned on his heel and made for the door, turning the wheel lock before striding out into the pelting rain.

Questions whirled around his brain, but something inside him knew better than to ask them.

The wheel-lock door slammed shut as Farren left, with Dothrael and Deel close behind him. All disappeared past the viewscreen and made their way down the reinforced iron stairs before Farren peeled off. Inside, Zaeroph and Gabrael waited patiently, listening to three sets of retreating footsteps.

'Keeping an untrained psyker close at hand,' said Gabrael when he was sure no one could hear them. 'Are you sure that is wise?'

'It is necessary,' said Zaeroph. 'Have some faith.'

Gabrael nodded as if convinced, but he felt the need to finish what he had started.

'You truly believe she will lure the xenos back to us?'

'Not for an instant,' said Zaeroph. 'These t'au are not imbeciles. There is a reason they rely on stealth so heavily. In a straight fight against us, they are hopelessly outmatched.'

'You think she has value in the wider work, then.'

'She may have seen our quarry first hand, even if she does not remember it,' replied the Chaplain. 'She may even have been affected by the device. If so, her brain will be of use to us.'

'Should we have Vaarad extract it?'

'No. Dothrael will keep her psyche under control, if necessary, and excise the answers we need after we remove her. You know full well what he is capable of.'

Gabrael nodded, looking out of the viewscreens to the stormclouds high above. They were beginning to part in places, revealing the star-studded vault and the livid purple weal of unreality that cut across it.

'Farren is still a dangerous liability, even with the asset in play,' he said after a while. 'He oversteps his bounds. This tendency is rooted deep in him.'

'He and his warriors are emblematic of a wider issue. One that gives the Adeptus Astartes new hope, even as it dooms our old ways to obsolescence.'

'Do you not say yourself that curiosity is an infection?' said Gabrael. 'One to be quarantined, moved into the vanguard, and dashed against the rocks of duty?'

'I stand by those words,' nodded the Interrogator-Chaplain. 'Their freedom of thought disturbs me as much as it does you. But the Lord of Ultramar outlined his vision very clearly at the Summit, and he watches from afar. This is his initiative.'

'His initiative, with the Primaris Marines as his eyes and ears,' said Gabrael. 'We tempt fate even by allowing them in our sanctums. Let them believe they are part of our Chapter for the sake of appearance if you must, but I implore you, Zaeroph, send them far away. Can you not speak with Azrael, or contact Ezekiel? Find a way to despatch these naïfs to another warzone entirely?'

'You wish for us to deliberately misinterpret the primarch's wishes? For us to refuse these new bodies, to keep the Ultima Founding from our ranks, would be as sure a way to invite the scrutiny of the Lord Imperium as if we directed our guns at Ultramar ourselves. We proceed with the induction programme as planned.'

'I suppose this is not the time to deviate from our course.'

'No indeed,' said the Chaplain, studying the ornate winged skull at the end of his crozius arcanum. 'We continue the hunt apace.'

'We have lost him already,' said Gabrael. 'I can feel it.'

'I too have my doubts. But we should not give up hope, lest despair diminish our perception. Our Thunderhawks are still searching the skies, as are the Nephilim, and the rest of the Ravenwing contingent are still tracing his spoor. We may find him on Saltire Vex yet. And if not, we will intercept him at his next destination instead.'

'Do we have an extrapolation of heading, at least?'

'Apparently so,' said Zaeroph. 'And according to the Ravenwing's last communiqué, the xenos are following him too. They are bound for the Scorpid cluster. If Autinocus is right, their blasphemous technology has a far greater augur range than ours. They will lead us right to him, and give us all the reason we need to strike at his destination.'

Gabrael nodded, deep in thought.

'The Scorpid star system is home to the Angels of Absolution's prime homeworld, Allhallow,' continued Zaeroph. 'We will trap him there, with our hammer crushing him against the anvil of Soul's Well.'

'This does not sit well with me, Chaplain,' said Gabrael. 'Employing the xenos in such a fashion.'

'We came close this time, old friend. Very close. If we keep up this pressure, he will overplay his hand soon enough, and then we will seize him.'

'What of the rigsmen?'

'They must be eradicated. The taint must not spread. Nor can word of its source.'

'I agree. But we cannot incur the world-fire without censure, even with the express consent of the Supreme Grand Master. We will draw undue attention from the Inquisition.'

'I realise that, Gabrael,' said the Chaplain. 'If it were at all possible, I would already have enacted it.'

'The populace of this outpost may already have spread to another site, even before we made planetfall, and spread the infection with it. And they may have taken incriminating information along with them.'

'The population is effectively quarantined already by their severance from the astropathic ducts. I have already seen to it that no more communication can be shared between Saltire Vex and Qaru Non, nor that which remains of the Imperium this side of the rift.'

'Then the problem will solve itself?'

'Essentially, yes.' The interrogator turned, the forbidding skull of his helm staring straight at Gabrael. 'Within a few months, the people of this world will be little more than statues of frozen flesh.'

High above Ferro-Giant Thetoid, there was a shimmer in the night sky. It rose high above the thunderclouds, and seemed to ripple, for a moment. Then the light from the planet's nearest moon caught it fully, playing across swept-forward wings and a pair of cannons jutting from a blunt nose cone of jet black.

The aircraft was deadly enough in itself, but inside it was a concentration of force like no other.

'They had their chance,' said the figure in the cockpit. 'And they failed to seize it.'

The pilot was a Space Marine, or at least an approximation of one, tusked in the manner of a beast. A vice-like apparatus of tubes and coils gripped his head as if holding it together from some grievous wound. The spark plug-like protrusions jutting from his strange crown crackled with black lightning.

Around his torso was a chain-link necklace of eight

rune-emblazoned skulls, each large and broad of brow. They were yellow-brown with age, and each had a patina of cracked shellac varnish. Seawater dripped from the gappy teeth of the most intact skulls, and small rivulets sloshed from the empty sockets of the one at the bottom of the chain.

To a simple man, the skulls were a grisly adornment, unsettling but crude. To one with the witchsight, they would appear as threatening as a string of time bombs, primed and ready to explode.

The cockpit smelt of salt and incense, with a faint tang of electrical discharge.

'They shot at me,' muttered the pilot. 'Shot at me as if I were some common mortal. Not so much as a word.'

The skulls clattered as he shifted in his seat, the sound of bone clacking against bone oddly out of place amongst the sophisticated instruments and dials.

'What?' said the pilot. 'No, they had no idea. Though they will find out soon enough.'

A trickle of seawater drizzled from one of the skulls, then beaded and floated away as the craft pushed its way free of the planet's gravitic envelope.

'I imagine they will, yes,' the pilot continued. 'They have proven tenacious. Those of you who are Mystai will understand that all too well. Besides, with the help of your talents combined, I intend to make my influence obvious.'

A distorted sphere of brine wobbled past the pilot's tusked helm, trailing smaller droplets in its wake.

'The Scorpid,' said the pilot gravely. 'Let us visit the lessons of the past on those who would rather forget. Lessons some of you will understand well, old friends. We shall show them what it means to be unforgiven.'

The skulls kept their peace. The black-winged craft shot on through low orbit and into space, its cargo of madness and death free in the void once more.

Company Master Gabrael's face appeared on the interior of the *Night Harrower*'s telemetry link for a static-laced second. *'We're to move out,'* he said. *'Thunderhawks inbound.'*

His image then disappeared again.

Moricani sat up sharply, combing his sandy hair with his fingers. 'Was that the dashing Master Gabrael?'

Farren laughed quietly. 'You'll get your chance to impress him soon enough, Pietr, but I'd advise against trying to do so with your wit.'

'But he seems such a light-hearted soul.'

'Don't they all,' said Vesleigh.

'You know as well as I that they have good reason for their attitude,' said Farren. 'There is little room for levity in an active warzone.'

'Certainly not with you as commanding officer,' said Moricani.

'Cease,' said Farren, consulting the skull-styled cogitator relay as it chattered out a studded length of parchment. 'We are still technically engaged, even if the enemy have fled. The Chaplain wants us to rendezvous over open water in thirty-three minutes.'

He thought about the debrief once more. Various odd phrases and fragments of information played through his mind over and over.

'But I have something I need to do before then,' he said, standing up. 'I need some answers.'

'You're not going to try to confer with the other officers again, are you?' said Moricani.

'Not them,' said Farren. 'Someone else.'

'Are you sure that's a good idea, lieutenant?'

'Trust me.'

CHAPTER THREE
TRIAL AND ERROR

Ferro-Giant Omicroid
Saltire Vex, Pelagic Industrial World
Chalnath Expanse

Omicroid's sea brig looked a dank and lonely place. Held suspended fifty feet below the underside of the promethium rig, the cuboid structure languished amidst a fug-like stench of unrefined fuel and rotting bivalves. The rough caulk of its walls was discoloured by strata of algae and caked salt, and long strands of bladderwrack hung from its underside like the beard of an undersea god.

Handhold by handhold, Farren swung by his arms under the rig's decking towards it. With his legs in a loose crouch, he had gripped the underside of the lower walkways by their grilles and grate-holes, reached out for thick pipes that looked solid enough to take his weight, and grabbed for the rung hollows of each intermediate stanchion whilst ignoring the trickles of promethium drizzling from above. Thus far, he was making good progress.

Behind him, the three Repulsors were smudges of dark green in the distance. By Gsar's estimate – and Farren trusted that implicitly – the tanks were too tall to make it under the rig when their engines were active, failing to clear it by a matter of a few infuriating inches. Besides, where a Repulsor made for an obvious sight, a single Space Marine had a chance of making it to the brig and back without being seen by inquisitive eyes. So, without so much as a moment's hesitation, Farren had taken the hard way.

Ahead the makeshift cell was a lump of dark, near solid black on the lieutenant's helm display. He could see a tiny trace of yellow through the air vents that hinted at the occupant inside. Doubt crept into his mind, the suspicion he should have stayed in the *Harrower* gradually coalescing in the shadows of his intent. But he could see no other way to the truth.

Reaching the framework of girders around the brig, Farren moved hand-by-hand around its periphery, taking care not to move too close to the ladder stanchion that led towards its circular vault-hatch. Above the brig was a grille; above that, no doubt, was the occupant's jailor. His breath quickened, and he pushed aside the pain in his wounded side as his breath came heavier.

The lieutenant knew he was taking a huge gamble in coming down here. He was risking being the brunt of another psychic attack, even by showing his face to the brig's occupant. But it was the thought of his superiors' reaction if they found him questioning their prisoner that was making his twin hearts pound. He was almost certain they would settle the matter in violence, swift and final.

The lieutenant dropped down onto the corner of the

brig, taking care to crouch with his impact so he didn't smash the whole thing into the waves. 'Who's there?' came a harsh, croaking voice, barely audible over the pounding surf. 'I've already told you everything I know!'

Farren knelt down, then laid flat on his chest atop the brig, leaning forward over the edge so his face was level with one of the air vents.

'Xedro Farren. Lieutenant Primaris, assigned to the Third Company.' He caught himself for a moment. 'From the hearing room.'

He could just about make out Deel in the darkness, huddled around a thermal battery that – according to his infrared – was all but drained of charge. Sitting there in a couple of inches of brackish water, she looked truly awful, her eyes staring white orbs in the shadows of a skull-like face.

'Sad to see the company master took his cloak back,' said Farren.

'It looked better on him anyway. Are you here to kill me?'

'No,' said Farren. 'Simply to talk, and check you are still whole in body and mind,' he said.

'I'll be dead by nightfall.'

'Did they torture you?'

'Yes. No. I don't know. I ache all over, especially my brain. And parts of my memory are just... missing.'

'Unfortunate,' said Farren. 'We are to withdraw in the next...' he checked his helm's chronometer '... eighteen minutes. There will be an extraction, not too far from here. If you answer my questions quickly, I will leave the top of this brig open. You can climb out, and begin to rebuild your home.'

'They have what they need, lieutenant,' she said. 'They won't leave Omicroid to freeze, it's too much of a liability. They'll torch this place as they go, and let the cold take care of the rest.'

Farren did not reply.

'One day my corpse might be found in the brig, I suppose. Maybe even identified. Evidence enough of mutiny, especially when the fact we colluded with the t'au comes to light.'

'That is the truth, is it not? Some might say you deserve punishment.'

'We had no choice, I already told you that! The whole thing will be put down to an insurrection rightly punished, its leaders slain by noble Adeptus Astartes, and the rest brought back into the Imperial flock. Just in time to die as dutiful sheep instead of vile heretics.'

'You have a strange way of looking at our rescuing of you from the xenos that were attacking you,' said Farren. 'I am sure you will be relocated from this planet and settled once more when your planet's winter cycle is over. I will make the arrangements myself if necessary.'

'Emperor's Throne, Farren. They will just let me die, and not think twice about it. Why aren't your brothers visiting the other rigs, then, if you're here to drive off the xenos influence? I saw that black craft come out of its hiding place, fleeing for low orbit. You Space Marines had better get after it, if you want to catch up.'

'What craft? What are you talking about?'

'The black winged craft with the twin cannons. Impressive tech. Not many craft can play submersible, then breach from underwater and boost straight into the sky.'

'No such craft is part of the Chapter's armoury,' said Farren. 'It must be Navy.'

'Whatever you say,' said Deel. 'It looked a good deal like the fighters pursuing it. And it had many of the same markings. Swords, wings, that kind of thing.'

'Really. Where was this craft heading?'

'Hard to say. It vanished within a few seconds of breach. Looked like it was headed for the Scorpid's Eye, that system's in roughly that direction. There's not much else within reach. The pilot was keen on escaping you, no doubt.'

'Falsehoods,' said Farren quietly. 'This is delirium.'

'At this point, I don't much care if you believe it or not. I'm dead either way.'

Farren looked back at the Repulsor, and glanced at his chronometer. Fourteen minutes.

'You know too much to just be left in here.'

'Is there any other choice?' she spat. 'You kept me alive, only to let me die!'

Farren looked up at the grille, then down at the surging waves below the brig. They had risen in height and intensity in the last few minutes, and now they were crashing against the stanchions and the underside of the brig with a steady rhythm. The cold salt tang of their spume filled the air.

Farren balled a fist and punched the vent as hard as he could, timing the impact just as a wave slapped against the underside of the cuboid to mask the noise. The metal buckled, one of the rusted-in screws along its length popping free.

Another wave broke, and Farren levelled another punch, this time forcing an inch-thick hunk of metal to stick outwards. A third wave came in, and Farren grabbed the protruding flap of metal, tearing it half-open with a dull clank.

As he was drawing back for another punch, the entire thing came spinning away into the water below. The toe of Deel's boot jutted from the other side of the vent for a second before disappearing once more.

The hole they had made was too small for a human to fit through, but in tearing the metal away, Farren had crumbled some of the rebar support beneath it. He grabbed the jutting metal struts and yanked them back and forth, dislodging even more of the pebbled stone.

Deel scrabbled at the mortar and slivers of rock from the other side. She scraped and pulled at the base of each strut, then took off her boot and used the steel toecap as a hammer, slamming it repeatedly into the stonework. Scatterings of pebble-sized stones fell away.

Gritting his teeth, Farren waited for the next wave to come in before violently wrenching the rebar left and right, clearing loose rock with his other hand and forcing jagged struts of metal aside with a grunt of effort.

'It'll do,' said Deel. 'Move aside. Please.'

Farren checked his lens chrono. Eight minutes. He was lingering too long.

Deel was already up at the vent's edge, reaching through to grab Farren's hand. He pulled her through as carefully as he could, but he could see her face was ashen with pain. She squeezed her hunched shoulders through the vent's widest part. He held his arm out, braced rock-solid with his power armour's support, and she clambered onto it as if it were the bough of a tree until his forearm was under her waist. Then, shuffling forward, he reached out as she fought to get her hips through, allowing her to bring her legs up and out.

Grunting with effort, Deel climbed over his pauldron and backpack, smearing blood from the dozen cuts and grazes on her arms and legs across the dark green of his power armour. With a final effort, she slumped atop the brig with a heavy sigh.

'No time for rest,' said Farren. 'We need to move.'

Six minutes left, and the waves were rising, getting fiercer.

'Arms around my neck,' said Farren. 'There's still a chance we can do this.'

Biting her lip in exhaustion and frustration, Deel wrapped her arms around Farren's gorget, locking one hand on her wrist and the other to the underside of his chest plate. She pressed her body to his backpack, but to Farren, her weight was nothing.

When he was sure she was secure, Farren launched off the edge of the brig and caught an H-shaped girder with the ease of a gymnast catching a bar. Riding his momentum, he let go with one hand, reaching out for the next grip. His fingertips caught it, but not by much. He felt a hot sensation in his side, near his psy-wound. He pushed the feeling away, and focused on going forwards.

Time was running short.

On and on Farren went, the engine of his enhanced physiology driving him forward. He was Adeptus Astartes. A *Primaris Marine*. He would not fall.

He glanced at the helm's lens chrono once more as it steadily ticked down.

'Hold on,' he said, hanging with both hands from a robust girder as he gathered his strength.

'Just get on with it,' said Deel through gritted teeth. He felt her legs wrap around his waist and tighten. He saw muscled arms in his peripheral vision as the rigswoman reached up and grabbed the girder herself to take some of the weight off.

'It's fine,' said Farren. 'I have this.'

'It's quite a way,' she said.

'I said I have this!'

He scowled and set off once more. For a minute he made good progress, but the woman's weight seemed to be growing with each passing minute. He checked his vital signs, and noted with a kind of abstract interest that he had lost a good deal of blood from the injury the human psyker had inflicted.

A wound in a Space Marine's physiology would normally clot and scab over quickly, the haemastamen's vital elixir conserving the fluids in a matter of seconds, but this wound had not been inflicted by any normal weapon. For some reason, the blood was not coagulating.

Fresh and unhurt, in the arid air of Mars, Farren knew he would be able to make such a journey three times over and feel little more than a pleasing burn of exhilaration. But here, after the exertion of a battle, with a human cargo skewing his balance and with a psy-wound open and bleeding…

Slowly, insidiously, the seconds on the chrono ticked down. Five minutes left.

Now the waves were slapping at his legs. He tucked them up as best he could, and pushed onwards. Swing, catch, readjust, swing, grab, swing.

Somehow, he had lost focus. He had not come this way, before. The girders here were slick with algal slime, and with each handhold, he felt his fingers slipping.

He had to make it to the next solid grip.

With a heave of exertion, Farren lunged for the promethium pipeline. He caught it easily enough.

Then a wave slammed into his legs, and he nearly lost his hold completely.

'Oh God-Emperor,' said Deel. 'Please tell me you can do this.'

'It's fine,' said Farren, tensing and relaxing his muscle groups to keep them from burning with the acid of exertion.

'Is it?'

Farren did not reply.

The Repulsor was still a full two-thirds of the rig's width away, and they were fast running out of time.

'Where in the Omnissiah's holy wilderness is he?' said Vesleigh, racking the bolts into his ammo clip for the ninth time in as many minutes. Around him the rest of the squad were seated in the passenger hold of the *Harrower*, each busy with his own thoughts or rituals.

'*He will make it back in time,*' said Gsar over the vox-link. It was a credit to his rapport with the *Harrower* that he had brought it back to full function after the battle, for the tank had taken several plasma hits and ion discharges on its outer hull. With the electrical interference still affecting its systems, Gsar's voice carried a strange tinny quality.

'No doubt he wants to make a grand entrance,' said Moricani. 'I imagine he will burst through that door at the eleventh hour, to our rapturous applause.'

'What if he doesn't?' said Thrunn.

'A valid question,' said Vesleigh, taking the bolts out of his ammo clip again. 'What if they've discovered he made an unauthorised sortie? That will not reflect well on us. We might even get reassigned altogether.'

'Then we shall excel, centre stage, in a different theatre of war,' said Moricani.

'Be serious for once in your life, Moricani,' said Enrod.

'We can't miss the muster. Farren's got us in enough trouble as it is.'

'I am being serious,' said Moricani. 'He will be back in time.'

'I hope you're right,' said Enrod.

Silence enveloped the interior of the *Harrower* once more, the only sound the regular tick-clack tick-clack of Vesleigh's bolts being racked, cleaned and re-racked in his rifle over and over.

Farren hung from the underside of the promethium rig, Deel's arms locked around his shoulders. She had brought her legs up high around his waist, now, and entwined her ankles and feet to keep from dropping down into the crashing waves.

The lieutenant swung his legs back hard, then brought them forward and turned with the motion, extending an arm to grab at the next stanchion. He found a solid grip, then rode the movement to grab for the next. He waited for a moment, tucking his legs as a crashing wave rose up to grab at him. Without the tide, Farren could have got into a rhythm, let the swing of his own momentum do much of the work. But with the waves against him...

'We're not going to make it, are we?' said Deel.

'We have to,' grunted Farren. 'Be silent. I must conserve my strength.'

Four minutes.

One slip is all it would take. Even if Deel managed to swim to safety once more, she would be frozen to death before long. Farren would die far sooner, plunging down into the depths like a stone.

Swing, grab, scrabble, shift.

The running joke amongst the Primaris brethren was that though a Space Marine would sink fast – his sheer muscle density and the weight of his battleplate would bear him down – his armour and physiology was so robust he could simply walk along the sea bed to the shore.

But on an ocean world, with a hole through his armour and a wound through his black carapace right into his abdomen, the pressure of the deep would claim him, just as it would any mortal man. His progenoid glands and the geneseed they contained would be irretrievably lost, leaving a hole in the annals of the Chapter forevermore.

Swing, grasp, breathe, reposition.

Three minutes left. They were still only half way back. And it had taken twelve minutes to get to the brig in the first place.

Farren reached up to a spar of metal girder where a patch of seaweed had taken root, and the brine paint had flaked away. Taking their combined weight on one hand, he hammered the most rusted part of the girder with the ball of his other hand. A few more times, and a jagged wedge of metal fell away. Farren caught it deftly before it fell into the crashing waves. He examined the long triangle of metal for a moment.

'Take this,' he said to Deel, holding it by the sharp end.

'Why?'

'Just take it.'

She grabbed hold of it without saying a word.

'Now drive it into my side wound. Aim for the heart.'

'What?' said Deel, her voice a disbelieving screech. 'Are you mad?'

'Just do it. It is our only chance.'

'You're insane,' she said. 'You'll kill us both!'

'Do it! You're wasting time! Trust me!'

Deel yelled out, a cry of anger and frustration. She slammed the long, rusted shiv into Farren's wound, all the way up, sinking it into tough flesh until it was buried deep.

Farren's lips curled, his eyes watering as the pain shot through him. His grip on the algae-slick girder grew weaker as he felt the rusted knife grazing his ribs, cutting at his right lung and puncturing his second heart.

It was enough. A huge rush of stimm chemicals roared around Farren's system as the implanted organ known as the Belisarian furnace pumped hard into full effect.

Triggered by near-fatal trauma, the furnace was designed by Archmagos Cawl to give the Primaris Marines one last burst of killing energy to let them claim revenge before their death in battle. Or in any extreme situation, come to that. Farren felt his strength return, flow through his limbs, every blood vessel tingling and pulsing as he pulled himself up once more.

With his eyes so wide he felt like they would never close again, Farren swung from girder to stanchion to pipe with jerking, desperate speed. He punched his fingers through rusted metal and crushed steel pipes as he made the straightest course between himself and the Repulsor. Deel hung on for grim life, arms and legs locked and hair whipping across her face as the wind and spume tugged at them.

The hungry waves reached up to grab at their legs, but Farren barely registered them. He breathed through froth that tasted of coppery blood, felt muscles sing even as his injured heart bled into his thoracic cavity.

He was dying, that much was certain. But the Repulsor

was close, and he was getting closer with every passing second.

Farren sensed something watching them, back at the brig; a sensation of disapproving eyes piercing his back niggled at the back of his mind. Then it was lost amongst the pain, and a growing sense of triumph.

Thirty seconds later, Farren was kicking at the *Harrower*'s door with the toe of his boot. The ingress hatch hissed open, and Vesleigh looked out, his handsome features a mask of confusion.

'Get her in!' shouted Farren.

Still hanging from the rig's underside, Farren shrugged Deel forward with his hip. She took the hint, and climbed into Vesleigh's arms. His battle-brother, too stunned to argue, carried her inside. The lieutenant swung in close behind, coming in so hard that he bowled Vesleigh backwards. Deel staggered away to rebound from Moricani's broad chest. Farren fell clattering to the floor of the Repulsor, clutching at his side. His hand was covered in half-clotted gore.

'Throne, Farren,' said Enrod. 'You stink of promethium and blood.'

'He needs help, you fool,' said Moricani, punching open the Repulsor's emergency cache and carefully extracting the dormant medi-skull inside it. He muttered an activation phrase – Hellblasters were no strangers to tackling irascible machine-spirits – and set the skull hovering free.

'He's shaking,' said Gsar over the intravox. *'His furnace has activated.'*

'He made me stab him in his wound,' said Deel. 'It was the only way, he said. Somehow it made him fight twice as hard to get back. I could barely hang on.'

Farren struggled to stay conscious as the skull-machine hovered down close, its syringe-tipped manipulators reaching for the red mess that was his side. A sharp spike of pain, and his entire flank became numb.

Dimly he registered his chronometer. Minus three seconds.

'Your anti-coagulants are working again, Farren,' said Moricani. 'We'll get you stable, then Vaarad and Autinocus can see to you when you get to the ship. We'll tell them it was embedded shrapnel. Rest now. Gsar, get us out of here.'

Farren nodded weakly in thanks, and let himself slip away.

CHAPTER FOUR
SHIELD OF UNTRUTH

The *Liminal Conquest*
Progress-Class Star Cruiser (Slipstream Enabled)
Flagship Of The Fourth Sphere Expansion

'High Commander Surestrike, most profound greetings of the T'au'va,' said Tutor Twiceblade. His eyes were cast down and his hands were held out towards his superior in the offering gesture of the gift-well-meant.

'The surviving teams are recovered. We have experienced the losses of two Ghostkeel warsuits and five stealth teams in total, with another three reduced below operational parameters.'

'Your candour and precision is appreciated, as ever,' said Surestrike. The regal figure standing in the flagship's underslung viewing dome did not look round. 'My thanks, loyal Sha'ko'vash.'

'I mean not to contradict you, but it is Twiceblade now, high commander.'

'I offer contrition. I had only recently reconciled your

last alteration. Perhaps such a long stasis demands frequent change, to keep things in balance.'

The high commander still did not turn, instead staring out at the stunning view below. According to the honour guard outside, Surestrike had not left his position for an entire rotaa. He had stood motionless, seemingly spellbound by the panoramic view of the ocean planet the gue'vesa called Saltire Vex.

Twiceblade could see why. Swathes of spiralling cloud over a jade and black ocean were dotted by the tiny orange pinpricks of the human rig-settlements, each circled by screeds of relevant data on Surestrike's vast command suite overlay.

Tutor Twiceblade knew the commander well enough to realise he was present in body and mind, but not necessarily in spirit. The journey through the sub-realm had taken a terrible toll on the commander. Ever since their re-emergence, his famous clarity of thought and deed had been compromised beyond recovery.

Some amongst the fire caste's least circumspect were saying the surety for which the commander had been named – that confidence with which he had carved a new destiny for the Fourth Sphere Expansion – had been shaken, shattered and cast away.

'The air caste report that the anomaly is leaving low orbit, commander. It has rendezvoused or docked with a larger craft, and is now bound for deep space. It is still baffling our scanners somehow, but the earth caste say they can still follow its heat trails.'

'Thank you, Sha'ko'vash,' said Surestrike. Twiceblade folded his hands over his solar plexus in the guard-against-offence at this second nomenclature gaffe, but the implied admonition was wasted. His superior did not see it.

'That is good news,' continued the high commander. 'Perhaps we can reveal the anomaly's location, and destroy it before it bears its taint to any other gue'vesa worlds. Or to any of the gue'la species, come to that. They are already corrupted a hundred times over.'

'That is true,' said Tutor Twiceblade. 'Rogue mind-science is toxic to the order from which the T'au'va is born. Doubly so amongst the uninitiated.'

The commander sighed, his head hanging. 'We cannot destroy every gue'vesa world, facility and ship, Twiceblade. Let alone every gue'la stronghold. Even should we make it back to the sept worlds, and even should we convince the aun of the righteousness of such a cause, it is not logistically possible.'

The tutor did not reply.

'Our very empire would turn against us to ensure our failure,' continued Surestrike. 'It is impossible.'

'What if we could show them the evidence, commander,' said Twiceblade. 'What if we could show them what we have seen?'

'They would never believe us. Not if we had a thousand recordings of the mind-curse to prove it. To deal with this poison, we must use the tourniquet, and the heated blade.'

'What if the curse spreads? What if we fail, and the main vector of infection spreads through another populace? These barbarian gue'la know not the meaning of quarantine.'

'We will not fail,' said Surestrike, still not looking round. 'We will cauterise it before it bleeds any more of its venom into the cosmos.'

'Should I tell the air caste to engage if they have the chance?'

'No,' said Surestrike. 'Identifying particular bodily remains in a debris field is all but impossible after the macro-level trauma of a naval engagement. For now, we follow. Maximum sensor range, plus fifteen per cent.'

'As you say, commander,' said Twiceblade, adjusting his stance to that of the protégé-at-attention. 'The siphon structure on Saltire Vex may still have infected gue'vesa upon it. Some of them are undoubtedly mind-cursed. Would you have us launch another strike and eradicate it completely?'

'No,' said Surestrike. 'No more overt action at this site.'

'With respect, we must stop them,' insisted Twiceblade. 'The gue'vesa exemplify the corruption of the T'au'va. Did I misunderstand your position on the subject?'

'We cannot risk open attack,' sighed Surestrike. 'If word gets back to the sept worlds that we are slaughtering human helpers inducted into the Greater Good, the Fourth Sphere initiative is as good as lost.'

'As you say,' said Twiceblade, doing his best to keep his tone neutral. 'Though perhaps, if the greatest concentration of the mind-cursed is upon the rig the gue'vesa designate Omicroid, we could engineer its destruction, and leave.'

'There is no need. I have already assured its destruction.'

'High commander?'

Surestrike moved a finger and slid it over a wide circular informational. He enlarged the view of the human settlement tenfold, tap-engaging satellite drones and complex starsun filters to cut through the clouds of water vapour.

Intrigued, Tutor Twiceblade approached Surestrike's

personal hex display and peered down at the crude structure. From above, its girders and supports came into focus; a skeleton made from ferrous ore, according to the earth caste analysis teams.

How the humans imagined that primitive iron structures would last amongst such a concentration of saline solution he did not know. Hundreds of such rigs dotted the ocean world's surface, their stout legs drilled into the planet's crust under the seabed.

'It is hard to believe that a thick coating of paint is the only thing between these facilities and the entropy of the ocean they parasitise,' mused Twiceblade.

'They stand against storm and tide alike,' said Surestrike, lifting the raised palm of the gate immovable. 'Proud and stubborn, yet locked in a war they cannot win. There is a strange beauty in that.'

Twiceblade was about to make a neutral reply when the image of the rig suddenly exploded, blossoming into a spreading flower of orange and black flame.

'Commander,' said Twiceblade. 'Was this the work of the *gue'ron'sha* Space Marines?'

'No.'

'Then you brought about its fate?'

'I ensured it in person. My Coldstar is subtle enough to evade detection by Imperial craft, especially in an active warzone, and deft enough to place explosives at critical points.'

'But… it was my understanding you never left this bridge, high commander.'

Surestrike finally turned, fixing Twiceblade with a strange stare.

'I will do anything for the Greater Good, Tutor Twiceblade.

But I will not turn the empire against itself, nor inflame the war between the T'au Empire and Humanity. To do so is to act against the T'au'va in a direct fashion. That is a far greater crime than allowing an abstract threat to survive. Now, if you will kindly leave me to my thoughts.'

Tutor Twiceblade averted his eyes, made the hands-clasped sign of the chagrined student, and left the viewing bridge without looking back.

High Commander Surestrike shut down the hex informationals and stared once more at the ocean vista stretching before him.

One of the recessed alcoves to Surestrike's left slid open. He did not look round.

'It is wise to have one who challenges your suppositions so close to you,' said a smooth, feminine voice. 'To have one who fears for a greater conflict, yet follows orders nonetheless.'

'I know this,' said Surestrike. 'That is why I give him audience.'

'Do you keep my counsel for the same reasons?'

'Your guidance is invaluable, most noble Aun'Shao, in ensuring the Fourth Sphere does not become a footnote lost to history.'

'The right words. Yet I feel there is nothing behind them.'

'There is nothing behind my eyes, either. You said so yourself, wise one. I remember it all too well. Perhaps I have more in common with our guest in the munitions deck than I like to think.'

'And yet you have a place in the Greater Good. An important one. Aun'Va saw something in you, and Aun'Wei before him. Your time is now, High Commander Surestrike.'

'This I know. It is why I am here, as the figurehead of this expedition, talking to you.'

'Then do not forget it. You have a duty to fulfil.'

The speaker in the wings of the dome made the gesture of the setting sun. With a soft hiss of an iris portal opening, she left for her own quarters.

Surestrike dismissed every drone attendant still hovering on standby, sending them away one by one with complex motions of his fingers. He stared unblinking at the vista shown on the command suite for a while longer. He paid particular attention to the tiny flames dancing above each of the surviving promethium rigs that dotted the ocean world of Saltire Vex, and the larger flame that was once Ferro-Giant Omicron. The flickering lights reminded him of something, something that made his soul ache with loathing and loss.

Then, when he was sure he was alone, he crouched down in a ball and keened in despair.

CHAPTER FIVE
WHITE LIES

Apothecarium
The *Executioner's Blade*

Xedro Farren opened his eyes, his hands automatically checking for his bolt rifle. It was missing, and with it, a great part of his calm. His augmented senses focused, relaying information through the fevered mist that threatened to consume his mind.

A bright azure light shone down upon him, directed right into his eyes. It was dimming, then narrowing, then dimming again, before blazing so bright he could feel his irises contract.

A firm hand pressed down on his neck, then on his chest, cool and certain. He felt a sharp pain in the side of his throat.

'Progenoids unharmed,' said a voice. It was so flat it was almost mechanical, with a definite rasp of augmetics. 'The same cannot be said for his third lung, nor his secondary heart.'

Farren struggled to speak, to sit upright, to tell them he was conscious. He found he could not move anything, not even his eyelids, or his pupils. Yet he was undoubtedly conscious.

'I still find this bio-architecture impressive, even for one of the Adeptus Astartes,' said the voice beyond the bright light. 'Every sinew is reinforced with these coiled metal springs. There is this bio-amplifier behind the hearts... And some manner of hybrid gland. I confess it is still a mystery. The rhythms do not map.'

'Just do what is required of you, Vaarad.' The second voice was familiar, registering in Farren's half-comatose mind as a malignant presence on some level. But with his bodily systems locked in a silent battle and his mind struggling to remain barely conscious under a cocktail of suppressants, Farren could not quite place it.

His eyesight was adjusting now. That omnipresent azure light was cast by something that floated, close enough to grab. Long, thick cables hung around a serried string of bone protrusions that reminded Farren of a dangling spinal column. As his mind slowly pieced together the meagre stimulus it could find, he realised that it was just that. A servo-skull, adapted for the use of sanctioned medicae.

He was amongst his Dark Angels brothers, then, in the apothecarium. He should have been reassured, but strangely, the tight feeling in his throat did not recede.

'We will have him at full combat efficacy within a day, perhaps two,' came the sonorous voice, the buzz of sibilance making it sound as if it was coming over a vox-link rather than from mere feet away. 'What of his battleplate?'

'Autinocus is seeing to it,' said the second voice. 'He will ensure it is returned to him in... an appropriate condition.'

'Has he mastered this pattern, then? This Mark X model?'

'He studied for years upon Mars' soil. If any amongst our circle can understand the craftsmanship of the Martian priesthood, it is he.'

'I feel, given the complexity of their biological and psychological systems, that he will find that a challenge.'

'That is his lookout. Concentrate on your own duties.'

'Of course.'

Farren saw something – a point of darkness – grow closer. It blurred, becoming a fuzzy black spot. He felt a sensation of proximity, and then a piercing pain right in the centre of his eyes, lancing to the back of his skull.

'Welcome back, brother!'

Farren felt some of his old confidence return at the sound of his old friend's voice calling from the communal space designated for Primaris use. He smiled, just a little. It was always amusing to him that Moricani could tell his approach purely by the rhythm of his footsteps.

Farren walked without even a trace of a limp, for his torso wound was already at operational parameters. The boots of his recently repaired Mark X armour thudded evenly on the vaulted chamber's alloy floor, their solid crump helping his surety return little by little.

There was Moricani, seated at a brushed steel mess table. His mad ivory smile was so wide his incisors were plainly visible in the corners of his mouth. The Hellblaster sergeant got up and strode forward as Farren made his way into the common vestibule, clasping the lieutenant's upper arms in the Terran fashion before making to deliver a sudden headbutt.

Farren jerked back, then broke Moricani's grip with a

shrug of his arms, in the same motion stabbing a pair of fingers up like a dagger to push hard under his friend's jaw.

'Omnissiah. You're as quick as ever, then,' said Moricani, swatting Farren's hand away. 'Just checking that psy-wound hasn't robbed you of your faculties.'

'You do anything like that in front of the others, Sergeant Moricani, and you will receive a swift and brutal reminder of why I carry a superior rank.'

'And every bit as serious!' laughed Moricani. 'I remember when you valued a quick test of reaction speed. It broke up the boredom of transit.'

'How long have I been out?'

'Two days, perhaps, not even that. We Primaris Marines heal quickly.'

'Did I miss much?'

'We are making for the Scorpid cluster, according to our brief,' said Moricani. 'Which, as hard as it is to imagine, was the briefest yet. We are to rendezvous with the Angels of Absolution before making our next attack. Ultimately we will face the greenskinned menace, I am pleased to relate. A simple, straightforward war of extermination – likely one that even you can wage without ending up on the slab.'

'Another jab, brother?' said Farren. 'I must leave myself open to them.'

'Usually.'

'Are we not to conclude our business with these t'au, then? Any news on why we withdrew so suddenly?'

'Not so much as a binharic screed.'

Farren's brow knotted. This behaviour was like no other strategic protocol he had heard of, within the Adeptus Astartes ranks or without.

'Odd. How is the… the *Harrower*? Is she still in the same condition as when I left?'

'She is,' said Moricani, his smile flashing wide. 'She is doing fine, inside and out, thanks to Gsar's ministrations.'

'The cargo, I mean?'

'Well enough, though a little shaken by the battle. Stowed away on the transport deck designated for us Primaris Marines, as though we're lesser citizens. She is down there with… all the other Repulsor transports, of course.'

'Excellent,' said Farren, smiling at Moricani's double-talk. 'We must make full use of the opportunities afforded to us.'

'You have been missed, Xedro,' said Moricani. 'By all of us. I will be more than glad to accompany you to check on the *Harrower*.'

'I will not refuse your company,' said Farren, his expression grave. 'Another painful memory came to me as I was out. Or it may have been a dream. I can barely remember it.'

'Oh? Was it the one where you gambolled through a field of tulips?'

'An intense light, ebbing and flowing. And pain. Lots of it.'

Moricani's expression curdled, turning from his habitual wry smile to a look of severe consternation.

'Brother? Is something wrong?'

'That light,' said Moricani quietly. 'Blue in colouration?'

'It was,' said Farren. 'Light azure, maybe white at times.'

Moricani put a hand to his forehead and rubbed it, staring intently at the grille of the corridor.

'Hmm. And the pain? Was it in the eyes?'

'It was,' said Farren. 'And behind them.'

Moricani met his gaze, and for a moment, he seemed like an old man.

'Enrod has been having the same recollection,' he said quietly. 'And Lenkatz recently confided much the same. I don't know if you noticed, but yesterday Vesleigh intimated that he too had a pain behind the eyes.'

Farren frowned. 'It must be an artefact of transition sickness. I would not pay it much mind.'

'I am not so sure,' said Moricani. 'When I mentioned it to Epistolary Dothrael, he said he had felt it too, and that it was common enough. But he did not look at me when he said it, and he changed the subject immediately afterwards. Isn't that a potential sign of duplicity?'

'We have to trust them, Pietr,' said Farren. 'We have no choice. They are acting in the best interests of the Legion, and so must we.'

'In the best interests of the Chapter, you mean.'

'*Chapter*, damn it,' said Farren. 'Old habits die hard.'

'And so do you, Xedro,' said Moricani. 'Maybe you'll even live long enough to eventually get the hang of the right nomenclature.'

'Thank you, sergeant,' said Farren drily.

'With the warp tides in our favour, it is only a matter of days before we reach our new hosts upon Allhallow. Perhaps you can bring some of your excellent diplomatic skills to bear upon them instead.'

'Perhaps I shall. We will see.'

'Shall we make our way to the deck, then?'

'Not just yet,' said Farren. 'I must meditate. Meet me at my cell in an hour, and we shall proceed from there.'

* * *

Farren tapped the release rune of his cell's alcove, and then pulled the heavy metal door until it slid closed with a dull clang. His mind was aching from the sheer volume of information he was trying to collate, to parse, to fit together. It was like trying to find a way through a dense fog at night. For some reason, the details just wouldn't fit. He sat on his spartan slab of a bunk and let his shoulders sag, pressing the heels of his hands into his eyes.

At least the wound in his side had closed over, seen to by Apothecary Vaarad. He took a quick look under the binding and its poultice, peering down through the headache to assess the damage.

The healing process had been hyper-accelerated so that a thick weal of pink and white scar tissue covered the fist-sized wound in his side. When he twisted to the right, he could still feel the damage done to his lung and heart by Deel's improvised dagger. Yet that pain too was dulled, and presumably the wound within him was also sealed over by the incredible recuperative properties of the Primaris physiology.

It was a testament to Vaarad's skills that Farren felt able to fight mere days after such a grievous wound – and to the skills of the Techmarine Autinocus that his battleplate was whole once more. Each separate piece was set into the alcoves within his cell, ready for re-attachment should the call to arms be sounded. He went over to the armour and lit the two sticks of preparation incense outside the alcoves, saying a placation prayer to the machine-spirit before taking the plates one by one and holding them to the lumen-brazier. He donned them carefully, feeling their interface ports click home into the sockets of the black carapace membrane under his skin.

Farren frowned. Not so long ago, Techmarine Autinocus had claimed to be unfamiliar with Mark X armour. Yet, the damaged midsection plate – which upon leaving Saltire Vex had a gaping hole in the side – was now sealed over, re-layered with ceramite, neurolinked, welded impeccably, filed, buffed, repainted in deep forest green and burnished to the same sheen as the rest of the armour. It was a feat of engineering that would impress even a tech-priest. It seemed to stretch credulity a little to think that the Techmarine had no prior knowledge of Mark X plate.

Better yet, the machine-spirit was placated. Farren had expected to have to spend hours appeasing it, if not long nights, as it was brought in harmony with his own bio-rhythms. But to him it seemed wholly at peace with the repair. Perhaps even docile.

Recalling the anomalies he had experienced in the battle on the promethium rig, Farren tapped through the armour's records to find the images of the xenos foe and the weapon of the human sympathiser.

The picts were no longer there. None of his battle data was there, in fact. The Mark X was as good as new, just as the Techmarine had promised him, but in the most literal sense. It was as empty of data and logged combat experience as when he had first put it on.

That in itself was highly irregular. A Space Marine grew with his armour, learned to trust it just as it learned to trust him in turn, like a knight of the elder times becoming one with the leather insets and padding of his mail until he and the armour moved as one. The armour, too, learned of its incumbent as the two fought together, its systems meshing ever more efficiently with the biology of the wearer until the two were all but inseparable. Yet here his Mark X plate seemed almost too polished, too clean to do its job at optimum performance.

Farren released the clamps at his jaw line, took off his helm, and rubbed his eyes with the heels of his hands.

What in the Omnissiah's name was going on?

Farren reached under his cell's bedslab, pulling out the thick half-shelf beneath it and taking an autoquill and synthvellum scroll from the recesses there. Pushing at the heel of his hand, he slid off his powered gauntlet with a hiss of escaping pressure valves. He depressed the heat rune on his small well of sealant wax, paused for a moment, and began to write, the only sound the scratching of the autoquill's nib as Farren's neat script unfurled across the page.

There was a loud knock on the jamb of his cell's archway. Moricani's voice came through the door.

'Is your hairpiece in place, lieutenant? May I come in?'

'One moment, my foolish friend,' called Farren, taking a blob of sealant from the wax well and pressing it onto the furled scroll of parchment. He pressed his index finger's print into the wax by way of an official seal. Then Farren stowed the scroll at his waist, opened the cell door by way of answer, and stared hard at his friend's wild grin.

'You're early, Pietr.'

'You present a commendably intense appearance, brother,' said Moricani.

'I'm not in the mood for sparring,' said Farren. 'My armour's recent data is missing.'

'It is?' said Moricani, his smile disappearing. 'Was it lost in the repairs?'

'I suppose so,' said Farren. 'But given that it was the right midsection that was being repaired, I fail to see why the helm would be compromised.'

'Let's talk about it when we get to the *Harrower*,' said Moricani. 'It's so much balmier down there.'

Farren shook his head and moved off, the Hellblaster sergeant striding to walk at his side. 'One day, Pietr, that sense of humour is going to get you killed. It is not a fit way for a Space Marine to behave.'

'We were taken before our prime,' said Moricani, 'made to fight one another, put under the knife for nearly a decade, and mentally reconditioned to become living weapons.'

'And that is amusing to you?'

'It is not amusing at all. Admittedly there is a certain irony to the fact we were made to save the Imperium, but even a glance at the skies betrays the fact we awoke far too late. We have not been welcomed as brothers, nor even as much-needed reinforcements, but tolerated as inconvenient reminders of an era long in the past. We now exist only to kill, or be killed. And my particular breed of murderer specialises in the use of a gun that can snuff out its wielder just as quickly as its target.'

Farren was too taken aback to say anything.

'Some of our kind embrace anger and bitterness, becoming addicted to war. I look for solace elsewhere, and attempt to bring some levity to this bleak existence of death, destruction and endless, grinding repetition. Tell me again, brother, what is wrong with that?'

'Nothing,' said Farren. 'My apologies, Pietr. Nothing at all.'

The air of the Repulsor dock was so thick with sacrament fumes and scorched oil that Farren found his eyes stinging. He replaced his helm, thankful for his rebreather. Moricani was quick to do the same.

'The dockers aren't mean with their reconsecrations, are they?' said the sergeant.

'The machine-spirits need the respect they are due,' said Farren. 'We'll be back in the fray before long.'

Stretching ahead of them was a low-ceilinged hangar. It had ten alcove docks stretching away, five on each side. Three of the nearest berths were occupied by the slab-sided forms of Repulsor transport tanks, their grav-units decoupled so they sat heavy as bunkers in the gloom. The two alcoves at the far end were occupied with single-person craft that were presumably from a previous mission – a duo-Aquila pattern Thunderbolt and a drab grey Arvus lighter.

Beyond those nimble craft was an airlock bay optimised for fast deployment. Its winking lights illuminated black and yellow chevrons that stretched out to form a safety perimeter.

Worker servitors idled nearby, turning their pallid heads and powering up their loading claws as Farren and Moricani entered. Farren made the sign of the cog as their bionic eyes read his noospheric aura. They recognised him as an ally of their tech-priest masters, and as one they entered a standby trance.

'We're here for the *Night Harrower*,' said Farren. 'My name is Primaris Lieutenant Xedro Farren.' He pointed to the closest servitor, a steel-jawed corpse of a thing with a hose for a right arm. 'You. Get that Arvus fuelled to maximum.'

The acceptance lumen on the servitor's temple flashed green. It thumped over to a stack of engine fuel cells. The others went back to dormancy, awaiting instructions.

'Let's board around the side,' said Farren quietly. 'It's

possible other eyes are looking through the optics of these servitors, and I am in no mood to answer any more awkward questions.'

Moricani held his palm up to the *Harrower*'s ingress plate, and the side door of the tank slid open, revealing the white, hard-edged metal interior within. Slumped in the far corner was Deel, her eyes sunken and her straggly, curled hair hanging down.

'From one prison to another,' she said.

'At least this one isn't swilling with cold water,' said Farren, climbing through the side hatch. She nodded gloomily by way of answer as Moricani joined them, pressing the panel that sent the door hissing closed.

'So have you finally come to kill me? Tie up that last loose end?'

'Not as such,' said Moricani. 'Quite the opposite, in fact.'

'I have something for you,' said Farren. He held out the parchment scroll he had prepared in his cell.

'What is this? Please tell me it's a pardon for treason.'

'Close,' said Farren. 'It is my personal vindicatum. It bears clear instructions for whichever Imperial servant you present it to. When you reach the astropathic nexus at Qaru Non, hand it over to whoever passes for a chamberlain master. The word of a lieutenant of the First Legion should be enough to see it expedited.'

Moricani stifled a cough at the term, but Farren ignored his rebuke and carried on nevertheless. 'We will set you on your way in just a moment. You must carry word of those stranded upon Saltire Vex to the relay. Restore the evacuation protocols before the cold cycle kills you all.'

Deel's eyes were wide, white and staring in the gloom. 'You think I can make it there?'

'Can you fly a light multi-atmospheric?'

'Well, yes,' she said, blinking slowly as if she were talking to an idiot. 'We don't have many roads on Saltire Vex.'

'Void capable?'

'I've made a few trips off world in my time. But how am I supposed to steal a ship? And what am I going to do when I get to Qaru? Start a new life whilst my friends freeze to death?'

Moricani opened the far side door of the *Harrower*, revealing the Arvus lighter at the back of the hangar before pressing the door closed once more. A haze of incense smoke wafted in, causing Deel to wave her hand in front of her face.

'That little fellow should get you to Qaru Non within the month,' said Moricani. 'We're most of the way to that waypoint already, and we've not yet reached the Mandeville Point, so we're still in real space. Farren thought it would be good to send you on your way when we were a little nearer to Qaru than Saltire Vex.'

Deel nodded. 'That would be better than good. You think this scroll will do it?'

'Almost certainly,' said Farren. 'The word of a Primaris Space Marine carries with it a strong association with Lord Guilliman.'

Moricani made an odd noise, somewhere between a laugh and a snort. 'Xedro likes to think he is closer to the primarchs than most.'

'We are forged from their lifeblood,' said Farren solemnly. 'That carries weight.'

'Well that's twice you have carried me, then,' said Deel. 'I will not forget it. If I can put in motion a large-scale evacuation, I'll make sure everyone knows it was your Chapter that made it happen. I'll make sure people know it was the t'au that attacked us, and the Dark Angels that came to defend. That the Emperor is beneficent after all. Over time, I think I can make a difference.'

'That would be welcome,' said Farren, feeling some forgotten emotion stir in his heart. 'It is good to hear that.'

'Enough of this,' said Moricani. 'Set her loose, for cog's sake, before I vomit in my respirator.'

'Every once in a while Sergeant Moricani is right,' sighed Farren. 'You should go. You're on your own from this point. I will cover the airlock protocols, and ensure the system recognises you as an authorised departure. It's up to you to get to Qaru Non and raise whatever help you can.'

Deel nodded. 'You have fuel? And food?'

'Your autocrat's chariot is being refuelled as we speak,' said Moricani, sketching a mock bow. 'But our particular brand of sustenance would do you more harm than good. There should be a decent survival pack in the lighter's cockpit, should there not?'

'Probably,' nodded Deel, standing up and stretching out her limbs one by one. 'Good. Let's go. I'm ready.'

Farren noticed her hands trembling, but did not mention it. Instead, he got to his feet, nodding at his battle-brother.

Moricani hit the far side door's release again, and Farren stepped through, staying in front of Deel to stare down the loader servitor that came to stand in their path. Moricani shielded the rigswoman from the second servitor with his bulk, grinning insincerely at the cyborg's recorder-lens as he passed.

When she was clear of the slow-moving servitors, Deel ran ahead and tapped a sequence into the exterior data-slate of the snub-nosed Arvus lighter. She bunched her fists as the code achieved nothing.

Farren loomed over from behind her and pressed his palm against it. The craft's rudimentary machine spirit recognised an Adeptus Astartes heat signature, and its pilot door hinged open with a hiss.

Deel flashed a smile up at Farren from under his arm, and clambered inside, linking her thumbs in the sign of the Imperial Eagle as she climbed into the cockpit and powered it up. He crossed his forearms over his chest in the double salute of the Primaris Marines.

'You're sure about this, Xedro?' said Moricani as the lighter's hatch thumped closed. 'Sure it's worth the risk?'

'To save a planet full of humans, even misguided ones, and bring them back into the Emperor's light? Yes, I think it is. Especially if it comes out amongst the system's rebels that she turned *gue'vesa*, as she put it, only to find that she belonged in the Imperium after all. The word of one like her will carry far.'

'I hope you are right,' sighed Moricani. 'But not too far, or we will pay dearly for it. It's one thing to work beneath the notice of our masters, but quite another to shatter their unwritten rules into pieces.'

CHAPTER SIX
THE LIVING WEAPON

The *Liminal Conquest*
Progress-Class Star Cruiser (Slipstream Enabled)
Flagship Of The Fourth Sphere Expansion

Tutor Twiceblade felt his pulse quicken at the prospect of disobedience, as he always did, but forced his unease back down. The hex-lift was coming to a smooth halt, the status display icon winking two levels from the bottom of its range.

'Ident needed,' said the hex-lift's drone intelligence. 'Please supply.'

Twiceblade pinched his finger and thumb over the sensor plate, rubbed them together, and blew softly. The plate turned from the slate grey of uncertainty to a healthy gold as fresh skin cells and breath droplets hit its bio-scanner.

'Greetings of the T'au'va to you, Tutor Twiceblade,' said the drone intelligence. 'Shall we proceed?'

He hesitated for a moment, weighing his options for the hundredth time.

'Yes. Please proceed, faithful helper.'

The hex-lift continued on its way, and a few moments later the status display icon slid to the lowest setting.

'Munitions storage,' said the drone as the lift doors slid open. 'May you find that which you seek, tutor.'

'My thanks,' said Twiceblade absently, venturing out. He realised his hand was hovering close to his pulse pistol, and forced himself to walk as if he had no more on his mind than retiring to his communal quarters after a long day of training.

The *Liminal Conquest*'s munitions contingency deck was dark, cool and sterile. It was the domain of the earth caste, a subculture including many who would gladly forsake sunlight, news of current affairs and the company of the other castes if it made their operational parameters more predictable. All for the Greater Good, of course, for it was their technology that underpinned the expansion of the entire t'au race.

Only the highest-ranking fire caste had clearance to venture into their domain at will. Even then it was usually by invitation, to inspect some prototype weapon or survey some ballistics results as the earth caste proudly displayed their next triumph of destruction.

Tutor Twiceblade made his way around the side of observation decks, through the alleys of ammunition warehouses and along gantries overlooking work areas. All the while he took care to stick to the shadows. When an earth caste work team thumped its way towards him on their heavy feet, he was quick to find an alcove, stack or hover bier to hide behind. His natural hunter's instincts made it easy enough to stay one step ahead of the myopic scientists that called this area their home.

The earth caste were excellent at focusing on matters which they were deliberately investigating, but they were famously poor at spotting anything outside their sphere of expertise. It was something Twiceblade had counted on many times as he went about his private work whilst the *Conquest* ploughed through space from one zone to the next.

Twiceblade ventured deeper into the bowels of the great ship, pacing along long corridors lined with lozenge lights. He fought to keep his demeanour casual, just in case he was observed or recorded by a micro-drone. No one challenged him. At one point, when the corridors narrowed, he had to shake off the memories of the passageways underneath Gel'bryn City, where he had waged his one-man crusade against the gue'ron'sha known as the Scar Lords. They were still as fresh as if he had experienced those events yesterday, despite the fact whole centuries of chronostasis had slid past.

It was not the first time Tutor Twiceblade had been down to the earth caste hangars since his recovery from his entrapment in the Imperial stasis field, but it was definitely the strangest. This time, the weapon he had come to inspect was very different. No t'au with rank less than 'O' even knew of its existence, and even then the aun had impressed upon them that the measure was only to be used in the direst of circumstances.

Tha'hasiro, it was called, on those rare occasions the fire caste whispered of it. A term that meant 'Living Weapon.' But it had another name, too.

Kais.

Making his way to Contingency Zone Eight, Tutor Twiceblade saw his destination; a tall cylinder that tapered towards the top in the manner of a primitive race's bullet. He stepped closer with great care, his breath coming shallow and uneven, and looked into the elongated oval that formed its viewing window.

The figure inside was relatively slight of build, his skin dark blue and wrinkled over a sparse muscular frame. His features were pleasing enough, yet somehow nondescript to the point of blandness.

Not much for the holographers of the water caste to use there, thought Twiceblade – his features were hollow and gaunt, a stark contrast to the noble countenances of his fellow Students of Puretide. After the aun's great experiment with Commander Farsight had failed, Shadowsun's warrior visage had been spread far and wide across the empire's informationals in his place. She had excelled in the role of exemplar of the T'au'va. But after his successful prosecution of the Fi'rios campaign, Kais had been allowed to return to his cryostasis cylinder rather than elevated to the status of a figurehead. With the water caste deleting all footage of his victories at the ethereal caste's request, he had soon after faded back into myth.

Only those who had looked Kais in the eye knew the truth of his quiet power. This was a warrior who had seen the face of madness and survived, who had consumed the darkness in his soul and made of it a potent weapon. To Twiceblade's mind, the commander in front of him was more lethal than any other t'au in existence. Even in dormancy, his tensed posture held the hair-trigger violence of a Fio'taun flintlock primed to fire.

Twiceblade had seen that violence erupt in person. It was a sight he would never forget.

The rest of the expedition believed Kais to be dormant,

held in between life and death as a hero who could be revived and unleashed on a particularly intractable foe if there was no other option. But Tutor Twiceblade knew better.

The first time he came to gaze upon the stone-cold features of the Monat Supreme – that warrior he had once thought of as his idol – he had seen a muscular twitch under the eye. That miniscule movement had hit him like a battering ram to the chest. The only conclusion was that cryostasis was not fully operative – whether that was by accident or design, Twiceblade did not know.

'Awaken, Monat-Kais. Please. It is Sha'ko'vash.'

The figure's eyelids flicked open, his mismatched irises of purple and black dilating as his pupils adjusted to the light. Twiceblade felt his stomach lurch – no matter how many times the awakening ritual took place, it still felt like a claw of ice clenching in his innards.

'Come closer,' whispered the figure in the stasis tube. 'I will not raise my voice to you, *tutor*.'

'Of course,' said Twiceblade, his heart thundering in his chest.

Long ago, hundreds of kai'rotaa ago, he had been Kais' first official teacher. He had personally tutored Kais when the commander was a cadet of no more than four years old. He had shouted at the young warrior to reprimand him for slinking away, chastening him in front of his fellow students on his very first cycle of training. Kais' eyes had hardened that day. Even now, there was something in the way the killer looked at him that said he had never forgiven him, never forgotten.

Tutor Twiceblade took a few tentative steps forward. He still felt his bones ache with the need to run whenever he stepped into the Monat's presence. It never went away, that feeling.

Shortly after Commander Farsight had given him the name Sha'ko'vash – 'fire's worthy cause' – and allowed him to make penance for his misdeeds as Sha'kan'thas, the tutor had launched a one-man attack on a Space Marine command echelon as atonement. Even that was not as daunting as approaching the Living Weapon. As a result of that strike Twiceblade had spent three hundred t'au'cyr locked in an experimental chronostasis field as a living monument to the Greater Good, apparently used as a motivational exhibit outside his own battle dome. He was a hero of the Fourth Sphere Expansion, lauded by his peers.

None of that mattered now.

All that was a lifetime away, an age, a soul's journey made long in the past.

'The gue'vesa curse is spreading,' said the tutor quietly.

'Of course,' came the reply. Kais' voice was emotionless, devoid of inflection or tone. His speech had no gestural component at all. To Twiceblade, it was as unsettling as if he was screeching from a mouth with no tongue or teeth to form the words.

'It must be stopped.'

'Then stop it.'

'I cannot. My commander believes that circumspection is the correct path.'

'Half measures are the refuge of fools.'

'He has not your clarity of vision. Yet I cannot convince him alone.'

'"Alone, a warrior cannot truly finish a battle. But he can start a war".'

'Master Puretide speaks through you, as ever.'

'He still has relevance,' said Kais. Inside the stasis pod he made neither inflection nor gesture, but Twiceblade could still hear the steel in Kais' voice.

'If the vector of the mind-curse could be isolated and destroyed, we could at least limit its spread,' said the tutor, making the circular motion of the guardian's perimeter. 'Then the work of cutting away the infected tissue from the body could begin.'

'Then release me. I am the sharpest of instruments.'

'I believe it. But once the vector is slain, how can we prevent the same curse from rising again from those it has infected?'

'The earth caste will answer that,' whispered Kais. 'Atmospheric poison. Chemical sterilisation. Planetary core disruption. All of these are viable.'

'That cannot be borne. The gue'vesa share their worlds with too many t'au, and the losses would outweigh the gains. As a commander, you should appreciate that better than anyone.'

'I am no commander.'

'You used to be. You have to be. That is why Aun'Va, the *Supreme Ethereal*–' at this Tutor Twiceblade stressed his words – 'placed you as a critical part of the Fourth Sphere Expansion.'

'I am a weapon,' said Kais, something fierce in his voice. 'I should be wielded as one.'

'Would you not prefer to be the hand that wields the blade?'

'No,' said Kais, the word cutting as sharp as an executioner's sword.

'We must transcend the notion of Monat as a lone warrior,'

said Twiceblade. 'We must make of that archetype a leader, an exemplar, a legend. I believe it was always Master Puretide's intent that you bring its philosophy to its natural conclusion.'

Kais stared at him with an intensity that Twiceblade felt might bore through the glass.

The tutor swallowed, and continued nonetheless.

'You must act as the leader of a lone force in the galaxy, acting in the name of the Greater Good, unseen and unheard. Yet you must do so with not one life, but hundreds of thousands. This the T'au'va demands of you.'

'Do not tell me what I must and must not do, *tutor*. I have planned your death more times than I can count.'

'Commander?' said Twiceblade, his blood going cold. 'I have only ever sought to aid you.'

'I have been fully conscious for three hundred t'au'cyr,' said Kais, his hissing tones fierce and clipped. 'An error in the cryonic process. My body was asleep, inviolate. But not my mind, *Tutor Sha'kan'thas*.'

The tutor was stunned into silence. To be trapped, motionless and locked in a prison of immobile flesh and bone, for so long... it was a chilling prospect.

'My mind was not allowed to age, to fall apart as all things do. I do not understand what manner of biostasis preserved it from entropy, yet left it active, able to parse what information I was fed and lay plans as to how best to use it. But I do know that the ordeal transformed me. At times I was permitted to roam, living waking dreams in which I commanded thousands of t'au teams and led them to victory. At others I fell, further and further, into the darkness.'

Twiceblade swallowed, his throat dry.

'Do you know how many decs that amounts to? Three hundred t'au'cyr? In that time, I have planned the death of my enemies a thousand times over, in a thousand different ways. It was the only thing that kept me sane.'

Keeping his peace as to his true thoughts, Twiceblade looked down.

'I built a war machine of causality, image by image, sliver by sliver,' hissed Kais. 'I have mentally rehearsed every permutation of every conflict against every known foe of the t'au race. Every strike, every manoeuvre, every possible angle or nuance I have analysed and memorised and perfected. In all those things, only one constant – I am alone. I am Monat.'

Kais stared, his eyes open a fraction too wide. 'And in many of those visions, I have seen you die over and over again.'

Twiceblade felt cold sweat on his wrists. The creature before him was no longer t'au, that much was obvious. But perhaps some trace of the Greater Good was left inside him.

He took a deep breath, and spoke.

'You know the mind-plague must be contained, quarantined and burned clean,' he said. 'The gue'vesa curse will spread if we do not limit it. This is why I stand before you, here, now. Surestrike's hesitancy will doom us all. You are the only one who can stop this. Tell me what I must do. Teach me. Let me be your exemplar, your protégé.'

'Unseal this device, and I will begin the work I was born to do.'

'You know I cannot.'

Kais flew at the viewing lozenge, face distorted into an animal snarl as he hammered at it with his fists. He slammed them into the plexiglass so hard they spread smears of blood across the inside. Twiceblade staggered back, his hand flying to his pulse pistol.

Then, just as suddenly, Kais stopped.

'I offer contrition,' he said, his voice perfectly calm. 'It is the stasis burn.'

'I… I see,' said the tutor. 'I shall consult with my contacts in the earth caste as to how to alleviate it.'

Kais nodded, his face a mask of composure as he somberly wiped away the blood on the inside of the viewing window. Twiceblade watched as the Monat cleansed every last spot of the blood, meticulous as a spider, without breaking his gaze for an instant.

The tutor re-engaged the cylinder's systems, backed away a few steps, and bowed his head with his hands forming the closing book gesture of the supplicant-whose-questions-are-complete. He turned on his heel and walked at speed back the way he had come.

Jensa Deel stood impatiently in the long queue of tattered pilgrims and scruffy supplicants that led to the choral node. The rib-like arches of the solar station Qaru Non stretched up around her. It had taken nineteen hours without food or rest to get to the front, with nothing to occupy her but the ache in her bones, the gnawing in her belly, and the fear that she would have a relapse of the mind-plague – that horrible, migraine inducing psyker-spasm that had afflicted her ever since the day she had swum too deep under Ferro-Giant Omicron. She had kept the fear away with detailed thoughts of how she would rescue the last remnants of Saltire Vex, then later resettle it in her own fashion, turning it from a drowning world to a thriving, fighting, killing engine of war.

Her stomach rumbled every few minutes, that hungry animal inside her waking up and beginning to prowl around her guts. She had found a survival pack in the Arvus Lighter after all, and its vitae-paste had filled a gap, but it had not lasted nearly long enough.

'Deel, Jensa,' intoned the gaunt, wrinkle-headed adjudicator at the top of the judicial lectern. She looked up sharply. The ancient had a collar of autocandle lumens extending from his ruff, and a tattoo of a third eye on his forehead, its rays of black and white faded to translucency with age.

'That is me,' she said. 'Present, I mean.'

'Rigswoman Jensa Mahlia Deel. Present your proposed missive before the masters of the choir.'

She stepped forward, eyebrows raised, and fixed the adjudicator with her most commanding stare. It was a look that had intimidated drunken riggers into compliance, usually promising a swift slap of her wrench on the side of the head. But here, directed up at an impassive judiciary some eighteen feet above her, it lacked something in the way of threat.

'I request the regular winter evacuation fleet be sent to Saltire Vex, for the cold cycle is growing close,' she said. 'This is a routine request and procedure.'

The wrinkled judiciary screwed up his face, making him look ancient beyond words. 'Have I not seen this exact request from Saltire Vex before, young lady? Have I not already given it a negative verdict?' He looked down at her as if she was no more than a clot of blood stuck to his shoe. 'You realise the penalty for wasting the time of an Imperial adept?'

'This time, you have little choice in the matter,' said Deel, grabbing Farren's scroll from her waist and holding it up. The adjudicator sighed theatrically, extended a multi-jointed limb from a hidden compartment in his lectern, and grabbed the scroll with a three-pronged claw.

The artificial appendage transferred it up to his wrinkled, bulge-knuckled hands. He tutted before checking its seal. Deel felt a warm glow inside as the pompous fool's expression curdled through confusion, to disbelief, to barely concealed awe.

'Emperor's grace,' he whispered. 'Is this... is this a Primaris seal?'

A susurrus of whispers spread back through the queue behind Deel.

'Yes,' she said, trying to make her voice as strident as possible. 'Read it, fellow servant of the Throne. I have no more time to waste.'

The adjudicator nodded, and unfurled the scroll. He drank in the information, his watery eyes seeming to bulge from his skull as he read and re-read its contents.

'I see. And you would have our astropathic choir send for evacuation craft to escort the populace of Saltire Vex to safety. Is that correct, Rigswoman Deel?'

'It is.'

'Unfortunate. I have a listed prohibition against that exact course of action somewhere here.' He sorted through the parchments on his desk, pulling one out to peer at it with eyes creased. 'And though it is vague as to its origin, it bears the hallmark of the Adeptus Astartes. The seal is authentic, though unfortunately the author did not deign to state his rank, nor his Chapter.'

'My scroll is not vague. As you can see, it comes from

Primaris Lieutenant Xedro Farren of the Dark Angels, formerly of the Indomitus Crusade, and it must be obeyed.'

'I must confess, if the rumours are true that the Primaris Marines are acquainted with Roboute Guilliman himself…' At this the adjudicator linked his thumbs and crossed his hands in the winged sign of the aquila. 'This sets a new precedent.'

'That is good to hear,' said Deel, a tiny flame of hope burning in her chest. She returned the sign, trying hard not to smile. 'Will you honour it?'

'This time,' said the adjudicator, his goldfish-like expression betraying the fact he saw Deel in a whole new light. 'I believe I will. Is there anything else, mamzel?'

'Yes,' said Deel. 'Kindly send a missive to the mercenaries gathered upon the neighbouring world, Saltire Non Aqua. A thousand drums of refined promethium to the first alphic-category warship to enter low orbit and establish a defensive perimeter above Ferro-Giant Thetoid. All I need is a parley. I will take it from there.'

'As you wish, mamzel,' said the adjudicator, his quill scribbling hard upon his data-slate. 'Mercenaries… fuel… thousand barrels of promethium… defensive perimeter.'

'Tell them to make haste,' said Deel. 'War will find us before the evacuation vessels bear us to safety, I am sure of it.'

'A war that requires an army of mercenaries.'

'Yes.'

'We have… contacts. A hireling alliance recently gained permission to bring one of their macro-class warships into Qaru nearspace. You will have your audience, Jensa Mahlia Deel.'

'Good,' said Deel, her eyes narrowing. 'Saltire Vex will not be caught off guard again.'

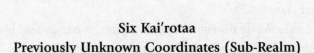

Six Kai'rotaa
Previously Unknown Coordinates (Sub-Realm)

High Commander Surestrike stared out from the viewing dome, focusing upon the tiny flames that flickered in the nothingness of the sub-realm. He had lately found them hypnotic. He could not shake the suspicion they seemed to move all the more when he focused on them.

Folly, of course. No living thing could survive out there, let alone detect his thoughts. Not even here, in the otherworldly space that few understood.

The Fourth Sphere Expansion had been sent out from the sept worlds to great fanfare and rejoicing. Like its last two predecessors, it had one of the Students of Puretide with it. This time, though, the Kan'jian alumnus had been in stasis instead of at the helm.

The Second Sphere Expansion had been led across the Damocles Gulf by the now-infamous Commander Farsight, specialist in the Mont'ka school of warfare, and the third led by the avatar of the Kauyon, Commander Shadowsun. The fourth carried with it the genius Monat known as Kais, but he was with them more as a totem than a leader, an exemplar of the Greater Good embodied in a soul that had sacrificed everything else.

Kais was the third of the trinity of young protégés that had studied under the Master atop Mount Kan'ji. It was said he had become so devoted to the Monat way of war that Aun'Va decreed he be alone at all times, lest others sully the purity of his vision. He was only to leave his cryostasis cylinder in times of desperate need. Though that seemed odd to a race that thrived on communality, the fire caste had of course respected that command.

Leadership of the Fourth Sphere Expansion had instead been entrusted to Surestrike. He had fought alongside Shadowsun on Mu'galath Bay, Voltoris and beyond, and earned the trust of the fire caste in doing so, earning the position of High Commander. Yet where Farsight had found infamy and Shadowsun earned undying glory, Surestrike had found his destiny swallowed whole by the vast interstellar anomaly known officially as the Greater Axial Rift.

Of late, the t'au had been using another term for it. The Mont'yhe'va. The Devourer of Hope.

Now the Fourth Sphere Expansion floated like a fleet expelled from a storm in foreign waters, carried like flotsam upon currents they had no way of understanding, let alone controlling. They were directionless, at the mercy of forces they barely understood. Only the grace of the T'au'va could carry them to their target now.

During the First Sphere Expansion, the earth caste had experimented with how to briefly oscillate between reality and that strange half-reality the gue'la called the warp. They had limited success, utilising only the surface of the deep, mysterious dimension they had first encountered in the Damocles Gulf.

Intrigued, but still not fully comprehending that which they were dabbling with, they toyed with the breakthrough technology, never truly understanding it, making short jumps as a stone skims along the surface of a pond.

During the Damocles war, the scientists and metatheorists had looked with awe and no little envy at the Imperial warships that disappeared from the void in a pulsing, roiling explosion of light, diving wholly into this alternate dimension, travelling great system-spanning distances upon its underwater currents and then surfacing again in real space without warning.

More often than not they did so specifically to rain hell upon their foes. It was just such a tactic that had seen the gue'ron'sha launch the invasion of Dal'yth.

Dal'yth, a war so violent, so sudden, so epoch-shattering that even its debris had yielded the key to a new future. That future had seen the Fourth Sphere Expansion built, modified for sub-realm travel, and now lost with all hands, Surestrike at the helm.

The high commander screwed his eyes shut hard as if to banish his failure. The Aun should have never trusted him to break new ground, to lead an expedition of billions of lives, let alone to find new horizons in the quest to expand the T'au Empire for the good of all. He was no Student of Puretide. He was a talented leader – he had to be, or else he would never have achieved O-rank – but when it came to the genius needed to lead an entire expansion, he could not help but feel that he fell short.

The nebula-like sub-realm outside the viewing dome roiled and spun. It seemed to Surestrike that it formed faces in the ether, hideous visages that grinned and howled and screamed.

PHIL KELLY

It was amazing how the systems of the mind played such tricks, enforcing pattern recognition on the most abstract of sights. Yet the phenomenon seemed strangely frequent, happening more and more with every passing dec.

Lights danced in the eyes of the phantom skulls out there, spinning like Vior'lan fireflies caught in specimen flasks as they played around the Fourth Sphere's becalmed fleet.

Surestrike could not shake the feeling the skeletal faces were mocking him.

CHAPTER SEVEN
DESCENT OF DARKNESS

Duskenwald
Allhallow, Scorpid Cluster

A murder of crows shot upward from the endless canopy of the Duskenwald. They squawked in alarm as they flapped, ungainly and scared, into Allhallow's evening skies. Something large but completely invisible was descending from the clouds above them, its retro-jets roaring low as it gradually came to a halt in the clearing below.

Gohorael narrowed his eyes, detaching his psy-crown and pushing it back into the cockpit's alcove recess as he guided the *Dagger* to halt. The crown's mental amplifier had made an uninterrupted planetfall almost too simple, in the end. Part of Gohorael longed for the signal bells on the cockpit's auspex recess to chime, for an aerial engagement in which to prove his power over the weak-blooded successor Chapter that called this world home.

The work of aeons was more important, of course. With

the crown and the relic from Saltire Vex boosting his psychic ability, he had excised his presence from the minds of any that sought him. Nonetheless he still had a nagging, scratching suspicion in the back of his mind, a sense that he was being followed – and not just by the deluded thinbloods that thought themselves true sons of the Lion.

He rearranged the octocraniad around his neck, ensuring the skulls all faced outwards. It would not do to rob the souls held within them of the view, not after they had done so much for him already.

The core beauty of Allhallow was its forests. Even Gohorael had felt something swell in his breast as he had flown over the rolling sea of its endless foliage. The trees were dense, coniferous, green-black, and in places cut through with beast trails that led to wide clearings. Gohorael had taken careful note of the glimmering lights of the planet's civilisation centres as he had descended, and avoided their greatest concentrations, instead seeking lesser settlements in the forest's midst.

In places, the trees of Allhallow had been cleared away to leave islands of fertile ground, areas claimed long ago by the indigenous people. Those great clearings were host to large keeps, watchtowers, citadels and castles, all linked together by hard-packed roads and trails that wound through the forests.

The greatest of the settlements by far was undoubtedly Soul's Well, the fortress-monastery of the Angels of Absolution. It was a mountain of concentric curtain walls reaching up to a high-walled fortress of black stone that pierced the lowest clouds. The time to pay that grand edifice a visit was a little way off just yet, but Gohorael would get there in time, bearing his own particular kind of gift.

There was no doubt this Chapter had chosen their homeworld for its resemblance to the long-lost planet of the First Legion.

Gohorael felt gratification mingle with a fierce sense of indignation. The symbolism was half the reason he had made the journey, but the planet's similarity grated nonetheless. Allhallow was unmistakeably an echo of ancient Caliban, though given the width of the beast paths, the monsters that hunted its forests were far less dangerous than those of the First's homeworld. A fitting analogue for its settlers, too.

Gohorael felt his blood curdle the more he thought about it. A successor Chapter, their blood even weaker than that of the so-called Dark Angels of the 41st Millennium, had the gall to claim an arboreal planet and fashion it in the image of his forefathers.

Worse still, and uniquely amongst the Unforgiven, this was a Chapter that considered itself literally absolved of the sins of the past through the purging of Caliban. Though they worked alongside their fellow Chapters and fought well by all accounts, they saw those ancient events as travesties committed by forefathers so distant they may as well have been another race entirely.

Gohorael snorted in disgust. No act, no matter how apocalyptic, could erase the shame, the terror, the immortal stain of dishonour that was known to the Adepts of the Imperium as the Horus Heresy. It was indelible, impossible to remove. Chaos was in everything, in every one of the Adeptus Astartes, and in every man, woman and child. This, at least, the upper echelons of the Dark Angels were finally coming to acknowledge, and to loathe themselves all the more for it, as was only right.

But for a brotherhood to pretend otherwise, to openly call themselves absolved of sin, this was an insult that could not be borne.

Gripping his staff of Calibanite oak, Gohorael set his jaw and made for the crenelated guard fortress on the horizon.

'Well, well,' said Landers Harasen, tapping a cracked data-slate fogged with the patina of bad maintenance. 'Come over, young Fenas. Look what the gate-skulls picked up on.'

Fenas, the lanky youth with whom Harasen had shared garrison duty for the last six weeks, came closer, peering over his shoulder pauldron with the expression of a mole that has burrowed up into the sunlight.

'Emperor's grace. It's one of them, isn't it?'

'Yes and no,' said Harasen, peering closer himself. It was hard to make out the figure in any detail, especially in the evening gloom, but there was something different about it.

'Not more bloody riddles,' said Fenas. 'Is it one of the Absolvers or not?'

'I doubt it,' said Harasen. 'Wrong heraldry. This one's battleplate is black as midnight.'

'The stories say they're white.'

'Yes,' said Harasen. 'I know that, boy. I told you that myself, remember?'

'I can't wait to see the look on the faces of those blaggards at Six North when we tell them that we got chose over them. That'll pay 'em back for the last Challenge all right.'

'But the Absolvers never come this far west. We're not good enough for the likes of them. Even if we won the Five Challenges they'd still find a reason to ignore us.'

'And yet there he is, right?'

'I told you, this isn't one of them! Emperor's teeth. Awaken the other skull, boy, you can work this thing better than me.'

Fenas fiddled with the runes on the side of the data-slate, humming a tuneless psalm of appeasement to its machine-spirit before knocking it with the heel of his hand. The screen glitched, fuzzed, and came into focus a little more.

'Throne above,' said Fenas with a shiver. 'Big brute, isn't he.'

'What's he wearing there?' said Harasen, pointing to the wreath around the figure's neck.

'Some kind of necklace,' said Fenas.

'Yes, I can see that,' said Harasen levelly. 'It does look a lot like... I don't know. Trophies of battle, maybe. Look, you can see the eye sockets.' He swallowed hard.

'I'm not sure I want to see them close up. Maybe he'll reconsecrate our gate-skulls, then leave.'

Without taking his eyes from the data-slate, Harasen slapped Fenas on the forehead.

'Look at him, boy. He look like a tech-adept to you? A servitor, perhaps? You think he's on an errand to swap out faulty servo-skulls?'

'So what is he here for, then?'

Harasen did not reply for a long moment.

'Nothing good.'

Seconds stretched past as the castellans watched the figure thrash his way through the undergrowth towards the dry-moat with long, powerful strides. A lizard-mule, startled from its lair, raised its frill in anger, then saw the intruder for what it was and slunk off for easier prey. The stranger had a long staff in one hand, and at his hip was a side-arm so large it would probably have taken all of Harasen's strength to lift it.

'Should we sound the alarm, do you think?'

'No. Not officially, anyway. It wouldn't go down well if he was an Absolver, if you take my meaning. Bearing news, summoning us to war, or similar. We should just... spread the word that we have company.'

'Right.'

The tall youth peered in close, taking in the tusked helm of the figure approaching the gate.

'I mean you should do it, Fenas! Go and tell the others!'

'Right, right.' The youth scurried off down the corridor towards the command hall, grabbing his halberd on the way past.

'Greetings of the day, my lord!' called out Harasen. He stepped forward from the shadow of the lowered draw-bridge, thumped his chest twice with a closed fist, then made as deep a bow as his starch-stiff tabard would allow. 'I am Landers Harasen, castellan of this meagre fortress. The honour you do us is too much!'

The Space Marine, still some fifty yards away, made his way towards them at an unhurried pace. Harasen cursed himself for a fool. Had the stranger heard him? Or had he simply announced himself too soon?

There was a stifled laugh from the battlements behind him. The men up there were enjoying his discomfort, no doubt. The most part of the fortress' guard was up there, gathered to see a Space Marine in the flesh. They were standing deliberately apart from the Icarus quad-guns at the corners so as not to offend their distinguished visitor.

Harasen glanced back for a moment; they were shielding their eyes from the setting sun, peering intently at the figure in black armour striding towards them. There was a part of him that would definitely have preferred them to be manning the guns instead.

Oddly, the stranger still didn't seem to have come into focus. The gloom gathered about him like a shroud. There was definitely something unsettling about him. The Absolvers usually came in massive transport vehicles or on rugged war bikes, but this Space Marine simply walked.

Harasen had stationed three men hidden in the gatehouse above the murder holes – a regulation measure, of course. Their lasguns would soon be pointing straight down, ready for a shot in the remote chance their visitor proved hostile. The men up there had complained bitterly, for everyone amongst them knew they would likely be the first to die if the Space Marine attacked, and have little to no chance of escape. But they had taken their positions all the same.

Directly behind Harasen, Fenas and a dozen of his fellow cadets were in full ceremonial armour, their halberds raised as those of an honour guard. Harasen had asked for them to keep their limber straps good and loose, just in case. And yet, in the face of the towering figure that had clomped across the drawbridge as if he owned the keep himself, the ten-foot polearms seemed little more reassurance than toothpicks.

Harasen felt sweat run the length of his spine, a palpable sense of dread overcoming him as the newcomer came within ten feet and stopped. Now he was in focus, every detail etched itself into Harasen's mind.

To say the newcomer was forbidding was a grotesque

understatement. He was almost eight feet tall, clad in ornate black power armour etched with silvered gothic script. He held in one hand a twisting staff of polished wood, its knots and stubby protrusions at odds with the baroque sculptures and smooth finish of his deep black plate. Age-browned skulls were worn in a wreath around his neck, some small, some so large they could not possibly have come from a human.

The figure's sheer presence was terrifying. But it was his visage that would haunt Harasen's nightmares.

'Tell me the name of this fortress,' intoned the figure. His voice was deep, cultured and smooth, emanating from a snout-like grille framed with large jutting tusks like those of a beast. Around his head was a complex apparatus of coils and spark plugs that gripped his temples like a vice.

'Er... it is simply called Sixth West, my lord,' said Harasen, casting his eyes down at the floor. 'We're not an old enough fortification to have a herald's name. For such lowly souls it is a signal honour to even speak with you.'

'It is serviceable.'

'G-good,' said Harasen. 'Glad tidings.'

'Are there any other Adeptus Astartes within a day's travel?'

'That is very unlikely,' said Harasen. 'The vast majority of them are still on campaign.'

'Engaged at the Cadian Gate, no less,' added Fenas proudly, puffing out his chest.

'Shut up, Fenas,' hissed Harasen over his shoulder.

'The Cadian Gate,' said the stranger, his voice a low growl. 'I see. But some have remained here.'

'Soul's Well has a garrison of Adeptus Astartes, I believe,' said Harasen, pointing to the sharp triangle of black stone that dominated the northern horizon. In truth, he was glad of the excuse to look away. 'We see craft coming and going. But we rarely see the Absolvers this far south.'

'Absolvers indeed,' said the stranger, raising his staff. 'They cast themselves as if they bring absolution, and tell themselves they are already absolved. Fear not. We will have them here soon enough, and teach them their place.'

The vice of pipes and cables around the stranger's head glowed bright for a second. Harasen felt a pressure in his head grow quickly from a pulse to an ache, then to a splitting, agonising migraine. He fell to his knees, his spine twisting in a senseless attempt to wriggle free of the pain. He ground his fist into one eye as the other bulged. Sights and sounds flashed through his mind like the flickering of a broken zoetrope.

The guardsman saw the stranger striding past him, glowing staff sweeping through the air. Tendrils of pink and blue light shot out to connect with Fenas and his fellow wallsmen. Harasen saw human bodies twisting and bulging, craniums distending and eyes bursting from heads in showers of nameless fluids. Screams filled the air as men's heads sank into their chests, arms elongated and grew extra joints. Liquid flame cascaded from the mouths of men who were gibbering and drooling in panic and terror. Fenas suddenly elongated as if being stretched on the rack, gangling limbs and knobbly neck stretching upwards before filling out with random bulges of muscle and jutting horn.

Desperately scrabbling to focus and draw his pistol, Harasen felt a ripping, tearing pain in his armpits. He fell forwards with a scream – not onto two hands, but four. Two strange glistening limbs shivered and buckled beneath his own, as pink as an infant's skin but heavy with muscle and cabled sinew. He was about to scream in horror, but it died in his throat. There was a shocking warmth in the lower part of his face. With mounting panic, he felt his jaws distend, his mouth filling with long needle teeth.

'Emperor save us,' said Harasen, his words distorted by his weird, needle-toothed mouth. 'Please. No.'

Hurried footsteps came from above – the guards atop the battlements, no doubt rushing to the Icarus quad-guns at the fort's nearest corners. Harasen looked up, eyes misted with tears. The stranger had spotted them running along the ramparts, and gave voice to a weird, sibilant phrase as he took something glass-like from his belt.

The stranger opened the phial and sent out a scattering of something that glinted in the twilight. In seconds the battlements echoed not to footsteps, but to screams.

Harasen saw a chink of black in the keep's wall as the sally port behind the west tower opened a crack. He shouted out and clawed at the kneepad of the stranger, hoping to distract him, but the Space Marine just brushed him away. He struggled to get up, but his centre of gravity was all wrong, and he stumbled forwards again, scrabbling on six limbs rather than four towards the newcomer. The stranger kicked him as if he were a troublesome dog, the impact so violent he felt his collarbone break and a couple of ribs along with it.

Crying out, Harasen twisted as he rolled, sharp agony jangling in his chest. He buckled over and curled in pain, catching a glimpse of Vallac Vandersen – one of the younger wallsmen – sprinting out from the sally port towards the treeline. For a second, he thought that his distraction had been in vain, and that the stranger had seen Vandersen disappear into the trees. But the giant was already striding onwards, the energies flickering from his staff focusing his strange magick on the garrison troops atop the crenelated battlements once more.

Harasen felt the edges of his vision turn black, the confusion and pain of the last few minutes threatening to rise up and take him into oblivion. Within less than a minute the guards of Sixth West had become awful, horrible mockeries of men, more like a freak show from the most demented of carnivals than a sentry patrol. Through it all strode the newcomer, resplendent in his black plate armour as he walked through the open drawbridge into the keep he had taken without so much as drawing his gun.

The stranger stopped on the threshold, looked up at the empty murder holes in the gatehouse, and turned back to the fleshy nightmares he had left in his wake. He was the last thing Harasen saw with his mortal eyes before they melted from their sockets, turned liquid by the sheer Chaotic power rippling in the air.

'Come back inside, then, brave men of Sixth West,' said the stranger. 'We have much work to do before our audience arrives.'

Vallac Vandersen ploughed onward at a stumbling run through the bracken of the Longfield Fallow, nettles stinging his shins and sharp rocks cutting into the threadbare soles of his ill-fitting boots. It had been two days since the horrendous events at Sixth West. Two days with no sleep, and no food either, other than the pine nuts he had foraged on the way. He was so sick of them now, sick of the smell of sticky amber sap and the sharp edges of the Duskenwald's pine cones. What he wouldn't give for half a roast pig.

For the fifteenth time that day he daydreamed of the juices of a thick slab of gammon, the mouth-watering smell of it. Then he thought of the stink of burning human flesh back at the fort, and his appetite left him completely.

Not long until he made it into the needle-trees again, Vandersen told himself. Not long until he was out of the moonlight and into the relative safety of the forest. If he could find a patrolling servo-skull, his chances of survival would increase tenfold; he might even be taken to a keep before nightfall to report on what he had seen. Maybe even Soul's Well itself.

And yet the fortress-monastery was still a long way off, said a nasty little voice in his head. Dozens of leagues away. Days and nights of constant travel, even if he some-how found a lizard-mule big enough to ride.

And if the thing that followed him didn't run him down in the night.

'Shut up,' said Vandersen to the voice. 'Leave me alone. I can make it there, it's not that far.'

The thing in his head laughed, mocking and cruel. He turned round, trying to shake the feeling that it wasn't just his imagination, but that he had actually heard it this time.

Some nameless instinct flared up, the same hind-brain warning that his forefathers would have felt when wych-wolves howled in the distance. The hairs on his neck, his forearms, his shoulders all stood and bristled, his mus-cles uncomfortably tense.

Vandersen could feel something, not so far away, looking at him. Looking *into* him.

The young warrior broke into a run, panting, thin trails of tears trickling from the corners of his eyes. He tripped, stumbled, cut his hands, and got upright once more, his awkward stagger turning into a run as he finally found a patch of solid ground.

He felt his lungs burn as the eaves of the forest loomed up ahead, then launched into a bed of bracken, scooping out with his arms like a champion swimmer at the Five Challenges as he fought through to the woods behind. Then he was through, bursting out like a startled boar onto a slight incline carpeted with tree-needles. He looked behind him, but nothing was coming through the bracken. The night air was still.

Finally safe, Vandersen told himself.

The nasty voice in his head snickered again, no doubt enjoying the sensation of him lying to himself.

'Not yet,' said a deep voice to his right.

'Aaaagh!' shouted the young guard, falling back awkwardly onto one hand so hard his wrist broke with an audible crack. He pushed away, scrabbling in panic through the pine needles as a massive shape loomed out of the shadow of the woods ahead.

The stranger from the keep.

'Do not run,' he said, his voice strange as he cocked his tusked head to one side. 'I bring a gift, to help you. Look.'

Vandersen felt himself compelled to look up at the monstrous giant, his baleful red eyes glinting in a bulky, broad silhouette. He was holding something out towards Vallac, the soft blue of the night sky shining from its rounded edges.

A human skull, brown with age and polished to a high sheen.

'This is a boon for you, mortal man,' said the giant. 'And it will bring gifts to others in turn.' He took out a wide strip of hessian and wrapped the skull in it, tying the cloth's ends together and tucking it roughly into Vandersen's belt.

'Do not lose it, or you will suffer the same fate as your friends at the keep, and be given a new body that you will not find to your liking.'

Vandersen looked uncomprehendingly upwards, his mind drowning in a sea of fear.

'You will be flesh-changed. Do you understand?'

'Yes, yes!' said Vandersen. 'Just let me live!' He briefly recalled seeing Harasen writhing on the floor, fleshy arms sprouting from his armpits as his eyes goggled in panic and pain.

The tusked stranger gave a sigh. 'Oh, you will live, little man. You have work to do.'

The giant reached out two fingers, each the width of a dagger's hilt. Vandersen, out of his mind with fear, froze like a winter corpse-rat as the giant pressed the tips of each finger against his temples, holding them there for a second before removing them with a slight shiver.

'Now. Get to it.'

Vandersen nodded vigorously before backing away. The stranger stood, watching him with those glowing red eyes. He seemed to be studying him intently, his manner as if he was a parent watching an infant animal take its first tentative steps.

Vandersen put a tree trunk between them, pressing his back against it in the hope that the stranger would leave.

Then he heard a faint hum of servo-motors as the giant turned and strode off, wood cracking and splintering underfoot as he went.

The guardsman ran for his life.

Half-dead with exhaustion, malnourished and so tired that his eyes kept rolling back in his head, Vallac Vandersen stumbled up the mosaic-paved road to Soul's Well.

Not long until he was safe, he told himself. But somewhere in his head he knew that was a lie.

Now and again a tattered supplicant who had come to gaze at the fortress' glory would wish him well, hold out a cask of stale water for him to drink from, or sprinkle him with cheap incense droplets as he passed. Even the thrall-guards and archer serfs in the towers looked upon his bloody feet and the smears he left behind him with approval. They saw only a pilgrim who had sacrificed much to come before them; somewhere Vandersen had lost his boots, and he had the weather-beaten, sunburned look of a man who had walked for days without rest.

Vandersen ignored them all. After all, he had work to do.

The main arterial route to the fortress-monastery, the Road of Supplications, stretched across the entire continent in one form or another. Here it was a wide mosaic-tiled pathway clean of all but dust and the gifts of vassal supplicants. It was flanked by long, fluttering banners that displayed the finest victories of eight thousand years of loyal service to the Emperor, each mounted on a tall pine tree denuded of its branches to better display its adornment.

High above them, crows circled and cawed, kept away from banner and mosaic by burning, crown-like braziers.

The high torches lit the gloom, casting an orange light down from each stripped-bare tree. Every so often the crackle and pop of boiling sap would send a flurry of embers trailing lazily through the night.

The fortress up ahead was built atop a mountain of astonishing grandeur. Soul's Well was rumoured to have a deep abyssal pit at its heart that led down to the water table beneath the mountain. Vandersen's grand-sires had always said the mountain had been cored by the arboreal god Ferna, its great pit scooped out by his vast gnarled hand so that he might quench his thirst whilst he sat atop the peak and marvelled at the planet's arboreal vistas. Now, only the Absolvers drank from that deep artesian well. They had taken Ferna's seat for themselves – as was their right as the rulers of the planet, and defenders of the Imperium.

Eyes cast down, Vandersen saw depictions of sacred scenes in the mosaics under his bloodied feet – of Ferna gifting the Mountain to the Absolvers, of the Crushing of the Green Beast, of the Time of Upheaval and the Smiting of Cardinal Bucharis. Each time he felt his spirits uplifted by the depictions of such glory, the horrible voice in his head would tell him the awful truth – the death toll, the confusion, the starvation and anarchy left in the wake of each conquest. The voice would not let him rest, talking to him every time his mind drifted off, and waking him back up every time he lapsed into a half-second of sleep, even as his feet shambled ever onwards.

Nearly there, he told himself.

Nearly dead, replied the voice.

Vandersen wandered into the shadow of the Portal of Soul's Well, a towering edifice that was as much water clock as it was gateway. Sculptures of saints, dragons and sacred engines of war ticked and swung and clattered into place, clashing lances against metal scales with faint metallic noises.

The Portal was one of the Wonders of Allhallow, beloved by all who hailed from there. Its main gates only swung open when the Imperial Knights came to pay homage from nearby Henchkeep; Vandersen had always hoped to see them in person one day. The personnel doors at the gate's base seemed tiny by comparison to those of the Portal, but they were the only chance Vandersen had of getting inside.

As he approached, a heraldic cyber-servitor, dwarfish in size but with a child's head upon its thickset body, descended from its gargoyle's perch. It was hovering upon a repulsor pack fashioned to look like wide silver pinions, and bearing a set of scales in one hand and a shortspear in the other.

'Halt-you… pilgrim,' it said, its voice tinny and oddly squeaky. 'Pay… respects… here.'

'I have work to do,' said Vandersen, his voice ragged and wheezy from exhaustion.

'You… will… halt,' said the seraph-servitor, its cybernetic eye whirring. Part of its chest fell away, a nozzle extruding from where its heart should have been with a tiny pilot light flaring in front of it.

'I bring news to the masters. News of a visitor. An angel of death, in black rather than white.'

'An…' The seraph paused. 'Explain.'

'This newcomer took Sixth West by force. He is one of them, I swear it. A Space Marine. A black angel.'

'Black… Angel,' said the seraph, its bionic eye unfolding

like a flower to expose a long lens that sent ruby light panning across Vandersen's face. 'Protocol initiated.'

'What is that light? I don't…'

There was a loud clank from the gatehouse ahead. Three heavily-built vassal warriors, their livery in the bone and black of the Absolvers, emerged from the shadows of the gate ahead. One stood right in front of him, the other two flanking him so that he had no way out. They lowered their ornate las-spears towards Vandersen's chest.

'What's in the hessian?' said the closest guard. Vandersen took it out of his belt and opened it to show the yellow-brown skull inside. He wanted to tell the truth of what had happened to him, let the words spill out in a jumble until the dreadful weight upon him had lifted, but for some reason he just couldn't get them out. It was as if his mind was stuffed full of fraying thread, confusing his thoughts any time he tried to focus on the recent past.

'A relic,' he managed, turning it over in his hands to show it had no augmetics. The guards nodded in assent; it was common enough for pilgrims to carry the bones of the revered dead.

'Congratulations, runt,' said the eldest of their number, a pox-scarred brute in ornate plate armour with a laurel wreath curling around his helm. 'You have yourself an audience.'

CHAPTER EIGHT
PLAGUE OF CHANGE

Soul's Well
Allhallow, Scorpid Cluster

Vandersen limped and staggered through the tall, vaulted corridors of Soul's Well, too tired to take in the beautiful tapestries and ornate autosconces that lined the walls. He was led through inner gates and along darkened tunnels, his escort the three vassals from the Great Portal. The fortress monastery was immense. It felt like he had been walking for the best part of a day since he had passed through its legendary gateway, and he had long ago stopped staring in awe at the spectacle and grandeur that surrounded him.

The older warrior marching in front of him, who Vandersen now thought of as Elder Pox because of his acne-cratered visage, was still staring straight ahead as he marched with clockwork precision along the cold stone corridors. By contrast, the two guards behind their sergeant were watching him like hawks. Whenever Vandersen veered close to a wall, hoping to rest his head on a buttress or stone memorial plinth, one of the two vassal warriors behind him would prod him with the butt of a las-spear, or simply guide him with a firm hand back on course.

After a while Vandersen came to realise that the one to the left of him was taking any excuse to hit him, whilst the one on the right was stern, but not violent.

They will beat you to death, you know, said the nasty voice in his head. *Once you have given your news.*

He risked a glance backwards, catching a glimpse of his two guards – one grizzled and bearded with heavy brown curls, one with a clean jaw and a nasty smirk. The smirker saw him looking and brought the end of his polearm up, catching Vandersen under the chin and rattling his brain as his jaws thumped closed. He half-fell as he turned, steadying himself with an outstretched hand before staggering onwards, almost falling into Elder Pox before resuming his stumbling walk. The bearded guard gave a tut of disapproval, but he was not sure if it was aimed at him or at Smirker.

Three more minutes and they had reached a massive vaulted hall, long columns reaching up to arc out and become the inner ridges of vast domes. Despite his exhaustion, this time Vandersen could not help but look upward, taking in the elaborate friezes and frescos that stretched up and around the domes. There was enough gold leaf here to feed a keep for a dozen winters.

'The grand atrium,' said the guard with the beard. 'Count yourself lucky, pilgrim. Few of your number ever get this far.'

'It's very... amazing,' said Vandersen lamely. 'But I have work to do.'

The cruel voice in his mind laughed, a high-pitched and mocking sound. He shook his head, trying to clear it out. His brain was hurting, now, a thumping headache that got worse every time he looked up at the frescos of Imperial saints and the gargoyle-like creatures they were impaling on their lances.

Thump, thump, thump.

Vandersen realised the noise was not his headache, but footsteps. Footsteps so heavy they echoed around the dome like the drums of war.

'Is this him, High Vassal Fiorenz?' said a voice from behind and to the right, rich and mellifluous.

'It is, my liege.' Elder Pox's voice sounded like a rough croak by comparison.

Vandersen looked around, and saw a figure from legend.

The Lord of Soul's Well was massively built, head and shoulders taller than Elder Pox and near twice as wide. His armour was every bit as ornate and exquisitely fashioned as that of the stranger who had attacked the fortress, but where that one had worn battleplate of black with ornate gold filigree, the Absolver lord wore fluted and sculpted armour of ivory white. An ermine cloak cascaded down from a gorget framed by two massive pauldrons, and a strange backpack of onyx rose behind his head.

His expression was not that of a king, nor even that of a guard looking down on him. He had an easy smile, and a glint in his eye that made Vandersen frown as if he should recognise him.

'Long day, my lad?'

'I... I have work to do,' said Vandersen.

'And what work is that? Can you not afford a respite, given the circumstances?'

'I bring a message for the Castellan of Soul's Well,' he replied, doing his best to shake his head clear of the chuckling that echoed through it. He felt himself shrink inside for a moment, the words bubbling out of him. 'There is one here who would make you pay for your pres… presump…'

'Let's take this somewhere a little quieter,' said the armoured lord, lightly placing a hand that could have crushed a human head upon Vandersen's shoulder. 'That will be all, high vassal. Please wait in the southern vestibule.'

'Of course, my liege,' said Elder Pox. 'Though your message said we were to escort the–'

'That will be all.'

'Of course.' The guard sergeant, his face twisted up into what he probably thought was a smile, backed away, motioning his men to do the same. They bowed as one, turned smartly, and made their way back the way they had come.

The Absolver, his hand still on Vandersen's shoulder, started slowly towards one of the side chambers that opened out from a wall full of sculptural scenes of battle. Half dazed, Vandersen walked alongside him, shooting occasional glances up at the lord's handsome features as he talked. Vandersen had to keep reminding himself the kingly figure was talking to him, and him alone.

'You have important news, I hear. Let's retire to this chamber before we speak of it.'

Vandersen nodded. He had a feeling that retiring anywhere would mean he was unlikely to come back out, but was too intimidated to disagree.

'I find the grand atrium to be excellent for bellicose speeches, my lad, but absolutely awful for personal discourse. I only chose it as a rendezvous to fulfil certain expectations.'

'Yes, but... I have work to do,' stammered Vandersen.

'So you say,' nodded the king, guiding Vandersen through into the chapel. 'And we shall see you to this work as soon as we can.'

Hard, confident footsteps filled the hall as another Absolver strode quickly up to them. He was clad head to toe in ivory battleplate, wax-sealed ribbons of parchment on each of his great pauldrons.

'Master Castellan,' said the ivory warrior, 'it is as you suspected. The recently translated fleet has elements of the First emerging from some manner of broad spectrum data-shroud. Their command echelon has already made planetfall, and only now is approaching us for an audience.'

'I have business to conclude here first,' said the king, 'for this young man speaks of an angelic figure in black. I am sure they would understand.'

The newcomer bowed his head. 'Of course.'

'Have Sergeant Nexa ready his hunters for despatch to their location, and tell him to act as necessary to ensure our shared agendas align. Use those exact words. Tell him to greet our visitors with due honour, and let them know I will be with them as soon as I can.'

Striking a fist upon his breastplate in salute, the messenger turned on his heel and marched back the way he had come. The king smiled down once more at Vandersen, guiding him towards the room at the edge of the atrium. The chapel was a visual feast, all statue-lined alcoves and elaborate chandeliers, but ultimately it was nothing next to the presence of the Absolver lord.

Vandersen still found it difficult to look away from him. His tanned skin wrinkled around the eyes, reminding Vandersen of his father. His teeth were white, but one was broken behind a swollen and slightly bruised lip. The lack of perfection made the Space Marine seem a little less frightening, more human than the statue-like saints of battle depicted in the keep's mosaics and friezes.

The armoured giant pressed his palm against a rune-slate as they passed inside, and a heavy door slid shut behind them.

'My name is Master Castellan Moddren of the Angels of Absolution,' he said. 'I have the honour of being the steward of this great fortress, Soul's Well. And you, my young guardian of the forest?'

'Vallac Vandersen of Sixth West.'

'I see. Tell me, Vallac. This work you speak of. Is it to bear me a message?'

'Yes!' said Vandersen. 'If you are truly the master castellan of this fortress.'

'I do indeed have that honour. Sometimes I even get to defend it.'

'Then I am to tell you this.'

The words came out in a strange groan, as if it were someone else speaking through Vandersen's mouth.

'You will wear your innate corruption for all to see,' he said in a guttural monotone. 'You and all those who consider themselves absolved, you will exhibit the sins of the fathers, and we will expose the truth within. There is no escaping it, the work of aeons has already begun.'

Vandersen suddenly collapsed to the floor, panting, with

sweat rolling down his temples. His throat felt hot, stinging, as if he were choking back vomit. Moddren dropped to his haunches, placing one large hand behind Vandersen's spine and propping him up.

'Where did the black angel give you this message, Vallac?'

'In the Duskenwald. I escaped through the sally port, but he tracked me down.' The words came in a rush, as if a dam had broken. 'I did not want any of this, I just wanted to escape, I don't belong here!'

'Catch your breath, son. No need to proceed until you are ready.'

'Aren't there other Absolvers coming to meet you?'

'In time,' said Moddren. 'If there is a hostile action levelled against our planet, no matter how small, then it has my full attention. They can wait.'

Vandersen gulped down air, sitting upright and nodding. After a minute had passed, he pushed the giant's hand to one side. 'I can continue,' he said, coughing to clear his throat as he got to his feet. His vision swam, churning like blood in a whirlpool. He staggered, but Moddren guided him to sit on one of the chapel's pews.

'You can talk sitting down,' said Moddren gravely. 'Go on. You say you escaped.'

'Yes,' said Vandersen, nodding again. 'He attacked us. But I'm not sure how. Some kind of witch-magic, I think. He didn't even fire a shot.'

'What did this magic look like, Vallac?'

'It changed them,' said the young man. 'It came out of his staff, and changed them into monsters.' He looked up to meet Moddren's eyes. The Absolver lord was gazing down, full of concern, the finger-thin beard around his mouth pulled into a triangle by his downturned lips.

Vandersen found himself caught somewhere between awe and dread before pulling his wits back together.

'I can continue,' he said, hugging himself for a moment before exhaling deeply. 'It's fine.'

'Good. This Space Marine, Vallac. He looked something like me, did he not?'

'No,' said Vandersen. 'Not really. He was… big, but he had all this gold script on black armour, strange tusks on his helm, and a weird device clamped around his head.'

'Did it have coils at the temple, and a kind of hood?'

'I think so,' said Vandersen with an involuntary shiver. The hairs on the backs of his forearms were sticking up at the memory. 'It's hard to explain. The hood lit up, before all the men began to… change.'

'That makes sense to me. He was using witchery. What else did you see before you ran?'

'Up on the battlements, the men were being attacked by something. I saw glimpses of something weird. Whatever they were just appeared out of nowhere. I could hear them, but I never saw them. I just ran.'

'Understandable,' said Moddren, nodding. 'But you say he came to you in the woods?'

Do it, pawn of lies, said the voice in Vandersen's head. *Do what you came to do.*

He felt his headache build to a peak.

'Yes,' he said, screwing his eyes shut. 'He ran me down as I was trying to get away from Sixth West. He came at night, and caught me up.'

His headache was splitting, now, robbing the corners of his sight. 'He told me to give you this message.'

Reaching out with his good wrist, Vandersen grabbed a heavy shriving iron from the end of the pew and brought it round hard towards Moddren's scalp. Quick as a snake, the master castellan caught his arm, squeezing so hard the wrought iron stick fell from his shaking hand. Vandersen could feel his bones grinding. He convulsed, nonsense spewing from his lips.

Let it flow, foolish curseling! screamed the voice in Vandersen's head. *Let it out!*

'I think that concludes our conversation. For now,' said Moddren, hauling Vandersen to his feet and sliding the chapel door open with his other hand. 'I have enough information to work with, high vassal!'

Vandersen swam in a hazy fugue, fighting to keep focus. From the other side of the grand atrium, he could see the trio of guards running towards him, their las-spears held at the ready.

'Escort this young man to a holding cell. Do so with great care. He is unpredictable, and likely mind-snatched by some entity that wishes us harm. He attacked me, or at least tried to. He still has much to offer us.'

'Yes, my liege,' said Elder Pox. 'If this is the best they can do, they have sorely underestimated us.'

The smirker moved quickly behind Vandersen and grabbed him by the wrists. He felt them yanked back before the cold metal of a finger-thick chain pressed against his flesh and pulled tight.

The master castellan pulled his helm from its mag-clamp at his waist and placed it over his head, its laurel-crowned face-plate glinting in the gloom. 'Command,' he said, the vox unit making his voice strangely mechanical, 'muster an immediate speartip strike force for Sixth West. Prime clearance.'

The bearded guard scowled disapprovingly in front of Vandersen, his las-spear's tip hovering close to his throat.

'Move, traitor,' he said.

Vandersen was pushed hard, and he staggered away, bullied across the mosaic floor of the Grand Atrium and into a dark corridor leading away from the light.

He caught a glimpse of Master Castellan Moddren as he left, staring intently at him as if he were a bothersome insect.

Vandersen was shoved roughly into a cell that was no larger than the inside of a privy. He was forced to stoop and crawl even to get his legs clear of the rapidly closing door, scrabbling to the back of the tiny room to gather his legs up against his chest. The door slammed shut with a resounding clang that made his brain rattle in his head.

'Make the most of it,' said Smirker from outside. 'That'll seem like paradise by the time we're finished with you.'

The bearded guard laughed, a peculiar cross between a grunt and a sigh. 'They aren't too kind to heretics, down here,' he rumbled. 'And rightly so.'

Vandersen shook his head as if trying to shrug off a bad dream, desperate to think of the words that would persuade the vassals outside to unlock the door. The low throb of pain in his forearm brought his mind back into focus; if he wanted to get out, he had to gather his strength. He stared down at his arm. Thick bruises, purple and yellow, were beginning to blossom where the king's gauntleted fingers had dug into his flesh.

It's no more than you deserve, basal wretch, said the little voice in his head. *Even this cell is too good for you.*

'Shut up!' said Vandersen, unconsciously scrabbling at the cloth bundle still tied to his waist. He felt something there.

'Shout and scream all you want,' said Smirker. 'We're quite used to it.'

Vandersen plucked at his waist some more. Something was making it difficult to sit down. His hands found something there, something large and round. He dimly remembered being given something in the forest, and felt a rising feeling between relief and mounting terror that the guards had not confiscated it. He took out the hessian sack at his waist, stared at it as if he had never seen the like, unravelled it, and looked numbly at the contents.

A fleshless human skull stared back.

'*Do as he says, little piglet,*' it said. '*Scream.*'

Vandersen screamed.

In the hearth chamber of Sixth West sat Gohorael of Caliban. The high-backed castellan's seat he had chosen for his throne was positioned at the head of the elder-table, and one of the keep's servo-cherub attendants hovered above each shoulder.

Before him were the remnants of the keep's defenders – those that had surrendered to him, suffered debilitating wounds, or been so overcome with fear they could do nothing but watch as their new master took his due. Not a single man or woman amongst them had kept their true form, each twisted by eldritch power into something far deadlier and more unsettling than a human being.

'Come forth the brave,' said Gohorael. 'You who would carry my message to the next flock, and the next.'

A barrel-chested creature with tiny, handless arms no thicker than sticks stumbled forwards. The distended sac of its cranium flapped like the bulging head of an octopus.

'I sherve,' it slurred, thick strings of drool pouring from

its discoloured jaws. It was repulsive, thought Gohorael, but the killing light of bloodlust was in its eyes. It would serve as a distraction, at least, and as a vessel for the infectious changes to come.

'So you do,' said the giant. 'I name thee Non Manus. You may spread enlightenment to the non-believers.'

At this, Gohorael took one of the age-browned skulls from around his neck. He untangled the cord wrapped though its eye sockets, and placed it around Non Manus' neck with the ceremony of a king bestowing a mantle of leadership upon his fondest arch-duke.

The mutant clacked its jaws, ropes of spittle flying left and right.

'Now bear that relic south, and make your way into the next keep you find,' said Gohorael. 'Use its power to destroy any who would resist the gift of our presence, then return it here.'

'Yesshhh,' said the creature, nodding as if it had only now seen the light.

'And who else amongst you would spread the word of the Architect of Fate?' said Gohorael, his arms held wide. 'This world is in grave need of his teachings.'

'I will,' said a long-limbed freak of a man, odd bulges of muscle protruding from his elongated neck. He seemed as if he had been crying, but stood proud nonetheless. 'I will bear this new truth for the betterment of all.'

'Ah!' said Gohorael. 'An eloquent one. How gratifying. Bow that mighty head, and inherit your destiny.'

The lanky creature knelt down, eleven foot of gangling muscle folding itself into a crouch by Gohorael's throne. The Space Marine took another skull from the octocraniad wreath, placing it over the mutant's neck.

'You were once called Fenas, were you not?'

'I was,' said the creature. 'But I have since seen the light. My mind is aflame, and I have been reborn.'

'So you have,' said Gohorael. 'You may keep your mortal name. I dub thee Fenas the Brave. You will make a fine spokesman. Go eastward into the night, carry that treasure with you, and spread the word of the Primordial Truth.'

'I shall,' said Fenas, unfolding himself before walking out of the hearthroom as if in a dream.

'May I approach?'

Gohorael looked askance at the next supplicant. He had the appearance of a normal man, older than the rest and running to fat, but for two things – his eyes were missing from their sockets, and a second pair of arms hung limply from his armpits.

'Ah. My would-be host.'

'Yes,' said the human, scraping a nail gingerly at the edge of the red-black pits that were once his eyes. 'Harasen. I was the one foolish enough to resist you.'

'And now?'

'I see things much clearer, my lord. You have my undying allegiance.'

'I can believe it. You are fortunate, for I am in a forgiving mood. Come to me, Harasen. I give you a new name this day.'

The castellan moved forward, easily avoiding the debris of the broken chairs and shattered candelabras that lay on the floor despite his blindness. He knelt in front of the improvised throne, and bowed his head.

'I name thee Truthseer,' said Gohorael, carefully taking one of the skulls from around his neck and placing the leather loop that bound it over Harasen's eyeless head. 'You above all others have looked upon the glory of change, seeing its light without mortal senses to cloud your perception. Go forth, head east at all times, and share your vision with all you meet, even when the unbeliever and the naïf tries to stop you.'

'Yes, my lord,' said Harasen. He got to his feet, a little unsteady, and headed for the gate.

'The work of aeons is underway once more,' said Gohorael. 'Now who amongst you has the courage to be next?'

In his tiny cell, Vandersen bit his lip, tears appearing at the corners of his eyes. The varnished skull was still staring at him, that maddening grin seeming to mock him.

'*Go on, moon-child,*' it said. '*Scream again. You're going to die here, friendless and alone. You know it to be true.*'

'No,' said Vandersen, pushing his fists into his eyes.

It was no use. The pain was still there, and the images. Oh, the images he had seen over the last few minutes. Even one of them was enough to scar the mind forever.

'*Let it all out, insignificant worm,*' said the skull. '*It's building up in your head. If you don't let it out, it'll burst.*'

'Leave me alone!' shouted Vandersen, his words reverberating around the cell as if it were the size of an empty cathedral.

'*But you are not alone, plague bringer,*' said the skull. '*I am in here with you. And I will have my sport.*'

'No!' said Vandersen, flinging the skull hard against the door. The door flew wide open, and the skull simply stopped in mid-air, turning to face him with a mocking grin. In the corridor beyond was Smirker, scrabbling upright from a half-slump.

'What in Ferna's chalice is–'

Vandersen found himself shivering, quaking, convulsing as his mind-wracking headache spread to encompass his entire body. His stomach convulsed, a wrenching feeling in his core as if an invisible claw clenched at his guts.

A stream of glowing white energy suddenly shot from his mouth, past the skull and into Smirker's open jaws, slamming him back against the corridor wall. Smirker spasmed and shook, limbs flailing as the outpouring of energy pinned him against the wall. The brickwork blackened and cracked around him, a halo of incendiary energy that left an inverse silhouette as if he had been shot by a heavy flamer.

Vandersen heard running footsteps, the sound somehow clear as day over the horror that eclipsed his mind. It was the bearded guard, disbelief slowing his pace as he witnessed the supernatural spectacle before him.

Vandersen bit down hard on the energy pouring from his mouth. The strange emanation beaming out of his craw ceased for a blissful moment.

Smirker slid to the flagstones, wisps of white smoke curling from his mouth and nostrils. The other guard turned to Vandersen with an expression of pure hatred, speartip pointed straight at his chest.

The floating skull turned in the air to stare right at Vandersen once more. His mind filled with flickering images of bloody carnage. He opened his mouth to scream. As the guard stepped forwards with his spear levelled at Vandersen's chest, another beam of light shot out, catching him in the neck.

The big man convulsed as the cascading beam travelled up over his chin and into his mouth, forcing its way in like a snake burrowing into a prey-beast's tunnel. He dropped the las-spear to the flagstones with a clatter and fell limp onto the recumbent, comatose form of his guardmate.

Vandersen gave an involuntary sob of fear and confusion. It became a rueful laugh, then a gabble of unintelligible syllables. Then, as Smirker and his bearded comrade clambered clumsily to their feet and stood vacant-eyed before him, his laugh turned into a horrible cackle that sounded as if it came from no living thing.

Fenas the Brave stumbled through the woods, the skull around his neck bouncing madly as he stooped under this tree and that. Forced to run almost bent double by his impossible height, he had scratches all over his arms and legs, some quite deep, and his throat was sore from crying.

He ploughed on regardless, driven by some nameless desire to… share. To propagate his gift.

Fenas felt his vision begin to clear. He slowed, then stopped altogether, staring in horrified amazement at his elongated, over-muscled limbs. Sobs rose in his chest, great wracking spasms of terror and panic.

Fear not, said the voice in his head, the voice he could swear was coming from the varnished skull around his neck. *The glory that you hold within you is more beautiful than the sunset. You serve a divine purpose. March on.*

Fenas nodded, choking down his anguish and making off again. There, on the horizon, he could see his quarry. A set of low walls, the remains of an ancient hill fort. Fires sent lazy trails of smoke into the evening air, and faint strains of viol music reached down to him, piercing the fog in his head. He recognised the tune – the Dancing Duke, it was called. It had been one of his favourites, before.

You are the bringer of truth, said the skull around his neck. *This night, they will dance to a different melody.* Fenas nodded, his grin exposing far too many teeth, and resumed his loping, ungainly run.

The vassal guard known as Jethred Ghaunn got unsteadily to his feet. For once, his habitual smirk was entirely absent. He was still in the corridor outside the holding cell, but his throat and chest were aching as if he had choked on a lungful of dank fire smoke.

Jethred had been looking forward to spending some quality time with the captive, Vandersen. Once that bearded oaf Trenton was off his attendance cycle, Jethred was going to practice a little with his knife, telling the high vassal the wounds he inflicted were in self-defence. Such little indulgences helped him forget what happened at the Five Challenges last year, if only for a while.

Instead, though, Jethred had been caught off guard when the door flew open, his spear up as some kind of servo-skull distracted him. The prisoner, Vandersen, had taken his shot. He had felt something hit him, pushing inside him before disappearing entirely without leaving so much as a bruise behind. The prisoner too was gone, his tiny cell empty of everything save a scrap of sackcloth. There was no sign of Trenton.

Jethred felt a rising need to flee, or at least to move away from that horrible cell, and find somewhere bright. Somewhere with lots of people.

The kitchens were a good place to start.

The vassal guard felt something burn in his chest as he set off. It felt like a very weak acid, but covering his skin as well as his insides – and it itched like fury. Each time he scratched it, it got worse. He could feel it moving up his throat, slowly but surely.

He heard heavy footsteps, the thunderous thumping of a Space Marine. He turned the corner to be confronted by a looming wall of white ceramite – one of the Absolvers, accompanied by three vassals.

'What happened?' asked the Space Marine, his vox-cast voice intense and angry. 'The autoseraphs are reporting a prisoner breach.'

Jethred was about to reply when a great torrent of burning white ectoplasm shot from his mouth, spraying the Adeptus Astartes and splashing onto the vassals nearby. The Space Marine fell back, clutching his helm. His attendants screamed, clawing at their clothes as the fabric clung to the molten flesh beneath.

All three of them began to shudder, strange growths jutting from their skin. Jethred drew his knife and stuck it right in the neck joint of the Space Marine's armour, aiming for his jugular.

The blade snapped. Then the Absolver backhanded him in the gut, sending him sprawling down the corridor.

Jethred rolled in a tangle of limbs. His stomach had ripped open inside him under the force of the blow; he could feel it as a queasy knot of horror and pain. It was so painful he could not help but let that feeling out.

His vision became a blinding white blur, the agonising light in his head turning his world inside out.

When he recovered his wits, the walls were streaked with glowing red-black lines, molten stone dribbling from their undersides. In the corridor before him, the Absolver had been cut into three smouldering chunks. One of the vassals was neatly bisected from shoulder to hip, his remains steaming gently in the corridor. The other two were staggering away, one clutching his stomach, the other grabbing at his head as if to keep it from splitting open. Glowing white ectoplasm dribbled from his mouth.

A good start, young dolt, said a voice inside Jethred's head. *But we still have work to do.*

CHAPTER NINE
HOPE YET

Ferro-Giant Thetoid
Saltire Vex, Pelagic Industrial World
Chalnath Expanse

Rigswoman del Aggio picked her nose absently as she stared through the monitor room's window. An Arvus lighter was coming through the rain, its stab-lights illuminating Thetoid's skyshield pad. She checked her manifest's data-slate for the incoming craft's credentials. No scheduled visit.

'What did I say, Markens,' she said over her shoulder to her colleague. 'No idents.' As was invariably the case when anything unusual needed doing, the big man was asleep at his station.

'Markens, you useless lump of sump-sludge!'

'Huh?' The sound of old recaff tins scattering around heralded Marken's return to wakefulness.

'We have company. The unscheduled kind. Might be bringing word about when we're getting off-world. I'm heading out to check it.'

'In this weather?' said Markens, shaking his head. 'Want me to come with you?'

'No, I've got it. No sense both of us getting the cold-ague.'

Del Aggio pulled her blankets around her shoulders like a cloak, then pulled a tarpaulin coverall over her head and struggled it down over the whole lot. She felt more like an ambulatory cone than a woman, her gloved hands poking out less than a foot on either side, but at least she would keep relatively warm.

As she neared the door, del Aggio grabbed her pulse pistol from the desk, secreting it under her blankets and tucking its handle into her belt. She had been dying to fire the bulky sidearm in earnest since the first shipment of weapons came in from the t'au. If needed it would burn through the blankets just fine to give any hostiles a nasty surprise.

Perhaps today was the day.

Fighting open the door against the howling, cutting wind, del Aggio stepped out into the cold of the gantry and gripped the icy rail hard as she descended towards the skyshield. Ahead the Arvus lighter had already landed; no mean feat of piloting in the howling gale. It was powering down.

Del Aggio brought one hand inside her blanket cloak and up to the handle of the pulse pistol, thumbing the slide so it powered up and became warm to the touch.

'Come on, Taker,' said del Aggio softly. 'Make your move.'

The lighter's rear hatch sprung up with a jerk of motion, coming to a halt before a well-muscled brown arm pushed it all the way open. Stepping out of the passenger bay was a tall, well-built woman with an expression like a storm about to break. Her dreadlocked hair was pulled back in a tight sheaf, and she had a bloody bandage wrapped around her neck as an impromptu scarf.

'Throne above,' shouted del Aggio, recognising the woman from last year's promotions briefing. 'You're Deel, right?'

'Yes! Can we get inside?'

Del Aggio beckoned her over. Together the rigswomen climbed back into the octagonal viewing room, Deel pulling the door closed behind her and re-sealing it with a clunk of the wheel lock. Del Aggio waved Markens down. The big man sat back in his prized recliner and lay down the heavy iron rod he kept in case the Takers came for him.

The weak blue light of the cage-lumens lit the three of them as del Aggio and Deel slumped into the nearest seats.

'Damnation, but it's good to see a fresh human face,' said del Aggio. 'Markens, this is Rigswoman Jensa Deel. Big name from Omicroid. According to the gossip traders, she literally breathes fire.'

'Well, I haven't done that in years,' said Deel with a tired smile. 'Though I can still remember the taste of promethium just fine.'

Del Aggio laughed. 'I bet.' She took a bell jar of moonshine from under her desk and held it out. 'I'm Kaita del Aggio. Chief rigswoman of this fine Imperial edifice.'

'Thanks,' said Deel, reaching out a shaking hand. She swigged from the jar before making a grimace. 'Throne, that's bad.'

'Better than your piss-weak Omicroid muck,' said del Aggio.

'Picked a nice night for it,' said Markens, throwing Deel

a ragged blanket. She wrapped herself in it with a grateful nod. 'No wonder you look beaten. Hey, Aggro, didn't you say Omicroid went up in flames?'

'It did,' said Deel before del Aggio could reply. She gulped uncomfortably as the moonshine burned its way down. 'I just flew over its smoking remains.'

'Emperor's fist,' said Markens. 'A lot of good souls there.'

'The scuttlebutt from Gammic said you lot were hit by Takers,' said del Aggio. 'Worst strike yet.'

'Something like that,' said Deel.

'They're taking their own damned time about getting the relief fleet here,' said Markens.

'That's because they cancelled it,' said Deel.

'What?' barked del Aggio, standing up with a jolt. 'They're leaving us here to die?'

'Very deliberately.'

'I don't...' del Aggio's eyes were wild. Markens sat forward in his chair, hands gripping its armrests tight.

'I'm working on it,' said Deel. 'There's a ship inbound that can get us all off-planet in one go. We need to let the other rigs know that single-point evac protocols need effecting if this is going to work.'

'Can't do that from here,' said Markens, shrugging. 'You need at least two senior staff from different rigs to...'

He stopped when he saw Deel and del Aggio both staring daggers at him.

'Oh yeah,' he said. 'Right.'

'Think of all those administratum slates we will have to wade through afterward,' said del Aggio, rolling her eyes.

'Which would you prefer,' said Deel. 'Death by boredom, or having your blood freeze solid in your veins?'

'Point,' said del Aggio. 'Before we get to all that, though...'
She frowned, and the serpentine dragon tattoos that formed
her eyebrows creased until their tongues were touching.
'How did you escape your rig going down?'

'Well,' said Deel. 'That's a long– '

She stopped, looking pale and stricken.

'You all right, girl?' said del Aggio.

'Can't handle her shine,' chuckled Markens. 'Told you
these 'croids got no guts.'

Del Aggio jumped back as Deel puked a great stream
of molten light onto the floor, the substance hissing as it
dribbled through the grate beneath her feet. She jerked
upright and looked straight at del Aggio. Her eyes and
mouth were lit by a fierce light, her face a horrifying mask
with three white holes aglow.

'Bloody hellfire!' shouted del Aggio, leaping up onto her
seat and scrabbling to get her pulse pistol out from the
tangle of her blankets. She fumbled it, the bulky sidearm
skittering into the glowing puddle of vomitous discharge
that was seeping through the floor grate. Markens grabbed
his iron rod, lifting it across himself to deliver a heavy
backhand, and swung.

Deel outstretched a hand, and Markens froze, unmov-
ing, his flabby bulk unbalanced but somehow remaining
held in mid-swing.

'Wait,' coughed Deel. 'I can... I can explain.'

'Can you?' shrieked del Aggio, scrabbling up the pulse
pistol. 'Aagh!' The glowing white liquid burned her skin,
and she juggled the pistol before pulling a sleeve over her
hand and regaining her grip. She desperately tried to get
a cloth-covered finger into the trigger guard, but her head
hurt, a sudden onset headache that made it impossible

to concentrate. 'Seven sockets of the Holy Throne, what on Terra is wrong with you?'

Deel took the pistol from her hand and set it down behind her as if relieving it from a child. Despite herself, del Aggio was too shaken up to resist.

'I don't really know what's happening to me,' said Deel, her hands trembling. 'But you need me alive, that I can tell you. Or we're all lost.'

'What do you mean?'

'It's not just some error or accident that they aren't going to extract us this time. They want us dead.'

Del Aggio paled. 'Why?'

'They know about the t'au. But you and I are going to make sure that every man, woman and child gets off this planet before we all freeze.'

'How? And what about... this?' She motioned at the still sizzling vomit on the octagonal chamber's floor.

'I... I ate food supplies intended for a t'au metabolism. It's fine. I had to eat something.'

'I knew this whole xenos thing would turn out bad,' said del Aggio. 'You heard about that alien mercenary warsphere in Saltire nearspace? The one full of cannibals?'

'It's getting nearer, apparently,' said Markens. 'No one knows why.'

Deel made a face.

'No,' said del Aggio, her eyes wide.

Deel nodded slowly. 'Oh yes. That's our only ride out of here.'

CHAPTER TEN
SIEGE BLITZ

Fortress Sixth West
Allhallow, Scorpid Cluster

'Battle stations.'

Xedro Farren opened his eyes, his hands automatically checking the critical points of his bolt rifle. His augmented senses pierced the amber gloom of the *Night Harrower's* hold.

His battle-brothers sat ranged around him, silent and still. Some of them were looking around, taking stock just as he was. The grinding growl of the Repulsor's grav plate engines filled the tank's interior.

Farren glanced at the data-slate mounted on the control interface. The *Harrower* was making its way through a thick coniferous forest with a long, winding path cutting the centre.

Farren leaned over and pressed the script-rune at the base of the data-slate, refreshing his knowledge of the mission parameters. They had made planetfall, the drop-ships landing in a vast clearing without incident. Now they were en route to a traditional-looking Imperial keep. It was a garrison point formerly held by the vassals of their allies, the Angels of Absolution, but according to the brief it was now in thrall to dangerous rebels.

Lately Farren had been longing for battle, and those who stood against the Adeptus Astartes upon their own home planets were in dire need of extermination. The sweet release of combat was close.

A stray thought surfaced, scratching at the back of Farren's mind.

On an Adeptus Astartes homeworld, couldn't the resident Chapter take care of one single fortress in rebellion?

'*Primaris of the Third Company,*' came Chaplain Zaeroph's voice over the vox. '*We are upon Allhallow at the request of our successor Chapter, the Angels of Absolution, who call this forest world their home. We are to extinguish the fires of a rebellion. The planetary sub-class is feudal, so we do not expect heavy resistance.*'

'We peasants should fit right in,' said Moricani. Farren shot him a look.

'*One of the Chapter's sentinel fortresses has turned from the light of the Emperor,*' said Zaeroph over the magna-vox. '*Squads Farren, Orenst and Parvell, stay the course on full ahead. You Primaris Marines will form the vanguard, attacking via the drawbridge and the gate. You are cleared to kill on sight anything that is not wearing battleplate. Make it count.*'

'Aye,' replied Farren. 'Understood. We will win glory for the Chapter, for Terra, and…'

He paused, frowning, before completing the phrase by invoking the holy name of Mars. Something was not right.

'*Engagement range in three minutes,*' said Gsar over the interior vox. '*I can see the target edifice through the trees, lieutenant. The site has extensively fortified outer walls, and a high keep within. Relaying pict.*'

Farren shook his head, dispelling his doubts as he took stock of Gsar's visual. A large fortress with a prominent gate house and a raised drawbridge behind a moat, it had Icarus batteries on each tower's corner and a high-walled keep at its heart, each fascia adorned with a sixty-foot carving of a faceless, hooded angel. He nodded as the battle ahead unfolded in his mind, planning his mode of attack in a matter of seconds.

'Lieutenant,' said Thrunn, 'I must ask. If this is a Chapter planet, why are we attacking it? Can they not see to their own business?'

'And were we not intending to engage an ork presence after transit?' added Gsar.

'Don't ask,' said Vesleigh. 'Just act.'

Farren nodded in affirmation, but said nothing.

'These Angels of Absolution are not the Lion's first sons,' said Enrod dismissively. 'They need an education in the arts of war, if they can't keep their own houses in order.'

'Does it matter why we are attacking?' said Lenkatz, Moricani's second. 'If we are told to take out a rebel strongpoint, then we take it out, and leave a smoking crater as a warning for the next idiots to entertain heretical thoughts. My gun's machine-spirit has been dormant way too long.'

'I know how it feels,' said Enrod.

Moricani smiled. 'Nothing like revolting amounts of firepower applied to heretics who consider themselves safe.'

'Just get the job done,' said Farren. 'And stay focused. I'm anticipating having to split our forces if we're to get all of them.'

'The Ravenwing will likely take care of any stragglers,' said Vesleigh.

'I'm not so sure,' said Farren. 'I can't recall ever actually seeing them in battle, and I'm beginning to think that's deliberate. Helms on. I'm going for a wide-spectrum view.' He opened the hatch at the top of the Repulsor and sprung up, catching himself before lifting his upper body smoothly upwards.

The grinding of the Repulsor tripled in intensity as it accelerated to combat speed, its anti-grav engines shaking the hull with a perceptible vibration. The black-walled fortress came completely into view as the *Harrower* turned a long curving corner on the forest path. With its battlements looming over the treeline ahead, Farren could see it was clearly designed after the classical fortress of Calibanite design, its walls canted and angled to deflect incoming shot with the minimum of structural damage.

From whatever avenue of approach the attacker's shots came, his assault would be blunted, and any who braved the killing field that had been established around it would present himself to the quad autocannon arrays mounted on each of its eight points. Each emplacement was mounted on a ball and socket gimbal so it could be brought to bear on any foe that dared approach. The main gate itself looked almost impenetrably thick, a giant slab of metal and stone emblazoned with stylised battle scenes. On a Chapter planet, such a gate would likely be proof against everything short of a multi-melta.

'Can you take down one of these trees so it falls away from us, Gsar?' said Farren. 'One of the really large ones?'

'*If I put the Icarus rockets to it as well, almost certainly,*' said Gsar. '*There are a few contenders. By my estimates the garrison here have been lazy with their axes of late. Want me to knock?*'

'If you would.'

'*Engagement range in three…*' said Gsar. '*Two… one… target.*'

The hull of the *Harrower* was filled by the screaming roar of its las-talon discharging. Twin bolts of crimson energy slammed low into the tallest, widest tree at the clearing's edge. Gsar fired again, the second dual bolt blasting into the base of the tree towering next to it.

The trunks came apart in an explosion of thick flinders. The first tree moved, then the second, ever so slowly leaning towards the path.

There was a *whoosh* from behind Farren's head, and two pairs of missiles shot out from the Repulsor's Icarus pod to veer upwards, striking each tree thirty feet from the tip of its trunk. The missiles detonated with an ear-splitting bang, their impact sending the giant coniferous trees back to topple straight towards the fort.

Gsar's calculations were impeccable, as ever. The first tree crashed down into the curtain wall with tremendous force, the tip of its hardwood trunk smashing down the battlements even as the other trunk crashed home. A great cloud of grey dust, needle leaves and spinning debris rose up, but the fortress wall remained whole.

Farren ducked back into the Repulsor just as the point defence guns on the battlements swung around to face him. He heard the *brak-brak-brak* of heavy autocannons firing, each punching impact ringing loud on the *Harrower*'s hull in a percussive storm of shells.

Moricani laughed, something wild in his tone. Farren savoured the feeling of the cocktail of stimulant chemicals flowing through his blood in response to his spiking heart rate. He thought of old Pater Cawl in that moment, of the contempt the ancient archmagos would have had at the very idea of an enemy hoping to stop a Repulsor tank with a volley of conventional shot.

No matter how many of their guns they brought to bear, it would not be nearly enough to save them.

The *Harrower* slewed across the clearing from the wide road to follow the forest's eaves. Its brother transports bulled forward together for the main gate. The *Dire Tidings*, transport of Squad Parvell, swept a killing volley along the battlements with its heavy onslaught cannon. Farren nodded in approval when he noticed that the tank's gunner, Ferendt, had fired in stuttering bursts so its bolts found the gaps in the battlements and not the crennelations themselves. The volley was rewarded with screams of pain from the garrison troops.

Not to be outdone, the onslaught cannon of Squad Orenst's transport – *Heaven's Troth* – poured a stream of bullets into the quad-gun array on the nearest tower. The heavy calibre shots knocked it off kilter, blew off two of its barrels, then tore it away completely in a scream of tortured metal.

The *Harrower*, having ground a path of mud and rock across the verdant clearing, was close enough to make a push for the walls. Farren took hold of the pintle-mounted cannon's manual controls and sent a long, sustained volley at the trees Gsar had felled, splintering away swathes of their outstretched boughs.

'Now or never,' he voxed to Gsar.

The Repulsor rose upon its grav impulsors and mounted the two fallen trees near their bases. The trees groaned, splintering and cracking as the tank's anti-grav field pushed down with immense weight, but Gsar's skill as a driver was such that the *Harrower* made the climb over the moat at an even pace.

The tank ground its way straight up the mighty trunks, its grav field snapping lesser branches and hurling great clouds of pine needles into the air as it pushed inexorably upwards. As it got closer to the battlements Gsar accelerated hard, the jutting stumps of the trees' broken boughs no impediment to the Repulsor's aggressive grav field.

Farren watched as the *Harrower*'s main armament canted upwards, its las-talon lining up with the quad-gun array that was tearing at its flank with raking blasts of auto-cannon fire. A dual blast of ruby light, and the quad-gun emplacement was reduced to a mangled claw of metal reaching up to the sky.

Then the Repulsor was up and over the wall. Farren's stomach lurched as the tank launched from the battlements. There was a moment of weightlessness followed by a strange, cushioned thump. The lieutenant unslung his bolt rifle and dropped inside, readying a frag grenade with his finger over the release switch.

'Now!'

The transport's frontal ramp flew open with a clang of pistons. Sunlight poured in. In the courtyard before them was a rag-tag assemblage of vassals, humans clad in defaced heraldry, many of whom were bringing lasguns to bear. Some of them were disfigured mutants, badly changed by whatever vile gods they worshipped in place of the Omnissiah.

Spears of ruby light shot out from their guns, glancing from the *Harrower* to little effect. Farren hurled his grenade at the thickest concentration of the rebels, the detonation sending a group of them sprawling in a cloud of blood and shrapnel.

'Traitors,' shouted Farren, 'your death has come for you!'

Enrod and Vesleigh were already firing, kneeling on either side of Farren. He took up his own bolt rifle and picked off one target, a three-eyed freak with too many chins. His second bolt took down the quadrupedal mutant to his right, and his third the elephantine brute behind him. Each round took a rebel in the centre mass before detonating to spray gore, bone and offal in a wide radius.

Farren heard the searing hiss of plasma shots from either side of the *Harrower*, along with Moricani's familiar barking laugh. The sergeant and his squad were taking a deadly tally of their own, burning spheres of superheated gas blazing out in tight volleys to vaporise the lasgun-armed mutants by the dozen.

This was not glorious work, thought Farren. Not a worthy foe. But it was necessary.

'Any moment, they charge,' said Farren, watching more of the mutant creatures spill from the spiral staircases, barracks and gatehouses around the edge of the courtyard. He could read the hatred in their eyes, the set of their shoulders, the snarls on their lips. 'Gsar, be ready.'

The rebels were gabbling, screaming and moaning in pain as they levelled a tattered volley of lasfire at Farren and his brothers. A four-horned mutant's las-shot smacked him in the leg, but the auto-reactive plate over his kneecap took most of the impact.

He returned fire, his bolt hitting the mutant in the nose.

The shot caved in his face a split second before exploding messily, leaving a headless corpse toppling into the dirt.

Farren looked left and right before scanning the top levels of the fortress. As he watched, a building-levelling explosion blasted away a massive chunk of the battlements from the top of the keep ahead. Through the clouds came a Thunderhawk gunship, low and steady, with its metal jaws agape.

'Here come the First,' said Vesleigh. 'High and mighty.'

'Focus on the enemy,' said Farren. 'The counter-attack is close.' Nearby the mutant creatures were massing into a throng, two of them carrying hessian sacks filled with bulky cylinders.

A great roar went up as the rebels rushed the Repulsor. Farren put a bolt into the bulging, distended neck of the nearest one carrying a sack-charge. He went down hard, his sack of dynamite spilling its contents across the yard. Vesleigh got the second mutant with a chest shot just as he hurled his explosives towards the Primaris Marines. A moment later, the rebel burst in a welter of red fluids.

'Fire in the sky,' said Moricani, loosing a bolt of plasma at the satchel as it arced through the air.

'Brace!' shouted Farren, turning his shoulder as his brothers followed suit. The satchels of dynamite detonated with a series of staccato booms. The blast wave flung mutant bodies backwards, painting the flagstones red as it bowled Farren and his brothers back into the *Harrower*.

There was a moment of stunned silence amongst the throng.

'Get back inside,' said Farren. 'We have seconds at most.' His brothers moved in with practised efficiency, some through the front ramp, others the side door.

Then, as if driven by a single overriding impulse, the remainder of the mutant mob charged with their voices raised in a chorus of hellish screams.

'Gsar,' said Farren. 'Do it.'

'Aye, lieutenant.'

The *Harrower*'s engines whined as if offended, then gave a coughing boom. A massive pulse of anti-gravitic energy burst out from its perimeter of bulky repulsion plates. The charging mutants were flung away by an invisible wave of force, tumbling back into the dirt or slamming into the walls of the garrison buildings.

'Go!' said Farren. He charged from the front of the *Harrower* with Enrod and Vesleigh close on his heels. Farren sent three bolts into three different targets, each of them within a dozen paces of the next. He was already searching out new hostiles as a series of detonations ripped apart those he had already doomed.

His squad claimed their own impressive tallies as they moved, killed and moved again. Loud hissing roars came from close behind as Moricani's Hellblasters took out the quad-guns pivoting around to draw a bead on the Primaris warriors.

There was a loud explosion from behind them as the *Heaven's Troth* and *Dire Tidings* finally took down the massive door to the keep. Shattered at the hinges by las-talon shots, the giant structure toppled in an avalanche of broken stone and dust.

The *Troth* was first through. The Repulsor's front jaws opened wide, and Orenst and his brothers charged out, adding their own bolt rifle shots to the one-sided firefight.

'Second level!' shouted Farren. 'Squad Orenst, you're

with me. There's a way into the keep up there. Moricani, take the right.'

'It would be my pleasure!' shouted back Moricani, far louder than necessary.

Farren darted into the leftmost corridor within the thickest part of the curtain wall. He turned the first corner, and took a lasgun shot right in his chest. It felt like a punch to the solar plexus, but he shrugged it off; he had taken worse on the dunes of Mars, and he was already running through it.

A silhouetted figure stumbled backwards in the corridor ahead. Farren shot him in the chest. The mutant sprawled as a crater suddenly appeared where his lungs should be. He fell back into the shaft of light from an arrow slit beyond to reveal a hideous mask of pink flesh.

Beyond the mutant's corpse was a wide set of stairs. Farren leaped the cadaver without breaking stride, Enrod close behind. The lieutenant was already half way up the flight of stairs when he heard Vesleigh's voice.

'What in cog's name is – aaagh!'

Farren spun round, looking over Enrod's shoulder. The mutant whose torso he had blasted open had risen up as if pulled by invisible strings. He was hanging in mid-air. A stream of white energy was pouring out of the mass of flesh where his face should have been, boring into Vesleigh's chest like a plasma torch. Shadows danced across the walls like fiends at some hellish bacchanal.

'Kill it!' shouted Farren. He pushed Enrod down, bringing his bolt rifle around to take a shot.

Too slow. Thrunn had already launched himself at the hovering corpse, bringing it down hard in a pit-fighter's slam hold.

Sickly white light poured out everywhere as Thrunn put his knee on the thing's neck, leaning all his considerable weight on it with a sickening crack. With one hand he grabbed its head, forcing it at an unnatural angle to point to the wall in case it vomited more energy. With the other he grabbed its collarbone, fingers sinking deep into its flesh. Then, with a great heave, Thrunn pulled the corpse's body one way and pushed its head the other, decapitating it in a messy burst of blood and ectoplasm.

'You could have just shot it,' said Enrod.

'Enough, Enrod,' said Farren. 'Vesleigh, are you fit to go on? That looks bad.'

The young warrior shook his head. 'I am compromised. I will take the rear.' He heaved as if to vomit, and blood spilled from his helm's grille. 'It's gone right through me, I think. My furnace... My furnace has been triggered. I must fight on. I cannot waste it.'

'Understood,' said Farren. 'I made it back from a Belisarian surge once. You can too.'

Vesleigh nodded stiffly, struggling his helm off and mag-clamping it to his waist. 'I need air,' he said.

'Come on.' Farren took the lead once more, taking the stairs three at a time.

'Wait,' said Vesleigh, screwing up his eyes. 'I don't think I'm going to–'

Suddenly, the young warrior convulsed, his back arching unnaturally far, and screamed like a man on the rack. He started to lash out, hands grasping like claws at his brothers nearby. To Farren's horror, his eyes started to glow white.

Thrunn struck him hard in the side of the head with the butt of his bolt rifle, and Vesleigh went down.

'Cogs above,' said Farren. 'That is psyker-mark, without a doubt.' He opened a secondary vox channel. 'Orenst, follow us up when you're able to and secure Vesleigh if you can. We must find whatever phenomenon it is that is causing this, and pull it out by the root.'

He turned to his brothers. 'We move, now, on me.'

Running onwards up the stairs with his brothers in tow, Farren made his way up towards a wide hardwood scaffold. He panned the barrel of his bolt rifle around as he reached the archway entrance, its bulk pulled tight against his shoulder. As he emerged, his eyes widened in disbelief. Before him was a scene from the Imperium's darkest nightmare.

From the corner of his eye, Farren caught a glimpse of a t'au stealther emerging from the shadows. Before he could react, the xenos' shot struck him in the head. Farren's world exploded.

CHAPTER ELEVEN
GRIM REVELATIONS

Fortress Sixth West
Allhallow, Scorpid Cluster

Sergeant Moricani sprinted hard up the stairs, his plasma incinerator's recharge coils lighting the stone corridor's walls a strange undersea blue.

'Time to die in flames, heretics,' he called into the shadows. There were sounds of battle in the distance, coming from the top of the keep, by his reckoning. No doubt Zaeroph and his veteran Dark Angels were up there already, having all the fun.

The Hellblaster sergeant reached a long stretch of tunnel and ran down it, Lenkatz and the rest of his men hard on his heels.

'No signal on this level,' said Darrodan, his forearm auspicator pinging. 'All this firepower, but no one to use it on.'

'So we go onward,' said Moricani. 'And up.' He ran up another flight of stairs, heavy footsteps pounding on the flagstones, and emerged on the top of the battlements. He checked down the line of his gun for signs of life, but saw nothing – the defenders of this section of the castle had been killed, and less than a minute ago by his reckoning.

'Energy weapons,' he said, looking down at a cadaver with a fist-sized hole in its chest. 'Plasma, by the look of it. Perhaps our Ravenwing or Deathwing brothers got here first.'

'Bit small for a plasma gun shot,' said Darrodan.

'I was thinking that too,' said Moricani. 'Pistol, maybe.'

Leaping the corpses of slain mutants, he ran over a hard-wood scaffold to reach the keep beyond. 'Do keep up,' he called back to Lenkatz and the others. They redoubled their pace, gathering around Moricani with their bulky incinerators aimed to cover all possible entrances.

Ahead of them was a large iron door, banded with sacred texts and info-locks. It was Proteus-pattern, by Moricani's estimation, and therefore proof against even a hydraulic battering ram array.

'Right,' said Moricani, holding his gun to his lips for a moment. He took a step back and aimed at the lock.

There was a high whine as Moricani ran his gun's plasma coils to maximum. It was followed by a searing bang, and a flash of painfully bright blue light. A wide hole appeared where the door's info-lock had been a moment before, the choking fumes of vaporised metal filtering through the Primaris Marines' helms to sting at their nostrils.

Moricani kicked hard just below the hole, and the door flew open with a loud clang. The sergeant was the first through, charging up a long spiral staircase that ringed the inside of the cylindrical keep.

High in the interior was an enormous bell, so thick

with dust and guano it had to have been silent for decades. The sounds of explosions and gunshots came from high above, and the giant bell rang dully on the cusp of hearing with the reverberations.

'Those are storm bolter rounds,' said Lenkatz. 'Double detonation. My money's on the Deathwing.'

'Then let's get up there!' Moricani shouldered his plasma incinerator and ran up the stone stairs three at a time, taking care to stick close to the wall as he made his way up the inside of the tower.

The sergeant heard the thunder and crack of battle much clearer as he got closer to the top of the tower, so clear he could make out the weapons being discharged. He could feel a glorious thrill of anticipation coursing through his veins.

Underneath his jests, he had often wondered what it would be like to fight alongside the finest warriors in the First Legion, to actively wage war shoulder to shoulder with the heroes of the Dark Angels. The thought made his blood pump far more than he would ever publicly admit.

Moricani reached the top of the stairs. A stout hardwood trapdoor barred their path. He put his shoulder to it and pushed hard, but the whole structure was reinforced with three-inch straps of iron. With only the smallest fraction of give, it felt as if it had been slab-bolted from the other side.

'A little room, please,' said Moricani. 'I am about to offend Phobossian's machine-spirit for a second time in as many minutes. If I have to have my name etched on the pillars of the Hall of Fire as a result, I would rather yours were not below it.'

Moricani retreated a couple of steps, kneeling and

raising his gun to an almost vertical angle before taking his shot. The trapdoor's right-hand side disintegrated in a shower of molten metal and burning flinders. He stood tall and put his shoulder to it once more, this time pushing it ajar as he brought his gun up with him, and fought his way up and out as best he could.

The sergeant had been trained for years to take in a battle situation, assess the best route to victory, and act decisively in the same moment. Yet the sight that greeted him on top of the vast bell tower was so unexpected it left Moricani all but dumbstruck.

The bone-coloured armour of the Deathwing stood stark against soot-black battlements. Nearby were the forbidding figures of Company Master Gabrael, Epistolary Dothrael and Chaplain Zaeroph standing with legs braced as they took killing shots with their plasma pistols at anything that came within range. Together with the veterans of the First, they were hammering fire into not one, but two breeds of enemy.

Stomping, screaming, running in every direction were misshapen mutants still clad in scraps of the fortress garrison's livery. Some of them were twice the height of a man, nests of tentacles thrashing from their necks and armpits as strange crustacean claws snapped and bulging eyeballs burst with the sheer intensity of the mutative energies wracking their bodies. They fought with no finesse or direction, bellowing like wounded bulls as they stormed through plasma shot and bolter salvo to fall upon those Dark Angels they could reach.

The other breed of foe atop the parapet was sleek, sophisticated and highly advanced, almost clinical in its attack. Moricani recognised the towering shapes of t'au battlesuits – not the near-invisible stealthers they had faced upon Saltire Vex, but gun-limbed giants twice the size of a Space Marine. They laid down pulsing bursts of fire into Deathwing Terminators and fleshy mutants alike.

The ancient, bone-coloured Tactical Dreadnought armour of the First's veterans was living up to its reputation; Moricani could only see two of the Deathwing that had gone down, and even they were firing their storm bolters from their slumped positions.

The same could not be said for the mutant creatures. Every volley of pulse rifle fire that struck one of them seared it to the bone, leaving deep red wounds in its flesh. The scent of sizzling, tainted meat hung in the air so strong that Moricani felt his diaphragm twitch and his gorge rise with the need to gag. He had heard tell of the stench of Chaos, but to feel it in the back of his throat was another matter.

He fought his horror back down, taking a deep breath through his mouth to re-establish his battle focus. A three-legged, slavering hulk with the lower jaw of a crocodile scrambled past, intent on the Deathwing behind. Moricani took a shot at its flank, blasting it away. It landed ten feet away amongst the steam of its own atomised flesh.

Another mutant was quick to replace it, a slender thing scrambling forth on all fours with its back arched high. It gave a thin, keening scream as a trio of Deathwing bolt rounds thudded into it and detonated in a spray of blood and bone. Each left a massive hole right through the creature, but somehow it kept on.

The thing's shrieks seemed to come from everywhere at once, from beyond the battlements as well as atop them. Several more of the mutants joined in the din, voices raised in madness and despair. The sound cut right through Moricani, as if thin needles of sound were piercing his soul. He shot a winged freak with too many fingers as it reared to pounce, blasting it over the battlements.

The ravaged quadruped nearby shook as if in the grip of a palsy, howling. White fire burst from inside it, pouring out from its eyes, its mouth, and the entry and exit wounds in its flank. Moricani ducked as one of the white beams seared overhead to strike a hovering t'au warsuit in the chest. He glanced back; the beam had cored it from front to back.

Incredibly, the xenos machine fought on for a few seconds, discharging more pulse shots into the spasming mutant before boosting backwards to slam into a battlement wall. The warsuit fell amongst toppling crennelations before becoming still.

Where the xenos gunner's beams had put holes in the creature, more white fire gushed out. Some of it struck other mutants, and they too shuddered, the strange effluvium shooting from their mouths and eyes to cascade across the ranks of the Deathwing. Moricani took one down, Zaeroph another, but the chain reaction was already out of control.

One of the veteran Dark Angels was hit in the thigh, and Moricani's breath caught as he saw the beam burning through to the flesh beneath, felling the bone-armoured giant. He had seen Tactical Dreadnought armour turn aside even a lascannon blast, but the psychic ectoplasm had melted it as if it were wax.

What manner of phenomenon was this?

'Sergeant,' came the voice of Nenst Lenkatz from below, 'permission to join the fray?'

'Get out here,' said Moricani, sending a blast of plasma into the nearest mutant before clambering out onto the parapet's flagstones. Lenkatz's head and shoulders emerged from the trapdoor, his heavy incinerator carried up and over as he came. 'But stay low,' said Moricani. 'This is a far cry from the battles we fought on Mars.'

'I can see that,' said Lenkatz, looking in awe at the surreal struggle unfolding around him. He raised his gun, overcharged it with a piercing whine and took a shot at the nearest t'au battlesuit. It hit the xenos machine under the arm, ripping the limb free in a spray of molten alloys and gobbets of alien plastek to expose the pilot inside.

The xenos warsuit crouched for a moment before boosting away into the air. Another giant machine thumped down from the skies to cover his retreat, streams of energy pulsing from its quad-barrelled cannons.

To the north, a squad of Deathwing stood over their fallen comrade, their storm bolters ripping apart the mutants that flailed towards them. Another clutch of the vile things were throwing themselves towards a trio of t'au warsuits to Moricani's left. Those that survived the xenos team's punishing firepower charged physically into the alien suits.

One of the giant machines kicked its assailant square in the chest with its hoof-like foot, sending him tumbling away to crouch low and vomit blood onto the flagstones. At the same time, another warsuit batted a mutant aside with the long-barrelled weapon system attached to its forearm. The mutant creature, its gangling limbs grasping, bounded back up again to grab for the t'au warrior's box-like head. It hung from the warsuit's neck like a jungle felid trying to bring down an ogryn.

Moricani took a shot, the sphere of superheated gas blasting the mutant apart and slamming into the torso of the battlesuit behind with force enough to send it toppling over the battlements in a crackle of energies.

'Good shot,' said Lenkatz.

'Thank you, Nenst.' Moricani stood up to his full height, deftly tripping up a rushing mutant only to stamp its distended head into the stone floor of the parapet a moment later. 'Though this is what you might call a target-rich environment.'

There was a muted bellow as a mutant with a pair of limbs jutting from its distended maw strode confidently towards Moricani, its halberd thrusting towards him. Moricani backhanded the flat of its blade, swatting aside the blow as his incinerator recharged. The mutant was quick, though, and spun the halberd in a full circle before thrusting once more. Moricani dived aside to avoid the risk of being spitted. Dropping his still-charging plasma gun, he drew his bolt pistol from his hip and put a round between the creature's mouth-arms before holstering it again in one smooth motion.

The mutant fell back as its head burst wide open. Then the screams that Moricani had registered on the cusp of hearing suddenly grew loud. They were so piercing they hurt the soul, but he still managed to scrabble up his plasma incinerator and whisper appeasement to its machine-spirit.

A swarm of strange fish-like creatures, much like the giant remora saprays Moricani had spotted in Saltire Vex's oceans, burst up from behind the battlements and soared into the air. They shimmered in the light, their bodies glistening as if covered in multi-hued oil. They were at once dark blue and all the colours of the spectrum.

Daemons. Not the red-skinned fiends Moricani dimly recalled fighting at Terra, thank the Omnissiah, for those creatures of blood and hatred had come on by the thousand. Even with a single glance, he could tell they were not of the natural world. They seemed somehow super-imposed over the reality of their surroundings, and the patterns of their flight emanated a raw otherness that made the sergeant's skin crawl.

One of the creatures suddenly burst apart into gobbets of what looked like quicksilver. A lash of emerald lightning crackled over Moricani's head – the work of Epistolary Dothrael. The rest of the creatures suddenly turned in mid-air, their previous upwards momentum into a steep downwards dive, then a swoop. Where the creatures plunged into the melee, their wings slashed limbs from torsos and heads from necks. With each pass they cut down mutants, t'au warsuits and Space Marines alike.

Moricani tracked one of the things as it rose back up, leading his shot a little before letting fly. The beast veered at the last minute as if it had known the attack was coming, turning its upward flight into a spiral and avoiding a salvo of bolt shells from the Deathwing below.

The sky-shark creatures winging behind it gave a triumphant shriek as they peeled away, swiftly coming back around to whip their mace-like tails at the heads of those Deathwing desperately trying to shoot them out of the sky. One of the Space Marines was bowled over, his helm crushed so badly the head inside must have been caved in. A pair of mutants fell on him to rip and tear at his neck.

More of the fiendish creatures slashed through the skies, screaming as they spun in strange helical patterns that dipped down to mutilate and slice those below. Moricani's plasma incinerator indicated it was at readiness, and he took another shot, this time singeing the tip of the leading daemon's wing. It corrected its flight and flew on with strange grace.

A salvo of t'au energy pellets hurtled up to meet the creatures, the bright little beads appearing in such profusion the leading daemons could not avoid them. They pierced the first two creatures through in a dozen places, their shimmering non-flesh quivering like jellyfish hit by a shotgun blast. A moment later, they discorporated in clouds of droplets. The ichor spattered down as acid rain to hiss and smoulder on the parapet, and the rest of the daemons dispersed through the morass, their piercing shrieks tearing at the mind.

'Audio dampeners to full,' said Moricani, drowning out the sound of that infernal screaming as best he could. He sent his next shot at the intersection where two daemons were likely to cross flight paths. He had read their movements well; one of the beasts took a direct plasma blast. It burst into a cloud of what looked like tiny silver fish spasming as they scattered in all directions.

'Farren,' said Moricani, 'if you can hear me, you're missing out on some weapons-grade strangeness up here.'

The sergeant dimly heard a shout of rage. He half-turned at the last moment to see a monstrous mutant with a bull's head and tentacle-fingered hands slam into him, lifting him off his feet with the impetus of its horned headbutt. Thinking quickly, he thumped it between the eyes with the butt of his recharging incinerator, then reached around for his bolt pistol. The creature's presumption in thinking it could gore him, especially when clad in the Cawl-marked miracle that was Mark X armour, was sorely misplaced.

With a cold shiver of apprehension, Moricani realised it did not intend to gore him after all.

The bull mutant had its tentacle-talons wrapped around him tight, and was about to bowl him over the edge of the precipice-like battlements and down to the rocks two hundred feet below.

There was a rush of hot air from above. One of the t'au warsuits dropped down to stamp on the horned creature's shoulders and neck. The creature crumpled into the flagstones, knocked cold.

Moricani fell backwards, catching a crennelation in the small of his back as he rebounded from the castle wall. He rolled away from the shimmering jet turbines of the xenos warsuit suddenly in front of him as the t'au warrior poured a stream of glowing energy beads into the fallen mutant.

Flat on his back, Moricani saw one of the sky-sharks diving down fast, its wings extended to slash at the t'au warsuit from above. He pulled his incinerator in close and fired vertically upwards, the plasma bolt vaporising the thing in a cloud of multicoloured mist.

'I owe you nothing,' he told the warsuit's back. It moved away without a word, driving back a pair of mutants with a focused inferno from its cylindrical flamer weapon.

At some unheard command, those t'au warsuits still aloft turned their guns on the daemons swooping overhead. Flickering streams of plasma fire and energy beads shot diagonally upwards to intercept the flying, swooping sky-sharks.

As Moricani got to his feet, he saw the earthbound t'au were focusing their fire on the mutants, sending columns of flame and heat-seeking missiles to incinerate and blast apart those fleshy creatures that still fought back. Together with the Dark Angels and Primaris Marines, they were regaining control of the fight.

To the west, Company Master Gabrael vaulted up onto a rampart, and from there onto the control revetment of an emplaced Icarus quad-gun atop the parapet. He swung it round with practised ease, hammering autocannon fire up at the swooping daemons in long streams of solid shot that glowed in the darkening sky. Three came apart in the space of as many seconds. The Deathwing added their own firepower, and the skies were soon clear.

As one the t'au began to pull back, firing their jetpacks to jump over the battlements and drift away. Many were still pouring firepower into the daemons and mutants alike as they neared the canopy of the trees.

Moricani and Lenkatz shared a glance, then both took aim at the nearest t'au warsuit. Their double volley caught the xenos warrior full in the chest, dropping him like a stone.

'Primaris contingent!' came the voice of Chaplain Zaeroph. 'Leave the t'au to flee. They are no longer a priority.'

'They are xenos, sergeant,' came Lenkatz's voice over the Primaris brethren's closed comms line. 'They must be annihilated. This rebellion is their work.'

'Obey your orders,' said Moricani, turning to Darrodan as he pushed up from the trapdoor to join the fight. 'Confine your fire to the rebels.'

With the t'au moving out of the fight, Moricani and the Deathwing brought their firepower to bear on the remaining mutants and daemons with terrible effectiveness. Now the Space Marines had the room to pick their targets at will, storm bolter shots shredded hideous grotesques and sailing sky-sharks left and right with methodical, contemptuous efficiency.

Moricani moved to fight alongside the closest Death-wing Terminator, kicking a half-dead mutant in the throat as he shot another in the back. Nearby the Librarian, Dothrael, made short work of those daemons that came too close with his crackling force sword, each carving blow cutting a swooping sky-shark apart. Those that kept out of reach he blasted apart with crackling arcs of bio-electricity that erupted from his eyes to whip left and right.

'Dothrael,' shouted Moricani as a knot of mutants, previously playing dead amongst the corpses, surged up to lunge for the Librarian's back.

Suddenly, Company Master Gabrael was at his fellow officer's shoulder. He cut down the mutants as if he was born to it, impaling and bisecting and lunging again and again with the ease of a Chapter champion in a practice cage. Each blow sent welters of blood sizzling to thicken the scent of cooked meat that hung in the air. Chaplain Zaeroph waded through the corpses to join him, simply bludgeoning those mutants that came within arm's reach. Each swing of his crozius arcanum snapped a spine or caved in a skull in a flare of actinic blue light. In a matter of moments, the fight was over.

'Moricani,' came a familiar voice from the sergeant's left. It was Darrodan, at the trapdoor with Lenkatz. 'What's happening?'

'Go back down below,' said Moricani, motioning to Darrodan as he made to approach. 'You too, Lenkatz. Something is going on here. I'll debrief you once I've gained a clearer picture.'

'If you are sure,' said Lenkatz.

'I am extremely sure,' said Moricani seriously. 'Given present company, Primaris troopers will not be welcome. Neither will our officers, come to that, but someone has to fill in for Farren.'

'Acknowledged,' said Lenkatz, following Darrodan as he climbed back through the trapdoor and onto the spiral staircase beneath it. Moricani heard Darrodan's voice as they went below.

'No jokes? It must be bad.'

Farren felt like his head was going to split in two. His helm was cratered so badly he could feel the wound pulsing in his scalp. He had rolled as fast and as far away from the source of the shot as he could, bolt rifle pulled in tight, and shook his head to clear it, but it had almost made him pass out instead.

Already he could feel his system pumping invigorating chemicals into his body to compensate. His Belisarian furnace had not triggered, thankfully, but he still felt like the inside of his cranium was on fire. He pushed to his feet, unsteady for a moment before steeling himself.

Muscle memory took over as he slid into a loose gunner's crouch. He submerged the splitting pain in the calm waters of the back of his mind, years of battle trance meditations pulling his focus together despite the ringing disorientation of the ambushing t'au's headshot.

Around him his squad had formed a tight perimeter, fighting against some unknown enemy. Their tight volleys were sent in staccato profusion, and the pain in Farren's skull flared a little with every bolt loosed from their rifles. Without his helm, the syncopated, percussive din of war would have been almost deafening. But the pain was ebbing, and his focus was coming back.

Around him was a scene of utter carnage. The wide, hardwood platform they had burst out onto reverberated beneath him, shaking under the armoured feet of a strike force of Angels of Redemption.

Dozens of their fellow Space Marines fought back to back, side to side, bolters hammering at the ghost-like forms that Farren dimly recognised as t'au stealthers.

He raised his bolt rifle and took a shot of his own at a chameleonic blur, missing his target by a hand's breadth.

'Cog damn it,' said Farren under his breath. 'Waste of a bolt.' Ducking, he forced his frustration down and took stock once more.

The platform was slick with blood, the gory remains of the keep's garrison spread liberally from one side of the scaffold to the other. Here and there the power-armoured forms of slain Angels of Redemption were strewn amongst the carnage, laid low by sustained plasma volleys or cored through by the same intense psychic discharge that had claimed Vesleigh. Some of them had eyes that were glowing white, a ghostly corposant playing around their sockets.

Farren shook his head and stood once more, hands automatically checking his bolt rifle. His helm recalibrated, presenting firing solutions on the nearest enemies.

Still plenty of xenos left for him to kill. A slowly rising lust for revenge swelled in his chest, demanding to be quenched in blood. He took a bead.

Then, in the space of less than a second, the t'au stealthers under his crosshairs disappeared from his helm display. Farren cast around, seeing strange ripples in the air for a moment. Then the xenos were gone completely.

'What in the Omnissiah's name,' said Enrod, the barrel of his gun panning left and right. Thrunn, too, had stopped.

'Where did they go?' he said, looking around in puzzlement.

Parvell was still firing. 'They're right there, lackwit!' he shouted. A pulse shot came from the shadows and hit him in the midriff. He cried out as the impact sent him clattering back into Farren. Parvell's bald head bounced off Farren's pauldron, hard enough to elicit a stagger, but Farren caught him and pushed him back into the fight. The t'au shot had been stopped by the layered ceramite of his Mark X armour, and he would shake off his disorientation fast. Farren loosed a double shot straight past Parvell in the direction he had last seen the stealthers.

'They're right there!' screamed Parvell, shooting his bolt rifle into the corner of the keep. 'Why aren't you firing?'

'Xenotech has attacked our machine-spirits,' shouted Farren.

A volley of pulse rifle fire came in from a nearby battlement, lancing in to strike Thrunn hard in the shoulder and burn his Chapter iconography down to the bare ceramite. He went down to one knee before getting back to his feet.

'Get in cover,' said Farren. 'We need to rethink this.'

His squad ducked back into the lee of a stone buttress, shoulder to shoulder as they reloaded and checked their rifles. Enrod primed a pair of frag grenades, hurling them out to cover their retreat. Thrunn slung his weapon and made to take off his helm.

'No,' said Farren, putting his hand on the younger warrior's arm as the grenades went off with a double explosion. 'I won't risk you taking a head shot.' He unclamped his own helmet with a hiss and mag-clamped it to his belt. 'Let Parvell and I tackle this.'

'That's ironic,' said Parvell. 'Considering your orders during the Glitchwar at the Noctis Labyrinthus.'

'That was during our training wars, Parvell,' said Farren. 'Against most xenos forces you expose yourself to needless danger.'

'But back on Mars you insisted all of us wear our helms, and in doing so you took us effectively out of the fight. Five of our brothers died.'

'This is not the time to bring up old ghosts,' said Farren tersely. 'In my experience nothing short of a headshot will convince you to value a piece of equipment designed to keep your brains inside your thick skulls. At least cover me, and cover your profile with a pauldron where you can.'

'Aye,' said Parvell, 'that's what I've been doing for the last sixteen months.'

A burst of plasma shot in, smacking off Farren's gorget and scalding his jawline. 'Gah!' he said, turning his shoulder and leaning out to return fire. He could see something shimmering out there now, standing in the lee of a stone tower. He put a bolt right in its centre and leaned back again, narrowing his eyes in satisfaction as he heard the muffled boom and patter of an armour piercing round doing its job in spectacularly gory fashion.

A dull murmur behind Farren grew to a shouting crescendo. The lieutenant spun on his heel, grabbing a frag grenade from his belt and priming it in one smooth motion. Sprinting towards them up the stairs from the courtyard was a motley throng of twisted, hideous mutants, still clad in the ragged scraps of the garrison's chainmail. Many were armed with a sword and shield in the ancient feudal fashion. Farren made out snatches of slurred war cries amongst the gibberish shouted by the rest.

'Destroy the traitors! Rush them!'

'Cast them back into the darkness!'

Farren's lips pulled back into a snarl as he lobbed the frag grenade. It bounced with a pair of solid thumps, its passage timed to perfection so that it reached the clutch of mutants just as it was about to detonate.

The foremost mutant, a bulging sack of meat and ragged chainmail, threw himself atop the grenade with a plaintive cry that was far too high-pitched for such a massively built frame. He flew apart a moment later as the fragmentation device detonated with a wet thump, its killing force choked by the rebel's sacrifice.

The creature's fellow mutants, coated with their comrade's remains, scrambled onwards. As they passed through the shadow of a circular tower Farren noticed there was something different about them – a light that set their eyes and mouths aglow in the gloom. Three white witch-fires glimmered in each fleshy head. Whatever was causing the garrison's mutation and orchestrating the rebellion was likely down there, in the dark of the keep's dungeons.

Farren raised his bolt rifle once more and set it to full yield, planning to shoot his way through the wall of trans-muted freaks to the truths that lay beyond. He had a lingering feeling of uncertainty in his gut.

He was beginning to think it was not flesh and blood they fought this day, but something far deadlier.

Moricani closed the trapdoor behind his men, and turned back to the Dark Angels atop the parapet. Chaplain

Zaeroph, Dothrael and Gabrael were standing in the middle of the circular tower, talking amongst themselves. Four hulking Deathwing Terminators stood in a rough semi-circle behind their officers. Two of their fellows were on one knee, having sustained serious wounds during the fight, but the barrels of their guns did not waver as they panned slowly across the canopy beyond the battlements. Moricani made out their words as he moved closer.

'What word from the Ravenwing, Interrogator-Chaplain?' said the Deathwing sergeant, a giant with a thunder hammer and two stylised wing-pennants curving from his shoulders.

'The quarry is contained,' said Zaeroph tersely. 'We still have the best vantage point up here. For now, we remain alert.'

The Deathwing sergeant saluted. He and his squad were surrounded by the strewn remains of dozens of mutant corpses, the scene reminiscent of some demented abattoir. The air smelled strongly of burning flesh, scorched bone, gaseous plasma residue and vaporised plasteks. Liquid ectoplasm still drooled from several of the mutant cadavers, glowing as it pooled beneath their shattered bodies.

The fifth Deathwing Terminator, his leg half-severed from his body by the beam of white psychic discharge, was shuddering as if in terrible pain. His eyes were glowing slightly – not the red of a battle helm in low light, but the same white as the unnatural effluvium.

Moricani was on the brink of saying something when one of the Deathwing stooped and, coils of energy wreathing his power fist, wrenched opened a fallen t'au warsuit that had been breached by the same psyker-stuff. He yanked away the multiple layers of the suit's outer armour with a series of loud metallic screeches, dismantling the warsuit's chest section to reveal the pilot inside.

The alien being within was comatose, but still breathing. He looked frail and malnourished, especially next to the Space Marine examining him. Moricani nodded to himself. No wonder the xenos race put so much stock in the technology of war, compensating for their physical weakness with the most impressive battleplate they could devise. But what were they without their suits? And what manner of soul could thrive inside such a paltry physical shell?

The thought of a xenos spirit did not sit well with Moricani, and neither did the idea of them carrying some manner of psychic curse. He saw traces of the strange ectoplasm that had blasted open the suit in the heat of battle, spattered across the inside of its control hub. He had half expected the t'au pilot to have glowing eyes like the Deathwing veteran, but to his surprise, the pilot seemed to be unaffected by whatever ague had claimed the Space Marine.

'Well?' said Dothrael.

'It's inert,' said the Terminator. 'As you surmised.' He reached in with his power fist, its fingers closing around the xenos' head. With a hum of servomotors, it closed until the t'au pilot's skull cracked, then collapsed in a revolting morass of bone and red flesh.

'They would likely be ideal,' said Dothrael.

'Ideal for what?' muttered Moricani to himself. As the Terminator finished his lethal examination and stood up to rejoin his fellows, Moricani noticed Gabrael move to stand over the injured Deathwing warrior. The company master seemed small in comparison to the fallen giant, especially without his trademark cape. He drew a power sword, an ornate broadblade with a black sheen.

'In the name of the Lion,' said Gabrael, 'I bring you deliverance.'

'Wait,' said the wounded Terminator, going rigid in an attempt to keep the spasms wracking his body under control. 'I can assist with–'

Gabrael's broadblade came down in an arc of hyper-disruptive energies. The powered edge, designed to cut through even layered ceramite, neatly took the warrior's head from his neck in a brief crackle of energy and a puff of atomised flesh.

'May he be cleansed in death,' said Gabrael, burning off the residue of the kill before sheathing his sword once more.

Unnerved, the Hellblaster sergeant made his way over to the officers beyond. 'An execution? Had he been tainted?'

'Yes,' replied Zaeroph.

Moricani thought of Farren's psy-wound, then, and felt his mind recoil from the implications. He approached the Dark Angels to find out more, expecting to feel the full force of their disapproval. Instead, he saw them all raise their eyes to look at something above and behind him.

Dothrael and Gabrael put their hands to their weapons, even as the Deathwing raised their storm bolters and assault cannons to a firing stance. Moricani turned, his plasma incinerator humming in readiness, to see what they were looking at. Zaeroph waved their weapons down, putting them on guard.

'Not yet. Just keep watch, inside and out.'

Descending from the skies was a xenos warsuit so large and statuesque it made even the hulking Deathwing look like children by comparison. It had an honour guard of its own – eight of the contoured stealther warsuits that Moricani and Farren had faced on Ferro-Giant Omicroid.

Amidst a dull thrum of xenos jetpacks they alit upon the battlements behind the white warsuit, taking position in a loose group around it. Their multi-barrelled gun-limbs were studiously pointed at the flagstones, a gesture of parley that even a peasant could understand.

Where the Dark Angels were spattered with blood, stained with soot and wreathed in the smoke of spent bolter shells, the giant xenos suit before them was spotlessly white. Its helmet had cleanly delineated red markings, and its primary, quad-barrelled weapon system hummed in an almost pleasing chord of energy discharge.

'We have a common enemy,' said the warsuit in perfect Low Gothic. Moricani recalled from his learnings after Saltire Vex that the t'au had excellent facility with language, and even had a whole caste of their society dedicated to such matters. 'Let us not waste our resources in destroying each other,' it continued, 'thereby allowing the infection to spread further.'

'They would be resources well spent,' said Company Master Gabrael, placing his hand on the hilt of his sword. 'Your destruction is only a matter of time. But we've already lost three men to this curse. Whatever is causing this white fire to spread, it is rapacious.'

'Not for us. Nonetheless, we do not know its nature. We are concerned as to that which it represents,' said the warsuit. 'It must be addressed.'

'Why are we treating with this xenos scum, master?' asked one of the Deathwing. 'And why is this one privy to it?' He motioned dismissively towards Moricani. The sergeant smiled without mirth by way of reply.

Zaeroph and Gabrael both ignored the Terminator veteran, instead giving their attention to the giant white battlesuit. 'When your kind are struck by this psy-product, you are unaffected. Just as was the case upon Saltire Vex. Why is that?'

'It is Humanity's disease, not ours,' said the warsuit. 'Are you not more concerned about eradicating the cause of this plague, rather than examining its effects upon more civilised races?'

'Knowledge is there to be seized,' said Gabrael.

'How interesting I find your choice of words,' said the xenos warsuit.

'The curse must be expunged,' growled Zaeroph, 'and the vector that carries it obliterated. Do not stand in our way.'

'I concur. However, for the vector to have taken such a toll on this site's inhabitants, it must have lingered here for some time. The entire planet may be compromised.'

Zaeroph looked at Gabrael. Moricani could tell an exchange passed between them without either of them saying a word.

'I fear he is right,' said Dothrael quietly. 'But as we discussed, we cannot level the blade against our own flesh and blood. Let alone bring it down.'

'We face a similar dilemma,' said the xenos. 'The ocean world is still compromised. Yet it is our allies that bear the infection, and we cannot openly fire upon them. The dictates of honour trouble our warrior caste as well as yours.'

'You have no conception of how honour works,' growled Gabrael, 'nor how insignificant you xenos are in the face of the Imperium's might. What do you know of our travails, insect?'

'We know that your race corrupts everything it touches, and perverts everything that seeks to realign it for the good of all. That has been made abundantly clear, both here and on the ocean world of Saltire Vex.'

'A world you claim to have saved. Yet you systematically attacked those people you once sought so hard to bring into your empire.'

'Those tainted by the mind-science plague must be burned from the T'au'va like a canker. Must we bear the burden of that truth alone when it is your kin who spreads it?'

A pregnant silence hung in the air. Moricani found his thoughts turning to Farren's psy-wound. The lieutenant had seemed unaffected by the psychic element of whatever had struck him – perhaps he had some natural resistance to it, or perhaps he had just been lucky.

'This is not over,' said Zaeroph. 'We have much to discuss, and will speak again, at the largest derelict in low orbit, once the immediate matter is resolved. For now, you will leave the demise of this site to us, and us alone.'

'If that is the only way we can work together against the greater threat,' said the warsuit. 'But this infection of the mind must be eradicated. Quarantined.'

'It will be scoured from the face of the galaxy,' growled Chaplain Zaeroph, the eyes in his skull-masked helmet glowing like red embers. 'That I assure you.' The skull-faced officer cast a glance sideways; for a moment, Moricani caught his visage full on before the Chaplain turned back to the xenos. 'And we will find you, when this is over,' he continued, levelling his crozius arcanum at the giant warsuit. 'We will find you, and we will extract the knowledge of how to defeat your entire race from your worthless minds. By the Lion, I promise you that.'

'Surely you have more pressing business than making unrealistic threats to potential allies,' said the xenos leader. 'Finding the traitor in your ranks seems a logical first priority.'

The Dark Angels did not reply, but Moricani felt their loathing for the xenos nonetheless.

'We will establish a perimeter one Imperial mile from this locale,' said the t'au leader, 'and eliminate any of the genetically aberrant creatures that cross it. The infection will be contained, for the greater good of all.'

Gabrael turned to Zaeroph, a moment of silent accord passing between them.

'We have not seen him make his move yet, even from here,' said Zaeroph quietly. 'He is likely still in the depths of the complex, burrowed as deep as a tick, much like on Saltire Vex. He sends his flock against us whilst he knows we are distracted. We must join the Ravenwing and bring this matter to a close.'

The company master nodded and turned away from the xenos as he made for the edge of the keep's battlements, the Deathwing close behind.

'You will leave unhindered,' said the Chaplain. 'Our interests align, for now. We will ensure the tainted ones are annihilated. We have business on the lower levels.'

The white t'au warsuit crossed its weapons in front of its torso in what Moricani thought was uncannily like a Primaris salute. It boosted away as smoothly as it had descended, the air shimmering behind its jetpack as it disappeared behind the battlements with its stealther escort in tow.

For a moment, Moricani felt Zaeroph's gaze upon him once more. It was an intense sensation, the glowering orbs of the Chaplain's skull-like faceplate etching themselves into the sergeant's mind.

'Epistolary Dothrael,' said the Chaplain. 'Accompany the Primaris sergeant here to his men. Link up with Lieutenant Farren, and from there descend into the lower levels. Aid them in finding and capturing the leader of this rebellion, no matter his nature or station.'

'Aye, Chaplain. It will be done.'

'Ensure any and all radical elements are dealt with accordingly,' continued the Chaplain. 'Then meet with Apothecary Vaarad and employ whatever assets you need to in order to bring the matter to a close.'

'Acknowledged, Chaplain,' said Dothrael, striding past Moricani with the heel of his ornate psyker-staff tapping on the flagstones.

Moricani turned and walked after him, wrong-footed by the events he was witnessing, but eager to rejoin his brothers. There were still sounds of battle from the courtyard.

'Inbound, Farren,' said Moricani over the Primaris level vox. 'We're to cleanse the lower levels.'

'We're already on our way down there,' came Farren's reply, tinny and crackling.

As Moricani neared the trapdoor Dothrael slowed. 'On reflection, you should first rejoin your squad, sergeant,' said Dothrael, gesturing for him to go through first. 'It is not ideal for us to assume leadership of a Primaris contingent. Doubtless you have your own protocols and war-cants that your brothers will respond to.'

Moricani raised his eyebrows in puzzlement as he slung his plasma incinerator and made to push himself back through the narrow aperture. 'My thanks,' he replied quietly. 'It will be an honour to fight alongside you, even at arm's length.'

As he turned to the trapdoor and began to pass back through to the stairs beneath, Dothrael placed a hand gently upon his plasma incinerator and muttered something under his breath.

'Epistolary?' said Moricani, half-turning.

'A blessing upon your wargear,' said the Librarian, inclining his head. 'I feel we will have need of it.'

CHAPTER TWELVE
THAT WHICH LIES BELOW

Fortress Sixth West
Allhallow, Space Marine Chapter Planet

Farren bludgeoned a charging mutant with a sidelong swipe of his bolt rifle. He dashed its brains upon the wall of the narrow tunnel before kicking it hard in the spine. This one had been covered in matted hair so thick it gave him the appearance of some primitive from mankind's distant past. It made Farren feel unclean just to look at it.

The lieutenant found a moment for a silent prayer to the Omnissiah. After fighting what seemed a dozen of the things on the stairs that led to the sub-levels – and in several cases, barely overcoming his assailants – he was glad of the reprieve.

'Spread out,' he said, motioning his squad to advance down the stone-walled stairs. 'Shoot first, worry about collateral damage second. I won't have another Vesleigh on my conscience.'

On reflex, he looked for the squad runes of Thrunn and Enrod in his peripheral vision, then realised that he and Parvell were still helmless. He was keeping it off for good reason, even down here in the gloom of the keep's dungeons; the t'au stealthers had caught him off guard once already. Parvell had a point, although he was loath to admit it. That said, the xenos had not attacked for some time, perhaps driven off by the throngs of mutants that burst out of every corridor and shadowed stairway.

'What are we looking for down here, lieutenant?' said Enrod.

'Enemies,' said Thrunn, helpfully. He kicked open a wrought iron gate, the metal screeching before ringing off the wall of the cell beyond with a deafening clang.

Farren shook his head and replaced his helm, reasoning that a sniper in the dark could see him silhouetted easily enough now Thrunn had revealed where to look. The big warrior had never really valued the concept of stealth.

'These rebels,' said Farren over the vox, peering around a column before stepping out to the next. 'These mutants. They are a grotesque distraction. Nothing more.'

'Lieutenant?' asked Thrunn. 'How so?'

'I do not know, to be honest. But the true quarry, that which I believe the Dark Angels are seeking, will be harder to find.'

'The xenos commander?'

'No,' said Farren. 'I don't think it's the xenos that the First are after, despite the conflict thus far. It will be the source of these mutations, and they are not of alien provenance.'

'So why are the t'au here?'

'Mercenaries,' stated Thrunn flatly.

Farren nodded. 'I think that might very well be the case.

That, or they are under the spell of whatever haunts this place.'

'Some kind of empyric curse,' said Enrod. 'Has to be.'

'Those who are struck by that white psy-discharge, they are infected by it themselves,' said Farren as he peered around a pillar. 'Then they either die, prove strong enough to ride it out or turn into those mutant things.'

'So Vesleigh's got that to look forward to,' said Enrod. 'If he survives.'

'Stop, Enrod,' said Thrunn.

'It was the lieutenant's call to leave him,' said Parvell. 'So we support him on it. Orenst's likely with him now.'

By way of answer, Farren ran his thumb along the illuminator rune of his bolt rifle as the gloom closed in around them. A thin but powerful beam of light speared out into the darkness. His squadmates did the same, and the stairwell was lit in stark white light as they reached the bottom. A corridor wide enough to fit a Repulsor down stretched away, dingy cells lining its walls on either side.

Farren could hear something in the middle distance; something like human speech. A verse and response, or some manner of chanting, perhaps. But only one of the voices sounded human.

Though the squalid, moisture-slicked cells on either side of him were empty – Thrunn, Enrod and Parvell had systematically checked them as they progressed – Farren was sure he could hear whispers in the darkest corners, maybe even the suggestion of cloth rubbing against flesh. It had unsettled him. He fought to keep his eyes straight down the tunnel, knowing that true danger would come from there if anywhere.

A new light source glowed at the far end of the corridor.

Farren squinted, making out the flickering of some strangely-hued fire in the distance. It sent green light down to meet them, giving a strange bio-luminescent glow to the heavy stone walls.

Some manner of vehicle rumbled far overhead, sending thin streams of dust trickling down from the ceiling. By Farren's estimate they were underneath the courtyard now, perhaps even beyond the curtain wall as the First engaged the rebels above. Moricani and his team were up on the parapet, according to Enrod's last scan, but with hundreds of tons of rock and stone between them the chance of clarion-level vox contact was slim to none.

The light coming from the far end of the cell-lined corridor was slowly getting brighter. Farren moved as quietly as he could to the edge of the corridor, gesturing for his brothers to do the same on the opposite side, but did not compromise his gun stance. He and his fellows were so bulky that to try to hide their approach altogether would be an exercise in futility.

There was something moving up at the end of the corridor, something gangle-limbed and inhuman. More than one figure, now, silhouetted against the light. They had such strange anatomies it was difficult to see just how many there were.

The things peeled away from the strange green flames beyond them, thin cackling laughs echoing down the corridor. Farren switched to infrared for a moment, and saw that the walls of black rock were crisping over with strange hoarfrost, fingers of cold spreading in fractal patterns towards the Primaris Marines.

'Now?' hissed Enrod.

'Now,' said Farren. He came out into the passageway

and strode forward, making himself an obvious target to bring out anything waiting in ambush.

He did not have to wait long.

One of the inhuman creatures emerged into the light of his torch, its impossibly long arms flailing. It had ten fingers on each of its hands, each finger a ribbed tube that trailed flame like a candle held aloft. Stranger still, its head was entirely missing. Instead a grinning, cackling mask of insanity spanned its chest, a mouth with a thousand teeth leering wide.

Farren felt his gut writhe at the sight.

He took his shot. The creature danced out of the way with surprising speed, but the lieutenant read its evasive manoeuvre, and sent another bolt in to greet it. It struck the creature right between its glimmering eyes, disappearing like a stone in water before detonating with a wet thump.

Split in half, the thing cried out in hooting dismay. Its flesh, pink and taut like that of a recent burns victim, peeled away, discolouring to a deep blue as it died.

Then something happened that stretched Farren's sanity to the limit. The two halves of the daemon creature swelled, unfolded, and stood up to reveal themselves as smaller versions of the first. They grumbled and muttered to one another as they loped forward, many-jointed fingers making strange arcane shapes that crackled with multicoloured sparks.

Another pink-skinned creature came capering from the end of the tunnel, a manic laugh spilling from the maw in its chest. This one was clad in gold-chased rubies; glimmering in the light of Thrunn's spear-torch, they looked like droplets of blood frozen in time. Thrunn put two bolts into it, one in each eye socket. That creature was ripped in half by the resultant detonation, and Farren felt a brief flicker of satisfaction at the sight.

'You do not belong,' said Thrunn. 'You should not exist at all.'

Farren's feeling of confidence ebbed away in a heartbeat as he saw three more of the gangling things, lurking behind the remains of the two they had just shot. Worst still, the corpse of the beast Thrunn had just put down was bubbling, seething, splitting apart. Bluish limbs pushed up from the pink-grey residue, thin to the point of disturbing emaciation.

Now there were four of the beasts coming for them; smaller, but just as horrible to behold.

'Where is a flamer when you need one,' said Enrod.

Farren grimaced and slid the rune node on the side of his bolt rifle to staggered burst. He opened fire on the strange blue creatures, his bolts finding their targets to send all four bowling backwards before detonating in puffs of flame. These too split, bifurcating into tiny flickering fire-monsters that danced and shrieked in indignation.

'I am not sure a flamer would do us much good,' said Parvell, priming a grenade.

Farren was about to shoot again when he saw a sheet of fire whoosh towards him. He turned his shoulder into it, covering his face, and felt a horrible wave of heat wash over his flank.

Though the flames were stopped by his power armour, his flesh suddenly felt sweaty, prickly and as itchy as if it had been washed in dilute acid. His cheek burned especially fiercely, feeling almost like it was riddled with shards of glass.

He took a shot down the corridor over his pauldron, the bolt smacking into the cackling daemon-thing at the end with a wet slap before detonating. Two smaller creatures spilled out of an explosion of warp-matter. Enrod put two bolts into their torsos, one after another, only for them to split into yet more of the tiny fire-creatures. Shortly after, Parvell's grenade went off, and the dancing fire-fiends were gone.

The smell of burning bodies filled Farren's nostrils for a moment, reminding him of the hit he had suffered. He looked down at his pauldron where the empyric flame had struck him.

The left flank of his armour had been transmuted to knobbled, porous bone. A single eye stared up at him, lidless and mad, before bursting like a soap bubble in a puff of atomised blood.

Another sheet of flame shot past, but instead of the roar of a conflagration it was accompanied by the tinkling of wind-chimes. Enrod stepped behind a vault pillar, narrowly avoiding being hit as the flame washed around it.

'Do not let the fires touch you!' said Farren. 'They are daemonic.'

'Daemons we faced on Terra,' replied Enrod. 'They are red of skin, and attack in a great onrushing horde. These are some vile species of xenos.'

'We have no time to argue this,' said Farren, opening fire with his bolt rifle once more. 'Just because we don't know about something, doesn't mean it's not true.'

There were more figures at the end of the corridor now, tall and thick-bodied. They had curving spines and gangling arms that stuck out like those of a scarecrow. The liquid fires that drizzled from the maw-like openings in their fists flared bright as they lurched forward amongst the tiny flame-creatures, the cumulative effect so bright that Farren had to avert his gaze.

More sheets of flame illuminated the corridor, this time setting light to the vault's pillars and walls. The prickly, itchy heat that came off them was unsettling in the extreme, but it was not that which was making his hearts thunder in his chest.

The sight of the strange eyeball staring up at him from his pauldron would not leave him. These daemons were a new breed, and more terrifying, in their own way, than the gore-dripping hordes they had faced in defence of Holy Terra. There was a strange intelligence mingled with the malevolence in their glittering black eyes.

Farren heard inhuman laughter from one of the cells behind him, then a whoosh of flame that crossed the corridor leading to the stairs. His breath caught in his chest as he realised that they were being penned in.

'Trapped,' said Thrunn.

A growl of irritation came from the vaulted chamber at the far end of the corridor, sounding like it came from a human throat – or that of an Adeptus Astartes.

'You are not of the First,' it said. The acoustics of the vault and the crackling of the flames licking around the walls only added to its forbidding timbre. It was a voice of dust, and bone, and hatred.

'We are,' said Thrudd. 'Now.'

'You are not,' came the reply. 'Neither are you amongst those who consider themselves absolved.'

'Come out, and we can discuss it properly,' said Farren. 'We can escape these flames together.'

'They will not burn me,' laughed the voice.

'This is your work, this empyric infestation?' said Farren. He could see a rune winking on his lens display. 'You consort with daemons.'

'With neophytes, there is little to discuss. You are guilty only by association.'

'The same cannot be said for you,' said Farren, checking his bolt rifle's ammo clip and striding forward as Thrunn and Enrod stepped out to flank him. There was a tall, black silhouette at the back of the far vault, a necklace of skulls visible as pale orbs in the gloom. Farren had heard whispers of rogue Space Marines, renegades that sought to tear down everything mankind had achieved; Cawl himself had spoken of them once, naming them the worst kind of traitors. By the look of the figure at the corridor's end, and the beasts of warpflame he conjured to his side, this one had fallen from the Emperor's grace a long time ago.

Farren took the shot, bolt rifle bucking in his hands.

The bullet exploded ten feet from the silhouetted figure, its explosion contained in a sphere of force that shrunk rapidly to nothing.

'And yet it is you that will burn for it,' came the reply.

Half a dozen multicoloured forms emerged from the archways, each a gangling, stooping creature that was shimmering and strange. They let fly twin torrents of flame from their claw-like hands. Farren dived headlong into one of the side cells, desperate to evade another horrible transmutation, then felt a pulse of shock as he realised he had given himself nowhere to escape to.

'Perhaps it is fitting you should die screaming in a cell,' said the traitor angel, 'like so many of my dearest kin. Your new brothers are unforgiven by more than just the Imperium, you know.'

Farren saw another jet of flame shoot past the entrance of his refuge, and heard a shrill scream of laughter as two of the gangle-limbed daemon creatures stepped into the cell opposite. Their fingers were alight with pink flame, and their eyes burned white.

The cell around Farren was becoming hotter, stifling air filtering through his rebreather even with his Mark X armour working hard to cool it. It was beginning to scald his lungs; he could feel it with each breath. Recalling lessons from the Omnissian monks about the temperature at which human flesh began to melt, he glanced at his helm's internal thermometer. The two values were becoming uncomfortably close.

There were faces in the flames – faces that seemed to be mocking him, almost daring him to run through them. The lieutenant screwed his eyes shut for a moment, then opened them, only to see the same thing even clearer. Despite himself, he looked down at the porous bone that had replaced the ceramite of his shoulder pad, and thought of the image of that singular eye staring back at him.

In the act of fighting on, would he turn into some grotesque mutant? Were he and his squadmates already doomed? He could not order them to run through that fire. Not when he knew what it could do.

Something akin to paralysis seized hold of Farren's spine, and would not loosen its grip.

'Lieutenant!' shouted Parvell from across the hall. 'What are your orders?'

Farren could barely see him, trapped behind a wall of flame in a cell opposite him where he had taken cover from the previous salvo. Against all reason, the sheets of flame between them were not dissipating, but forming ever thicker barriers that rippled with etheric power.

'Lieutenant!'

Farren felt something dark and horrible close over his mind. Doubt, perhaps, crippling and stifling. It was robbing his surety, his ability to think straight. Was it weakness that this fiery phenomenon had caused? Had it merely highlighted something frail and worthless in Farren's soul?

Was that all there was, behind his swollen physique and precious armour? Just a scared child, naive and powerless in the face of an uncaring universe?

Farren felt he was drowning in a tide of merciless time that would suffocate him. It would crush him and render him no more important than a speck of dust flickering to nothingness in the heat of a thousand dying suns. There would be no escape, not in this life. Only pain, infinitely slow-burning and intense enough to render him an imbecile.

Agony and suffering, said a voice in his head. The mental image of a burning skull hung before each of his eyes, crossing over, blending, then separating again. *Pain, machine-child, for the rest of your life.*

Farren dropped his gun, his fingers numb with the dark chill of despair.

There was a sudden crash as the ceiling above the corridor caved in. Farren looked up dumbly, stupefied for a moment. He felt a distinct sensation of cold tendrils withdrawing from his brain.

A vast swathe of earth and rock tumbled down to bury and extinguish most of the witch fires that lined the corridor. The noise was almost unbearably loud as an avalanche of burning brickwork cascaded down the corridor.

A vast silhouette flew overhead, something so familiar in shape it triggered a surge of hope and pride in Farren's mind. A Thunderhawk gunship, capable of felling a fortress wall with a punitive salvo from its dorsal cannon.

The rockfall was closely followed by a trio of hulking black shapes plunging through the sudden shafts of light. They landed with a series of heavy thumps in the corridor before revving their engines and careening, riding the cusp of control, down the corridor.

The riders opened fire as they came on, the bolters mounted underneath each angel-wing firing thumping twin shots into the capering daemons at the far end of the passageway. The detonations, mind-wrackingly loud in such close confines, ripped one daemon after another apart. They poured more fire into the daemons that hatched from their remains, and yet more into the strange sentient flames that came from them.

Another black shape shot through the skies revealed by the landslide, its swept-forward wings and blunt, stubby shape unfamiliar to Farren. It twisted mid-flight, strafing the corridor with such vigour that Thrunn had to leap back into the cell from which he was emerging. The twin pathways of the flyer's ammunition stitched down the centre of the corridor to the vault at the end, eliciting a cacophony of thin screams from the flame-spurting creatures.

The squadron of bikes, riding at speed down the corridor, slewed to a halt just outside the vault to make impromptu barriers with the chassis of their bulky metal steeds. The Ravenwing riders cast about themselves, looking for their quarry even as they opened fire point-blank at the daemons. By the way their helms darted left and right, Farren could tell they had not found what they were looking for.

'Xedro!'

Moricani's voice, and close by. Farren leaned out of the cell, wary of the hellish flames bursting back to life at any moment, and saw his friend at the bottom of the stairs that had led them down here. Never before had he been so glad to see that grinning, manic face.

'Moricani,' shouted the lieutenant. 'Guard the exit!'

'It would be my pleasure!' the sergeant shouted back. Farren found his spirits lifting at the sound of his old friend's habitual irreverence, and felt his head begin to clear, just a little.

Something glimmered in Farren's peripheral vision. A blur, dull black and glinting like a living statue made of onyx. Opposite him, it was moving from one cell to another – with his helm's motion tracker at full, Farren could just about make it out amongst the flames. The figure was passing through the walls of the cells, in and out, straight through rock and flame without so much as a twitch of concern as the mutative fires cascaded across it.

'There!' said Farren, rune-marking it on his helm's display and communing the data with the machine-spirit of Moricani's own armour. 'That's the orchestrator. A psyker, he has to be.'

'What on Mars are those creatures at the end?' shouted Moricani.

'They are taken care of,' shouted Farren, 'just make sure nothing escapes!'

'Understood,' said Moricani. The telltale blue-white of charging plasma coils lit the end of the corridor as

Lenkatz, Darrodan and the others came in behind their sergeant. They let fly with a barrage of plasma that seared down the passageway at the darting black figure, but they did not hit their mark, for he was already elsewhere.

Up ahead Farren could see the daemons hurling coruscating clouds of fire at the Ravenwing bikers. The black-armoured riders swerved this way and that to avoid them. Pink fire dulled to blue, thinned to yellow, then dissipated entirely as thunderous volleys of bolter shots filled the vault at the end of the corridor. The din was all but unbearable as the bellows of wounded Space Marines mingled with the high-pitched screams of daemons caught in the Ravenwing's lethal crossfire.

The flames penning Farren in were thinning. He gritted his teeth, sending the rune of command to Parvell so he would take the mantle of leadership in his stead.

'Emperor, Omnissiah, Motive Force, watch over me,' he said. 'Protect my wargear.' He took a deep breath. 'This I do for you.'

Shoulder first, Farren ran straight into the mutative flame.

Sergeant Moricani saw his brother Farren burst out of the cell ahead and to the left, wreathed in oddly burning flames. He put the sight out of his mind – power armour was proof against the vagaries of fire, even able to withstand a close range promethium blast. The real threat was elsewhere.

'Block the exit,' said Moricani to Lenkatz. 'Cover that gaping hole that used to be the ceiling. Anything trying to get out needs bringing down. The Dark Angels seek the leader of this rebellion, and we are not going to disappoint them.'

'Understood,' said Lenkatz.

Moricani winced, scanning the cells on either side in the hope that the target rune Farren had sent across would flare.

There, to the side. Something was–

A sudden blast of black lightning slammed into Darrodan, hurling him backwards in a storm of malfunctioning plasma energies. The ceramite of his armour struck sparks from the rough stone of the staircase behind as he fell to the flagstones.

Moricani raised his plasma incinerator and spun on his heel as he depressed the trigger to maximum, dropping to a crouch. Another bolt of black lightning shot overhead. The incinerator whined in anticipation as it powered up to maximum capacity.

'I am not here for you, child of the Red Planet,' came a sepulchral voice. 'Not this time. Let me pass. I must teach these pale reflections of our primarch about the true nature of their kindred.'

Moricani looked for the source of the voice. To the right, the targeting rune on his helm display flickered like a dying firefly over a patch of darkness.

'No,' said the sergeant. He swung his incinerator and depressed the trigger lever to full, intending to send a superheated sphere of killing energy right at the head of the black figure in the shadows.

The plasma weapon screamed. It exploded in a white fireball that incinerated a full third of Moricani's body in a single searing instant.

'No!' Farren staggered, multicoloured flames still licking from his armour, down the cell-lined corridor. He had emerged from the fires a little scorched, but essentially unscathed – perhaps his quick prayer to the Omnissiah had been answered.

The same could not be said for Moricani. Farren was horrified to see what was left of his friend swaying as if hit by a knockout blow. The Hellblaster sergeant had always prided himself on knowing the tolerances of his plasma incinerator to the smallest degree.

Yet here it looked as if the weapon had killed the wielder.

Fingers of despair pushed into Farren's mind as he saw the Hellblaster sergeant topple over, his battleplate burned clean away across the right half of his body to leave behind a hideous, red-black mass. From nowhere a black shape leaped over him, a shadowy gargoyle that landed with a clang upon the third stair of the spiral staircase before taking them four at a time to disappear from sight.

Ignoring the billowing inferno slowly claiming the corridor, Farren hunched down and ran to the end of the passageway to Moricani's side. Even his friend's helm was half-molten, his face burned back to the skull across his jaw and left cheek.

'Is he dead?' said Lenkatz, his voice tight with stress as he laid down a burst of suppressive fire from his incinerator. Three small spheres burned down the passageway, each hurling back a half-formed daemon where they struck.

'Very nearly,' said Farren, taking a couple of snap shots down the corridor at the nearest fire-creature, 'but his rune is still active on my helmview.'

'His furnace,' said Thrunn. 'It'll trigger.'

'He's likely too far gone for–'

Moricani sat up suddenly and got back to his feet with a half-strangled roar, lurching around to run back up the stairs. Lenkatz went after him without another word.

Farren felt something hit him in the back, and spun around. A hideous, leering monstrosity cackled as it ripped at him, one ten-fingered hand closing over his helm and yanking at it as it tried to get at the flesh beneath. Farren kneed it hard in the mouth, feeling long teeth break even as he brought both elbows down in an overhead strike. The thing buckled and went down. He stamped hard on the bulging mass of its face, again and again.

'Just die!'

'We live!' it screamed back, its pink flesh separating under his boot as it bifurcated into two grimacing blue creatures, hideous and nightmarish. They grasped at the lieutenant's legs.

Farren kneed one aside, flinging out a boot to pin it to the wall as he shot the other one point blank. The bolt threw its remains in all directions, and the largest chunks turned into shrieking fire-daemons that danced around each other, drizzling flame. Their faces were contorted and cruel, as if they were beside themselves with anger.

Farren ignored them, turning to put the clip's last bolt into the torso of the second bluish creature. It too turned to flame. Then Thrunn appeared at Farren's side, stamping the fire-creatures to scatterings of sparks. As one of the crescent-shaped daemons bounded in close, Farren drew his sword and impaled it through its mouth before punching the side of its head repeatedly. It dissipated with a wail. Nearby, Parvell took the rest of the fire-sprites out with two carefully measured shots from his bolt rifle.

'What are these things?'

PHIL KELLY

'Chaos,' said Thrunn.

'Some manner of servitor creature, I think,' explained Farren, 'summoned from the empyrean, perhaps, by that warrior in black.'

'The one Moricani went after,' said Enrod. 'He had the look of a traitor.'

'I know,' replied Farren. 'Let's get up there.' He cast a glance down the corridor towards the Ravenwing, still hammering fire into the strange flame-beasts in the vault at the end, and hesitated for a moment. Then he remembered his old friend toppling over, and sprinted up the stairs.

Farren burst out onto the upper scaffolds of the fortress, bolt rifle panning around in three quick movements to cover the corners where a shadowed enemy could skulk. Thrunn, Enrod and Parvell emerged behind him, their own rifles moving smoothly left and right. Ahead was Epistolary Dothrael, his psy-stave crackling with coils of deep green energy, and Gabrael, holding a charged plasma pistol at his side.

'Where is he?' said Farren.

'You don't have him?' said Dothrael, his tone urgent. 'But–'

A black blur shot past them, sprinting for the vault door that led to the bell tower. Farren was the first to fire. His bolt sped true, but just as it was about to strike the traitor angel it detonated in a burst of flame. The guns of Thrunn and Parvell boomed behind him, but their bolts met the same fate. Even the ball of plasma unleashed by Gabrael splashed like liquid flame across the invisible dome that protected their foe.

Dothrael suddenly dropped to his knees, clutching his head and crying out in a voice that did not sound even vaguely close to human.

'Pathetic,' said the traitor angel, suddenly visible next to the battlement. His image was distorted, hidden behind a shimmering field of force that made it look as if he was underwater. Farren took another shot, and another, a storm of bolts hammering out from the Intercessors behind him. They too burned to nothing on the face of the psy-shield. The lieutenant grimaced and thickened his fire.

Under the crack-boom of discharging bolt rifles there was a roar like that of an enraged grox. Moricani came barging out from the vault door with his arms spread wide. He made for a hideous sight; one half of his body was scarlet ruin, the right side of his face a stinking morass of molten flesh.

Farren recoiled as his old friend plunged through the rippling psy-shield and struck the traitor angel from the side at full pelt, the momentum of his sudden charge enough to slam the psyker staggering sideways. With his foe caught in a thrashing grapple, Moricani heaved onwards, pushing with all his might. Farren watched in disbelief as he bowled the traitor straight over the battlements, following close behind.

'Gsar!' shouted Farren over the vox, 'get in close as possible to the tower! Now!'

The growl of the Repulsor's anti-gravitic engine rose up nearby, getting closer. Farren ran in a series of long strides, extrapolating the course of the *Harrower*'s rune, then leaped through the two nearest crennelations. He heard Parvell shout behind.

'Follow him! To the ramparts!'

Farren had a brief sensation of falling. Then he slammed feet-first into the top of the Repulsor tank, rocking it with his weight as it cushioned his fall on its anti-grav field. In a heartbeat, he was already up, his bolt rifle at his shoulder.

There was the traitor angel, fighting hard amongst a blood-slicked mess of mutant corpses, his necklace of yellowed skulls bouncing crazily around his neck as he punched Moricani over and over in the face. A shattered wooden staff lay nearby, its splintered remains fizzing with blue and pink lightning. The sound of the sergeant's wild laughter rose high.

Farren breathed out slow and pulled the trigger. This time the bolt slammed under the traitor angel's pauldron, the explosion of its impact rocking him, but not dislodging the death grip he had taken on Moricani's throat.

Then Gsar added his own fire, a stream of high-impact bullets from the *Harrower*'s onslaught cannon slamming into the traitor's side. In a cloud of sparks and smoke he was bowled away from Moricani, who slumped back unconscious.

The traitor rolled, coming up braced with one hand outstretched as if to crush something. There was a scream of tortured metal as the front of the Repulsor buckled. Farren leaped clear, landing with a thud a moment before the entire tank was lifted into the air. It slammed back into the monolithic stone blocks of the curtain wall behind, then pitched onto its side.

With practised swiftness Farren reloaded his rifle, ejecting the spent clip even as he grabbed a fresh one and slammed it into the rifle's breech. He saw Dothrael, drifting cruciform with arms outstretched into the court-yard. The Epistolary's staff crackled with energy, sparks leaping from the eyes of the horned skull at its tip.

The traitor angel, intent on buckling the front of the *Night Harrower* with a twist of his outstretched hand, was struck in the side of the head by a bolt of glowing force from Dothrael's staff. The black-armoured psyker went down amongst the mutilated flesh of his former acolytes – and so did the *Harrower*, falling to the ground with a thunderous crunch.

Farren darted right, firing a fresh bolt at the traitor angel as he writhed in pain. The psyker flung out a hand at the last moment, and the bolt disappeared in flame a full three feet from impact.

'Omnissiah's rage!' shouted Farren. 'Why won't you die?'

With a cry, the traitor angel suddenly stood, leaning forward as if into a gale. Dothrael's helm, held in the vice-like apparatus of his psychic hood, suddenly burst into flame. He was flung backwards into the twisted remains of a shattered portcullis.

The traitor angel grabbed an avian skull from the neck-lace garlanding his throat. He ripped it free, hurling it hard into the flagstones to shatter in an explosion of bone fragments.

A cloud of blue smoke billowed upwards, shot through with crackling bursts of light. The smoke formed into two columns, then gathered together at the peak to form a twisting arch. Reality seemed to ripple with it.

Farren could just make out a hellscape of maddening crystal angles beyond; it made his eyes hurt to look at it. A series of piercing pains cascaded across the muscles of his shoulder beneath his transmuted pauldron of bone.

Out from that archway came a giant bird-like claw adorned with jewelled bangles the width of half-track wheels. It was followed by a screeching head, its shape somewhere between that of an eagle and a crocodile. There was a horrible malevolence in its beady eyes.

Up on the rampart, Parvell, Thrunn and Enrod opened fire, their volley thundering into the creature's flesh. To Farren's eyes it seemed as if the bolts turned to blobs of quicksilver a moment before impact, doing no more harm than a shower of summer rain.

Still hauling its bulk from the smoke portal, the creature waved its colossal claw. The three Primaris Marines on the rampart suddenly froze. A moment later they burst into flame, their paralysed bodies quickly turning black as tiny, shrieking flame-daemons crawled up their armour towards their helms.

There was a shriek of turbine engines, and a black shadow with the angular wings of a Dark Talon passed over Farren. A split second later the monstrous creature emerging from the arch was struck by a beam from the round-barrelled cannon under the fighter craft's nose. Blinding in its intensity, the light was every colour and none, all at once.

The monstrous avian spasmed as if caught in the grip of a terrible palsy, desperately trying to fend off the light. The Dark Talon was angling its jets downwards, hovering low like a bird of prey set on the kill. The kaleidoscopic beam from its cannon was relentless. For a moment, Farren thought he saw the daemon tear open, and the air around it tear with it, as if it were no more than damp parchment.

The gigantic daemon gave a shriek of rage and denial

that seemed to ring through every bone of Farren's body as if they were glass chimes. Then it was gone, the traitor's arch of smoke dissipating in wisps of sparkling light. Cries of triumph and relief came from the ramparts above as Farren's brothers found the flames consuming them suddenly snuffed out.

The lieutenant scanned the courtyard. The mind-blasting light was gone, but to his dismay there was no sign of the traitor angel. It had all been for naught. All that sacrifice and suffering. Farren felt like his heart had been plunged into a bottomless lake of cold, black oil.

Then the *Harrower*'s onslaught cannon opened fire, pouring bullets at an oblique angle to slam into something across the courtyard as it passed into the shadow of the curtain wall to the gatehouse.

The traitor fell out of the shadows, black tendrils of pure darkness trailing from its limbs. He turned, eyes blazing red with anger and defiance.

Farren was already half way across the flagstones. His confusion and despair had turned to pure, undiluted hatred. It was a driving force, an irresistible imperative that made him run as hard as he could. Gone was the Xedro Farren that analysed, reviewed and made the kill with a hunter's precision. He drew his blade from its scabbard, activating its disruption field as his run turned into a sprint.

This Xedro Farren wanted to cut, and impale, and hack his enemy apart face to face.

The traitor drew his own blade, an ornate charnabal sabre in the ancient Terran design, and sketched a salute.

Farren charged in, his vicious swing deftly batted aside with a ring of impeccably forged metal. The traitor angel weaved to one side as Farren's momentum carried him past, but the lieutenant spun swiftly with his blade outstretched to make a slash at his adversary's waist. This time he felt the parry jar his wrist, the sabre flicking around his heavier broadblade to stab at his neck. Only the Mark X's raised gorget stopped the sword from opening his throat.

Farren rode the impact, making a jab that tapped the side of his opponent's blade. On instinct the rapier was drawn across to block. Quick as a snake the lieutenant twisted the tip of his sword underneath to come in for a killing thrust on the opposite side.

The traitor gave ground, three quick paces taking him away so his back was to the wall.

Then the shadow of the Dark Talon flitted over him, and a weapon from before the Age of the Imperium tumbled out of its yawning hold.

The archaic bomb struck the traitor angel a moment before his outflung hand could ward it off. The rippling burst of its detonation became a shimmering implosion of light, and for a moment the psyker was caught in that same pose, arm outstretched, yet completely immobile.

Dothrael ran across the courtyard, with Chaplain Zaeroph sprinting from the bottom of a set of stairs to join him as they converged upon the time-frozen angel.

'Stay back!' shouted Zaeroph, motioning for Farren to give them space as the Dark Talon came in low. The craft, its engines blasting hot and buffeting winds into the courtyard, dropped slowly with impeccable precision to land on the far side.

Farren kept his blade pointed at the traitor angel nonetheless, convinced that any moment some other sorcery would be invoked to turn the tables. Dothrael was letting psy-energy play out from his staff, the tendrils of crackling force binding their captive even as he slowly began to move in the remnants of the field.

With the winged edges of his crozius arcanum, Chaplain Zaeroph gingerly lifted the necklace of skulls from around the traitor angel's neck. With the utmost care he held it out to Gabrael, the company master taking it reverently before handing it to one of the Deathwing that had entered the courtyard. The Deathwing sergeant strode up to the traitor, a bandolier of strange vice-like devices held in his grip.

'Such is the vengeance of lost Caliban,' said Zaeroph as the sergeant approached. A matter of feet away, the sculptural bas-reliefs of the landed Dark Talon slid apart along their length to reveal a dark space inside it lined with crackling coils. It was a cell, of that much Farren was sure.

'I hereby claim you in the name of the Lion,' said Zaeroph. He walked around to the other side of the traitor angel, interposing him with the aircraft's secret cell on the other side.

'The primarch was a lie,' said his captive. His voice was slurred by the aftermath of the stasis bomb, but he seemed to recover with every word. 'Whilst I languish in the cold dungeons of the Rock, I can warm myself with the knowledge you will be forced to slay your spiritual sons on this planet. Just as the Lion slew his upon Caliban.'

'We will become far better acquainted, you and I,' said Zaeroph, his tone sinister. 'For now, though, you will wait.'

He raised a foot and booted the traitor angel as hard as he could in the chest, sending him staggering back into the cell-like interior of the Dark Talon. The bas-relief statues of the cell's doorways thunked shut a split second later with the sound of pneumatic bolts, a thin trail of smoke drifting from the hairline crack that had formed the door.

The Dark Talon took off a second later, its engines at deafening intensity as it lifted from the flags and rose into the darkening skies. Within seconds it was bracketed by a pair of the nimble craft Farren recognised as Nephilim jetfighters. A few seconds after that, the huge and blocky hull of a Thunderhawk flew overhead, following the trio of fighters as they rose into the clouds.

Farren watched the strange squadron of aircraft go for a moment, wondering what in Mars' name he had just witnessed. Then he turned his attention back to the Dark Angels in the courtyard.

Moricani was out cold, unlikely to survive without a lengthy stay in the apothecarium. Parvell, Thrunn and Enrod were gone from the battlements, presumably already on their way down.

Nearby, Dothrael had donned circuit-lined gauntlets that looked to Farren like elaborate power fists. Close to him was a Ravenwing rider with swept wings upon his helmet. The Librarian was taking the skulls one by one from the captive angel's necklace with the utmost care, and setting them within vice-like artefacts, handed to him by the Deathwing sergeant, so that the pads of the devices gripped the skulls' temples.

The Librarian shot Farren a glance, daring him to say something. Farren read his unspoken cues just fine, and remained silent.

'Withdraw all units,' said Chaplain Zaeroph, striding over to Farren as Parvell, Thrunn and Enrod emerged from the bottom of the nearest tower. 'This is over. We cannot risk further contamination.'

'Chaplain?' said Farren. 'We have brothers still active, brothers down, and the Angels of Absolution have engaged the rebel survivors on the upper levels. Their attack has been swift and efficient, but we should–'

'Withdrawal. Now. Rendezvous with your transports outside the main barbican and leave.'

'With respect, Chaplain, I–'

'Just do it, lieutenant. This is not the time for impertinence.'

Farren shook his head, eyes wide inside his helm. 'This can't be in the Emperor's name. I refuse to believe it.'

'I just received a personal missive,' came Parvell's voice over the Primaris solovox. 'They said if you don't effect the order immediately, they'll give me a field promotion and ensure I do it instead.'

'They can't,' said Farren, but he knew already that was a lie. Something inside him that had been twisted, battered and chipped away by the events of the last few months finally broke.

Thrunn walked past him, not meeting his gaze. 'I'll get Moricani. Enrod, you should meet up with Orenst and get Vesleigh whilst we still can.'

There was the chug of a bike engine behind them. Farren turned to see one of the Ravenwing Knights staring right at him, the plasma talon mounted on his bike's fairings pointed straight at Thrunn.

'No he shouldn't,' said the black-armoured rider. 'You are withdrawing, just as the Chaplain says. Make for your intact Repulsors and leave the warzone immediately. We will see to Sergeant Moricani, and recover your lost brother.'

Farren felt his defiance wither inside him. A sense of implied threat hung in the air, the gaze of the Ravenwing rider as unwavering as his guns. The lieutenant had long ago lost his grip on what was happening, but he had a distinct feeling that to go against these orders would lead to violence. And when Primarch Guilliman heard of it – and he no doubt would, even if Farren did not send word himself – that strife would escalate to censure of the most extreme kind. Perhaps it would even lead to civil war.

Somehow the sensation of utter defeat felt familiar.

'We withdraw, brothers,' he said. 'Now.'

CHAPTER THIRTEEN
THE WITNESS

Apothecarium
The *Executioner's Blade*

Moricani had been engaged in a silent battle against his own bio-system for hours. He was desperately trying to find a measure of calm as the after effects of his triggered Belisarian furnace raged within him.

The potent cocktail of hyperstimulants, anaesthetics, pain suppressants and hormone boosts supplied by the implant next to his twin hearts was a heady mix. Whilst it raged around the system, it made him feel truly invincible. But even should he fight through whatever had dealt that grievous wound and find help from his company's Apothecary, it might not be enough to save him.

Not that that was the purpose of the implant. Pater Cawl had given it to his Primaris creations so they could wreak the maximum amount of havoc upon the enemy before their expiry. And though his memories of the battle at Sixth West were hazy, Moricani was fairly sure he had done well at that.

What it would be to feel the furnace's rush without the crippling, typically fatal injury that triggered it. What it would be to harness that power. Perhaps, if he lived through this ordeal, he could find a sympathetic bio-magus who could help him out with an autonomous trigger. In fact, if he made it back to Mars, he was fairly sure his contacts in the…

Moricani opened his eyes, just a crack, at the sound of power armoured feet thumping towards the apothecarium. Something made him close them again, taking as deep breaths as possible as two sets of Adeptus Astartes footsteps clumped into the chapel-like medical centre.

'Two, this time,' said an augmetic-fuzzed voice. Moricani recognised it as Vaarad's. The insectile buzz of the Apothecary's lumen-skull grew louder as it scanned the warriors on the slabs within the candlelit alcoves. A wash of azure light came over Moricani; it was his turn.

Azure light. Something felt familiar in Moricani's mind about that.

'One of them is that Lion-damned sergeant of the plasma gunners,' said the voice of the Apothecary's companion. It sounded familiar. Not Dothrael; it was too casual in its sentiment for one of the Librarius.

Gabrael, perhaps?

'Somehow I feel sure he will be brought into line soon enough,' said Vaarad.

'So we'll make a useful bullet shield out of him yet.'

Moricani fought the urge to raise an eyebrow. That was Gabrael all right.

'Are you sure we will not be disturbed?' said the company master.

'Yes,' said Vaarad. 'All of the incumbents should be unconscious or worse, according to my data. This area is shut off. Zaeroph is busy humouring one of Guilliman's spies.'

'Good. He has much potential, that one, but entirely misplaced. Servitor, bring in the asset.'

There was a low purr, and the scent of auto-sanctic incense as something large – an autobier or hover-throne, by Moricani's estimation – entered the apothecarium.

'Look at this,' said Vaarad. 'This one took a psy-wound to the chest, and a bad one. One Danic Vesleigh, according to my auspicator.'

'The ape with the eyebrows? Farren's adopted squad?'

'Yes. I'm scanning for empyric residue.'

Moricani heard the telltale chimes of a psyoccular auspex, undercut by the rising whine of a plasma pistol.

'Unaffected,' said Vaarad. 'At least nothing that I can detect.'

'Odd,' said Gabrael. 'Not that we should be complaining. What manner of curse is it, do you think?'

'The plague appears to spike quickly, creating explosive psychic discharge, then recede to a dormant state,' said Vaarad. 'Whether it disappears altogether I cannot say. I hypothesise that in most cases it uses the psychic potential of the host body in the act of infecting others around it. Some are killed or rendered unconscious in the process. The results here certainly imply that to be the case.'

The plasma pistol's whine descended once more.

'It is those who survive to transmit the plague that I am concerned about. Unchecked psychic ability is the gateway to damnation.'

'Will this one live?'

'Unlikely. His second heart is almost as compromised as the first.'

'But he might, though.'

'It's possible.'

'Then we can't take the risk. Rig up the cannulas. And if that fails, we ready the incinerator. Ultramar be damned.'

'Give me a moment, company master.'

Moricani fought to keep calm as the Apothecary cut into Vesleigh's neck at the base, then pushed a finger deep inside.

'Yes, his progenoids are still intact. These sinew coils are remarkably effective as protective measures, as well as in lending mechanical strength to muscle contraction.'

'All the better for them to take a bolt on our behalf.'

'Quite. Rather than looking over my shoulder, Master Gabrael, would you be capable of administering the sedatives to the second patient whilst I treat the first?'

'If I can find a vein, yes. Though why we do not simply allow Epistolary Dothrael to wipe their minds clean I do not know.'

'It is an imprecise technique. To obtain optimal results from these ones, they need to fight at peak efficiency. I flatter myself to think that my psycho-hypnotic adjustments are more productive than total mnemonic obliteration.'

'As you say.'

'The requisite materials are on that tray. Please make ready. I have more specialised work to do, and a limited window in which to do it. After these we still have the others to do, and the process takes time.'

'Of course,' said Gabrael. 'Let us proceed.'

'Servitor, bring forth the asset.'

Moricani heard the lopsided shuffle of a servitor on the

move, accompanied by the hum of a hover-throne. It was followed by the sound of tiny autodrills whirring, and the faint sucking of fluids being drawn through a tube. With stimulants still raging around his body, Moricani could not resist opening one eye, just a little.

The scene was blurred, right on the extreme periphery of the sergeant's vision, but it was soon etched into his soul.

A network of thin transparent tubes jutted from Vesleigh's head and throat. They were bunched at his shoulder, tied into a thick cable filled with fluids that bubbled pink and red. Less than three feet away, the tubes were joined in a similar manner to the neck of a naked, over-muscled hulk with a heavy metal visor and metallic cat-o'-nine-tails whips in place of its hands.

An arco-flagellant. The perpetrator of some unforgivable crime, mind-wiped and turned into a super-weapon at the hands of the Adeptus Mechanicus' most inhuman surgeons.

Moricani had seen a pack of them in action during the daemon wars of Terra, going from drooling inactivity to screaming, berserk frenzy at the utterance of a simple trigger phrase from their Ministorum masters.

'Now,' said Vaarad, tapping a sequence into the rune nodes on the side of his servo-skull. The azure light began to pulse, flashing arythmically as the Apothecary leaned in close. 'Danic Vesleigh. You do not clearly recall the events of the attack upon the fortification known as Sixth West. In fact, you do not wish to dwell on the events of the past at all. They are hazy and painful to summon to mind.'

A figure moved in close, blocking out the light. Moricani shut his eye completely once more, fighting the urge to spring up and fight – an urge that would almost certainly get him killed.

Vaarad continued to talk from the alcove across the apothecarium.

'Should you feel any surge of cerebral activity that is unusual, you will return to this state and remain comatose. Furthermore, when you hear a certain phrase you will immediately make ready for conflict, and concentrate only on those events about to unfold.'

Moricani felt a pain in the side of his neck. Just as his senses began to blur together, he heard Vaarad confirm a dark suspicion that turned him numb with betrayal and shock.

'That phrase is "battle stations".'

CHAPTER FOURTEEN
AWFUL TRUTH

Apothecarium
The *Executioner's Blade*

Farren strode through the corridors of the Dark Angels battle-barge as it made its way from Allhallow to deep space. He had received his orders only a matter of hours ago, and had not thought about much else. No matter how long he dwelt on them, they made as little sense to him as when he had first heard them.

The entire Dark Angels strike force was to return to the planet Saltire Vex, this time to destroy its installations utterly for the sin of being tainted by xenos.

The notion of returning to a former warzone rankled in Farren's mind, especially after making the long haul from that location in the first place. There was something in the mindset of all Adeptus Astartes that demanded they kept going onward at all times; kept momentum so the enemy never had a chance to prepare for their devastating assaults.

That said, with him having let the woman Deel go free, there was every chance the people they sought were no longer there. The whole affair could be an exercise in futility, or worse, a witch hunt with him as the traitor on trial.

But that was not the part that rankled the most to Farren's mind. To attack the very people they had formerly bled for, striven for, given their lives to save from the xenos invaders that were preying upon them seemed galling in the extreme. Yet they had willingly left the Emperor's light to embrace the alien, and that was rightfully punishable by death. The dissonance made his jaw clench.

The apothecarium was not far, now. Less than an hour ago, Chaplain Zaeroph had told him not to disturb the healing process by entering the chamber. He had told him that Moricani was making a full recovery, and that a lieutenant's duty should be in planning those attacks to be made in the future, rather than dealing with the fallout of those made in the past.

The words had weight, at the time. But Farren could no more ignore Moricani's plight than he could forget the sight of his brother's ruined flesh after the plasma malfunction.

He had sent Thrunn to the Chaplain within minutes of his return to the Primaris contingent's quarters. The young warrior had questions of his own about what they saw in the dungeons of the keep, and sometimes the most honest and compelling motive of them all was a need for the truth.

Whilst the big warrior kept the Chaplain busy with simple questions that all had very complicated answers, Farren had time enough to seek out some truths of his own. He had already gone through the ritual of ungirding in his cell, padded out into the corridor in a woven robe and headed for the apothecarium to see his old friend.

Or what was left of him.

All plasma weapons were volatile; it was why they had such a reputation in the armed forces of the Imperium. To be entrusted with their use was as much a curse as it was a blessing. But the Primaris Hellblasters knew their weapon tolerances better than even the plasma gunners of the Adeptus Astartes, for they were trained in the use of that one weapon above all others, and were at one with their machine-spirit. To suffer such a catastrophic malfunction at a critical time – it had to be the work of the psyker that had summoned the ether-spawn to distract them as he escaped. The black armoured figure they had run down in the keep.

What had become of that figure since he had been incarcerated in the Dark Talon's stasis hold, Farren did not know. Presumably he was languishing in a cell somewhere, if he had not already been executed. There was no way the lieutenant would be entrusted with any information as to his fate, that much was obvious. Zaeroph and his fellows were not the giving type, and they seemed especially reticent to give any details when it came to the rebellion's leader.

The corridors leading to the apothecarium were wide, far wider than those of the Primaris contingent's quarters upon the *Blade*. The faint smell of counterseptic tingled at the back of Farren's nose as he passed a large vestibule area and approached the door.

As a lieutenant, he had clearance to make his way in, though should Vaarad be inside at the time he would no doubt have a difficult conversation ahead. The Apothecary was as tight-knit with Zaeroph as Gabrael and Autinocus, and would not look kindly upon an unsanctioned visit. Should word reach Zaeroph, the resultant interrogation about his motives would not be pleasant.

The thick lintel of the apothecarium's entrance was framed by two skeletally thin caryatids that Farren at first took to be sculptural. When one of them whirred into life and stared at him, he was taken aback for a moment, but hid his discomfiture with the sign of the Holy Cog.

'Primaris Lieutenant Farren,' he said.

'Denied,' said the servitor, its voice as dry and rasping as two pieces of groundglass parchment rubbed together.

'*Lieutenant* Farren,' he said. 'Formerly of the Indomitus Crusade.'

'Denied.'

Farren's eyes narrowed as he recognised the servitor's mech-pattern. He reached up to the servitor's neck, peeled away the outer casing of two of the many tubes running from the cogitator pillar behind it into the back of its head, and carefully squeezed them flat with finger and thumb. Bereft of its mind-link chemicals, it squawked in alarm for a few moments, but was unable to send for help. After a while, it fell still, black liquid drooling from the side of its slack maw.

'The tech-priests of Mars send their greetings,' said Farren.

The apothecarium's vault doors ground open, the noise loud enough to have Farren darting a glance over his shoulder despite his attempt to appear in command of the situation. He strode through, looking left and right for any sign of Vaarad. To his relief, there were only wounded warriors in the bay, each strapped to a slab with cannulas and wheezing resp-tubes attached to their torsos and necks.

Farren passed a prone Dark Angel whose legs were missing from the knees down, then the cybernetic replacements propped on a nearby lectern of dark green marble. To his right was a Space Marine who should by rights have been long dead, for his entire chest was caved in as if by a massive boulder. A nest of pipes and wires was connected to the plugs in his black carapace, sucking and glugging as they took out extraneous fluids and added back in those needed to keep the warrior alive.

The lieutenant raised his eyebrows. Any Apothecary skilled enough to bring that severe a casualty back to active service was worthy of the name twice over.

Farren's hearts thumped as he scanned the rest of the beds. There was Moricani, strapped to a med-slab at the back of the pillared hall. Despite his height and broad shoulders, he seemed shrunken, robbed of his easy posture and wry smile by the terrible wound that had laid him low.

Almost as if he was already a corpse.

Farren walked closer, his gait that of a thief trying his best not to make a sound. Even at a glance he could see Moricani's wounds were awful. A morass of red, pink and black flesh, marbled with white streaks and the odd gleam of bone, covered his entire right side. In places even his black carapace was burned away, the ribs and lungs beneath open to the air. The soft pink tissue beneath puckered and flexed, puckered and flexed, whilst ribbed and cartilaginous tubes gurgled softly from his torso.

'Pietr,' said Farren softly, 'well met.'

He waited for some sarcastic reply, but the figure on the bed lay still, motionless apart from the very faint motions of its breath.

'Pietr. I have come to wish you well. Can you hear me?'

A moment passed.

'No,' came the faint reply, right on the cusp of hearing.

Farren felt the guttering fire of hope in his soul flare to life once more.

'Thank the Omnissiah you're alive,' he said. 'Even if your sense of humour is still intact.'

'Barely.'

'What happened, Pietr? I don't believe for one moment you overcharged your incinerator that badly.'

'Didn't.'

'So why did it come to this?'

'Sab… otage,' said Moricani.

'Who would do that?'

'The First.'

'Not possible,' said Farren, but even as he said the words, he knew that was not the case.

'I saw… some things, Farren.'

'What? Something you were not meant to see?'

'Yes. There was… an accord. In battle.'

'You mean the daemon creatures?'

'No,' said Moricani. 'Listen, Xedro. Just listen.'

Farren cast a glance behind him across the apothecarium, but all was as he left it.

'The First,' said Moricani. 'Talked… with the… xenos.'

'A parley?'

'No,' wheezed Moricani, shaking his ravaged skull an imperceptible amount. 'A pact.'

'How so? Did they unite against a common enemy?'

'Yes,' said Moricani.

'The daemons?'

'Not… exactly. They… intimated… they needed… the t'au.'

'What for?'

'To... attack... Allhallow.'

Farren stepped back, his mind whirling. Moricani had to be delirious. To side with a xenos force over a Successor Chapter... it was unthinkable. There had to be some mistake.

'What? Why do this?'

'The... Angels of... Absolution. They are... tainted... by a psy-plague.'

'Tainted?'

'That... white... psy-fire. It is... infectious to... other Adeptus... Astartes.'

'Not all of them,' said Farren, gesturing to his side.

'It... appears not. We... must be... made of... stronger stuff.'

'And the Angels have become infected?'

'Yes. But we... cannot... purge it... ourselves.'

'And the t'au can? I hardly think they–'

'*Yes,*' interrupted Moricani, exasperation quickening the wheezing of his breath. 'They are... all but... psy... inert. Dim souls. Immune.'

'So the First are sending xenos against their own successor Chapter? That can't be right.'

Moricani's left eye, bloodshot and crusted with yellow discharge, slid over to meet Farren's gaze. For once, there was not an ounce of humour in it.

'But why stray so far from the light?' said Farren. 'Why not inform the Inquisition, and have them deal with it?'

'Old secrets,' said Moricani. 'Must be... kept.'

'And why would the t'au even agree to such a thing?' Farren's mind was already racing as it sought the answer. He thought of the stealther t'au they fought on Saltire Vex, of the strange psyker-plague they first encountered there, and of their orders to head back and purge the site for good. The events had to be connected. More than that, they were cause and effect.

'The t'au want us to attack their human allies in return,' said Farren as realisation dawned. 'They want deniability, so they can keep up their pretence with every other human world they've lured into their empire. That's why we are heading back to the ocean world. We are to be their proxies, and finish the riggers for good.'

Moricani nodded, grimacing as the movement opened a furrow of wounds on his neck. Whitish-yellow pus leaked out of the tiny chasms that appeared by his collarbone.

'Who would make such a deal with a xenos force? What would bring the First so low?'

'The... quarry,' said Moricani. 'Its secret... must be... worse.'

Farren narrowed his eyes. 'A quarry that summons daemons to his side? That would be worse, in my book.'

'True.'

'But to keep all this from the Inquisition,' said Farren, frowning as the pieces fitted together in his mind, 'that implies...'

Moricani's left eyebrow raised, just a little, a perfect curve of hair in comparison to the burned and slug-like weal of flesh on the other side.

'The quarry... is one... of us,' said Moricani, lifting a claw-like finger to point at the winged sword emblazoned upon Farren's robe. 'A Dark... Angel.'

Farren felt sick. From the start, their enemy had not been a force of alien invaders, nor a rebellion, nor a psychic curse.

It had been one of their own.

'That cannot be. All this death. All this war. It cannot be for the sake of one lone traitor. I refuse to believe it.'

Moricani struggled to sit up, his tubes straining as flesh and skin cracked in shining red deltas across his burned flesh. 'You... know... it is... true!' he hissed.

Farren's eyes went wide. 'Calm,' he said, gently placing his hand over the side of Moricani's face that still looked vaguely human. 'Calm, my friend.'

The sergeant allowed himself to be pushed back down, his good eye sending spears of accusation at Farren even as the white orb of his lost socket leaked whitish fluids across the ravaged flesh of his burns.

'If this is true,' said Farren coldly, 'I will keep the spark of this truth, and nurture it until it becomes a flame, then an inferno. I will burn this conspiracy from the heart of the Chapter if it is my last dying act.'

Something shivered in Farren's mind, a sense of famil-iarity, and a vision of strobing lights and faces peering down. He was about to dismiss it when he saw his friend's good eye creased with effort.

'There is... more. The... memories,' said Moricani. 'You... told me. You have... them too.'

'The nightmares?'

'The... *memories*,' hissed Moricani. 'I heard... Vaarad. And... Gabrael. Working on... Vesleigh.'

'When?'

'Not... sure. They thought... I was... out.'

Farren said nothing, a chill sense of dread closing over him.

'They were... using fluids... from a battle servitor...'

'To accelerate the healing process?'

'To… mind-wipe… Vesleigh. Then… then me.'

Something sank in Farren's stomach.

'What?' he said. His mouth tasted of ash, and of cold, dead things.

'They remove… our memories,' said Moricani. 'They… mind-wipe… us all.'

'No!' shouted Farren. His arms felt full of burning bio-fuel, his hands ready to rip and tear as hyperdrenaline thundered through his system.

'They take… our memories… and send us… to war… over and… over. But… they didn't know… about our… furnace. Keeps us… half-awake.'

Farren felt the floor of his mind fall away for the second time in as many minutes.

It made so much sense. The sensation of waking, as if from deep meditation, when they were going into battle. The flashbacks, the dreams, the sense of figures looking down and shining azure lights right in their faces. The fact that almost every one of the Primaris Marines had experienced the same thing at some point.

They were being used as puppets. As distractions. As shields of flesh and bone to be hurled against a convenient enemy whilst the real work was being done behind the scenes.

'It's all lies,' said Farren. 'This whole Chapter is built on lies.'

Moricani said nothing, his tubes wheezing as he stared up unblinking at Farren.

'What do we do now?' said Farren softly.

'Get to… the heart… of it,' said Moricani. 'Expose… it all.'

Farren nodded sombrely, something hardening inside his soul.

'Yes,' he said. 'That I can do.'

CHAPTER FIFTEEN
SAVAGE MEASURES

Saltire Nearspace
Kroot Warsphere *Vawk Karaow*

Jensa Deel pushed the Arvus to its maximum speed. Once they had left Saltire's orbit, she had been able to see her reflection against the starlit void, lit from below by the wan illumination of the cockpit displays. The visage there was that of a stranger, perhaps twenty years older, the skin more like a washed-out grey than her normal healthy brown. More than once she had seen her long-dead mother in that reflection.

Now the introspection of the void was a rapidly vanishing memory, eclipsed by the immensity in the middle distance.

A kroot warsphere. Part space station, part migratory city, part battleship. And entirely inhabited by ruthless alien cannibals that sought their strength from eating the bodies of the dead.

The xenos ship was slate grey and gunmetal, a little like two ringed city-domes cut from a planet's surface and welded on either side of a massive spindle. It was oddly fascinating in its ugliness. No hint of streamlining or grace could be found here, nor even the jutting, pugnacious arrogance of Imperial craft. This was an alien vessel in the truest sense of the word, built to satisfy sensibilities and desires that no human could truly understand.

'I can't believe you're taking us onto that Throne-damned monstrosity,' said del Aggio. 'Especially with your, *whatever it is*, Deel. Your *sickness*. This is total madness.'

Markens nodded. 'She's not wrong.'

'So is staying behind,' said Deel softly, steering the Arvus lighter towards the winking ingress lights she had been told to aim for by the mercenary xenocrats of Qaru Non. 'So is waiting for death.'

The rigger lined up the transport with what she assumed was the warsphere's docking bay. She engaged the craft's machine-spirit, rudimentary though it was, to help guide her in safely, and focused hard on the approach.

The warsphere grew steadily until it completely filled the viewscreen. She cast a glance down at the recommissioned pulse carbine she had stashed under the seat, reassured by its lethal lines.

'Oh-kay,' said Deel, huffing out a long breath through pursed lips. 'Anyone know anything about kroot that we haven't already covered?'

Markens spoke up. 'Remember that water caste operative back on Thetoid last summer, Aggro? As he put it, "they have a distinctive scent".'

'So they stink,' said del Aggio. 'Bad.'

No one laughed.

The warsphere loomed even larger now, the details on its surface visible. Everything about it was wrought on a massive, crude scale, as if it had been built by some cyclopean race of titans. In parts the outside of the sphere seemed to be overgrown by cables, winches and badly welded girders, a separate and more organic superstructure yearning to get out. It reminded Deel of the pict-captures that had fascinated her as a child, her visualbook images of majestic, column-like arboreals throttled by parasitic vines of bright green.

The ingress lights blinked in series, silently guiding them in to the pipe-lined passageway that led inside. To Deel's fevered mind, the ingress point looked a lot like the gullet of some strange cybernetic beast.

'In we go.'

'So your plan is to persuade them to help us with a single barrel of promethium,' said del Aggio. 'And you think that will be enough to convince them to face down whatever retribution is sent our way.'

'Up to and including a strike force of Space Marines,' added Markens.

'Do you have any more realistic ideas?' snapped Deel, balling her fists to keep them from trembling. 'Any old friends in-system that could make a difference?'

Del Aggio said nothing.

'So we go in,' said Deel. 'Just… don't say anything to them.'

'That's not her forte,' said Markens.

'What if you… what if you have an episode, like before?' said del Aggio. 'I've had a headache ever since.'

'Then I reckon you'll have to take it up from where I leave off,' said Deel. 'Saltire Vex is counting on you, even if it doesn't know it.'

Another long silence. Deel guided the Arvus lighter further in as the ingress portal led them to a massive, dark hangar. A double set of vault doors irised open and shut as the lighter passed, and the lighter's pressure gauge flashed as they formed an airlock.

Dimly lit, the inside of the ship seemed half derelict. Around the edges of the wide, low-ceilinged dock were the scatterings of ships from half a dozen races, each dormant and part-disassembled at the edges of sight. A strange black discolouration, a little like the oil mould that clung to the lower layers of the rigs, had claimed a fair few of them, and some even boasted small clusters of vegetation.

Here and there, condensation dripped from the rust-spattered ceiling. The columns of lights that had guided them in turned through ninety degrees and winked towards a wide, empty berth.

'Guess we set down here then,' said del Aggio.

'Where is everyone?' muttered Deel. 'Some welcoming committee.'

'Fine by me,' said Markens. 'You need someone to watch the lighter, of course. I hereby volunteer.'

'Not a chance,' said del Aggio. 'You're gonna make good friends with that barrel, hauling it up any stairs, pushing it up ramps, carrying it over rope bridges, whatever we find.'

'*If* I do that,' said Markens, 'and *if* we make it back, and *if* our ship hasn't already been stripped for parts, then you have to officially make me Rigsman Second Class.'

'Eurgh,' said del Aggio. 'Fine.'

The Arvus lighter set down hard with a triple clunk, the pneumatic hissing of its landing gear audible even inside the cockpit.

'Sorry,' said Deel. 'Bad landing.'

'You're not vomiting white gunk today,' said del Aggio. 'So as far as I'm concerned you're doing fine.'

Deel unclipped her harness and made her way to the back of the lighter before stepping out into the hangar beyond. The air was humid, horribly so. Already she could feel sweat pricking at her back, her armpits, the old wounds in the backs of her legs.

'It's hot as a burnsman's forge in here,' said del Aggio.

'Smells even worse,' grunted Markens, manhandling the promethium barrel they had taken from Thetoid and rolling it out of the back of the Arvus with a loud clang.

Deel waved them quiet, but the big man had a point. The place was truly foul, home to an acrid stink that stuck like rancid fat to the back of the throat. Deel flexed the muscles in her nose to block her nostrils from the inside; an old rigger's trick. It made her voice sound as strange as if she had ignifluenza, but it had saved her from nausea a hundred times over, especially when mucking out the drops.

'Just deal with it,' she said in a nasal monotone, 'and keep your eyes wide.'

The ingress lights suddenly changed, winking in a new pattern that led them into the cavernous rear of the hangar. At the back was a corridor, roughly oval in shape and ridged with thick stanchions that reminded Deel of the rings of cartilage reinforcing a human trachea. Long pipes and ribbed cables ran along its length like tendons and veins, reinforcing the impression they were venturing into the innards of some immense steel giant.

With Deel taking point, pulse carbine held ready, the three riggers made their way onwards into the gloom. Jensa cast a glance backwards. Del Aggio was at her shoulder, watchful eyes under a tattooed scalp, her pulse pistol concealed somewhere under her raincape.

Markens was dutifully rolling the promethium barrel along in front of him, trickles of sweat on his heavy arms and fat-rolled neck. The heavy steel drum made a low, grinding rumble as it traversed the passageways – audible even under the bass thrum of the warsphere's engine units, it put them all on edge.

'Should have lined its ridges with packer's tape,' muttered Deel. 'Too late now.'

There was a strange, guttural caw from ahead. All three of them stopped for a moment, their attention fixed on a shadow that flickered in the flashing light of the ingress lumens. A hunched avian cocked its head at them, ruffling its mangy feathers. It shook the sheaf of quills behind its beady eyes and a long and jagged beak.

'Right,' said Deel. 'Probably some kind of pet–'

There was a flicker of movement.

'Or a distraction,' she continued, slowly lowering the barrel of her gun. 'Don't make any sudden moves.'

She turned slowly to see four figures dropping down from the pipes above, their olive green anatomies lithe and sparse. Clawed feet like those of birds clanged onto the metal floor of the corridor, and long rifles, each of which was tipped at either end by vicious blades, whipped around to point right at them.

Deel felt oddly proud that two of the four were pointed at her, leaving one each for del Aggio and Markens.

The xenos stared over their blunt beak-maws with penetrating black eyes. The nests of quills that jutted from the back of their heads fanned up, as if to make their silhouettes larger. The quills rattled, whilst some tinkled where nuts and metal trinkets had been woven in amongst them. The kroot were clad in leather and covered in what looked like thick, fatty grease; in places, it was dark, and streaked like warpaint.

'We are here to parley,' said Deel in Low Gothic. She felt something lift one of her dreadlocks from behind, and turned just a fraction to see the tip of a rifle blade an inch from her eye. The blade tugged a few more dreadlocks free, its owner making the approximation of a cackle before letting it fall.

'Par-lay,' cawed the kroot in front of her, a scarred brute some eight feet in height. He was missing a large portion of his skull, and had a scorched black augmetic in its place. 'Sal-taw Vec-kas,' he trilled, his pointed black tongue sticking out from his blood-encrusted jaws.

'Saltire Vex, yes,' said Deel. 'We want to hire you.'

The kroot threw back their heads, making shrill cawing sounds that Deel was almost sure were mocking her. She smiled insincerely.

'Carm toh see mas-tar shay-par,' said the kroot leader. He shouldered past her roughly, his fellows close behind. The bodily contact left a smear of evil-smelling fat on Deel's shoulder. Under the grease, his anatomy had been hard, strong; little more than muscle over bone. It felt… hungry, somehow.

'Deel?' said del Aggio softly.

'I think he said "come to see master shaper…"'

'Huh,' said Markens. 'That sounds like who we want, right?' He put his weight against the promethium drum and started rolling it once more. The kroot ahead clicked and cawed to one another, making the shrill mocking sound once more as they went.

'I hope so, Markens,' said Deel, noticing a patch of stitched pink leather dangling from the rearmost kroot's belt. The hairs on her neck and forearms stood up as she realised it had eyes, nostrils and a mouth.

'I really very much hope so.'

The cavernous space of the kroot leader's court was huge. Oppressively hot and stinking of acrid xenos flesh, it was lined with hundreds of tall, branching structures, each somehow reminiscent of Deel's old arboreal pict-book – yet this jungle was made of girders, coiled wire and iron stanchions twisted out of true.

Lithe, quadrupedal shadows slinked in its reaches, jaws agape, whilst dozens – no, Deel thought as she looked closer; *hundreds* – of kroot-mercenaries leaned against, sat near and dangled from the steel trees. They were hard to make out – deliberately so, for their grease-painted skin was streaked with dark discolouration by way of camouflage. Tendrils of actual vegetation hung from the structures in places, and strange multi-jointed insects buzzed and fluttered in shafts of light that stabbed down from above.

The largest beam illuminated the king of this strange assembly. Seated on an immense pile of captured weapons and bone trophies at the heart of the cavernous space, he was massive even by the standards of his looming kindred. The sheaf of greyish quills that protruded from his skull stuck out in all directions, each spine-like appendage adorned with complex metal jewellery, and his eyes were covered by complex infrascopic goggles that would have looked more suited to a Space Marine Scout than a barbarian warlord.

A hunched, elderly kroot perched on his haunches on

a rickety platform at the warlord's side, wearing a cloak of long feathers and a stylised leather mask holding his own sheaf of quills. He stood unsteadily, propping himself on a gnarled staff of lacquered heartwood.

'Yu-mans bow bee-fore the Grey King,' he said in a harsh croak.

Shivering, Deel bowed low. Markens followed suit after shoving his barrel upright with a clang that sent a hundred bladed rifles clattering upwards to focus on him. He froze mid-bow, not daring to stand again.

'That wun not bow,' said the feather-clad speaker, motioning at del Aggio.

'That's right,' said the rigger loudly, 'I do not. Far too much–'

A shadow moved nearby. The hilt of a kroot rifle thumped into del Aggio's gut, hard enough to send her to her knees in a wheezing, red-faced ball.

'You doo now,' said the speaker. The Grey King gave a croaking, bass caw that was a little too much like human laughter for comfort.

'Yoo come as food,' said the speaker, cocking its head. 'Small flesh,' it added, its quills dipping in disappointment.

The pungent stench of the place was getting thicker. It was so foul it was beginning to make Deel's eyes water. That was what she told herself, at least.

She was definitely not tearing up through fear.

'We come as employers,' she said, keeping her voice steady. 'To enlist your services as mercenaries. All of you.'

A great cacophony of cawing, barking, hooting and clapping of hands came from all around as the metal jungle came to life, the sound deafening in its sudden intensity. Deel waited for it to subside. Sure enough, the Grey

King raised a giant clawed hand, and the assembly gradually fell quiet.

'Yoo want to hi-yer us,' said the speaker, his tone harsh. The feathers on his back fanned out, and Deel realised with a start that they were not a cloak, as she had first thought, but wings. 'Watt could you poss-ab-lee offer us?'

Willing every ounce of her self control into keeping her hand steady, Deel held up a finger. She took out the hip flask and tinderswitch she had seconded from del Aggio from her jerkin – a dozen rifles swinging around to cover her as she did so – and unscrewed the top.

'Al-ca-haul?' said the Grey King, his posture stiffening in his chair. He snorted like a rhino about to charge.

'No,' said Deel, swigging a big gulp from the flask whilst fighting the urge to vomit. She flicked the tinderswitch and, lips pursed, breathed out a great cloud of promethium droplets.

They caught instantly. A massive pillar of flame and greasy black smoke shot up from her lips to the ceiling, sending crazy shadows dancing in the metal trees and sending the assembly into a hooting, cawing cacophony once more.

'Promethium,' she said, kicking Markens' barrel with a steel-toed boot. It gave a pleasingly loud clang. 'Pure, undiluted firejuice.'

'We have that,' said the speaker. His tone was still harsh, but his wings were folded back again, and his eyes were bright. He flung out a hand. 'We are war-sphere, *Vawk Karaow*. One bar-ral is nuth-ing.'

'This is just a quality sample of our goods,' said Deel. 'We have literally tens of thousands of barrels of the finest stuff. Tens of thousands. All you need to do is land, and we roll it aboard. One berth, one barrel.'

'One berth one bar-ral,' said the speaker.

'Yes. Then we debark at the next system along, and leave the goods with you. You'll have all the fuel you need for years, decades. And there's room enough on this vessel for all of us.'

'Isss there,' hissed the Grey King.

'Yoo have weap-ons of t'au ser-vant,' said the feathered speaker, pointing at her pulse carbine. He had made 't'au' two staccato halves, and mangled a few syllables, but the more he spoke to her, the better his facility with Low Gothic seemed to get. She had heard of the kroot's ability to mimic others, but to see it in practice was truly impressive. No wonder they made such adept mercenaries.

'We are not bound to Great Good,' the speaker cawed, something close to disdain in his eyes and the cocking of his head. 'Here away from septs, we do as we see fit.'

'The T'au'va is a noble ideal,' said Deel. 'And it united our planet, once. But there are those amongst the t'au that would see us dead, just for the crime of being human. What kind of unity is that?'

The rhetorical question hung in the air. Deel could not tell if it was the silence of contemplation, or whether the kroot had lost interest and were thinking of their next meal.

'We come to you as independents,' she said, pressing on. 'As a people with much to offer, but no allies to offer it to.'

There was another long silence.

'One berth, one barrel,' said the speaker, tilting his jaw back.

'Yes.'

He nodded, running a string of finger bones through his talons. 'Tell more,' he snapped. 'We make pact.'

Deel felt a cold shroud lift from her heart, fluttering above it, but ready to descend once more.

'Halt it,' said the Grey King.

Down came that shroud, over Deel's heart.

'Hau do, we-know,' said the warlord. 'Hau do you tell truth we know.'

Deel frowned. 'I don't lie. Check the quality of that barrel's contents if you don't believe it's the good stuff.'

'Not enough,' said the speaker, slowly shaking his head. 'To risk war-sphere. I say to you, no, we cannot.'

'Come heer,' said the Grey King, extending a long talon and beckoning Deel closer. The talon was like the claw of some ancient saurian, scaled and black-nailed. It had three other claws ready to grasp, to rip, to plunge into human flesh behind it. 'Come.'

Deel stepped forward hesitantly, then caught herself and strode, confidence radiating from her every step despite the fact she felt nothing but pure terror inside.

'Giffft me,' said the warlord, motioning at her fingers. 'I will taste-trooth.'

Every instinct in Deel's mind screamed at her not to hold her hand out.

She held her hand out anyway.

The warlord grabbed it, enfolding her brown digits in his giant claw. His grip was a wrench-vice, inescapable. The warlord leaned in, his acrid stench overpowering. His eyes, though hidden behind the high-spec Imperial sniper goggles, seemed to bore into her.

Then the warlord's massive, jagged beak, more like that of a snapping turtle than a bird, darted forward and clipped off two thirds of Deel's little finger in a single motion.

Deel's lips curled as she fought with all her being not to scream. She yanked her hand back and pinched the stem of her severed finger to save from drizzling blood all over the makeshift throne.

The warlord sat back, licking the edge of his beak clean of Deel's blood. She heard the crunch of her own finger-bones as the master shaper chewed thoughtfully on her flesh.

'Hah,' he said eventually, as if surprised.

The feathered speaker clicked and whistled in the unintelligible kroot tongue.

'She is, trooth-teller,' said the Grey King in response, nodding. 'And psy-spiced.'

'Psy-ling?' said the speaker, his eyes glinting as his quills rose high. 'Good meat, for shay-man.'

'No,' said the king, shaking his head. 'Too use-fuel.'

The shaman's quills drooped once more.

'One berth, one bar-rel,' said the giant xenos thoughtfully, looking down at Deel. She was shaking now, uncontrollably.

'Y-yes,' she said. 'Just get us off Saltire Vex, and put us down somewhere safe. Warm. We don't care where.'

'You seek warm,' said the kroot monarch, eyelids lowered.

'Yes,' she nodded. 'Please.'

'Done.'

A flood of relief washed over Deel as she backed away, bowing low. She saw the black spots return at the edge of her vision, and fell back, only to feel del Aggio catch her and carry her back over to Markens.

Whilst del Aggio tore off a strip of cloth from her cuff and bound the finger-stump as best she could, Deel leaned heavily against Markens' reassuring bulk. The smell of his stale sweat was reassuringly human after the olfactory assault of the kroot's stench-grease.

Deel frowned. Come to think of it, she could hardly smell the vile stench of the kroot. It had all but disappeared.

'Go now,' said the speaker from atop the podium. 'Ready your people. We will come for you on fifteen day from here.'

'Fifteen days,' said del Aggio pensively. 'With the evac protocols already in place...' She paused, counting on her fingers. 'And by then, the waters around the rigs will already have started to floe...'

Two heavy-set kroot approached Markens and yanked the promethium drum away from him, cawing harshly in triumph as they carried the barrel between them to the rear of the warlord's throne.

'All yours,' said Markens. 'You're welcome to it.'

Jensa felt her senses swim back into focus as the kroot king waved them away. She leant heavily on Markens as they made their way back to the lighter.

'Deel, my girl,' said del Aggio, the dragons on her eye-brows kissing as she frowned. 'I think I might just love you a little bit.'

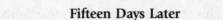

Fifteen Days Later

The vast sideways domes of the descending starship were blurred by the punishingly cold winds that whipped across Saltire Vex's ice floes, but Jensa Deel could see them growing clearer by the minute. Well over a mile from the tip of one dome to the other, the vessel was as incongruous and unsettling as a vast metallic meteor hanging suspended in the sky.

Yet to the people of Saltire Vex, the arrival of the warsphere was their salvation.

Deel looked back to see long columns of huddled refugees stretching behind her, thousands of riggers shuffling across the ice floes that had slowly, inevitably formed over their ocean. The floes were a sign of the deathly temperatures the planet would plunge to as it continued on its elliptical journey away from the star Saltiros; amongst the riggers, it was said that if you saw an ice floe, it was already too late. Now that supposition was being put to the test.

The rigger families making their way from the lowest pontoons of the rigs were wrapped up so completely they looked more like columns of penguins than people. Deel knew that some of them had made the trek from one rig to another across dozens of sites, using them as staging posts for a far larger pilgrimage towards the rendezvous point of Ferro-Giant Thetoid.

Many had made their journey on boats, ferries or low-altitude flyers; others had crossed on ice-skiffs or even canid sleds as the floes had closed their grip around the promethium rigs. Each of them bore a barrel of promethium, though some were larger than others – the terms that Deel had laid out to her fellow chiefs were clear enough, but she had not specified the size. The strongest amongst the refugees rolled barrels even larger than the one Markens had carried to the warsphere by way of an example, whereas the children carried barrel-shaped pails that sloshed with half-frozen promethium sludge.

It galled Deel to think that hundreds of riggers had already died in this great exodus – fallen through the ice, perished from exposure in the storms that lashed them every week, or simply frozen to death as their bodies gave up entirely. Yet thousands more had made it to the rendezvous site in time. Great crowds of her people stamped their feet, hugged themselves and stared up at the sky as the warsphere gradually made its way down towards them.

Deel pulled out the auspicator tube she had taken from Thetoid's surveyor nook and focused it on the colossal starship as it grew ever closer. The lower strata of its composite hull was now discoloured with some weird manner of caulk, no doubt an insulating material of some kind intended to protect it from the imminent landing.

On the cusp of hearing Deel could make out the sounds of her people crying out; some in outrage, others in awe, or in sheer grateful disbelief that their arctic nightmare was about to end.

'Ungrateful bastards,' said del Aggio, shivering hard. She had been copiously sick the night before in their shared bunk, and had not had anything positive to say ever since. Deel could not shake the image of white ectoplasm gouting and spraying from between del Aggio's teeth as she tried desperately not to let the psychic energies roiling inside her fly out of control.

'Not all of them,' said Deel. 'And you can bet your last coin that none of them will stay.'

'I'm looking forward to getting back into that stinking nest,' said Markens, blowing into his cupped hands. 'At least it's warm in there.'

The three riggers watched in silence as the warsphere slowly, majestically lowered itself into the ice floes with a grinding bass crunch. Jets flared from dozens of ports on the outside of the dome rings, slowing the descent, but still the landing was anything but elegant. The thing threw tidal waves of freezing water into the air as it bellied down, vast sprays of spume erupting. Clouds of steam wreathed its underside as the heat of its atmospheric entry was counteracted by the ice water.

For a long while, nothing happened. The susurrus of awed whispers amongst the populace began to rise, with some louder voices shouting out in impatience.

Then, just as Deel feared a riot might break out, several massive chunks of metal folded away from the warsphere.

They hinged down, coming to rest upon the larger ice floes in a spray of ice crystals.

'Right then,' said del Aggio.

'Right then,' replied Deel. She cast a look at Markens, and he shrugged.

'Let's get off this icy deathtrap,' he said. 'I for one won't miss it.'

Somehow, Deel knew the big man was lying. But that was all right.

CHAPTER SIXTEEN
CONFRONTATION

Saltire Nearspace
Approaching Kroot Warsphere
The *Executioner's Blade*

A servo-skull drifted into the communal space where the Primaris Marines sat around their mess table, its spinal cord waving like a tentacle.

'Lieutenant Farren,' came Apothecary Vaarad's tinny voice from its augmitter. 'Sergeant Parvell. Brother Gsar. Brother Thrunn. Brother Enrod. Please report to the apothecarium immediately for routine psy-scan.'

Farren took a deep breath, sharing a look with his brothers. Even Enrod cast him a glance, his usual studied indifference replaced by genuine concern. It had not been long since the lieutenant had visited them in their cells and passed on what he had learned from Moricani.

'Here we go, then,' said Thrunn.

'Yes,' said Farren. 'Time for the routine procedure we discussed.'

'Is there no way around this?' asked Parvell.

'Sadly not. We cannot afford to lose that which we worked so hard to gain.'

The lieutenant turned to go, and as one the Primaris Marines filed out behind him. Nothing of their usual surety remained in their step, only a profound unease. To Farren, their expressions were those of condemned men going to the gallows.

'This shouldn't take too long,' said Farren. 'Gsar, you have what we discussed?'

'Aye,' he said, rapping his knuckles on the combat knife under his robe. The amount of anger and disappointment the Repulsor driver managed to convey in that single syllable was impressive.

They followed the servo-skull with its weird, dangling spinal cord for a full fifteen minutes, passing through vaulted corridors and echoing munitions halls as they made their way from one side of the *Executioner's Blade* to the other. Not another word was spoken until they reached the apothecarium.

The smell of counterseptic reached them before the med-suite's caryatid servitors came into view at the end of the corridor. As Farren recalled, there was a small vestibule area off to the side, an area where those who were yet to seek the Apothecary's services were encouraged to wait in meditative contemplation of the procedures to come.

'In here,' he said, motioning for his brothers to go inside. They filed in wordlessly.

The macabre servo-skull drifted in after them, its flickering azure lumen dimly casting a pool of illumination across the floor.

'Procedure imminent,' it buzzed.

'Kindly inform Apothecary Vaarad we are here,' said Farren, 'and relate to him that we are finding a constant bio-rhythm in preparation for his procedure. It is a Primaris-specific ritual. We will be ready for psy-scan in precisely six minutes.'

The servo-skull nodded in mid-air. 'Six minutes. Acknowledged,' it said, turning to slide away with a soft hum of anti-gravitic motors.

'Is that enough to fire it up?' asked Enrod once the apothecarium's door had slid closed behind the floating skull.

'Trust me,' said Farren. 'I am well aware of the timescales here. Gsar, your combat knife please. We need to make this quick, and subtle.'

Gsar unclipped the combat knife – sixteen inches of razored hypersteel so sharp it could saw through an iron stanchion – and flipped it, proffering it hilt-first to the lieutenant.

'No,' said Farren, pushing the blade back towards Gsar. 'We each deliver the wound to another.' He raised his arm and pointed to the dent beneath. 'Through the armpit into the heart. Close it quick, so it has time to clot. By my calculations, that will be easiest to conceal.'

He looked at Enrod, expecting him to call out the plan as madness, or even denounce it altogether as he strode out with not so much as a backwards glance. His battle-brother simply met his gaze, and nodded. Parvell, to his left, crossed his forearms in the Primaris salute.

'Gsar,' said Farren, turning his flank. 'Do it.'

The tank driver lunged.

'Hnnngh!' Farren felt a blinding white pain burst in his mind as the long-bladed dagger sank to the hilt in his armpit. It scraped bone before pricking his primary heart.

Gsar took the dagger out, slicked red from hilt to tip with the lieutenant's blood, and passed it to Thrunn. As the big warrior took it and lined up the point under Gsar's raised arm, Farren could already feel the chemicals pulsing through his bloodstream from his Belisarian furnace. They were pushing his system into overdrive, a rapid response to the blade's intrusion into the meat of his heart.

Thrunn put the heel of his hand against the blade's hilt and pushed it home into Gsar's chest. The tank driver grimaced and breathed quickly in and out, his eyes watering and tendons standing out on his throat as his ribcage was penetrated and his heart was pierced. He shook, as if in revulsion, but he still stood. The combat blade slid out of his torso, then Thrunn passed it to Parvell.

The bald sergeant nodded solemnly as Enrod raised his arm and turned his head away. 'This is a true bond of brotherhood, you realise,' said Parvell as he placed the tip against Enrod's bare flesh. 'This is different from the kin-lines of the Chapter, or even of loyal allegiance to the primarch. This bond is ours, and ours alone.'

Parvell pushed the long knife hard, its impossibly sharp tip slicing through sinew coils and black carapace alike. Enrod stifled a cry, biting his knuckles so hard they bled, but he kept silent, only gasping when the blade came out once more. Then it was Thrunn's turn to have the blade push into his heart, and finally Parvell's, with Farren wielding the knife.

The five Space Marines stood with blood dripping down their flanks. Their chests were heaving as if they had each gone twenty rounds in the practice cages as their Belisarian furnaces pumped a heady mix of stimms around their bloodstreams. Farren could already feel the veins in his arms and thighs pulsing, becoming acutely aware of blood clotting under his arm as the hypercoagulant chemicals of his haemostamen went to work.

'Five minutes,' he said. His jaw clenched involuntarily. 'Clean up any blood splatter before that cog-damned skull comes back. And keep your bio-rhythms from spiking, if you can. Just ride it out.'

The Primaris Marines went to work, each one dabbing at the clot where Gsar's blade had gone into their flesh. So sharp was the combat knife, so resilient their flesh, that the wounds were all but invisible when their arms were lowered, just as Farren had hoped. Yet the operation had not been a precise science; none of them were apothecarium trained. By the blood trickling from his armpit, the combat knife had severed one of Thrunn's major veins.

'Just hold it tight,' said Farren, his vision pulsing slightly in time with his heartbeat as his furnace went to work. 'We only have to get in there.'

Even as he spoke, he knew it was a lie. How did they ever hope to disguise all the blood from a trained Apothecary, especially one as adept as Vaarad, less than a minute away from examining them? Four of the wounds had clotted, but the fifth...

'Six minutes,' came a metallic voice from behind Farren. He spun, almost knocking into the floating skull and spinal column that formed Vaarad's med-familiar. 'The apothecarium is ready to heal you.'

Farren cast a glance back at Thrunn. The big warrior took his hand from his armpit, the rich red of fresh blood still obvious in his palm.

'No choice,' he mouthed.

The five ventured into the apothecarium, Farren at their

PHIL KELLY

head. He could feel his blood thundering in his veins as he saw the berth where Moricani still lay, a dark velvet curtain drawn across it. No doubt he was being kept on the threshold of consciousness until the time was right to use him as a weapon once more.

Apothecary Vaarad was at the far end of the chamber, bent almost double over the corpse of a dead Space Marine. He was suturing closed the hole where the progenoid glands had been; as he finished, he placed a full gene-flask carefully on the desk.

'Back to the Chapter,' he said in his strange rasp, his augmetic jaw glinting as he turned. 'The ultimate fate of us all.'

'Just so.'

'Just so indeed, Lieutenant Farren. Though in the fullness of time you will undergo a similar procedure, today you and your brothers are here for a psy-scan. It is a routine procedure after exposure to an unsanctioned psychic presence. There is nothing untoward about it.'

'I see,' said Farren, fighting to keep his tone level. 'Brothers, to the slabs.'

Wordlessly the Primaris climbed onto the level berths, one in each alcove. Farren felt his pulse thunder all the harder as he saw Thrunn trailing bright spots of blood in his wake.

'You are wounded, Battle-Brother Thrunn,' said Vaarad, kneeling to examine the blood. His servo-skull flew in close, its azure light turning the spilt vitae black.

'My fault,' said Enrod, holding up his knuckles. They were red with blood, flesh peeled back where he had gnawed on them to stifle the pain of their furnace-triggering pact. 'A slight disagreement, settled in the warrior fashion. The others broke it up, but I proved myself to have the more compelling argument.'

Vaarad hissed through his teeth, turning away in disgust to run his hands over a tray of syringes. He selected one, attaching it to the primary manipulator arm of his servo-skull. 'You will keep that temper in check,' he said, his voice passionless as that of a Kataphron battle servitor, 'if you wish to earn your true place in the Dark Angels Chapter.'

'Of course,' said Enrod, his tone contrite. Farren caught his eye; there was something unfamiliar there, under the too-wide stare of one whose furnace burned hot.

Collusion, perhaps.

'A little cortex sedative, now,' said Vaarad, 'administered to prepare you for the psy-scan.'

Vaarad's servo-skull hovered in close to Farren, the syringe glinting in the bluish light of its lumen. He bared his throat, knowing that in doing so he approached the precipice of amnesia. Furnace or not, there was a distinct possibility he would forget everything, waking once more in the hold of the *Night Harrower* with his hands checking his bolt rifle for the hundredth time.

'Just let yourself relax,' buzzed Vaarad as azure light shone brightly into the lieutenant's eyes. 'This will not take long, and then everything will be as it should.'

Inside, the beast caged behind Farren's heart raged wild.

CHAPTER SEVENTEEN
THE BLADE UNSHEATHED

Viewing Dome
The *Liminal Conquest*
Progress-Class Star Cruiser (Slipstream Enabled)
Flagship Of The Fourth Sphere Expansion

Tutor Twiceblade stared balefully at the holovis suite as
his high commander replayed an airborne view of the
events transpiring on the primitive planet far below. The
site was visible as a green smudge on the viewing dome's
voidscape, but it was shown in pinpoint detail on the
subsidiary hex informationals. It looked forbidding, for
a primitive structure, especially swathed in smoke. Upon
entering the system, Commander Surestrike had impressed
upon all of Vre rank or higher that such sites were to be
treated with extreme caution.

At one point, Twiceblade had not known why. What
harm could such a primitive, even feudal government pose
to an advanced civilisation such as that of the t'au? Yet

now, watching the relay unfolding before him, he began to see just what such planets represented.

Anarchy, raw and infectious as a suppurating wound.

The fortress that Surestrike had descended to in his Coldstar was once a formidable defensive position, albeit static, but he had left it little more than a smoking ruin. The high commander had already transloaded his drones' war footage to the fire caste's information web, and Twiceblade had memorised nearly every detail of the recordings, even editing together the relevant sections in a flagrant breach of caste protocol. He and Surestrike had resolved to understand every nuance, just in case they had missed something about the gue'ron'sha and their strange servants.

On the hex informationals, thick black smoke belched from the fortress' towers, its walls, the stairways that led to its subterranean levels. Its courtyard was strewn with the remnants of mutant human bioforms, some ripped apart or mangled so violently they appeared savaged by a pack of great knarlocs. Figures staggered or fled from the tumbled walls and shattered gatehouses of the primitive megastructure for the woods around. Some were cut down by explosive rounds as they fled, others making it to the apparent safety of the treeline.

'Observe this pattern,' said Surestrike.

The display zoomed out, rushing backwards as the drones that assembled the footage took a new vantage point. The fleeing humans were lit with various designators and target locks as they fled. After reaching a mile or so from the site of the carnage, many of them were snuffed out, their designators disappearing. Others were consumed by sudden white fires that blazed bright before their designators turned from silver to red.

'This footage is from the last diurnal rotaa,' said the commander, a note of sadness in his voice. 'We already know the quarantine has not been effective. Those infected by the mind-plague have proven to be… highly unpredictable.'

The footage zoomed out again. Several other structures were on fire within a twenty-mile radius of the first, columns and palls of black smoke trailing westward in the prevailing wind.

'And there is no way of tracking down those elements that have escaped whilst they are still relatively contained?' asked Tutor Twiceblade. 'Surely the earth caste have some manner of delineator.'

Commander Surestrike made the downward gesture of the saddened soul. 'They have nothing we could use.'

'Then the infection will spread,' said Twiceblade. 'We cannot engage and destroy every craft that leaves a gue'ron'sha homeworld without initiating a full-scale war.'

'That is true,' said Surestrike. 'And the gue'ron'sha delegates we spoke with upon the derelict space station already realised that.' The high commander turned, a strange light in his eyes.

'That is why they gave us *this*.'

Surestrike motioned to the artefact held aloft on a cushion of anti-gravitic energies, projected from a hover disc that Tutor Twiceblade could have encompassed with his arms. The human relic was a yellowed skull in a vice of metal. To Twiceblade, the macabre thing seemed blunt and simian, its powerful jaw, wide orbits and a heavy brow the hallmarks of a primitive but effective hunter.

'They believe this can be used to seek out those who are infected,' said Surestrike, 'be they gue'la or gue'ron'sha. Yet they cannot be the ones to do it.'

To Twiceblade, the human skull seemed a vile and ata-vistic thing. Yellowed with immense age and surrounded by a mechanism of primitive pincers and coils, it seemed all the more anachronistic next to the clean, high-tech lines of the hover disc that held it upright. Gaping sock-ets stared up at the tutor, the whole artefact seeming to laugh at him with its maddening rictus grin.

'Is that purely some manner of primal, fetishistic arte-fact,' asked the tutor, 'or does it have an actual use?'

'It may seem too surreal to contemplate, given its lack of technological embellishment,' replied Surestrike. 'But according to the mind-science specialist Dothrael, it will emit a signal of some kind whenever a psyker is close.'

'No doubt it has circuitry laid into the actual bone,' said Twiceblade.

'As you say,' nodded Surestrike sagely. 'Though having seen what we witnessed in the sub-realm, there can be no surety as to what measure of mind-science infects it.'

Twiceblade suppressed a shudder.

'Ultimately, it is largely irrelevant,' continued Surestrike. 'We have not the sanction to use it from an elemental council, nor the tools needed to track down and slay every infected human on a stronghold planet of highly trained elites.'

Nodding absently in agreement, Tutor Twiceblade said nothing. His thoughts had turned to the tale of Com-mander Farsight, as they often did. Farsight, and his darker counterpart.

'I must talk with the aun immediately,' said Surestrike. 'All of those we have left, that is. I have already petitioned for an audience, and they have granted it, for it is no secret that I need their guidance.' He made the gesture of the lost swan before continuing. 'Please feel free to use this viewing dome as your own, tutor, and meditate upon your own course. I shall be taking my saz'nami with me, of course, so you will be without guardianship.'

'I... see,' said Twiceblade, subconsciously making the sign of the dutiful servant. It was an uninspired choice, but it would have to do, for his mind was already racing.

'I know I can trust you to do the right thing for the T'au'va,' said Surestrike, holding Twiceblade's gaze for a long moment.

Then he turned, and walked away through the viewing dome's main portal. His saz'nami bodyguards followed him in a swirl of ceremonial cloaks, leaving Twiceblade alone with the disturbing Imperial artefact.

It stared up at him, grinning as if he was the only fool in the world that did not appreciate the joke.

Tutor Twiceblade felt a chill pass over him as he advanced from the corridor that led from the battlesuit bay into the atrium of Contingency Zone Eight. He had felt on edge for almost a full cycle, ever since his return to the viewing dome where he had spoken to Commander Surestrike and his subsequent... unauthorised requisition of the Imperial artefact. He held it close, wrapped in a thick cloak and cradled under his right arm. The feeling of nervousness he got when he was disobeying orders was reaching fever pitch.

There it was, the stasis cylinder that haunted his dreams, its shape that of a piercing projectile from a black powder age.

A 'bullet', the gue'vesa called it. Even the word sounded compact, aggressive. A final, swift and thoughtless answer that could be made to conclude every possible disagreement.

Twiceblade shook his head. He could not afford to think like that.

Like *him*.

Ghosts of concern flickered through Twiceblade's mind as he approached the cylinder. He had been expressly forbidden by Surestrike to seek out their resident stasis guest, on pain of demotion and instant exile. That in itself told Twiceblade much about the true status of their guest, and about Surestrike's understanding of the Monat.

He could not blame the high commander, however. One could not walk in the light of leadership and the darkness of the singular predator at the same time.

Those who studied the Way of the Lone Soul paid a high price for their learnings. They would never again feel the true companionship of their fellows, the soul-affirming camaraderie between t'au, the reflected light of a team-mate's victory or the deep emotional connection of the ta'lissera.

But in return, they learned of autonomy, independence of spirit, and – though it was never said aloud – a knack for knowing how to circumvent the rules and suppositions of those less enlightened by potential. It was known as the Freedom of One.

Yet here, in this moment, that philosophy felt not so much like freedom, as a trap. It was not the opprobrium or censure of his master Surestrike that blotted Tutor Twiceblade's mind like a spill of cephalopod's ink, threatening to darken and stain everything it touched. It was fear, plain and simple. Fear of the thing in the canister.

Kais, the Living Weapon.

Tutor Twiceblade approached the cylinder as if it were an improvised explosive on a kinetic hair-trigger. He placed the bundle of cloth containing the strange Imperial artefact on the floor with the utmost care, and stood back up. The next part of the ritual was vital, and it had to be observed correctly, or else he risked igniting Kais' temper.

That rage was less obvious, perhaps, than Farsight's famous ire. Twiceblade knew full well the fire inside Commander Farsight, for he had been burned by it more than once; it was exothermic, an honest conflagration that shed light as often as it did destruction. The very name that Twiceblade had given Farsight in the battle domes of his youth – '*Shoh*' – meant 'inner light'. By contrast, the anger of Shadowsun was internalised; it was cool, measured and slow burning, inevitably culminating in meticulous revenge.

The temper he had seen exhibited by Kais was more terrifying still. It was more like the sudden formation of a black hole – an utter absence of motion, a deathly silence, followed by a dramatic burst of killing violence that sucked in everything around it, yet was still somehow immutable law. It was like a metaphysical equation unfolding with the authority of the cosmos behind it, an onyx detonation that annihilated everything even close.

Though he had never admitted it to another living soul, Twiceblade feared it above all else.

'Awaken, Monat-Kais,' he said softly. 'Please. It is the one you know as Tutor Sha'kan'thas.'

The figure's eyes flicked open. The mismatched eyes were hooded, emotionless, like those of a void mantis suddenly aware of nearby prey. Twiceblade felt the familiar sensation of dread blossom within him. He used every iota of his focus to meet that gaze, to swallow the terror inside him so it could not spill out of his mouth.

To show fear now would be as sure a road to ruin as to draw his bonding knife and cut his own throat.

'Tutor,' said Kais, his voice as level and cultured as that of the eldest scholar from the academies of the T'au sept world. 'You come to set me free at last. My thanks.'

'Perhaps,' lied Twiceblade. 'But first, master, we must talk.'

'*Master*,' said the t'au in the stasis cylinder. 'I am still not used to that form of address.'

'I seek your aid.'

'Do you.'

'Much has transpired since we last spoke.'

'Then speak of it.'

'The mind-curse,' said Twiceblade, touching his forehead with all eight fingers. 'It spreads.'

'The planet we orbit has formidable defences.'

'It… it does, yes. It is a homeworld of the gue'ron'sha.'

'And you wish me to destroy it.'

'Not exactly,' said Twiceblade. 'It… it has become infected by the mind-curse. It has affected gue'la and gue'vesa alike, causing spontaneous mutation of the mind as well as the body. We withdrew at Commander Surestrike's command, but I saw many of those infected fleeing from the inception site into the forest.'

'Then you must hunt them down.'

'Surestrike believes that planet is already lost.'

'Likely he is right. Let it die.'

'We cannot, master!' He too felt a strangeness at the shifting of the power dynamic, and tried once more to recall Kais as a young man, but it was like looking at a razored steel blade and trying to see the chunk of ore in its past. All trace of the cadet was gone, and all sense of empathy with it, if it had ever existed at all.

'The greatest likelihood is that the mind-curse will cause other infections,' said Twiceblade. 'Especially if allowed to spread unchecked. If even one of the vectors reaches a gue'ron'sha world and infects the humans there, the toll upon the T'au'va could be intolerable.'

'How can a human mind-curse possibly harm the T'au'va,' said Kais, his expression as still as that of a corpse.

Twiceblade centred himself, recalling the nine meditations before continuing.

'The journey to this part of the galaxy was eventful. Whilst you were in cryostasis, we fell into darkness.'

Kais did not so much as flicker an eyelid. 'Speak on.'

'The earth caste. At the behest of the ethereals, they were tasked with finding a way to cross interstellar distances at a fraction of the traditional speed.'

'They skimmed the sub-realm.'

'No,' said Twiceblade. 'Not as such. The aun wanted more than even that. The debris from the invasion of Dal'yth… amongst it was a large Imperial warp drive. It had certain similarities with the engines of an archived kroot warsphere, harvested long ago without the pech'vesa's knowledge.'

'Wise,' said Kais. 'They are protective of what remains sacred to them, and they are one of very few threats that could tear the sept worlds apart.'

'The ethereals demanded that a new sphere of expansion take place, and within a punishingly narrow timescale. The earth caste obliged, of course. By combining insights from Imperial and kroot warp technology, they created the Slipstream drive.'

'Which is no doubt a miraculous advancement. But not perfect.'

'As I understand it, it harnesses the massive amount of energy resultant from matter and antimatter colliding, and uses it to rip a hole in the fabric of space and time.'

Kais frowned, just a little. 'That is epoch-making technology.'

'It is,' nodded Twiceblade. 'But not for the good of all.'

'You near the heart of the matter,' said Kais, his eyes narrowing. 'I can see it in your eyes.' He leaned forward. Unconsciously, Twiceblade leaned back, his hands forming the half-warding, half-pleading shape of the storyteller-seeking-peace.

'The earth caste staged a demonstration of their new invention,' he continued, 'attaching the Slipstream drive to an XV65 Marlin. A small craft, and nimble. The test was a success. The Marlin slid from one side of sept space to the other in an incredibly short amount of time.'

'The water caste were overjoyed.'

'They were. Every caste was jubilant, master, save that of the earth caste who invented it. Their warnings that it was fit only for small craft fell upon deaf ears.'

'The aun ordered it replicated on a grand scale before it was refined.'

'They did,' said Twiceblade, his own brow furrowing. 'They claimed it was integral to the conquests of the future, and that nothing should stand in its way.'

'And the earth caste did as they were told, despite their misgivings.'

'They did, yes. They had been entrusted with a sacred duty by the aun themselves, and they would not be seen to fail.'

Kais nodded, just once. 'So the ethereals demanded the Slipstream drive be attached to an entire fleet, and a Fourth Sphere Expansion driven deeper into coreward space than any before. This much was inevitable.'

'Perhaps,' admitted Twiceblade, impressed at Kais' insight, 'for they are always seeking ways to increase our influence upon the stars.'

'By your tone, I can tell this grand endeavour ended in disaster.'

'Worse,' said Twiceblade.

Kais closed his eyes, just for a moment, before transfixing Twiceblade once more.

'The Fourth Sphere Expansion was gathered and ready,' said the tutor. 'A greater assemblage of craft has never been seen since Farsight's address outside Gel'bryn City. The ethereals announced its readiness, for each ship – whether t'au or that of an allied race – had been fitted with an upscaled Slipstream device. The *Liminal Conquest*, upon which we now stand, was at the fore.'

'The earth caste were strangely subdued that day, no doubt.'

'They were, master, yes.'

'And yet the launch went as planned.'

'No.'

'Speak of it.'

'As the ethereals gave permission for the fleet to launch, and the Slipstream devices were triggered, something terrible happened.'

'There was a loss of millions of t'au lives,' said Kais. 'And the ethereals maintained that such was the price of progress.'

'Not immediately,' said Twiceblade. 'Space itself seemed to

unravel, the spiral arms of the galaxy shuddering. A purple light burst out wherever the shimmering skies began to buckle and tear. There was a splitting and unfurling of the sky, something like flowers of sickly light blossoming from a slowly splitting gut. The *Mont'yhe'va* had come. The sight caused us all to wail in disbelief and horror – to us, it seemed as if the universe had ripped along its axis.'

'That was how it felt to me, too. I saw visions that day, and not my own.'

'In an instant, we were gone. Something pulled us through that rift – perhaps the fact of its very opening. I saw only lights, crashing past in their thousands. To those of the septs viewing the phenomenon it must have seemed as if the rift yanked us into its gullet like a Dal'ythan cetacean drawing in a shoal of shellmites.'

'And the ethereals did nothing.'

'They had no idea whether that was the anticipated result,' said Twiceblade, his tone aggrieved. 'High Commander Surestrike, given leadership at Shadowsun's explicit recommendation, told us to simply hold to the same heading and let the Slipstream device do the work. So that was what we did.'

'And continued to do, until people began to die.'

Twiceblade let his head hang. There was a part of him that railed at Kais' extrapolations and comments, at his interpretations of their actions before he had been informed of them, for they were never flattering. Yet they were all correct. There was another part of the tutor's soul that agreed with him, that felt the same sense of disillusionment at the course they had been forced to take.

'The first to die were the mercenaries,' he said softly.

'That is usually the case.'

'We were caught in there for whole Kai'rotaa,' said Twice-blade. 'It was almost impossible not to look out of the viewscreens at... whatever it was that roiled outside. It was hypnotic. If it was the empyrean spoken of by our gue'vesa contacts, it was deeper than we ever suspected. We had only skimmed the surface of that great ocean before, but now, with the Slipstream... We were in its depths, and with no cartography to guide us out.'

'How chilling,' said Kais.

'More than you know,' said Twiceblade, feeling a cold sense of injustice flow over him. 'They did not come for us, not for the pure t'au ships. No,' he said, a deranged smile spreading on his face. 'They had other prey in mind.'

'Who had prey in mind?' said Kais. His eyes narrowed to slits, one black, one purple. 'What were these predators?'

'To this day, I have no idea. But they came from the nothingness, circling the convoy ships in their millions. They had no real form.'

'Yet you saw them.'

'Only when I did not look directly at them. They were more like wisps of nothingness, drawn into approxima-tions of the t'aunoid physique. Some had wings, some had tentacles. Some had elongated heads, or horns, or serried ranks of teeth, or split stomachs, or looked like gue'ron'sha with helms like flaming skulls, or wielded blades that looked like slivers cut from the void... they were so strange that earth caste mind-helper teams came for those who looked upon them too long.'

'And one day, they attacked, for their *kauyon* was complete.'

'It was. But they did not attack the *Conquest*.'

'This I know.'

'They went for the mercenary warships, master. We saw

them flock around the lineships of the greet, the winged discs of the ostense council, the cruisers and cutters of the humans, the warspheres of the kroot. Around the dhows of the nicassar, they massed as thick as a swarm of alkali-gnats.'

'Did you intervene?'

'When we had a clear shot we took it. It proved no more effective than firing an arrow into the crashing sea.'

'How did they survive, these creatures, in the void of this sub-realm?'

'I have no idea,' said Twiceblade. 'I can only assume they had some manner of bio-tech in their blood. But the same could not be said of their victims. They ripped open the craft of our allies, physically carving them apart with blades, axes, their bare hands, even their mouths. It was... distressing in the extreme.'

Kais seemed entirely unmoved, but Twiceblade was caught in the telling of the story, reliving it with a desperate intensity.

'As the rotaa clicked by, they feasted. All those who acted as honour demanded, those who took their vessels or even their Coldstar battlesuits into that swirling sea, were soon taken. There was nothing we could do but watch as our allies were slowly torn apart.'

'There was nothing you could do.'

'No,' said Twiceblade coldly. 'And I for one am glad that some of us survived, to witness that which was to come.'

'And what manner of fate was that?'

'We were becalmed,' said the tutor. 'No chance of escape.' He drew a finger around the palm of his hand, making the swirling gesture of the whirlpool inescapable. 'We had been sucked into the dark heart of that sub-realm, where even the currents themselves are devoured. Then, as the decs slid by, we began to hear a scraping noise.'

'On the outside of the hulls.'

'Yes. It was interminable. The bridges of each of our ships showed the same thing – no forward movement. No momentum of any kind. The things out there were laughing.' Twiceblade shuddered at the memory. 'The swirling faces, the creatures scrabbling at the hull… they were laughing at us. Of that I am sure.'

'Taunting you, as a poorly disciplined hunter does his cornered prey.'

'Yes.'

'And in doing so, they allowed you to escape.'

'To this day I am not sure how.'

'Describe it.' Kais' eyes were narrow once more, hungry for data. The tutor had seen that same expression the very first day the Monat's tutelage had begun.

'It is almost impossible to describe it,' said Twiceblade carefully. 'There was something out there amongst the swirling nebulae, something vast. More of an impression of a sentience than an actual creature.'

'Larger than these beasts attacking the craft.'

'Immeasurably so. It had… many arms, I think. Some of those were made to nurture, or to provide, others to destroy. In physique it was familiar to us, for it was built much like a member of the aun.' He paused, lost in the memory, and his shio'he wrinkled. 'Though in retrospect it was bulkier, and many of its hands had five digits. As if the notion of human beauty had mingled with the optimal form of the t'au.'

'And did this hallucination speak?'

'It did not. It had no face, only a blank and impassive

mask. It was somehow familiar to me, reassuring even, yet it was repugnant at the same time. And I can assure you it was no mirage.'

'Really.'

'Every member of every vessel saw the same thing, though as with all the forms in the sub-realm, it could not be recorded.'

'So there is no proof that it occurred. There is such a thing as collective hallucination.'

'Perhaps,' said Twiceblade. 'But this… entity was our saviour. It looked down upon us. I felt something of good in it. Some twisted form of altruism, or communality, perhaps.'

'And yet your voice trembles to speak of it,' said Kais.

'I found it strangely calming to behold, master, But I also felt its hunger to grow, to spread its many limbs from the tip of one of the galaxy's spiral arm to the other. To remake everything in its own image. I remember feeling that, and then feeling like it peered directly into my soul.'

Kais scowled, and Twiceblade felt a far more real, immediate fear rise up within him.

He took a deep breath before continuing.

'Just when I thought I would ignite from the inside, it reached out with its many limbs, and ripped a hole in the swirling nebulae that had becalmed us.'

'It tore a hole in the sub-realm itself,' said Kais.

'Yes. But not like the rift that had opened before us to swallow the Fourth Sphere Expansion. It was more like a tunnel. The thing reached through it, then seemed to fade away. The tunnel swirled before us, drawing us in – at first, with almost imperceptible slowness, but as we neared the hole, it drew us in at great acceleration.'

'An anomaly within an anomaly,' said Kais, his face emotionless. 'To get out, you had to go further in.'

'Exactly,' said Twiceblade, making the hands-wrapping sign of the quandary within the enigma. 'We had little choice. But we angled our craft towards it as best we could, and rode the forces drawing us in. We heard something, then. A chorus of howls, of shrieks, as if the creatures that clung to the exterior of our ships were in terrible pain.'

'How pleasing.'

'Even those took their toll,' said the tutor heavily. His hand made a cutting motion before he could stop it, an old tutor's sign of displeasure at an inappropriate line of enquiry.

Kais' lips curled, just a little, to show a sliver of perfect white teeth. Twiceblade felt something at the base of his stomachs twitch at the sight.

'Continue,' said the Monat.

'The funnel that drew us in,' said Twiceblade, 'it was painful even to look at on the *Conquest*'s viewing bays. Its walls were spiralling vortices of colour, of screaming faces, of the constellations and the spiral swirl of the galaxy all mixed into one twisting tube. It felt as if we had been in there for entire kai'rotaa by the time it finally spat us out, but the data suites insisted only a few decs had passed by the time we re-entered mundane space.'

'And your ships were intact.'

'Largely,' agreed Twiceblade. 'Though most of the t'au inside them bear some kind of mental wound at the experience. Sleep is rare amongst those of the Fourth Sphere, of that I have proof. I still see that sub-realm every dark cycle, when I close my eyes to meditate, and that entity looming within it.'

'You have a theory as to what that creature was,' said Kais, 'and you abhor the conclusion you reached.'

'I do,' said Twiceblade. 'It is the reason no gue'vesa can be allowed to live. Nor can any allied race of the t'au, come to that.'

Kais raised one bald eyebrow, just a fraction. 'That is not what I expected to hear.'

'I have studied the works of Commander Farsight in the past. As his original mentor, it has always pleased me to see where his conclusions lead him. There are hints, in those writings, and messages between the lines. Hints as to another type of creature abroad in the galaxy that is not flesh and blood.'

'Ghosts,' said Kais. 'Kauyon-Shas, the one you know as Shadowsun, was always over-fond of them.'

'No,' said Twiceblade. 'Not the spirits of the dead. Something else. Some kind of echo animus given life, given form.'

'You believe that such a thing is possible then,' said Kais. 'You believe that this entity is… an echo of t'au souls.'

'Not as such.'

There was a sharp intake of breath audible through the communion relay.

'Then you think that entity to be a coalescence of t'au belief.'

Twiceblade shook his head. 'No, master, I do not. That entity was not the culmination of the wholesome beliefs of our kind, as strong as that force may be. Neither is it the avatar of the T'au'va, as some have suggested. I believe that it is instead a corruption of the Greater Good. A twisted reflection.'

'How can that be?'

'The other races that were with us,' said Twiceblade. 'They were preyed upon by the creatures in the sub-realm far earlier than us. They must have been seen as more desirable prey.'

'Because their souls were louder, brasher. Because they could not pass by unseen.'

'That was my conclusion, too,' said Twiceblade. 'They are of that realm, or connected to it, somehow. The echoes in the sub-realm... they are the reflections of those races that possess mind-science. That which exists in two dimensions at once. This is what Commander Farsight speaks of in his reminiscences, infers between the lines of those texts forbidden by the aun.'

'The entity you witnessed. It was a human god.'

'In a way,' said Twiceblade. 'That entity was the gue'vesa's conception of our faith, given strength by the other psychic races that believe in the same tenets.'

'We have no god!' spat Kais, his lips curling back.

'We do not, and rightly so,' said Twiceblade. He was shaking, but he had come too far to go back now. 'But to them, even a philosophy can be worshipped. To them, the line between faith in concept and faith in a divine being is thin. Perhaps even non-existent.'

'They have created a false god,' said Kais. His eyes were wide, his veins standing out as if he were trapped in hard vacuum. 'The mind-science races have created a god in the image of the T'au'va.'

'They did not do so intentionally,' said Twiceblade. 'It is testament to the water caste they believe so strongly in our ideals. Truly believe. And that entity saved the Fourth Sphere Expansion, or what was left of it. Perhaps, if our teachings had not been so convincing, the entity would not have had the strength to open the wormhole. The tunnel through which we passed from one side of the galaxy to the other, and ultimately, founded the Nem'yar Atoll.'

'It matters not,' said Kais. 'This cannot be borne.'

'I agree. They must die, every one of them, before they corrupt the ideals of our kind still further. Those who gave rise to this alien conception must be destroyed.'

'That is why we attacked the gue'vesa ocean world.'

'It is,' said Twiceblade.

'Word of this cannot reach sept space,' said Kais. 'We would make enemies of our allies as well as our foes. We would be disavowed, and exiled, much like Mont'ka-Shoh.'

'Almost certainly.'

'The aun have their own conclusions. The views of the fire caste upon matters supernatural would not be welcome.'

'It would not.'

'Then we of the Fourth Sphere must eradicate all alien auxiliaries. Anything with the least presence in the sub-realm must die. It is the only way the T'au'va will remain pure.'

'I share the same views, as does High Commander Surestrike.'

'But we must do so without the septs having knowledge of our agenda.'

'We have been making extensive use of stealth tech thus far,' said Twiceblade. 'We show ourselves only when absolutely necessary, and we act through agents wherever possible. We must have plausible deniability if challenged by the aun of sept space.'

'Agents,' said Kais. 'You intend to stoke the Imperium's wrath. To turn it against those that have strayed from its tenets.'

'That work has already begun. We have contacts in an elite force of gue'ron'sha known as the Dark Angels. They are to finish what we started.'

'And they asked something of us in return.'

'They asked that we exterminate that which they cannot be seen to engage. They have a similar quandary, in that their overseers cannot learn of the destruction they intend to unleash upon their own kind. Their fragile notions of brotherhood and sanctity could not sustain it.'

'And the site we are to decontaminate is one that is badly infected by the mind-curse.'

'This much is true, perceptive one,' nodded Twiceblade.

'Thinking is all I have done for the last eight lifespans,' said Kais. 'I wish to put my Monat theory into practice. I am well versed in operating on the fringes of a war effort to achieve its true goal. I will hunt and eradicate those who bear the mind-curse. This I promise you.'

Kais leaned forward in his claustrophobic confines. 'But first you must let me free.'

Twiceblade nodded. 'Yes,' he said, tapping the authorisation codes he had obtained from his earth caste contact into the cryostasis cylinder's control pattern. 'I believe I must. And I bring you a gift for just that purpose.' He held up the cloth-wrapped skull with both hands in the gesture of the guest's gift.

The cylinder began to hum, low and ominous. A light-bar that covered half its height slid from charcoal, through gunmetal, iron and steel. Tutor Twiceblade felt his pulse race as it moved through copper, then bronze, then silver, and finally gold.

There was a bright chime, and a soft hiss of equalising pressure as the door swung ajar by the tiniest amount.

Kais flew out of the stasis chamber like a starving ghoul, his face a mask of rage. He balled a fist and slammed it hard into Twiceblade's throat. The tutor's world exploded into pain mingled with primal terror. He went down onto his rear, struggling away in utter shock as he desperately tried to draw breath.

'If I had meant to kill you, you would already be dead,' said Kais, suddenly calm as a mountain lake as he sat on his haunches. 'That blow will merely render you silent for a moment, for I have grown tired of your voice. In less than a minute your windpipe will open and you will be able to breathe once more.'

Twiceblade stared up, goggle-eyed and too frightened to move.

The Living Weapon stooped, picking up the strange cloth bundle that had been placed to the side of the cryostasis cylinder. Twiceblade saw thin wisps of condensation rise from the naked warrior's hide. To the tutor his lean, cabled frame looked not like that of a healthy t'au, but more like a weapon in a t'aunoid form – a weapon forged in the distant past and ready to be quenched in the blood of the present day.

Kais unwrapped the cloth-shrouded artefact deftly, taking out the vice-framed skull inside. He frowned slightly, examining the apparatus as if it was a weapon for which he could not find the trigger.

'This is something I did not foresee,' he said flatly. He looked down to Tutor Twiceblade as he struggled to his knees. 'It appears I must tolerate your voice a little longer if I wish to learn its function.'

Twiceblade nodded, making the slowly pushing hands of the worthy lesson yet to be imparted. Then he held up a finger and thumb, the sign for a microdec's indulgence.

Kais sighed through his nose. As he waited, he ripped a long strip from the cloak that had encased the skull and twisted it tightly before tying it into a knotted garrotte. Satisfied with his handiwork, he wrapped the rest of the cloth around his groin to form a loincloth reminiscent of those worn by first documented hunter-tribes of the Fio'taun Plateau, and tucked the garrotte in its folded-over waistband.

'I have paved the way for you, master,' croaked Twiceblade.

Kais raised an eyebrow, his body canting forwards to radiate threat.

'That device,' said Twiceblade, his voice as strangled and thin as if he had travelled a desert for days. 'The Imperials called it a *psyoccule*. It triggers whenever one possessed of mind-science ability is close.'

'Useful,' said Kais, nodding. 'Especially given the perversion of the T'au'va you spoke of.'

'These gue'ron'sha were Imperial shas'vre equivalents,' he wheezed. 'Maybe even shas'o. They admit to their own incompetence, and wish us to exterminate those they cannot catch.'

Kais nodded again. 'That is acceptable.'

'I have ensured you have the tools. The corridor at the far end,' said Twiceblade. 'It leads to the battlesuit hangars.'

Kais made to move off, his economy of motion that of a dancer, or an assassin.

'Wait,' said Twiceblade.

The Living Weapon turned back.

'There is one battlesuit in there that you will find open, and initiated with my own leadership signature. It is a model that I feel you will appreciate. A far more powerful extension of the stealth suit you once used.'

'An XV95,' said Kais.

'Yes,' replied Twiceblade. 'How did you... how do you know of it? It did not exist at the time of your stasis interment.'

'The prototypical specifications of the Ghostkeel were remotely downloaded to my chamber's edification suite eighteen hundred and six point nine rotaa ago.'

Twiceblade frowned, suddenly feeling adrift once more. 'What? That is whole generations ago. Before the Ghosts of N'dras were even revealed to the septs.'

'Nonetheless. They were uploaded by one using a Fio'O ident dating back to the beginning of the Second Sphere Expansion. I have made myself more than familiar with the battlesuit's capabilities, and that of its drones. Is there a designated vector ship assigned to it?'

'There is,' said Twiceblade. 'An Orca, authorised with my own command signature. It has an automated *y'eldi* helper-program supplied by an air caste contact of mine. You need only mention the destination, and it will bear you there.'

Kais cocked his head, reminding Twiceblade of a raptor sizing up its prey. 'Why are you doing this?'

'For the Greater Good,' said Twiceblade. 'Of course.'

Kais made the sign of the T'au'va. Somehow, it had never seemed so terrifying.

Twiceblade swallowed. 'I will be observing from an inverse telepresence suite via one of the XV95's stealth suit drones.'

Kais narrowed his eyes, his top lip curling back.

'All I ask is to watch and learn,' he said. 'I will not interfere.'

'If you do, it will cost you your life,' said Kais, something in his voice as cold as a winter grave. 'It may even cost mine.'

Twiceblade nodded. 'Understood.'

Kais turned on his heel and left without another word.

Telling when the Living Weapon had left was difficult, for he made no sound as he moved, but Twiceblade had patience to spare. After a stretch of two full decs he finally rose to his feet. Two decs later he left the munitions bay, holding on to the rail inside the hex-lift as if it were part of a life raft in a stormy sea.

He glimpsed, just before the hex-lift door closed, an oval panel on the far side of the hangar slowly sliding back into place. There was a figure inside, slender and elegant. Then the doors closed, and the vision was gone.

CHAPTER EIGHTEEN
TO STRIKE AS ONE

Duskenwald, Near Soul's Well
Allhallow, Scorpid Cluster

The survivors sat huddled around a meagre campfire, passing around the remnants of a flagon of sour wine. Around them, beyond the mouth of the cavern in which they had sought shelter, the woods pressed in. They were composed of thick, ancient needle trees that were in some cases over five centuries old. Though widely spaced, their branches formed a canopy of entwined branches so thick they all but blotted out the harvest moon glowering down from above.

All three of the ragged figures around the fire were hunched over and heavy-lidded, every one of them a grotesque, mutated in some manner or other.

Fenas knew he was the worst. He reached up a gangling arm that was more tentacle than human limb and banged a flat hand against his ear, trying to somehow dislodge the tinnitus rising within it. Every day, a new trial. It was bad enough he was an eleven-foot freak with bulging, misshapen limbs. Going deaf was just adding insult to injury.

'Pass me that wine, Harasen,' he said. 'On your left. Sooner I can drink myself to death, the better.'

'I know where you are, boy,' said the flabby, pale-skinned man to his right. 'I'm blind, not stupid.' He turned his ravaged, empty sockets on Fenas and bared his teeth, but held out the flagon nonetheless.

'I should get the most of that swill,' said the third of their sorry group. 'It was I that liberated it.' Jethren had escaped from the Absolvers' fortress, way up north, whilst they had been preoccupied with the outbreak ravaging the inner corridors of their sacred stronghold.

'You and your vassal chief there,' said Fenas, nodding over at the decapitated head at Jethren's feet. Horseflies were fussing around its orifices, seeking a convenient place to lay their eggs. Jethren shooed them away. 'Old Fiorenz here was helpful enough, after a bit of persuasion,' he grinned nastily, 'and I needed his eyes, as it were. But he doesn't get any of the good stuff. He's given me nightmares enough without seeing wine dribble out of his tubes.'

'At least you don't have the memories of those skulls to get rid of,' said Fenas. 'I can't sleep for seeing my one, staring at me. Worse than you, even, Harasen.'

The eyeless man just nodded. 'Just be glad they chose someone else to latch onto,' he said. He too was fiddling with his ear, sticking his little finger deep in there and wiggling it around. Fenas sympathised. It was hard to hear even the crackle and snap of the fire with the ringing noise growing steadily more intense.

'I suppose… I suppose whatever ghosts lingered inside them gave us up as bad prospects,' said Fenas. 'No keep nor castle on Allhallow will let in the likes of us, not nowhere. Especially not after those rumours of aliens, and new lights in the sky not two days ago. I tell you, those weren't Imperial.'

'I'm all right with that,' said Jethren, gesturing at the badly skinned crawhog they had roasting on a spit over their meagre fire. 'Keep our heads down and let the demigods sort it out. I can live off the land well enough.'

'Can you eat it without it falling out your belly?' asked Harasen, gesturing vaguely in the direction of Jethren's gaping stomach wound.

Fenas couldn't help but look. The gash still hadn't healed so much as solidified, and even over the course of their short acquaintance it had turned into something vaguely resembling a mouth. The sight turned Fenas' own guts. Thick goop and clear liquid alike drooled out of the jagged, pink teeth that lined the vassal guard's torn-open abdomen.

'What are you babbling about now?' asked Jethren. 'Can't hear a damn thing for some reason.'

Then, right in front of Fenas' eyes, Jethren disappeared from the waist up in a cloud of pink mist.

'What in the–'

Harasen leaped up, scrabbling at his blunt halberd. Then he too seemed to vanish, his entire right side disappearing to leave only a tapering wedge with one arm flailing uselessly. It toppled into the fire, the thick stink of burning human fat reaching up into Fenas' nostrils.

'Go on, then!' shouted Fenas into the woods. 'Get it over with!'

He saw something, then, out of the very corner of his eye. It was a technological monster of some sort, a shimmering blur in the moonlight near twenty feet tall. Its outline looked more like one of the legendary Dreadnoughts of Allhallow than one of the Space Marines he had been expecting. Disc-like distortions rippled in the air behind its broad shoulders.

Fenas felt his diaphragm convulse, and he heaved a great stream of psychic ooze, the projectile vomit splashing across the trees on the west side of the fire. His eyes watered, but he strained to see what had become of the monster nonetheless. He could not make it out. All that filled his head was that damnable ringing.

Then he felt something behind him. He turned around, ectoplasm dribbling from between his teeth, and snarled.

Fenas the Brave died on his feet.

Kais scanned the skies with one eye whilst the other zoomed in on the part of the clearing where the trees thinned. Independent focus was a trick he had learned lifetimes ago, and it had improved his kill ratio ever since.

Briefly he recalled a young Kauyon-Shas teaching the technique to him on the slopes of Mount Kan'ji, with Mont'ka-Shoh sitting cross-legged in the dappled sunlight nearby. It was strange to think they had gone on to become the legendary commanders Shadowsun and Farsight. Mont'ka-Shoh had chuckled at Kais' discomfiture as their team-mate had dropped two leaves in front of him that spiralled in different directions, then demanded he follow both of them at once.

He banished the memory, fixating instead on the readouts spooling across the interior control suite of his XV95

Ghostkeel. It was a lethal machine indeed, and he had plans for it. But it was yet to fully prove its worth.

In the darkness of the trees, picked out by the spectrographic overlay of his target lock, was the mouth of a large cavern. It was hidden by a thick drape of moss and bracken that had grown over a curtain of roots from the largest trees overhead. To a common warrior, it would have seemed much like any other part of the forest, but Kais had noticed its hidden potential immediately.

There was water seeping from within it, making the ground boggy in places before spreading out into a dozen trickling rivulets that led further into the woods.

On the Ghostkeel's screens the space behind the curtain of vines and roots registered cold blue and black, implying a great depth amongst the ambers and duns of its surroundings. Kais noticed something else as his eyes flicked left and right. He zoomed in on the stem of a fern a hundred feet away. It was broken, albeit only a little, with the fronds now facing away from the root curtain. One of the gue'la had emerged from inside; some two rotaa ago given the hardened state of the sap that had leaked from the broken stem.

It had to be the human with the strange stomach wound, thought Kais – one of his companions was too tall and ungainly to exit without causing much more damage to the flora, and the other, having no eyes, would likely have been even clumsier.

Kais triggered one of the sensor orbs in the Ghostkeel's head to pan across to the relevant corpse. The guard wore the tattered remains of a heraldic uniform, its colours and iconography mapping as a variant of an archived gue'ron'sha cadre.

Another sensor orb slid, like the eye of some arachnid hunter, to the massive mountain citadel that reached up over the treeline to shimmer on the far horizon.

The gue'ron'sha stronghold.

The Ghostkeel stalked over to the curtain of roots, the two vaned discs of its X5 Stealth drones hovering close behind it. Calling up his echo location suite with a deft flick of his pupil, Kais sent a hypersonic pulse into the darkness.

A heartbeat after the echoes had returned, a glowing blue sonographic map of the tunnel network appeared on the Ghostkeel's destination hexscreen. Every crack and fissure emanated from a wide arterial passageway leading into the depths of the mountain.

Narrowing his eyes, Kais pushed through into the darkness beyond.

Almost an entire nocturnal cycle had passed before Kais reached the first true line of resistance. They had been sentry guns, of a sort, hidden in darkened fissures and cracks with tiny laser optics on a hair-trigger alert. He had pursed his lips in impatience as his battlesuit located and automatically target-locked, knowing even that measure was unnecessary.

Kais had outwitted point defence drones on the first day of his training under Tutor Sha'kan'thas, when he was but four years old. Now, with the XV95 at his command, even the most advanced Imperial drone was an insult to his capabilities. He had walked past them without breaking stride, the full-spectrum countermeasures of the giant battlesuit baffling the sentry guns to such an extent they perceived nothing more than a sliver of glitching confusion. To all but the most advanced machines, the Ghostkeel was a phantasm in the wind.

The second trial had taken the form of a vast chasm, water spattering down from a thin tunnel above it. Had he left his battlesuit, he might have climbed upwards, following the trickle of water vertically until it led to another river. But Kais would not leave a weapon like the XV95 behind, not if there was another way. Firing up his jump jets, he bounded across that thirty-foot wide fissure with no more effort than a kroot hound leaping over a puddle.

On the other side, Kais had followed the channel that cascaded as a set of miniature waterfalls through the pitch-black tunnels until it became a rivulet, then a stream.

Now he found himself at an underground river. The source was a wide subterranean lake, with murky water dripping into it from the stalactites high above. On impulse, he opened his olfactory relay and breathed in the cool, damp air of the cave. He savoured it like a fine elixir. It had been so long since he had been able to truly appreciate a natural environment, it was all he could do not to open the Ghostkeel's plexus hatch and drink it all in in person.

Amongst the stalactites was something that looked like a cyclopean well of ancient, chisel-dressed stone, but inverted, built into the ceiling by primitive human masons. Light spilled from within. Kais smiled coldly and initiated the Ghostkeel's jet pack, proximity-locking his stealth drones to follow his exact trajectory. He manoeuvred the XV95 to ascend through the inverse well, taking care not to so much as scratch its chameleonic alloy as he went. Moments later he was rising to the top, the drones beneath him.

He rose into a wide octagonal chamber at the top of the giant well. Seven of the walls had alcoves, each holding a statue of some hooded gue'la saint. The eighth had a vast vault door. A cursory scan revealed that it was slab-locked, a retinal recognition scanner built into the eye of a bare skull the intended method of unlocking it.

Kais was quite used to the Imperium's displays of disrespect to their ancestors, but had no wish to engage with human remains. He simply raised his fusion collider and melted away the vault door's slab-locks – adamantium cores, dressed stone and all. Molten goop bubbled down the side of the door. Kais sent a tight beam electromagnetic pulse from his sensor-arm, and the entire edifice hinged slowly open to reveal the corridors beyond.

Kais was glad to see there was room enough for the Ghostkeel to traverse the passageways beyond. The Imperials were so fond of their own warsuit equivalents – the squat and slow machines they called Dreadnoughts – that the lower levels of their principal fortifications were built to house them. He sent an echo-pulse to see if there was anything to kill close by, and when it came back negative, pushed further in with his bafflers at maximum saturation.

After half an hour of prowling the corridors, the so-called 'psyoccule' skull artefact that Tutor Twiceblade had given him – and that was sharing the Ghostkeel's cockpit – began to shudder of its own accord once more. Its lower jaw rattled unsettlingly in the wire apparatus that held it upright. After staring at it for a moment Kais turned the Ghostkeel this way and that, listening for the skull's shivering to grow more intense, as it did when it was facing the direction of the nearest psychic presence. The psyoccule seemed more agitated than ever when he faced east.

So east he went. He bypassed dull-eyed, slack jawed servitors with their limbs entirely replaced by crude heavy weaponry, stalking past them without eliciting so much as a blink. When he entered a corridor network with a pair of gue'la chattel on patrol, the first thing they knew of his presence was a tight beam from his dual fusion blasters. The weapon systems gave no more than a faint hiss as they vaporised the humans' disgusting, hairy bodies.

Now, as the skull shook with manic intensity, he could feel an imminent danger tingling behind his eyes.

The heart of the gue'ron'sha keep was not far away.

The iron-bound skull's teeth clacked together with horrible animus. Suddenly, a nonsensically strong smell clung to it, somehow, filling the control cocoon of the XV95 with the scent of brine. Kais paid it no mind. Let Shadowsun obsess over spectres and phantasms, he thought. It was not his way. As the Ghostkeel padded forwards with the smooth gait of a stalking lion, the Monat commander focused instead on the stone archways and alcoves of the corridor ahead.

The prey was close.

There was the unmistakeable sound of heavily armoured feet marching into the atrium up ahead. Kais pinged another hypersonic pulse, his XV95's echo-location software building the architecture ahead in impressive detail. He bounced a spread of high-density data harvesting pulses towards the figures in the middle, refining his picture of their disposition. The atrium was a choke point and a crossroads all at once, and according to his readings, a team of five gue'ron'sha had chosen it as their place to die.

Kais thought through the coming engagement's problems one after another, the optimum solutions unfurling from the stasis of his memory without so much as a frown of concentration.

Subjects: five gue'ron'sha with mass reactive ballistics, all aware.

First data point: one obvious point of egress, covered.

Second data point: targets in heavy powered armour.

Third data point: mind-science evident according to foreign sensor reading.

One bio-reading implication: centremost not wearing helm.

Hypothesis: target with missing helm likely to be psychic threat.

Kais blinked, just once. A very close analogue was the kill pattern he had designated Mono-Imperial Scenario 2934/E during his cryostasis – it was one he considered challenging, but by no means lethal. He swung the Ghostkeel into the recess of a vaulting alcove and prepared his strike with a series of darting eye movements.

The skull chattered loud, as if beside itself with excitement at the prospect of the kill.

Solution one, thought Kais. He sent in a volley of blind-pulse flechettes that whipped around the corner. The gue'ron'sha cried out in alarm, opening fire.

The flechettes burst in a multi-spectral explosion of light and sound. Imperials could almost always be relied upon to have hair-trigger fingers, and this group was no exception. His control cocoon's autotrans spooled their leader's words.

'– – BROTHERS – IT IS AMONGST US – –'

Solution two. The Monat swung round the corner of the alcove, data blossoming on his target lock as the white-armoured Space Marines reeled from the debilitating burst. The nearest two gue'ron'sha were all but obliterated in a silent storm of energy. The clattering of their disembodied limbs upon the flagstones was the only sound to mark his fusion collider's wrath.

Solution three. One of the targets started to shake, white energy pouring from his eyes and mouth as it rose off the ground. It was shouting in its guttural tongue.

'– – IT MUST DIE – –'

Hypothesis proven, thought Kais. He was already airborne, his boosters hissing as he leaped into the vaulted ceiling of the atrium. He pivoted mid-jump, stabbing the icon of his left-hand drone to decloak its stealth field and suddenly reveal itself amongst the Space Marines.

One of them cried out a warning, shooting from the hip; Kais swerved, and the high-calibre bolts ricocheted from the curve of his armour. The other raised his firearm and added his own volley. Two shots hit Kais in the hip, exploding to knock him back.

The Ghostkeel sent a ballistics report blossoming upon his damage control suite. Kais scanned it with one eye as he blink-triggered the fusion collider with the other, blasting the nearest Space Marine to red ruin just as the XV95 reached the apex of its leap. The other Space Marine twisted away with surprising speed, priming a grenade and hurling it at him.

Kais flicked his eyes to designate two targets at once. One of the twin fusion blasters mounted on the battlesuit's shoulders took out the grenade in mid-air. The other turned the gue'ron'sha warrior to a burning stump and a dissipating red mist a fraction of a microdec later.

The psyker, unsteady on his feet as white effluvium

poured from his eyes, nose and ears, screamed in two voices at once. The sound would have been unsettling to a normal t'au, Kais thought, but for him it was an invitation for the kill. He dropped down and stamped one of his suit's hoof-like feet into the gue'ron'sha's unprotected skull, crushing it like an egg.

The close quarters attack was an indulgence with all his weapons systems still registering in gold, and Kais knew it. But then he had been incarcerated for the most part of three hundred t'au'cyr. He could afford to relish his work a little. If he was honest with himself, every killing movement was as close to joy as Kais had ever felt.

The next likely site of organised resistance, according to Kais' preliminary echo-location, was a long hall that appeared empty of targets. He scanned it nonetheless, and sent a drone ahead on optimum stealth recon.

His command suite built up a comprehensive picture. Ending in a broad set of stairs that curved upwards, the hall had walls of glass as much as rock, each gleaming barrier covering one of eight alcoves. These each had a faceted glass façade wrought with lead lining, the patterns and figures they depicted presumably intended as a primitive form of art. Above the alcoves were lance-like protrusions hung with long cloth banners, much like those that once fluttered from the fortresses of the Fio'taun. The zone had all the trappings of a feast hall; all that was missing was a long table made from some species of hard flora.

How these gue'ron'sha liked to venerate their inglorious past.

Kais was cautiously pushing his Ghostkeel inside when an energy readout spiked hard on his emission reader.

The Monat's brow creased. The pattern was an unknown form to him, and he did not like that at all.

Leaning back hard in his control cocoon, Kais boosted away just as a blaze of azure energy erupted in the centre of the grand hall. A pair of missiles shot through the air where he had been standing a heartbeat before, tearing a chunk from the doorway arch. Almost simultaneously a storm of mass-reactive bolts hurtled in, many less than two feet from his carapace hood.

Eight warriors materialised out of nowhere. The strange teleport technology of the Imperium, the envy of the earth caste, phased them into the hall in a crackling dome of lightning.

The psyoccule shivered its teeth, indicating another psychic presence. Kais had already taken stock of his situation by the time he had twisted his Ghostkeel back into the corridor, sliding it out of sight with an impressive grace for something of the XV95's hulking size.

They were heavily armed, these ones, and far larger than the previous targets. Two had bulky missile arrays upon their shoulders, whilst two more had rotary cannons slung under their right arms. Kais saw them as lesser reflections of the mighty Broadside; they were not a lethal threat to a cutting edge XV95 at a distance. At close quarters, if they brought the crackling powered gauntlets on their left flanks to bear, that assessment would soon change.

Subjects: eight gue'ron'sha with explosive ballistics, four heavy, all aware.

First data point: one obvious point of egress, covered.

Second: targets in Broadside-equivalent armour, melee adapted.

Third: walls adorned with primitive weaponry.

Fourth: mind-science residue detected. No specialised equipment apparent.

Kais twitched his shio'he in thought. The situation mapped against Mono-Imperial Scenario 2991/D, or a close analogue thereof.

He stepped out of cover, triggering the battlesuit's entire spectrum of holophoton countermeasures before letting fly with a volley of fusion energy.

In that moment the Imperials found themselves confounded a dozen times over. Kais knew what they would be experiencing on their own targeting screens. They would be plagued by images of overlapping, independently acting Ghostkeels moving in all directions, layered holograms of the gue'ron'sha from the previous chamber firing at them, stroboscopic orbs of light flashing at frequencies designed to disrupt biological perception, and insidious waves of static that caused their ammunition feeds to back-cycle.

Every aspect of the earth caste's artifice in taking apart the enemy's technology, replicating it and learning how to hijack it was brought to bear at once. For an entire second, the gue'ron'sha elites were stunned into inactivity.

It bought Kais all the time he needed.

Prioritising those amongst them with the heaviest weaponry, he hit the cannon-armed warriors first with his fusion collider, swiping his arm across the rest of the squad so the heat of its discharge cooked off the ammunition on the shoulders of their missile-armed brothers. The gue'ron'sha were ripped apart in a messy series of explosions as their own munitions detonated atop their armour. Typical of the Imperium, to use guns that could so easily kill their owners.

The four surviving members of the squad charged, voices raised in a wordless battle cry. Kais moved left, smashing through one of the compartmentalised windows to shrink his profile and let the first one past. He came back out at an angle to shoulder barge the second of the Imperials, knocking him out of the way and overrunning him as he turned back around to shoot.

He almost made it.

Kais felt the slamming impact of an energised fist under his cocoon as he passed. His own readouts fuzzed with static as the weapon's disruption field spooked the Ghostkeel's readouts for a moment. Kais hit the suit's flechette launcher and countermeasures suite at once to buy him time. The resolution of his screen crystallised a moment later, revealing another recovered gue'ron'sha drawing a bead with his snub-nosed, double-barrelled gun.

Kais crouched, extrapolating a ballistics trajectory in the space of a millidec. He used the Ghostkeel's armoured thigh to deflect the incoming bolts at just such an angle they did not detonate upon his carapace, but upon the glass wall beside it. There was a tinkling explosion of ancient glass as the window across the archway came apart.

Kais looped the sound waves of the shattering glass on his audioscopic suite and analysed their resonant frequency with one eye. He directed a blast from his fusion array at the gue'ron'sha brawler with the other even as the brutish creature came in with a wild punch.

Just as the warrior disappeared in a flash of superheated energy, Kais sent a sonic pulse from his countermeasures suite. It shattered every glass pane in the entire hall in a single crashing moment.

Two of the three surviving gue'ron'sha turned their heads as broken shards clattered across them. Seeing an opening, Kais stepped past with a half-turn, backhanding one of the Space Marines with his blunt electrowarfare limb to send him sprawling. He panned the fusion collider's shimmering beam across the staggered warrior, and he was blasted to nothingness before he hit the flagstones. The other raised his gun, thundering a salvo at Kais' head, but the Ghostkeel's alloys were proof against it. A shot from one of Kais' shoulder mounted fusion blasters was turned aside by some kind of energy field, but the other tore the Space Marine apart.

The last gue'ron'sha warrior stood before him, defiant to the last.

'– – YOU WILL DIE HERE XENOS SCUM – –' the autotrans relayed.

'– – THERE WILL BE NO ESCAPE FOR YOU – –'

Kais summoned up the death scream he had recorded from the psy-tainted gue'ron'sha and broadcasted it at mind-splitting volume in response.

Snarling, the white-armoured warrior raised a long, powered blade and charged. He was amazingly fast, far more dextrous than Kais had expected.

Kais took a long step backwards, but it was not enough. The broadsword arced down, its disruption field hungry to rip right through the XV95's torso and impale the pilot within.

At that moment one of the Ghostkeel's drones shot forward. The blade cleaved right into it, cutting it in two with horrible ease. Kais shot the Imperial warrior point-blank, ribbons of gore and steam splashing across the hall's flagstones as he died in a single blinding instant.

Frowning as his drone's hex informational turned charcoal grey, Kais moved on to the end of the hall. He listened for the jittering teeth of the psyoccule to increase in their frequency, and was rewarded when he neared an archway-shaped panel on the wall. Zooming in, he found a hairline crack and two areas with flaking plaster that implied hinges.

Cycling his fusion collider to full, Kais took a shot at the door where a gue'la would think to put a lock. The door cracked in half along its middle.

A swift kick from the XV95 and it fell in completely, revealing a bound figure behind – far larger than a standard gue'ron'sha, and shackled from maw to toe. The psyoccule gnashed and clacked; likely this was the psyker it sought.

The figure's eyes began to glow white. His suspicions confirmed, Kais took the shot, vaporising the figure in an instant.

Kais slid the olfactory relays of the battlesuit to maximum as he took in the aftermath of a long-calculated strategy put into lethal effect. The air stank of vaporised blood, burned alloy and ozone.

He inhaled the scent deeply, and moved on up the stairs to the uppermost levels of the fortress.

Master Castellan Moddren of the Angels of Absolution stood surrounded by his trusted veterans, his powered broadsword drawn and his storm shield canted against his thigh. A scowl marred his patrician features, lit by the candle-lumens of the Great Octagon. Above him was the Dome of Saint Ahtoa, the painted cherubs and seraphs smiling down as they brought water to Ferna of the

Forest, and winding around him was the incense of his most pious servitor attendants. As the master castellan of Soul's Well, he had a duty to defend it with his life and limb, leading the garrison troops to victory over whatever malignant forces were acting upon it.

With the fires of outrage burning at his heart, Moddren felt more like an angered animal than a leader of men. The urge to kill was upon him. His sanctum, his fortress, had been infected by a plague that had already claimed a dozen good men. And now – according to the Hidden Brotherhood – an alien champion was loose in their midst, running riot in some manner of stealther warsuit.

'We will engage it in here,' said Moddren, his tone cold and certain. 'It is nothing more than an assassin, and I will not run from it.' He put two fingers on the exterior nodes of his displacer field, checking the temperamental device was still active, and nodded to himself.

'Aye, my lord.' Moddren's company champion, the stocky but dextrous bladesman known as Brother Jalamus, brought the hilt of his Terran greatsword to his helm before whipping it away in a diagonal slash. 'I will cut its limbs from its body, and deliver it to you, so that you may have the pleasure of dealing with the pilot inside.'

Moddren nodded. 'Please do.' He motioned to his hand-picked team of veterans to take their places around the edges of the room. 'Though I make no apologies if I spit it on my blade first. Epistolary Thorne, ensure the bait does not get under our feet, or exhibit any behaviour that will complicate our work. This will be no easy fight, and our locations are of vital importance.'

The master castellan checked the glowing triangles upon his helm relay; all was in position above as well as below.

He cast a glance at the Devastator squad he had stationed in the Whispering Balcony, behind the ornate balustrade that lined the upper stratum of the mosaic-lined dome. He nodded, satisfied they were hidden well enough. Then, despite himself, he found his eyes drawn once again to the three astropaths in the centre of the massive octagonal hall.

The psykers were bound one per side to the grille-like facings of a tripartite truthfinder rack of ancient design. They had their eyes hidden with iron masks and their mouths clamped with the long-forsaken devices known as scold's bridles.

The brutal instruments were still thick with dust after being brought out from reliquaries that had lain undisturbed for millennia. They were amongst those few relics of the past that the Angels of Absolution did not like to venerate. But the master castellan knew well from the events of the last few days that the psyker-plague could appear in moments, causing one afflicted by it to expel a vile liquid that spread it to all those it touched. Only a member of the Librarius could keep infected psykers under control, and he had summoned Thorne to his side for just that reason. But to Moddren it seemed a physical blockade against such effects was a wise additional precaution.

'Master castellan,' said Thorne, 'I can feel its approach. It will be here in less than a minute at its current pace.'

Moddren touched the aquila tattooed upon his temple, and closed his eyes, just for a brief moment.

'Then may the Lion bless our swords,' he said softly.

Tutor Twiceblade monitored Kais' progress from the safety of the *Conquest*'s relay throne. He was couched in an ergonomically optimal posture designed to promote wellbeing, yet his eyes were sore from staring, and his veins were thumping fit to burst.

The surviving X5 stealth drone that accompanied Kais' infiltration, boosting the chameleonic properties of his Ghostkeel in the process, was still beaming up every aspect of his progress through the gue'ron'sha fortress. The Monat neared the mountain's heart now, having bypassed nearly every hazard that stood in his way. Kais was a far more lethal weapon than any missile, macro-pulse cannon or high-calibre railgun, a leader in deed rather than word and arguably one of the three finest warriors in all the T'au Empire. In all likelihood, he would achieve his goals with utmost efficiency; Tutor Twiceblade had learned a lot just by watching him.

But he was also one of the three famous Students of Puretide, an icon of the T'au'va that was of consummate importance. His was a genius of such insight he could secure victory for expeditionary forces time and time again. He was irreplaceable, of paramount value to the Greater Good.

To lose him to an unauthorised sortie would be amongst the worst crimes against the T'au'va imaginable. The infamous punishment of the Malk'la ritual, levelled only at those commanders who committed a criminal waste of resources, would only be the beginning. But whatever censure was brought against him, it would be nothing next to the scouring soul-pain of a truly grotesque failure. The disgrace of getting Kais killed would eat him from the inside out until his final end.

It was too late. The deed was done. As he watched, Kais drove further into the gue'ron'sha citadel.

Tutor Twiceblade sat forwards in his seat, hands like claws digging into the quasi-foam of the throne's armrests. The Monat was steadily approaching the centre of the gue'ron'sha fortress and the complex energy signatures that lay within.

Transfixed, the tutor did not notice the icon for one of the gue'ron'sha ships in low orbit slowly relocate on the display's macro-informational, moving until it was directly above the giant fortification.

Kais sent a complex pulse of hypersonic sound along the corridor and into the massive chamber he could see just beyond. Octagonal, ringed by a balcony and with a tall dome at its peak, it had a simple rotational symmetry that was pleasing to the Monat's eyes. Such structures were easy to process and even to weaponise, mapping well over his root calculations concerning engagements concluded within interior spaces. It could provide up to a 3.4 per cent efficiency enhancement to his kill-to-duration ratio, and hence met with his full approval.

Within the octagonal space were more gue'ron'sha warriors, some present at the heart of the chamber, others stationed in ambush around the gallery in its upper levels. They believed themselves hidden – it was an amazing feat of naivety, given that they were wearing brightly coloured, heavy-emission powered armour that made a constant low thrum.

At the heart of the chamber was a trio of figures wearing little more than robes and elaborate necklaces. The iron-bound skull shivered vigorously next to him, the constant *clackclackclackclack* of its teeth an additional layer of information that Kais was glad to process. To hear a sound first hand was unusual, and made a refreshing change from the second-hand, pre-parsed data of the XV95.

He waited, as immobile as a mantis. It would not be long before the gue'ron'sha gave into their need for mindless, tribal chatter, providing their own distraction – and he could wait as long as necessary. Patience, as Shadowsun had taught him so long ago, was the brother of silence and stillness, together the most lethal weapons of all.

Sure enough, it was a matter of less than a dec when the most elaborately armoured of their number turned to talk to his subordinates. Kais knew enough about the gue'ron'sha mindset to know that as soon as the celebrated leader figure spoke, every warrior's eyes would be on him out of respect.

The Monat called up his countermeasures and darted down the corridor for the kill.

Master Castellan Moddren turned to his brothers, and spoke. 'When the xenos moves into–'

The room suddenly exploded into blinding light, a thousand contradictory images appearing on Moddren's helm display. His artificer armour's machine-spirit screamed in pain and confusion, but he was already moving, darting behind Brother Jalamus to cover Epistolary Thorne with his storm shield.

His instincts were proven correct. The shield suddenly crashed backwards in a burst of energy, the backwash of heat so intense Moddren could feel it through his armour. He was fighting blind, riding his momentum to skid into the lee of the nearest pillar even as he listened for the engines of the giant xenos machine.

There it was, under the multi-tone scream of his machine-spirit – a faint hum of engines, coming in to skirt the edge of the chamber.

Moddren's vision cleared in time to see the astropaths disappear in a blaze of light and flame. All three of them simply disintegrated from the waist up, along with the top half of the truthfinder rack. Blood spurted from those arteries not cauterised by the blast, a cluster of tiny fountains that turned the psyker's robes from green to crimson and black.

'West flank!' he shouted. 'Kill it!'

The company champion, Brother Jalamus, charged past Epistolary Thorne and on towards the shimmer of energy at the wall. His movements seemed to blur as he passed the chanting Librarian. Jalamus leaped, evading a sudden blast of energy to plant his feet on the side of the chamber, then pushed off hard with his greatsword outstretched for a killing thrust.

He passed straight through the warsuit-sized shimmer of energy to collide hard with the mosaic beyond it, staggering away before regaining his feet.

A mirage. Grimacing, Moddren ripped off his helm. At least he could trust his eyes.

'No!' shouted Thorne.

Moddren ducked just as a column of energy shot over his head, the smell of his own burning scalp mingling with the dry, choking fug of burned stone. He ducked and rolled again, suddenly aware of the looming warsuit to his left, then came up with his shield before him. He did not so much deflect the second blast as rush into it, trusting to the storm shield's ancient force field to protect him, then broke left and swung his broadsword in a rising diagonal sweep.

The warsuit raised its shin to intercept the blow even as it blasted Jalamus to atoms, but it did not evade. The sword bit deep, all but cutting the limb free in a spray of white sparks. The warsuit boosted high, nearly yanking the blade from Moddren's hands, before kicking him so hard he skidded across the flagstones on his back. The master castellan felt a savage sense of relief when he realised his sword was still in his grip.

Epistolary Thorne was suddenly above him, conjuring a burst of blue fire that raced out like a vengeful ghost. It swathed the xenos suit's multi-lensed head in blistering fire. The xenos thing recoiled, and Thorne moved in for the kill, but a heavy disc-like drone raced in to smack hard into the Librarian and send him sprawling.

There was a crack-whoosh from above as missiles arced down from the Devastator team on the Whispering Balcony. The disruptive electro-gheists the xenos was sending out had done their job all too well, for to Moddren's horror, the krak missiles struck Thorne instead of the warsuit. The Librarian fell in a blackened, torn heap, blood seeping from his rent armour.

'Helms off!' shouted Moddren, his sensation of outrage mingling with a growing suspicion the situation was already long out of his control. 'It's confounding our machine-spirits!'

He jumped upright as the warsuit opened fire upon the Devastators in the gallery above. The killing beam from its strange tripartite weapon vaporised the balustrade and much of the pillar, taking with it two of the heavy weapon troopers behind.

Moddren charged, slashing his powered broadsword into the jet vents of the xenos warsuit. At the edge of the chamber, Veteran Sergeant Paethen raised his plasma gun and took his shot, only to fall back in an explosion of light a moment later. Crying out, Moddren swung his sword hard and carved a wedge from the thing's arm before dodging away, moving to its blind spot, and striking for its torso.

The blade cut in, its tip digging deep, but it did not find the pilot inside. The xenos creature's armour was a formidable defence, even against a powered weapon. But Moddren had not truly expected to make the kill with his sword.

The xenos thing had moved close, now, to the centre of the room.

Close. So very close.

Tutor Twiceblade felt himself shake with emotion. His mind was swamped, a tide of frantic hope crashing against cliffs of stone-cold fear. As he watched, Kais was taking apart the gue'ron'sha command echelon with consummate skill. It was like witnessing a master bladesman go through steps long rehearsed, each movement leading to a trap, an illusion, a killing strike that made his opponents seem clumsy and slow by comparison.

Twiceblade shook his head in amazement as the tempo of the dance sped up, the gue'ron'sha slain in ones, twos and threes like the inevitable culminations of a string of mathematical equations.

To the tutor's mind, this was the supremacy of the T'au'va writ large.

A tiny chime came from the orbital distribution suite. He spared the hex-screen an irritable glance for a fraction of a heartbeat, idly noting that the gue'ron'sha ship now positioned directly over the mountain fortress – despite that ship facing directly away from the nearest t'au monitor vessel that was observing it – had turned red.

The lethal, warning red that denoted target lock.

Twiceblade's eyes grew wide with horror.

Kais dodged out of the path of the shimmering blade of the gue'ron'sha leader, sliding left as another hacking sweep came in. A glancing blow, it carved a thick wedge of alloy from his arm, but did not compromise the systems beneath. A few moments before the swordsman had landed a heavy blow upon his jet pack, but by Kais' calculation that was acceptable damage. In such close confines he could afford up to a thirty per cent loss of efficacy before lack of vertical mobility became a hindrance.

A gue'ron'sha to his right fired a blast from some manner of plasma weapon. The control cocoon grew painfully hot as the superheated energy penetrated the machine's flank, burning all the way through to the interior.

Without diverting his attention from the gue'ron'sha leader, Kais hit the recessed panel by his feet that ejected the suit's pulse pistol, took it up with his off hand, and pointed it through the steaming hole to shoot the plasma gunner in the head.

The Space Marine leader came in hard, his blade leaving crackling arcs as he hacked at the Ghostkeel's plexus hatch. Kais ran a swift recalculation, blasting the gue'ron'sha with a dual beam from his shoulder weapons to force him to raise his shield. He kicked the crude protective slab hard, sending the warrior sprawling to buy him enough range for the kill. The gue'ron'sha wasted a valuable second replacing his helm. A foolish error of judgement, thought Kais, especially now that his EMP reservoir was nearly at full. First the pulse, then the kill, then he would make his escape.

'– – NOW – –' read the autotrans as it rendered the human's command.

'Kais!' came the voice of Tutor Twiceblade, emerging painfully loud from the speaker-nodes of his control cocoon as alert signals flared on his command and control suite. 'They have orbital–'

The Monat felt his concentration flicker and go blank, just for a moment. Just as he was rerouting all his power to the XV95's emergency force shield, his focus was shattered by the one element he had not factored in his calculations.

Aid.

In that same moment, the beautifully painted dome above them came apart. A column of killing energy lanced down from low orbit, and Kais' perfectly calculated rampage died in a storm of light.

CHAPTER NINETEEN
THE BATTLE WITHIN

Saltire Nearspace
Kroot Warsphere *Vawk Karaow*

'Battle stations.'

Xedro Farren opened his eyes, his hands automatically checking the critical points of his bolt rifle. Slowly, his augmented senses pierced the amber gloom.

He was not within the *Night Harrower*, as he had somehow presumed, but held tight in a harness on the side wall of a Goliath-class boarding torpedo. He let his hands run over the exquisitely crafted rifle once more, mentally preparing for the battle to come.

Then something changed.

Like a radioactive sun breaking through the murk of a cold winter dawn, the events of the last few weeks began to coalesce in Farren's mind.

Everything. The fate of Saltire Vex. The plight of its riggers. The twisted victims of Allhallow. The jet black armour of the traitor angel. The news of a pact made by the Dark Angels with the xenos, an arrangement that would let them attack their own successor Chapter by proxy, and do the dirty work of the t'au in return.

And worst of all, the revelations of Pietr Moricani – and the implications of his absence, for he was not present on Farren's rune display. No explanation, no status register entry. Just an empty berth. It did not bode well.

Farren watched the expressions of his brothers around him change as they too came around from Vaarad's botched mind-wipe. Realisation began to dawn, after a moment of taking in their surroundings. He saw vague confusion give way to slow outrage on Enrod's pinched features, smouldering anger becoming visible upon Thrunn's broad and uncomplicated face. Gsar's thin lips peeled back to reveal a grimace of disgust, whilst Parvell clutched his bald head in his white-knuckled hands.

Despite it all, Farren's plan had worked. At the critical moment, the Primaris Marines had pushed their augmented biological systems so far into overdrive that their furnaces had burned out whatever baleful chemicals had been pumped into them.

This time at least, the mind-altering treatments of the Dark Angels apothecarium had failed to erode their memories entirely.

Chaplain Zaeroph's sepulchral tones came from a ruby-eyed servo-skull at the far end of the torpedo, static lacing his every recorded syllable.

'We will not be returning to the heretic planet of Saltire Vex this day,' said Zaeroph through the skull. *'Ill-discipline within our ranks has allowed its traitorous populace a chance to escape, and to spread their heresy still further.'*

'You're the traitor here,' growled Farren under his breath, but he did not trigger his vox. Instead he made his lips into a tight line. He knew well, as a lieutenant surrounded by his men, this was not the time. A collapse in morale, the confusion and doubt that would follow, could be disastrous in an active warzone.

Perhaps, thought Farren, the Interrogator-Chaplain and his coterie were counting on it.

'Be calm, brothers,' said Farren over the Primaris vox link. 'If we are to seek justice, we must survive.'

'The Emperor has revealed the truth to us through his Divine Tarot,' continued Zaeroph's voice. *'It is the Pawn of the Void we seek this day. These traitors to humanity have taken refuge upon a mercenary ship codified as a kroot warsphere.'*

Farren felt the tightness in his throat get worse. He knew next to nothing about the enemy they were about to face. Even the priests of Mars had not had much to say about such exotic warships, other than that they should be destroyed at range if at all possible.

'Many of the unsanctioned refugees aboard the warsphere have contracted a psychic plague,' continued the message. *'Do not let their emanations touch you under any circumstances, and give the Emperor's Mercy to those that become afflicted.'*

Enrod spat a gobbet of acidic saliva on the bulkhead opposite. It hissed gently as it scarred the armaplas, filling the air with an eye-stinging scent.

'You Primaris Marines of the Third Company have been given the honour of the vanguard assault. We will attack from another vector, and make for the engine cores. Together we will destroy this nest of corruption, this offence against the Imperium's rightful domain. Or we shall die in the attempt.'

The message cut off abruptly. For a while, the only

sound in the boarding torpedo was the dull thrum of its passage through space. Then the proximity alarm at the boarding torpedo's tip gave a loud, bright chime.

'Brothers,' said Farren. 'We will do our duty here, as Dark Angels, and as true sons of the Lion. We will lead by example. We will destroy the enemies of the Imperium, as we were born to do.'

Thrunn nodded, but other than that, his brethren remained still. The chime at the fore of the boarding torpedo rang out once more.

'Remember this is a plague site, and that the infection it bears could affect countless other worlds unless we destroy it,' continued Farren. 'Do not let your focus be robbed by the truths we have uncovered. We can deal with that situation properly upon our return.'

None of the Primaris Marines replied. Farren chose to take their sullen silence for acquiescence, if not agreement. Perhaps this was what it truly was to be a Dark Angel. To be a dour and stoic force of destruction, fighting not for glory, nor for the joy of battle, but for duty, and duty alone.

The proximity alarm's infrequent chime became more strident, more insistent, until it rang like an inferno monitor at full blast.

'Ready your weapons, brothers,' called out Farren.

There was a deafening boom and a tremendous, bone-shaking impact as the boarding torpedo slammed home into the side of the xenos craft. Farren felt himself yanked forwards and then hurled back, the torpedo around him filling with a fierce roar as the circular melta array behind its tip burned through the outer hull of the warsphere.

Then, with a ringing, slamming impact, the tip of the boarding torpedo hinged outward into the enemy craft. The harnesses holding the Primaris Marines shot open with a fierce hiss of hydraulics.

Farren was the first out, as ever, his bolt rifle at his shoulder as he burst through the smoke looking for movement. His brothers were close behind. The corridor they had emerged into was dark, misted and almost surreally humid, its sides and ceiling not walls so much as a thick mass of cables, twisted girders and coiling pipes.

Far too many crawlspaces, thought the lieutenant. Far too many places for an–

Farren had already shot the first kroot on instinct before he had fully registered its presence. Its rangy body toppled down from the pipelines, one ankle caught so that it dangled upside down with its sheaf of head-quills scraping the grilles of the floor.

Enrod took another further down the corridor a split second later, his expertly placed bolt striking the gangling green-grey xenos in the chest just as it drew a bead with a long-barrelled, spined rifle. Thrunn took a hit in the shoulder from above, growling in wordless anger before threading a shot into the gantry overhead to fell a third avian xenos.

Farren's helm display showed no hostiles. 'Clear.'

Parvell came up beside him, his bald head glinting in the green light of the buzzing lumen-spheres that were dotted seemingly at random along the strangely organic corridor.

'You realise the t'au make use of kroot as snipers,' said Farren.

The sergeant nodded. 'Good point, lieutenant,' he said, unclipping his helm from his waist and sliding it smoothly over his head.

Farren was taken aback at the bald man's acquiescence, but he said nothing.

'Should I take point?' said Enrod. 'If they use snipers, you should not be at the fore. We cannot afford to lose your leadership. Not now.'

'My thanks,' said Farren. Though it rankled to see another take the risks on his behalf, it did make sense tactically. 'Omnissiah bless your aim, then, Enrod. And go well.'

The lieutenant could not help but smile as his squads moved on, Enrod at the front and Parvell clad in full battleplate from head to toe. A fierce sense of triumph filled his chest. Maybe they had a chance after all.

'Move swiftly, brothers,' he said, standing straighter than he had done for the first time in years. 'We have an example to set.'

Pietr Moricani felt something shift inside his mind, a wyrm of consciousness wriggling in his forebrain. It was disturbing his long, deep sleep. He made a fist in his mind, enfolding the wyrm in his ethereal grasp and hoping to squash the life from it. But all that came from between his fingers was light.

He opened his eyes, just a fraction. Vaarad's mutilated visage stared down at him. The Apothecary had a look on his face as if he was examining a bacto-culture dish, and one that had not yielded the results he expected. The metallic jaw that dominated the lower half of the Apothecary's face moved an inch to one side, giving him a disappointed leer.

'It appears, by the movement of the subject's pupils, he is conscious.'

Moricani made to contradict that statement, purely out

of sheer contrarian habit. All that came out was a strange gurgle.

'The after effects of the asset's cerebral fluids are still powerful,' said the Apothecary. 'He senses his surroundings, but does not fully register.'

Moricani's spirit laughed inside. He felt his chest twitch, a slight vibration at first, but then a swelling, a shaking, and the approximation of a true laugh.

'Interesting,' said the Apothecary, beckoning to his servo-skull. 'Dacius, record this, please.'

Moricani felt his breath fill his lungs, his intercostal muscles flexing as feeling returned to his chest. Whatever sedative he had been given was wearing off fast.

'You are...' said Moricani. His vision swam for a moment, then came back again.

Vaarad recoiled. 'I am what?' asked the Apothecary, his eyes narrowing.

'You are not as... clever... as you think,' slurred Moricani, smiling dumbly in triumph at managing a whole sentence.

'Oh really? And why is that, Sergeant Moricani?'

'We gave the riggers a way out. And we know,' he said, nodding slowly. 'We know what you do in the Lion's name.'

'What are you talking about, sergeant?'

'We,' he said, screwing his eyes up. Why was the damned medicae making it so difficult? 'We Primaris Marines,' he said, awkwardly jabbing a thumb at his own chest. 'We know.'

'And what do you claim to know?'

'About the mind-wipe,' said Moricani, his eyes open crazily wide. 'About the asset, and the traitor angel.'

Vaarad's face – those parts of it that were still flesh and blood – suddenly showed an unhealthy pallor. For a moment, he did not speak, move, or even breathe.

'Subject is sadly delirious,' he said matter-of-factly, turning his head towards his servo-skull. 'These babblings are of no logical use. Codify the last two minutes under enigma protocols and archive dump at the first opportunity.'

The servo-skull gave a short blurt of acknowledgement.

'We know!' cried out Moricani, his thoughts crystallising as his smile broadened. 'More than you realise. We know your secrets. And you know less about the works of Pater Cawl than you think.'

Vaarad looked thoughtful. He pulled on the straps binding Moricani to the table. They were tight as ever, not allowing more than a single inch of free movement. Then the Apothecary stood up to his full height and made his way over to a corner of the room, his servo-skull drifting after him.

Moricani heard him speak from the far corner of the room, his voice almost too faint to hear.

'Psyvox relay initiated,' he said. 'Extremis protocol.'

The sounds of static drifted across the room, accompanied by a distant wailing.

'Brother Dothrael,' said Vaarad. 'The asset was not as we thought. New contingent aware. Recommend immediate Mortis program.'

Moricani frowned. What was he saying?

'Repeat. Recommend location of following subjects during active service. Recommend premature termination of subjects Farren, Thrunn, Gsar, Parvell, Enrod. Prioritise reclaim of listed Primaris active gene-seed.'

A dark cloud of misgivings rumbled across the horizons of Moricani's troubled mindscape.

The feeling only increased when Vaarad's face swam back into his line of sight. The Apothecary was red-faced, flushed almost, his eyes slits of disapproval bordering on hatred.

'You'll get what you deserve soon enough,' said Moricani. 'We Primaris Marines are the future, and we will be the death of you.'

'Experiment terminated,' said Vaarad, taking his drill-tipped narthecium from a steel shelf under his med-lectern. 'Subject irreconcilable. On this day, Brother Pietr Moricani died of his wounds.'

The bulky apparatus had the white helix of the healer emblazoned upon its side, but there was no doubt as to its primary barrel's true function.

Moricani thrashed and spasmed, hoping against all reason he could break from the heavy straps that held him to the slab. Some of them gave a little, but most were so tight to his body they did no more than creak in protest.

The last thing that Hellblaster Sergeant Pietr Moricani ever felt was the cool tip of the Apothecary's narthecium placed upon his right temple.

Interrogator-Chaplain Zaeroph smashed the last kroot out of his path with a backhand sweep of his crozius arcanum. Ropes of electricity coursed across the alien's broken body as he kicked it out of the way, its hollow bones breaking under his boot with a satisfying crunch.

'That's the last of them, for now,' he said. 'A shame.'

'There will be more,' said Company Master Gabrael, wiping the gore from his blade with the hem of his new silken cloak.

Behind them, the gantry was thick with alien corpses.

Many had been bludgeoned to death, the scorch marks of the crozius' disruption field surrounding each shattering blow. Some had been hacked apart or cut in two by brutal sweeps of Company Master Gabrael's power sword, their corpses gently smouldering.

The victims of Autinocus' clinical attacks lay here and there, cored through the chest by spheres of superheated gas, hacked apart by his cog-toothed axe or mangled by the grasping, merciless grip of his servo arm. Yet more were burned to the bone as if they had stood too near a raging blast furnace – in many ways they had, for when his battle ire was up, the psychic wrath of Epistolary Dothrael was something to behold.

The trail of corpses stretched all the way back to the Thunderhawk, perhaps a quarter of a mile distant with its landing apparatus mag-locked to the outside of the warsphere.

'That's the engine core, up ahead,' said Autinocus. 'The edge of it, at least. It is a well-preserved example of its kind, reliable but primitive. And easy enough to destroy.'

'Excellent,' said Zaeroph. 'Make ready the detonation.'

The Techmarine nodded curtly and went to work. His servo-arm peeled back layers of insulation to get at the giant cylindrical core beneath as he took a string of melta charges from his waist.

'Interrogator-Chaplain,' said Epistolary Dothrael. 'A moment, please.'

Zaeroph turned to Dothrael as the Librarian held up an arch-shaped relic. Within it was a yellowed cranium covered in the patina of extreme age. The skull's teeth were clacking as if it was trying to communicate. Dothrael held it close, staring into the empty sockets and cocking his head as if he was straining to hear. Blood began to seep out of the skull's eyes, but he seemed to pay it no mind.

Zaeroph too ignored it. Only for now, he told himself. Only for now.

'Vaarad sends word from the *Blade*. It is not good. He says the asset is no longer working as we thought, and that the subjects are aware. He requests we engage the Mortis program.'

Zaeroph felt his ire build to truly volcanic levels. The Primaris contingent, under the capable but troublesome Lieutenant Farren, had stumbled over secrets that should never come to light. And that, as any member of the Inner Circle knew well enough, could not be borne.

'Finish up swiftly, Autinocus,' he said, his voice as serious as the grave as he located the Primaris runes on his helm display. 'We make for the central chamber. We must pay the lieutenant and his men our final respects.'

Xedro Farren emerged from the corridor network into the light of the ovoid chamber beyond. After several hard-fought skirmishes against small groups of kroot, he was spattered with stinking xenos blood and low on ammunition. Still, he had a buoyant confidence in his step that he had not felt for months. In his experience, the black and white realities of combat had a way of drowning out an unquiet soul.

The artificial cavern they found themselves inside was lined top to bottom with cables, girders and tree-like constructions festooned with actual vegetation, together forming an industrial forest all around its edge. The overall effect meant that the area felt more like a wood-lined clearing than a space aboard an interstellar craft. Right in the centre was a mound of captured weapons and skulls, atop which was a throne.

Gsar, redeployed in Farren's squad whilst the *Harrower* was undergoing repairs, had quickly surmised the warsphere was built along a strong central axis. After that he had led them to their destination with an unstinting sense of direction and purpose. Already it was paying off. His hypothesis held out when they found the corridors fanning out from a central point, like the spokes of a wheel; it was a primitive but effective design, and not hard to navigate, despite the clustered jungle of pipes and struts that cluttered its corridors.

'Spread out, brothers,' said Farren, despatching his squads left and right with a gesture. 'These xenos like to believe they specialise in ambush. They will attempt to confound us with stealth.'

A great yapping cacophony, like the howling of mutant hounds, emerged from the corridors stretching away on the other side of the artificial cavern. Suddenly a living tide of beasts came pouring through the corridors to spill out and fill the space with horrendous noise. They were lithe, long-beaked creatures that looked half way between kroot and giant, bald attack dogs.

'Or perhaps not,' said Farren. 'Fire at will.'

Farren and his brothers began to put down the creatures with clinical efficiency. Every shot fired bowled one of the beasts over before spreading its remains wide in the ensuing explosion. Soon enough, the site had turned into a blood-maddened tableau of butchery that had more in common with some hellish daemonic visitation than a clean military exercise.

Farren reloaded his clip, picking off kill shots once more

as Gsar reloaded his own rifle and thickened the volley beside him. On Mars, they had relished such situations, the quadrupedal servitors of the tech-priests expended in great measure only to have their brain canisters recovered at the end of each exercise and vat-grown a new body overnight. The training was intended to teach them how to refine target priority and ammunition conservation in the face of superior numbers.

If only Pater Cawl could see us now, thought Farren.

When Farren killed the fifth beast in a row, his bolt rifle clicked empty once more, the last of his clips already expended in the butchery since they had boarded less than twenty minutes ago.

Gsar, Enrod and Parvell needed to reload, too, but they had made every bolt count. By the time the last beast-packs had made it half way across the artificial clearing they were starting to waver. Most of them had turned and ran, the explosive deaths of their brethren enough to send the rest packing once their impetus was lost. Only three of the creatures had made it to the Primaris line.

Farren unsheathed his power sword and sliced one of the beasts in two, with Gsar stabbing another mid-leap with his combat knife. Nearby, Thrunn caught the third beast by the jaws and ripped its skull in two with an ursine grunt of effort.

As an attack wave, they had left a lot to be desired.

But as a distraction, they were excellent.

Even as the last of the hounds were despatched a dozen heavily ornamented kroot stood from amongst the pile of trophies in the centre of the clearing. There was a motley assortment of humans with them, mercenaries and traitors who opened fire alongside the kroot.

Weapons and skulls cascaded down around their legs as the ambushers took their shots. Caught in the open, the Primaris Marines had no immediate reply. Enrod went down heavily, his right eye shot out through his lens. Farren was hit in the neck, stumbling back with the command to take cover dying in his throat. Gsar took three bullets at once, and was knocked off his feet, hitting the deck with a loud clang.

Then the giant grey kroot at the heart of the pile of trophy weapons levelled a long, sling-held plasma rifle with a blade jutting down from its tip. He aimed carefully, and put a sizzling blue bolt right through Thrunn's chest.

Farren drew his powered broadblade from its scabbard and charged. He turned his shoulder to take two sniper's bullets on his pauldron as he closed the distance. He felt the pain in his throat subside as the shock of the sniper's bullet passed, and a swell of anger rose in his chest as he pointed the tip of his blade towards the giant grey-quilled xenos in the midst of the enemy.

'Face me!'

The challenge came out as more of a strangulated rasp than the bellicose roar he had hoped for, but its message was clear enough. The grey-quilled giant stepped out of the trophy pile completely, its taloned feet clacking as it took a warrior's stance. Farren pounded towards it, arms spread to make himself large and hence keep its attention. Just a few more metres…

The bladed plasma rifle came at him, fast as a whip. He had barely begun to parry when it smacked hard into his head, smashing his focus right out of him. The rifle came around again at terrible speed, clanging from his gorget so hard it nearly toppled him over. The third blow hit the heel of his palm. It took the power sword from his grip, sending the blade spinning away.

The xenos had strength, speed and reach – far more than Farren, especially with his broadblade a few strides distant. He dodged the grey monster's next blow, but the rifle came back fast in the opposite direction. The hooking sweep took his legs out from under him, and he landed heavily in a pile of long-rusted lasguns.

The kroot warlord rose over him, a horrible barking laugh emerging from its blunt terrapin-like beak.

Jensa Deel winced as she watched the Grey King take Farren down in a matter of seconds.

She had recognised the lieutenant's distinctive helmet the moment he had come into the cavern, and felt a wash of mixed feelings even as the kroot hounds bounded past her and their ambush began in earnest. He had saved her, back on Saltire Vex, and in doing so given her and her people a real chance at survival. She could not repay that with an attempt on his life. Instead she had shot at the stanchions above the Primaris Marines, missing on purpose, but not by such a margin that the kroot would later call her on it.

With three of the Primaris Marines down already and Farren on his knees, she felt as if she had made the right choice. She lowered her pulse carbine and stepped back, her eyes fixed on the duel.

'Deel,' shouted del Aggio as she took a shot at the Primaris Marines converging on their position. 'What the hell are you doing? Take them down!'

By the rigswoman's side, Markens was letting fly with a flamer linked straight to his old barrel of promethium.

Each giant plume of flame filled the air with greasy black smoke as it billowed towards the Space Marines recovering and reloading their guns in the middle of the clearing.

'They are allies,' she protested. 'At least, they were.'

'Hu-man,' said the winged kroot shaman as he glided in from the false trees to land behind her with a crunch. He grabbed her arm roughly and raised her carbine to point at the Primaris Marines once more. 'Must kill. For good of great.'

Deel grimaced, shaking the bird-like creature off, before taking a few more desultory shots at the nearest Primaris Marine.

Whatever happened here, she had a feeling it would not end well.

Farren scuffled back towards his broadblade, sliding amongst the scrap as a blast of plasma melted a steaming hole between his legs. The grey giant was shooting at him now, presumably considering the duel over barring the execution.

The creature's very arrogance gave Farren a pulse of pure, Emperor-given hatred. His hand touched something sharp in the trophy pile, and before he knew it he had hurled a jagged xenos knife hard at the creature's head. It batted the blade from the air with the end of its rifle as if swatting away a fly.

It was an opening, at least. Farren made full use of it, springing forward with a roar to catch the towering xenos around the waist and bear him down into the trophy pile in a crash of limbs and scattering weapons. The giant grabbed his head almost immediately with its scrabbling claws, wrenching his helm this way and that so hard that Farren felt his neck would tear open and his head come clean off. The creature had one leg locked around his arm, pinning it to his body. Its frantic, crocodilian thrashing, combined with the thick greasy oil of its skin, made it almost impossible to gain purchase in return.

Farren felt one of its talons pierce the neck seal of his helm and push up underneath to penetrate the soft flesh under his jaw. He found purchase with one of his feet and pushed hard, breaking the creature's questing finger. The thing's grip was back in a moment, pinning his other arm with its knee as it hammered a saw-bladed knife at the neck joint of his armour over and over again.

Any moment and that blade would be stuck right through his neck. Incredible as it seemed, he was losing the fight, mere seconds away from death.

The fire of frustration within Farren, stoked to a raging conflagration by the events of these last few weeks, blazed bright. He felt a wash of molten strength cascade through his tired limbs, a cascade of chemicals that made a surge of adrenaline seem pale by comparison.

His Belisarian furnace burned.

The lieutenant stood up with a cry of pure, animal rage, hauling the giant xenos with him into the air in one vital feat of strength. He broke its leg with a sharp movement of his arm, then toppled it sideways to slam the beast into the jutting angles of the trophies below with all his considerable weight.

Farren's hand shot up, catching the creature's wrist as it raised the combat knife for a stabbing deathblow. He squeezed, the hypersteel coils around his sinews contracting hard as they brought their terrible composite strength to bear. One by one he felt the creature's bones break in his grip.

The jagged knife tilted, then fell from its quivering claws. Farren grabbed it before it could land and slammed it so deep into the creature's eye socket that only the hilt protruded. The grey giant's pointed black tongue stuck out, long and quivering, as it fell back with a loud death rattle.

Out of the corner of his eye, Farren could see Enrod and Gsar opening fire upon the shadowy figures in the artificial trees around them. Three fell, their bodies bursting apart. It was enough. The kroot began to melt away and disappear.

The lieutenant peeled his fallen foe's death grip from his arm and stood atop the pile of trophies. It was all he could do not to raise his eyes to the ceiling and cry out to the Omnissiah as the savage energy of victory coursed through his limbs. He took in his surroundings like a barbarian king surveying his new domain, pleased to see that his enemies had fled before him.

And saw the face of a ghost.

Interrogator-Chaplain Zaeroph emerged into the massive artificial clearing, his command squad close behind him. As he made his way through the strange, twisted trees that lined the periphery, he saw a strange vista.

There, amongst literally hundreds of dead kroot-forms, stood the Primaris Marines he sought. Their leader, Farren, was atop a pile of what looked like discarded weapons – trophies, no doubt. Before him was a figure all too familiar.

Jensa Deel, chief rigger from Saltire Vex and architect of her planet's exodus.

'Let us leave the lovers to it,' said Gabrael. 'We can detonate the charges, and claim collateral damage.'

'Imprecise, with respect,' said Autinocus, his outstretched plasma pistol steady as a rock. 'I have a bead, Interrogator-Chaplain. Which one should I kill first?'

'Neither,' said Zaeroph. 'Let's see how things transpire.'

'Deel,' said Farren, 'you're alive.'

'Yes,' she said, 'thanks to you. Our only chance for survival was to link up with these mercenaries, and to get as far away as possible. Thousands of us made it aboard to the outer decks, cramped but safe. And you gave us that chance.'

'What? I thought you wanted to wait out the great cycle, then return.'

'We cannot,' she said. 'You know as well as I do that we would need to be quarantined. That weird psychic plague... it lies dormant for now. It has some kind of lifespan, burning bright, then passing on, but how long before it is back?'

Farren said nothing.

'We are striking out for pastures new,' she said. 'Let us go. Please. We will find a place far from the Imperium, and settle that instead. A new beginning.'

'You have not the requisite Warrant of Trade,' said Farren coldly. 'Nor the primarch's grace to claim a world in the Emperor's name.'

'What else can we do?' shouted del Aggio. 'We have families on this craft, hundreds of refugees, and a trade deal that will see us to safety!'

'You fired on us,' said Farren, looking sidelong at Markens as he tried to hide his flamer amongst the scattered trophies underfoot. 'You fired on us, and sided with the xenos over your own kind.'

'I fired to miss,' said Deel.

'I will not,' said Farren, reaching out a hand behind him. Enrod, his eye socket bleeding, placed a reloaded bolt rifle in the lieutenant's hand. Farren nodded his thanks.

'I saved your life on Saltire Vex,' he said, looking down at Deel. 'I saved it again by getting you off planet. I will not save it a third time, so you can stoop even lower and spread your treason to more deserving worlds.'

'Wait,' said Deel, desperately, a single tear appearing at the corner of her eye. She absently wiped it away across the side of her face. It left a glowing white streak in the gloom. 'This will all be for nothing if you–'

Farren shot her in the head. A heartbeat later, Gsar turned his rifle on del Aggio and gunned her down even as Enrod shot Markens in the chest.

'Let's get this over with,' said Farren, turning away and walking towards the core of the xenos ship.

'Lieutenant Farren,' said Zaeroph, emerging from the treeline with Company Master Gabrael, Epistolary Dothrael and Autinocus close behind. 'Brother Gsar, Brother Enrod. Well met. We observed your measures here. Most effective. Perhaps the link you provide with the Cult Mechanicus can be put to good use after all.'

Farren nodded, but could not bring himself to meet the Chaplain's gaze.

'It is time to leave,' said Gabrael. 'Autinocus has primed melta charges upon the engine core in such a fashion it will trigger a chain explosion. You and your men will accompany us to the Thunderhawk *Pride of Lions* and return with us to the strike cruiser.'

'Acknowledged,' said Farren dully.

'Have faith, lieutenant,' said Zaeroph, laying a reassuring

hand upon his pauldron as he guided him towards the exit. 'Your deeds this day have not gone unnoticed. Not by the Emperor Himself, nor by your immediate superiors.'

That is what I am afraid of, thought Farren. But he did not say a word.

Farren felt the pressing weight of acceleration as the Thunderhawk *Pride of Lions* shot from the exterior of the kroot warsphere like an eagle soaring from a mountain peak into the open skies. When it was some distance away, its pilot, Autinocus, sent a tight-beam psalm of activation to the munitions he had sown within the warsphere's core.

Tapping an appeasement rune, Farren brought the warsphere into focus on the faded disposition data-slate within the transport hold. The ugliness of the xenos fortress and the events that had transpired inside it made his soul ache. Then, as he watched, light began to stream out from the insides of the giant spacecraft. It began to fall in on itself, then come apart in a stately collapse that left it no more than a field of void-claimed debris.

Not one of the thousands of screaming voices that accompanied its destruction could possibly have made its way across the void of space, but Lieutenant Xedro Farren felt he heard them nonetheless.

EPILOGUE

Master Castellan Moddren came round slowly, screwing his eyes shut hard before blinking away the searing, blinding afterimage of the orbital strike. His displacer field, an irreplaceable relic of his Chapter, had teleported him away at the moment of the orbital lance strike, and in doing so had unquestioningly saved his life.

The octagonal hall stank of acrid smoke, burning paint and ionised stone. Apart from winding trails of dust, nothing moved amongst the ruin of rubble, torn bodies and collapsed slabs of ceiling. Several of his brothers were buried under the detritus, including those he counted closest to him. It was a heavy price indeed.

There it was, the architect of all this destruction. The xenos killing machine, finally revealed as the giant white warsuit it truly was. Even broken and splintered, even half-molten and gouting smoke, there was something elegant about its contoured plates and sweeping lines. The T'au Empire was getting more advanced, more dangerous, with every passing year.

Moddren stood up, staggering as rubble shifted under his feet. His body ached in a dozen places, and he could taste blood on his gums, but he was alive. It was more than could be said for his company champion, his foremost Librarian, his trusted veterans and his finest Devastator squad. Here and there a white-armoured limb stuck out from the rubble, but few life signs registered upon his helm display.

Though he hated himself for it, there was one life sign he cared about most of all.

Moddren made his way over to the torn-open xenos warsuit, his blade – still clutched in one numb fist – held ready. Should there be so much as a shiver, a twitch of an eyelid, he would haul that xenos bastard out from his nest and make him pay a thousand times over.

Somehow, the master castellan knew he would be sorely disappointed, even before he placed a boot on the flank of the ruined warsuit and hefted it onto its side. Sure enough, the cockpit inside was empty.

Almost.

Moddren was about to turn away and begin the long and painful work of rebuilding when he saw something odd within the contoured, over-luxurious cocoon. He frowned, reaching down to take the object from beneath an ejected drawer cast in the negative image of a bulky pistol.

Smooth, round, and held clamped within a vice of iron, the artefact was unquestionably a yellowed skull.

To his disgust, its teeth bit together in a strange, irregular rhythm – *clack, clack-clack, clack, clack*. He snatched up a length of heraldic banner that had once hung from the chamber's wall, and started to bundle the relic away from sight.

As he wrapped, it was not the skull itself, but the familiar icon on the side of the iron device that made Moddren's blood run cold.

It was the symbol of their parent Chapter, the Dark Angels.

'It appears the tutor succumbed to his obsession with the student,' said Aun'Shao. As she approached the empty cryostasis cylinder in Contingency Zone Eight, Commander Surestrike watched her make the slashing finger motion of the wounded soul. 'As we knew he would,' she continued. 'Though their roles are soon to be reversed once more. Their connection has a strange beauty, poised as it is between symbiosis and mutual hatred.'

'We of the fire caste are often ruled by our hearts,' said Surestrike, tilting his head in agreement as he came alongside her. 'It is our greatest strength, and our deepest weakness.'

The commander watched, a feeling of numbness spreading within him, as the ethereal placed her hand on the jamb of the cylinder's cryolock and held it there as if to feel its heartbeat.

The two stood in silence, the emptiness before them echoing the void in Surestrike's chest. The void at the heart of the entire expedition.

'Do you judge the *Tha'hasiro* a success, honoured aun?' said Surestrike eventually.

'Oh yes. I am no warrior, but I have seen enough of the footage to appreciate the potency of the outcome. Against gue'ron'sha, no less.'

'A true display of the fire caste's mastery of war,' agreed Surestrike.

'It is only a shame that O'Vesa cannot know just how sound his theories proved to be, all those t'au'cyr ago.'

'Sound enough to replicate the process?'

'Certainly,' said Aun'Shao. 'My peers and I shall determine just how that is to be done before the matter is taken to an Elemental Council. I should think an even sixty-four *Tha'hasiro* should be a good place to start, should we be able to find that many Monats of the requisite potential. It will take at least a few generations for them to yield results, of course. But upon the culmination of the process, we will have an army like no other in the galaxy. It will be my legacy to the T'au'va.'

'And will Tutor Twiceblade be sentenced to the Malk'la for his crimes?'

'Of course,' said Aun'Shao, turning with a look of mild confusion. 'That is what the ritual is for, after all.'

'Even though we deliberately allowed him to transgress? Though we led him to the act of unleashing the Living Weapon by the manner of its forbiddance, and ensured that none stood in his way?'

'Even so.'

'I see,' said Surestrike, his tone cold.

'How could it be any other way, after what he took it upon himself to do?' asked Aun'Shao, the deep pools of her eyes wide. 'After he committed to such a flagrant gamble with the T'au Empire's resources? We can attribute the source of his behaviour to his stasis anachronism, and to the fact he once fought at the side of the Rogue Commander Farsight. Looked up to him, if the records of Dal'yth are true. Tutor Twiceblade will become an exemplar as to why taking the initiative in inter-caste matters is to be discouraged. If he survives his Malk'la, of course.'

'As you say.' Surestrike summoned his nerve, finding the remnants of his old confidence within himself before continuing.

'Aun'Shao,' he said. 'Might I be allowed to enter cryostasis myself, in the conventional manner? I would greatly value a chance to rest, body and spirit, and help the T'au'va of the future instead of the present.'

That way he might be free of the ghosts that plagued him, thought Surestrike, and the memories of the souls he had consigned to oblivion. Since the ordeal of their expansion, the limbo of timelessness had seemed infinitely preferable to the trauma that haunted his mind every dark-time dec.

Though the commander did not speak of his feelings, something in Aun'Shao's eyes told him she understood his motives very well nonetheless.

The ethereal made the sign of the flower petals closing at dusk, sighing gently before continuing. 'Oh no, commander,' she said, 'you are far too valuable as a focal point for the Fourth Sphere Expansion for us to allow that. You must know this.'

Surestrike cast his eyes down.

'You and I witnessed something in the sub-realm,' continued Aun'Shao. 'Something unnatural and twisted that needs to be destroyed. None amongst us may rest until the T'au'va is pure again, even should that take us to the winter of our lives and beyond. Now, put into motion the location and recovery of the Living Weapon. He is too useful to lose.'

'Of course,' said Surestrike, maintaining his mask of composure as he made the sign of the dutiful servant.

Inside, his soul was screaming.

Deep in the secret heart of the *Executioner's Blade*, Lieutenant Farren, Brother Gsar, Brother Enrod and Sergeant Parvell stood shoulder to shoulder in a rough circle. They were surrounded by tall, sputtering candles, each ringed with the iconography of the First Legion, and the scent of incense hung in the air. A strange, half-cyborg servitor with a skull for a head scratched at the walls with a hammer and chisel, engraving something into the furthest corner of the room.

'I had my misgivings,' said Zaeroph as he walked slowly around the four warriors. 'Sore misgivings. But you have proved more than useful to our cause. You have proved... discerning. Resourceful. Lethal. Unstoppable in your duty. These are qualities we value highly in the upper echelons of our Chapter.'

Farren felt his spirits rise, just a little, at Zaeroph's words, though the thunderclouds that had gathered around his psyche still rumbled in the back of his mind.

'More than that,' said the Chaplain, coming to a halt in front of Farren and looking right into his eyes, 'you have proven resistant to the energies used by our direst foes. Able to heal from them without corruption. That is of immeasurable value to us.'

Farren thought of his psy-wound, then, and the vile mutating fire that had burned itself into his memory to haunt his meditations at night. Had the Dark Angels known about them all along?

'There exist many structures and ranks within the Chapter that you have not been made aware of,' said Dothrael. 'They have stood for millennia, primarily to enable us to hunt down and redeem those souls who were once trusted brothers, absolving them of past crimes.'

'The traitors,' said Farren.

'Yes,' said Zaeroph. 'The Fallen.'

'Yet we cannot elevate you to the brotherhood of huntsmen,' said Dothrael. 'Not without the consent of Supreme Grand Master Azrael himself. Instead,' at this, he pulled out a golden aspergillum and flicked blessed oil at their feet, 'you will be incepted into a new brotherhood entirely, until the Chapter's elders can decide on the ultimate fate of your kind. But you have proven too useful an asset to waste.'

The hairs on Farren's neck stood up at the Librarian's choice of words. For a moment, he thought of his friend Moricani, and the manner of his death. But he said nothing. He had a feeling that within the brotherhood of the Dark Angels, keeping silent would prove the most useful skill of all.

'The Circle Primaris,' said Zaeroph, touching his crozius arcanum on Farren's shoulders one after another, then doing the same to Gsar, Parvell, and lastly Enrod, whose new bionic eye whirred quietly as it focused on Zaeroph's skull-like mask.

'You will pursue leads that we cannot,' said the Chaplain. 'Not only within the Ultima Founding and the works of the Primarch Guilliman, but also the Martian priesthood. You will put the agendas of the Chapter, as stated by your superiors, before all other concerns. All that which you witness from this point on belongs to the Chapter, and the Chapter alone. Do you understand, aspirant brothers?'

'Aye,' they said as one.

'Then welcome to your new lives.'

Farren bowed his head, conflicting emotions tearing at his heart and mind.

'It is common practice, in these circumstances, for you to be given new names, those of sainted warriors from the dawn of the Chapter,' said Dothrael.

'But as a mark of this historic moment, and of your unique origin, you will instead be allowed to keep a version of your own names.'

Uttering a phrase under his breath, Zaeroph bade the skull-headed servitor in the corner of the room shut down. It sank into itself, becoming little more than a pile of rags and bony armatures that folded away into a small heap. In doing so, it revealed the words it had been etching into the walls.

Brother Ropan. Brother Galus. Brother Lason.

And Brother Xedro.

'Welcome, at last,' said Interrogator-Chaplain Zaeroph, 'to the Dark Angels.'

T'AU WORD	BEST TRANSLATION
Aun	Ethereal/Celestial
Aun'ar'tol	Ethereal caste high command
Be'gel	Ork
D'yanoi	Twin moons
El	Second highest t'au rank
Fio	Earth
Fu'llasso	Overly complicated situation (lit. 'cursed mind knot')
Ghoro'kha	Death hail
Gue'la	Human
Gue'ron'sha	Space Marine (lit. 'engineered human warriors')
Gue'vesa	Humans who have joined the T'au'va (lit. 'human helpers')
J'kaara	Mirror
Kais	Skilful
Kau'ui	Cadre
Kauyon	Metastrategy of patience and ambush (lit. 'Patient Hunter')
Kavaal	A temporary grouping of contingents (lit. 'battle')
Kor	Air
Kor'shuto	Orbital city
Kor'vattra	The t'au navy
Kor'vesa	T'au drone (lit. 'faithful helper')

Ko'vash	To strive for (lit. 'a worthy cause')
La	Lowest t'au rank
La'rua	Team
Lhas'rhen'na	Euphemism for noble sacrifice (lit. 'shattered jade')
Mal'caor	Spider
Mal'kor	Vespid (insectile mercenary race)
Malk'la	Ritual discipline meted out to leaders who fail the T'au'va
Mesme	Combination
Monat	A solo operative (lit. 'lone warrior')
Mont'au	The Terror – a barbaric time of war
Mont'ka	Metastrategy of the perfect strike (lit. 'Killing Blow')
Mont'yr	Blooded (lit. 'seen battle')
Mor'tonium	Highly reactive alloy used as key element of ion weaponry
M'yen	Unforeseen
Nont'ka	Time of Questioning (concept used by Ethereal caste only)
O	Highest t'au rank
Or'es	Powerful
Por	Water

Por'sral	Propaganda campaign
Rinyon	Metastrategy of envelopment (lit. 'Circle of Blades')
Rip'yka	Metastrategy of cumulative strikes (lit. 'Thousand Daggers')
Run'al	Observation post, small blind or bunker
Saz'nami	Ethereal honour guard/ enforcer of the T'au'va
Shas	Fire
Shas'ar'tol	Fire caste military high command
Shas'len'ra	Cautious warrior
Shi	Victory
Shio'he	Olfactory chasm, t'au scent organ equivalent
Shoh	Inner light
Shovah	Farsighted
Ta'lissera	Communion/Marriage/ Bonded; sacred ritual for t'au groups
Ta'ro'cha	Unity of a specific trio (lit. 'three minds as one')
Ta'shiro	Fortress station (spacebound)
T'au'va	The Greater Good, cornerstone of t'au philosophy
Tio've	Contingent
Tsua'm	Middle
Ua'sho	All forces of a given caste in one location (lit. 'command')

Ui	Second lowest t'au rank
Vash'ya	Focused on more than one thing (lit. 'between spheres')
Ves'ron	Robotic being
Vior'la	Hot blooded
V'ral	Undercut
Vre	Middle t'au rank
Y'eldi	Gifted pilot (lit. 'winged one')
Y'he	Tyranid (lit. 'ever-devouring')

A NOTE ON T'AU UNITS OF TIME

A **T'au'cyr** is an annual cycle on the core sept planet **T'au** (each is approximately 300 Terran days).

A T'au'cyr is comprised of 6 **Kai'rotaa** (each is approximately 50 Terran days).

A Kai'rotaa is comprised of 80 **Rotaa** (each is approximately 15 Terran hours).

Each Rotaa is broken down into 10 **Decs**. Decs are either light-time or dark-time.

Most t'au need only 1-2 Decs of sleep per rotaa (each is approximately 1.5 Terran hours).

ABOUT THE AUTHOR

Phil Kelly is the author of the Space Marine
Battles novel *Blades of Damocles*, the Warhammer
40,000 novel *Farsight: Crisis of Faith* and the
novellas *Farsight* and *Blood Oath*, as well as
the Warhammer titles *Sigmar's Blood* and
Dreadfleet. He has also written a number of
short stories. He works as a background writer
for Games Workshop, crafting the worlds of
Warhammer and Warhammer 40,000. He lives
in Nottingham.

YOUR NEXT READ

THE LAST HUNT
by Robbie MacNiven

When one of their recruiting worlds comes under threat from
a splinter fleet of Hive Fleet Leviathan, Joghaten Khan leads the 4th
Company to protect the planet from the rampaging tyranids.
But all is not as it seems…